Loving the Worst Man

JENNY FYFE   NATALIE MURRAY

JN
ROMANCE

Copyright © 2023 by Jennifer Fyfe and Natalie Murray

All rights reserved.

No part of this book may be reproduced in any form or by any electronic or mechanical means, including information storage and retrieval systems, without written permission from the author, except for the use of brief quotations in a book review.

Publisher's Note: This is a work of fiction. Names, characters, places, and incidents are a product of the author's imagination. Locales and public names are sometimes used for atmospheric purposes. Any resemblances to actual people, living or dead, or to businesses, companies, events, institutions, or locales is completely coincidental.

Loving the Worst Man / Jenny Fyfe & Natalie Murray - 1st ed.

Paperback ISBN: 978-0-6458830-2-2

Hardcover ISBN: 978-0-6458830-3-9

Cover design by Ink and Laurel

CONTENT WARNING

This book contains scenes depicting grief over loss of a parent and discussions around substance abuse. We have done our best to handle these topics sensitively; however, if these issues may be triggering for you, please take note.

To Natalie, Love Jenny

To Jenny, Love Natalie

CHAPTER ONE

DYLAN

I don't remember her name.

I should because she told me what it was at the bar last night before I ordered the cab to bring her back to my place. And it makes me a total dick, but every time I look at the redhead curled up in the corner of my bed, all I can think is: Miss Susie.

Which definitely isn't this woman's name.

Because *that* name belonged to my kindergarten teacher, who also happened to be my first crush. Whatever happened to Miss Susie? She must be about fifty by now. She had the most gorgeous ice-blue eyes. And that sandbox in the corner of her classroom was the highlight of my day. I really loved that sandbox. So much better than the water table.

The woman tangled in my sheets rolls over, her foggy eyes surrounded by a layer of smudged black eyeliner. I offer her a lazy smile, even though I have a mountain of stuff to do today and lying around in bed with this woman isn't on the list.

"Morning," she says, her voice raspy from all the

karaoking she'd done last night before landing on the stool next to mine. Her sleepy gaze takes in my jeans and T-shirt. "What time is it?"

"Eight o'clock."

Her brows come together. "Why do you look so awake?"

Because I'm a morning person—not that she needs to know that since this will be the only morning we spend together. "I have to get to work."

"Isn't it Saturday?"

"It sure is." The joys of self-employment. Doesn't matter what day it is, there's always something to do.

She lifts to her elbows, and the white sheet around her slips, revealing the soft swells of her breasts. "Don't you work from home?" Her gaze falls on my Nikon F2 sitting on the nightstand, the first camera my dad ever gave me.

Yeah, I work from home. But that doesn't mean I get to lounge around whenever I want. If I did that, I'd get nothing done. The first thing Dad taught my sisters and me about owning your own business is the importance of a schedule. Usually, I start work at eight—meaning I'm already seven minutes late.

"I do, but I have a lot of meetings scheduled today." First, I have to introduce my favorite mug to a fresh cup of coffee; next is a meet-and-greet with a pile of emails. After that, I need to swing by the camera shop to pick up the new Leica super wide-angle lens I've had my eye on. And when I get back, I'm meeting with a vat of developer and three rolls of film I shot earlier in the week.

"Oh, okay. Sorry. I'll get out of here and let you get to work." She gives me the same sultry smile that had me asking her back to my place. When she rolls out of bed, the other reasons I asked her are on full display.

"Can I get you a cab?" I call after her. There's no way she's going to be walking anywhere in those four-inch stilettos lying beside her black thong. I'm not sure where she lives, but the bar where we met had been across town, so more than likely, it's nowhere near here.

"That'd be great. Thanks." Not-Miss-Susie whips her dress off the back of the chair where she'd straddled me last night for an impromptu lap dance and heads toward the bathroom.

I order a ride share to meet her at the front of the apartment building in ten minutes. Wouldn't want her lingering too long and making things awkward with idle chit-chat. I don't want to know how she likes her eggs or how she takes her coffee. I don't need to hear about her parents' divorce when she turned seven or about all her terrible ex-boyfriends.

I have my baby sister Hayley for that sort of drama.

Hayley calls me at least once a week crying because her latest shithead boyfriend cheated on her, or another ghosted her, or some other prick said she wasn't the kind of girl he wanted to bring home to meet his mother.

What kind of person says that shit? Honestly. My sisters are lucky I live in Texas because if I was anywhere close to New York, where Hayley lives, or to the rest of my family in Maryland, those assholes would be dead, and I'd end up in jail, and our mom would get upset and it'd be a whole thing.

If you're not interested in dating someone, you say it flat out.

If you're not going to stay faithful, don't call a woman your girlfriend, and don't even think about proposing.

It's really not that fucking hard.

Not-Miss-Susie pads out of the bathroom in the same

slinky black dress I peeled her out of only a few hours ago. "I had a lot of fun last night," she says, her cheeks staining pink.

"Yeah. Last night was great."

She twists her palms together like she's nervous. Which is crazy to me, considering we've both seen each other naked. "Do you...um...want my number?" she asks.

I can't say I want her number because, A: I don't, and B: Even if I did, I wouldn't know what name to put it under. "Redhead with great tits who looks like Miss Susie" doesn't exactly scream "She's the one" to me.

"Last night was great," I say again, "but like I said at the bar, I'm not looking to get involved with anyone right now." Been there. Done that. *Not* interested.

She tucks a strand of hair behind her ear, and her gaze drops to her heels. "Oh, yeah. Of course. Sorry."

Another apology. Who is this woman and what did she do with the one who told me she wanted my balls in her mouth? "No need to apologize," I say, right when my phone buzzes with a notification. "Looks like your car is here." Thank god. Shit was about to get awkward. I hold open the door and give her a peck on the cheek because I'm not completely heartless. "Have a good one."

Her smile returns. "Thanks, Dylan. You too."

Well, shit. Now I feel like even more of an asshole because she remembers my name. Still, I give her a friendly wave before she disappears into the elevator, her eyes holding mine right until the doors close. Relief spills through me when I shut my own door. Nights out are fun. The mornings after? Not so much.

Maybe I should stop inviting women over and just go to their place. Then I can leave whenever I want. Not that I'd sneak out in the middle of the night. Hayley had that happen once and cried about it for a week. I'm not *that* guy.

But staying over means sleeping on someone else's mattress. I may only be thirty, but I need my beauty rest.

I shuffle into the kitchen to make myself a quick cup of coffee, grab a yogurt from the fridge, and head straight for my laptop on the island.

While waiting for my inbox to refresh, I bask in the warm sunlight streaming through the wall of windows overlooking Congress Avenue. There's something cathartic about living in one of the tallest buildings in a city like Austin and being able to sit back and watch the world go by, knowing you don't have to be part of it if you don't feel like it.

My stomach lets out an angry growl. I'm not sure peach yogurt is going to cut it today. You know what sounds good? A plate of biscuits and gravy from that diner a few blocks over. Although their coffee tastes like toilet water. Would it be rude to bring a mug of my own brew from home?

A flood of new messages pops up on my screen, distracting me from my hunger. This is why I can't take a day off. If I don't take care of these, come Monday morning, I'll be swamped and end up spending half of my day playing catch-up. I'd hire an assistant, except the thought of having to spend that much time with someone I don't know makes me want to hide in the darkroom and never emerge, like that weird hairless creature from the Lord of the Rings.

The thought turns my stomach.

Or that could be the two shots of tequila that Not-Miss-Susie and I took when we got here. My sisters would murder me if they found out I'd forgotten a woman's name while she was still in my bed. Not my finest moment, I'll admit.

I delete the handful of junk emails that have found their way into my inbox, despite the filters that my sister Alex (short for Alexis, but don't ever call her that unless you want her to throw your favorite hat into a fire) put in place.

Looks like my royalties from the stock photo sites I've listed with have doubled since last month. And one of the photos I took in Nashville a few weeks back has been shortlisted for another award. If I win, it'll be another one to add to the resume—not that I'm asking for more work. Half the emails I receive are from people looking to hire me to photograph their products, aspiring models wanting headshots for their portfolio, or magazines asking if I'd be interested in freelance work.

Being tied down with contracts and deadlines sounds like my own personal version of hell.

If something really interests me, I'll take it, but most of the time, I shoot what I want and see what happens. Probably not the best business model, but I'm not short on cash, and even if I were, my trust fund is always there to fall back on.

I've just made myself a second cup of coffee when Hayley's name pops up on my phone. Saturday morning at nine o'clock—right on schedule after a Friday night out. I answer with a laugh. "Hey, Buttons. I was wondering if I'd hear from you today." That's right. I call my baby sister Buttons because she used to collect them. And I don't mean casually. She had multiple boxes of the things.

Her broken sob bursts through the speaker. I rub my hand down my face and sigh as I close my laptop. If this is anything like the last time, it's going to take a while.

I decide to pre-empt whatever rant she's about to go on and show my support like a good big brother. "Yes, all men are assholes—even me. We all belong in the pits of hell with our dicks on fire. We definitely don't deserve good women like you. And no, I don't know where the good ones are hiding, but if I hear anything, you'll be the first to know." That should about cover it. I take a sip of my coffee and —*dammit*. Burn my fucking tongue.

For some reason, my words don't make her laugh the way they usually do, which makes me sit up straighter. "Hayley? What's wrong?"

"It's Mom and Dad," she sniffs, her voice breaking.

My heart stalls in my chest, and my hands begin to shake.

"They're gone, Dyl. They're both gone."

CHAPTER TWO

JADE

I glue my eyes to my phone in a silent SOS, but Mrs. Horne doesn't take the hint.

She shuffles closer to the counter, leans over the cash register, and continues telling me in excruciating detail about her clock collection while my thumb swipes through the dismal string of matchups in my dating app.

"All of them have very long pendulums," Mrs. Horne says.

I snicker at the timing of that comment and pause on the profile of a cute guy in a paramedic uniform. Mrs. Horne keeps talking, and I try to pay attention because she's clearly lonely, which is why I always greet her with a smile. But grandfather clocks don't exactly get my pulse pumping. You know what does? Customers spending money in my family's convenience store so we can make our loan payment this month. And Mrs. Horne—who's come in daily ever since she moved to Still Springs eight weeks ago—hasn't bought so much as a stick of chewing gum.

When she finally wraps up a spiel about Danish Bornholm clocks and my eyes are glazed over, I point at the fluffy Pomeranian scuttling around her short heels.

"We just got a new brand of organic dog food in this week," I offer hopefully. We make good markups on the fancier brands.

Mrs. Horne's nose scrunches. "Oh heavens, no. Minnie only eats home-cooked organ meats. But I will have some water for her, please. She's thirsty after our morning stroll, aren't you, cherub?" She reaches down to pet her dog on the head while I suck in a breath and slip off the stool.

Glad I can be of service. Anyone else need anything while you're browsing in here without spending a dime? A foot massage, perhaps? Want me to go fill up your gas tank or do your taxes?

I tell myself to stop being a bitch and pour some water into a bowl in the kitchenette before sliding it beneath Minnie's lapping tongue. After Mrs. Horne heads back outside clutching only her rehydrated pooch, I slink back onto the stool and sigh at my phone.

I really need to restock the shelves in aisle three, but that cute paramedic got my attention. As I scan his profile, my chest sinks. Damn. He lives in DC. I barely have time to shower these days, let alone drive three hours for a coffee. But I've had to widen my search lately because the dating pool in Still Springs is way too shallow. I've been on exactly two dates in the past year—one with the guy from the gas station who called his mom halfway through dinner to tell her how well it was going. The other was with a guy I went to middle school with. When I told him I still work at my family's store, he said: "I'm usually attracted to girls with more ambition and drive, but you're so pretty that I'm still holding out for that kiss." *On a cold day in hell, dickwad.*

The only half-decent option left in town has messaged

me a few times since he found me on the dating app—Officer Nate Williams, our town's deputy sheriff. To me, though, he'll always be Nate the Nark, a nickname he earned in high school after he got our basketball team's entire starting line-up suspended for attending a keg party. He's still a straight-laced, socially awkward wallflower, but there's no denying that his police uniform is kinda hot. The fact that he lives around the corner is another tick in the plus column, but after what happened with my sister a few months ago, I have to be careful about dating a local in this gossip-riddled town. The Quinn Brothers store that's been in my family for three generations is already gasping its last breaths—one more family scandal and we'll be done for.

Since the merger we'd planned with the old Harringtons restaurant next door fell through, Dad's having to come into the store every other day instead of retiring. Even worse—he's started talking about selling. Every time he says those words, my eyes sting, and I have to push away a throbbing urge to call Ruby.

Apart from Dad, my sister is the only person who understands how much this store means to me. She and I basically grew up within these concrete walls. One of my earliest memories is balancing on Mom's knee while she taught me how to operate the cash register, and she'd always be sitting here waiting for Ruby and me to arrive each day after school.

In second grade, when I was asked to draw what I wanted to be when I grew up, I drew myself running the store. Mom pinned it to the fridge, and that dream of mine never changed—all I've ever wanted was to inherit the store one day and be my own boss. But lately, Quinn Brothers has been hemorrhaging money as more and more locals shop at the larger, cheaper Kings superstore outside town.

I just need to stay focused and put everything I learned in college into practice. *You got this, Jade. You against the world. Screw the haters.*

The bell rings as two middle-aged women step through the door in wide-brimmed hats and khaki shorts. Definitely tourists.

"Can I help you with anything?" I offer with a smile.

"No, we're just browsing," one mutters, eyeballing the display of organic soaps artfully arranged in reused wooden crates. Each time she picks one up and sniffs it, only to put it right back, my heart sinks a little more. When they head back outside empty-handed, I heave a sigh.

Should I swap out the display?

Maybe our prices are the problem. I should swing by and see how much Kings is charging. I don't know how they always seem to get it right, but that whole family walks on water. Hayley King has been my best friend since the third grade, and I love her to bits, but she's the definition of living a charmed life. She left for a fancy college right after graduation and now works in New York City as an art gallery assistant because she adores art rather than needing the money. When we were kids, she was the first of our friends to get her own cell phone. And the day she turned sixteen, she woke up to a sports car sitting in her driveway with a gigantic red bow wrapped around it.

I tell myself for the thousandth time to stop trying to compete with the Kings. If I had gobs of money to throw at everything, this store would be a cash cow too.

With a fortifying inhale, I decide to hunt through my Pinterest boards for cool window display ideas with zero budget. When I go to shut down my dating app, I spot a new message from Nate.

> @OFFICERNATEWILLIAMS
>
> Hi Jade, I hope you're having a fantastic day
>
> I don't know if you heard, but there's an Italian food fair coming to town next weekend
>
> If you're free, I'd love to take you there for dinner
>
> Best regards, Nate

Best regards?

I reread the message. Thinking about woodfired pizza and lemon gelato makes my stomach growl in protest like it hasn't had a decent meal in months. Funny how that works when it actually hasn't.

I swipe up to Nate's profile pic—a snap of him leaning against his police cruiser with his arms crossed. His dark red hair is neatly combed to the side, just like in high school, and he still gives off such a straight-ass vibe that he'd probably be as suited to the priesthood as he is to law enforcement. But what the heck. Maybe a bit of social company is what I need to get my head out of this store mess for a few hours.

Stop overthinking it. And you need lemon gelato to live.

> @JUST_JADE
>
> Howdy, Nate
>
> Fantastic would be a strong choice of word, but have had worse
>
> Hope things are well with you!
>
> And that's a kind offer, grazie... I love Italian food

> You're on :)

I ask him to send more details, then slip my phone back under the counter. *Focus time.*

But first: coffee.

I grab my pink skull-and-crossbones mug and carry it into the kitchenette. I've only had two cups, and I need three a day, minimum, to qualify as human. Maybe that's why I was in such a grumpy mood with Mrs. Horne.

I scoop coffee into the filter and lean back against the counter while it brews. A choked gurgle sounds behind me, and I spin around, gasping at the sludge spurting all over the counter while the coffee machine has a conniption.

"No!" I switch it off at the wall and burn my fingers trying to figure out what's going on.

I can't survive without coffee. And I definitely can't afford a new coffee maker right now. *Shit.* I head back into the store and down aisle two, grabbing a jar of instant.

I'm stirring a teaspoon into my mug, grimacing at the dirt-water, when my phone rings. After taking a quick sip and gagging, I dash back to the counter and find Hayley's name flashing on the screen.

"Hey, fancy-pants." I smirk into the phone. "How's city life?"

"Hey." Her voice comes out thick and drained.

"What's wrong?"

She gasps a sob. "It's Mom and Dad."

My stomach drops. "What about them?"

Hayley makes a broken sound, and my breath lodges in my lungs.

"They were in a car accident early this morning on the highway outside Still Springs. It was a head-on collision with a truck, and...they...they didn't make it."

My hand flies to my mouth. "Oh my god, Hayley." I burst into tears. "I'm so, *so* sorry."

I slump onto the stool, and for a few stunned minutes, we cry together while painful memories flood my head of the moment I found out my mom had passed. Even though she had terminal cancer, her death was still sudden—she contracted pneumonia while in the hospital and went downhill fast.

There is nothing on this earth that can prepare you for that feeling. And to lose *both* your parents at once... My eyes fill up again. Hayley's parents were always so kind to me—especially her mom, with her infectious smile. And her dad had the quirkiest sense of humor. I can't believe I'm never going to see them again.

With my phone shaking at my ear, I listen to Hayley quietly explain more about what happened and that the funeral will be here, in Still Springs.

"Would you like to stay with me?" I offer through sniffles. "I'm living at my grandma's place now that Ruby's moved out, and there's lots of room."

Hayley sighs. "Thanks, but I might need to be at the house with my sisters and brother. But I'll let you know if I change my mind."

"Of course."

She promises to keep me posted on everything, and after I tell her over and over how sorry I am, we say a choked goodbye that leaves my heart burning in my chest.

Holy shit.

This doesn't feel real.

A sharp need to hug my dad and my sister grips me everywhere. I may be trying to run a business that's failing, but things could always be worse. There's nothing like an event like this to put everything into perspective. My gaze drifts over to the framed picture on the wall of Mom and Dad smiling in front of one of those aqua-blue lakes in Alaska. It's one of the only vacations they ever took together, always agreeing that they'd travel when they retired. Another sob rises in my throat, and I brace my hands against the counter, swallowing it back down.

Any motivation I had to work on the window display evaporates as I brush my knuckles beneath my eyes, my chest aching for Hayley and what she's lost.

I open Facebook on my phone and swipe through to Hayley's photo albums. My heart clenches when I reach a family portrait from her oldest sister's wedding. The bride, Iris, is leaning into her new husband, and to her right stands her parents—Steve and Martha King—wearing proud smiles. Hayley looks beautiful in a blush-pink bridesmaid's dress, and her other sister, Alex, is grinning playfully in a silk jumpsuit.

On the other side of Alex stands Hayley's older brother, Dylan, his tattooed thumbs gripping his pockets, his eyes hidden behind a pair of Ray Bans, and his dirty-blond hair swept up messily in the wind. Not that I've ever seen it look neat. Despite being suited up for the wedding, the guy still looks like he just fell out of bed. He was wild-looking even when he was a teenager and I was a little kid running around Hayley's swimming pool, secretly hoping he'd scoop me up and toss me in.

When swiping through the images becomes too painful, I back out of the app and open my bank account. I have just enough in there to send Hayley some flowers—money I'd earmarked for groceries this week, but I can always borrow more stock from the store and pay it back later.

Biting away tears, I order the flowers, then find the courage to call Dad to tell him the devastating news.

CHAPTER THREE

DYLAN

"This is really stupid," Hayley groans.

I ignore my baby sister's rude comment the way my therapist, Sarah, told me to and continue staring out the car window at the sign until the tightness in my chest begins to ease. Every so often a car whizzes past, but I keep staring while we're pulled over on the shoulder.

Welcome to Still Springs
Population: 1,212
EST: 1862

Will they deduct two from that number now that Mom and Dad are gone?

I blink back the tears that have been plaguing me since yesterday's phone call while Hayley taps her manicured nails against the steering wheel. "Come on, Dyl, we're already late."

This is exactly why I wanted to rent my own car. But she said that would be pointless since we were both flying into Baltimore. I'd offered to drive, but she refused to let me behind the wheel of her cherry-red Audi A3 that she can't seem to keep between the lines.

"One more minute," I say, tracing each golden letter with my eyes as the breath locked in my throat slowly pushes through my lips.

Still Springs. The town where we all grew up. A place I loathe with every fiber of my being. If it weren't for most of my family living here, I'd never come back. Usually, it's straight to Mom and Dad's for whatever holiday we're celebrating, stuffing my face until I can't eat anymore, and then it's right back to Texas.

As soon as the funeral is over, I'm gone.

"You good?" Hayley asks.

I take one more deep breath. "Yeah, Buttons. I'm good."

She throws the car into drive without another word and whips onto the road.

I massage my aching chest and do my best to regulate my breathing as we drive past our old high school, the lone gas station, the car wash—nothing has changed. Not that I expected it to. But still. It's unnerving.

I close my eyes and lean against the headrest, counting the number of breaths I take until Hayley slams on the brakes.

"We're here," she says.

When my eyes open, and my parents' three-story brick colonial fills my vision, a fresh wave of panic crashes over me. "This isn't the funeral home." I'm not ready to go inside yet. Not when Mom and Dad won't be waiting at the door to greet us. I thought I'd have another hour, maybe two, to prepare myself.

"Alex thought it'd be a good idea to meet here first," Hayley explains.

"Why?"

"Family meeting." She says that as if it should be obvious.

Except it isn't obvious because Mom and Dad were the only ones who ever called King family meetings. And they aren't fucking here.

I force myself out of the car and head straight for the porch.

"Aren't you going to bring in your stuff?" Hayley calls from the rear of the car.

"I'm not staying here." That's where I draw the line. I can't see Dad's ratty old armchair sitting empty every time I set foot in the living room. I can't open the fridge and not find one of Mom's "famous" apple pies waiting for me.

My hands begin to tremble, and I stuff them into my pockets. If only I could stop the cold sweat from beading along my hairline.

Hayley heaves her suitcase from the trunk and sets it down on the driveway. "Where do you think you're going to stay?"

"The farmhouse." My parents own a wedding venue outside of town with a beautiful, sprawling farmhouse on the property.

Hayley presses a button on the trunk, and it slowly eases back into place. "You can't. It's being rented all week for some family reunion. And there are weddings, like, every other day until November."

Well, isn't that fantastic?

The wheels on her bag are loud as hell as she breezes past me.

The door opens right when Hayley reaches the first step. My legs lock up, and I freeze in the middle of the driveway. Alex and Iris rush out and throw their arms around our youngest sister. Surprisingly, all their broken sobs don't make me want to cry. Seeing my sisters with tears in their eyes makes me want to fight the whole fucking world.

But you can't fight death and hope to win.

"You have to do it, Dyl. None of us will be able to get through a single sentence without breaking down. Please."

A man doesn't stand a chance against three King women on a good day. When they're all teary-eyed and sniffling? There isn't a hope in hell.

Do I want to do my parents' eulogy?

Hell no.

Am I going to do it anyway?

Of course. Because having some asshole truck driver slam into my dad's car at seventy miles an hour has left me as the only man alive in the King family.

Not to mention that I'm the oldest by eleven months, so shirking this duty isn't in the cards. I'll have to find some way to breathe through the gripping tightness. It's either that or make a fool out of myself in front of everyone.

"Fine."

Three pairs of arms come around me, pulling me into yet another hug. I've held it together through two viewings and the shitload of people who've come over to Mom and Dad's to "pay their respects," but this speech might be what finally breaks me. My eyes burn, but I refuse to let any tears leak out. I need to be strong for my sisters.

"Mommy?"

The small voice at the door breaks up the sob-fest.

Iris dabs at her eyes with a balled-up handkerchief that

used to belong to our dad. By the time she kneels to wrap her arms around her daughter, she's smiling again. The smile may be brittle, but at least it's there. "My little sunshine. You don't know how much Mommy needed this hug."

"Pappy always said my hugs were magical."

So much for not fucking crying.

"They really are," Iris whispers.

Ella blinks up at me from over her shoulder. "You want a hug too, Uncle Pickle?"

Oh, yeah. That's me. Uncle Pickle. Don't ask.

"Only if it's a really, really big one. Bigger than the one you gave your mommy because you secretly love me more." I bend to scoop up my giggling niece, her tiny arms squeezing my neck. I'm jealous of Iris, with her husband and daughter to distract her from the shittiness of this situation. Any time I'm alone, I start thinking about all the stuff that Dad and I had planned on doing but never got the chance. Like taking that cross-country trip on our bikes. Or heading out to the salt flats for a race. Then there's the McAllen International Carfest. Should've fucking gone.

When Ella says it's Alex's turn for a healing hug, I set my niece down and excuse myself. I find a quiet corner in the choir room at the back of the church to type out a few notes on my phone while my sisters speak in low tones about the dinner that's happening after this back at Mom and Dad's. Thankfully, only a handful of close friends and family are invited. All I have to do is make it through the funeral, burial, and then dinner.

With any luck, after we meet with the lawyers for the reading of the will, I'll be on the first flight back to Austin.

A short while later, the pastor quietly steps in and tells us it's time. When he asks who's doing the eulogy, I reluctantly raise my hand. We get into a line and file down a dark hallway and out to the vestibule. Somber music filters through the speakers as the door opens, and Hayley leads the way into the packed sanctuary.

I keep my head down, managing not to make eye contact with anyone as we shuffle into the front pew. Every time I try to swallow, my throat refuses to budge.

I can't bring myself to look at the gilt-framed photo of my parents resting on an easel beside the pulpit. Instead, I stare blankly at the two matching caskets Iris picked out, pretending I don't know who's inside. That gets me through the depressing songs and the short sermon, but then Alex squeezes my knee and it's time.

I push to my feet and adjust the black tie squeezing my throat. A collective murmur lifts from the crowd, but by the time I step behind the pulpit, you could hear a pin drop. Given my reputation around town, they're probably all waiting for me to burst into flames inside this holy place.

I can't look at my sisters because seeing them cry will make my own tears spill, and that'll be all people will talk about. God knows, I've already given this place enough fodder to last a lifetime.

As I stare down at my phone screen, my throat locks up. Why did I let my sisters talk me into this? They owe me.

I raise my head and glance over the small sea of ashen faces, my gaze halting on a pair of clear, green eyes watching me. The young woman's golden hair falls in soft waves over the shoulders of her sensible black dress.

Jade Quinn. Hayley's childhood best friend.

Unlike most of the people sitting in this church, there's no judgment on Jade's face, just a sad but encouraging smile.

I clutch the wood of the pulpit, inhale a deep breath, and begin.

"When he was in high school, my dad was one heck of a football player. He still holds the state record for the most touchdowns in a single season. I remember worrying that he'd be disappointed when my promising football career ended at seven years old with a broken ankle." That was when he gave me my first camera to distract me from having to be in a cast for a month.

"But the disappointment never came," I go on. "Dad was never anything but proud of us. During our weekly phone calls, he'd spend half the time asking about my life and the other half telling me what was happening with Iris and Alex, and where in the world Hayley was off to next. Even though he was a successful businessman, we rarely spoke about business. He just wanted to talk about his family because that was his legacy. Not the stores or real estate or investments, but his wife, children, and Ella, his granddaughter. The light of his life."

My teeth dig into my bottom lip, and my eyes burn.

One down. One to go.

"And Mom..." *Don't cry. Don't cry. Don't cry.* "I'm sure you'll all agree that Martha King was a friend to everyone she met, a pillar in this community, and a saint for putting up with all four of us without losing her mind."

A light chuckle sounds from one of the rear pews, and my gaze falls back on Jade. Her amusement quickly fades, and when she reaches up to wipe her cheeks, the man beside her offers her a tissue. Is that Nate Williams? They're sitting awfully close together. Don't tell me that Jade is dating that prick.

Focus, Dylan.

I glance back at my phone, skimming my notes to try

and remember where I left off. "I think my sisters would agree that Mom could bake a boxed apple pie better than anyone on the planet. And she gave the best hugs, always holding on so long that it got awkward."

I hear Hayley's choked laugh, clear as day.

Time to wrap it up.

"Through the years, my parents were invited to all sorts of charity events and parties. Whenever Mom would get tired, she'd give Dad a wink. That was their signal. He'd wink back, then tell whoever he was speaking to that it was time to go, and they'd leave together. I don't think it ever crossed their minds to go their separate ways, not even for a night."

My throat tightens, and I reach up to loosen my tie so I can get through this last part.

"Just like all those parties," I say, "Mom and Dad had to leave this world together. And knowing that makes all of this a little more bearable."

I'm such a fucking liar. Having them both die at the same time has been torture. I couldn't have chosen one over the other. I just want one of them here to help us through this shit.

"Mom and Dad," I say to the coffins, "We love you and will never stop missing you." I collect my phone and return to where my sisters are sobbing, still fighting the sharp stinging in my eyes.

CHAPTER FOUR

JADE

I swipe my knuckles over my cheeks as Hayley and her sniffling sisters shuffle down the aisle, trailing after the pallbearers carrying the caskets. Hayley's brother Dylan is at the front of the pack, the edge of his dad's coffin resting on one shoulder, his stricken eyes concealed by sunglasses.

The overhead speakers crackle like someone's fiddling around with the sound system, and a second later, "I Can't Get No Satisfaction" by The Rolling Stones floods the air as mourners begin filing out of the church.

My brows fly up at the choice of song, and I exchange a glance with Nate. After we'd arrived at the funeral at the exact same time, the deputy sheriff had followed me into one of the back pews and sat quietly beside me for the service.

"Hayley's dad was a rock n' roll fan," I explain in a whisper while slipping the funeral booklet into my purse.

Nate leans closer, bringing a strong whiff of aftershave. "At least it's not 'Another One Bites the Dust'." The corner of his mouth twitches.

Holy smokes, was that a joke from the world's most

poker-faced police officer? Ordinarily, this sort of breaking of character would thrill me, but I shoot Nate a subtle look for making that joke at a time like this.

The forty-minute service had felt like forty hours to me, with Dylan's heartbreaking eulogy churning up memories of my mom's funeral that made my palms sweat against my knees. Back on that awful day, I'd sat in the front pew grinding my teeth and forcing myself to think about things that wouldn't make me fall apart, like how many separate blocks of wood had been used to make up the parquet floor.

The unwanted flashback disappears when Nate gets up beside me. We wait for a gap in the parade of funeral-goers before falling into step behind them.

"This is not what I expected for our first date," Nate murmurs. "I would have preferred the Italian festival with some pasta and perhaps a glass each of chianti." The way he pronounces chianti as chee-anti is like nails on a chalkboard.

"Yeah, the whole grief thing really takes the romance out of the air," I deadpan.

He snickers, his body so close to mine that our arms brush. "You do look beautiful, though, Jade."

Oh, jeez. I drape my long, blond hair over my shoulder, suddenly self-conscious in the tailored black dress I bought for Mom's funeral and hadn't worn again until now.

After thanking Nate for his compliment, I dash outside into the comfort of the fresh air, although there's a cool bite to the September wind. The Kings' popularity has attracted a sizable crowd, and it takes a few seconds for me to spot Hayley over near the funeral cars. I weave my way through to her with Nate still shadowing me.

Hayley's puffy eyes brighten a little as I approach, and I fold my arms around her and give her a big squeeze. Nate steps forward to offer his condolences, and as the two of them chat a little, I overhear the reason he's here. He attended the car accident that killed her parents while he was on duty, and he wants to pay his respects. I can't even imagine how awful that must've been. I definitely wouldn't have the stomach to be a police officer.

Out of nowhere, the Burner triplets burst through the crowd and dart between us, nearly knocking me on my ass.

"Is that where the dead bodies are?" asks the rattiest-looking triplet, pointing at the hearses.

Gasps ripple through the gatherers except for one voice behind me that breathes a light laugh. Dylan edges past, bringing a faint waft of something fresh and musky, like expensive men's soap.

"Fuck, I needed that," he murmurs about the boy's macabre comment, then says something to Hayley about the burial arrangements. My gaze catches on a beautiful image of flying birds tattooed vertically up the side of his neck.

"Are you coming back to the house with us, Jade?" Hayley asks. She'd mentioned a small dinner for close family and friends in a text this morning.

"Definitely."

Dylan twists around and his eyes lock on mine, sending heat to my cheeks. *Ugh, I hope he doesn't think I was staring at him like a creeper.*

"I'm so sorry for your loss," I mumble to him, my blush deepening.

A faint smile edges his mouth. "Thanks, Jade."

His blue eyes hover on my face, and I hide my strange embarrassment by turning back to Nate and giving him a soft smile. Nate's looking only at Dylan, with his jaw so tight that it could snap into two pieces. Dylan doesn't so much as glance at him.

The preacher steps forward with Hayley's older sisters

and asks if the family is ready to start making their way to the cemetery. Tears swell in Hayley's eyes as she nods, and Dylan curves a hand around her shoulder.

The family heads off toward the cars, and Nate waits beside me as I watch them go. "You and Hayley have stayed close?" he asks.

I nod. "Still the best of friends, even though we don't get to see each other very often." We make a point to call each other at least once a week, although she's usually the only one with news.

His teeth dig into his bottom lip. "So, you know the brother well, too, then."

"Dylan? Not really. I think he lives somewhere out west." And by "I think," I really mean, "I know for a fact that @dylan.a.king lives in Austin, Texas." Not that I stalk him or anything. Because I definitely don't. His location is right there on his Instagram profile for everyone to see.

"Thank goodness for small mercies," Nate mutters.

My brow pinches. "What do you mean?"

He presses his lips together.

I wait for more, but his gaze drops to his watch. "Can we talk about this another time? I have to get to work, so I won't be at the burial." He shoots me a look of regret. "I'm already late."

My cheeks pull up. "Baddies to catch and cities to protect."

He chuckles. "More like a drawer full of paperwork." His cheeks flush pink. "Are we still on for the Italian fair?"

As if I'd ever turn down Italian food. "We better be. Because today really did suck as a first date."

His smile stretches wide, but then his lips tighten up again. "Will you do me a favor, Jade? Stay away from Dylan King. That guy's trouble."

I snort half a laugh. "Sure, Dad."

Nate just passes me an unsure look before he turns and strides away with his hands balled into fists at his sides.

What the heck is his problem with Dylan King?

AFTER THE BURIAL, I SWING BY THE STORE TO CHECK on Dad. When I find him struggling to unpack a giant box of frozen goods, I end up sending him home to rest his sore back and then have to stick around until closing time.

Before I lock up, I lightly press my palm to the picture of Mom and Dad to say goodnight to her, the same way I do every day. Outside, I jump into my car and floor it toward the King residence, hoping that Hayley got my apologetic texts about being late.

The Kings' mammoth home sits tucked away in a beautiful, forested part of town that overlooks the springs. The front door is unlocked, as always, and I cautiously step inside to find Hayley and her sisters sitting around the marbled dining table with half-filled glasses of wine. They still look shell-shocked, but I'm relieved to see Hayley almost smiling. She helps me fix a plate of pork chops with baked vegetables and mash. It's just a few of Hayley's sister's friends here, her sister's husband Justin, and me. There's no sign of Dylan.

While Hayley and I talk as I eat, I take in all the parts of the dining room that have changed since I was last here. The abstract artworks lining the eight-foot-high walls are new, and I assume Hayley had a hand in choosing those. I used to come over to this house all the time when I was little, but back then, I'd mostly grab Hayley's hand and we'd bolt upstairs to her enormous bedroom, locking ourselves in with her vintage record player and hours of boy talk.

"It's so good to see you," she says, and I tilt my head into her shoulder, wishing it could be under any other circumstances.

"Did you come to the funeral with Nate the Nark?" she adds, poking my side.

I snicker. "No, we kind of sat together by accident. But I am supposed to be going out with him this weekend."

"What?" She whacks my arm and I laugh, even though I feel guilty talking about dating on the day of her parents' funeral. But Hayley seems drawn to the distraction, and we chat more about Nate's fuddy-duddy vibe, but agree that he's not *not*-cute, and he does have an impressive job.

A chill dances up my bare arms, and I shiver.

"Are you cold?" Hayley asks. "I've got sweaters upstairs in my suitcase."

She yawns as she goes to get up, but I tell her I don't mind getting it myself.

I give her wrist a squeeze and wander up the staircase coated in plush carpet, my chest constricting when I pass by the photo wall of family pictures. I force my gaze off her mom and dad's beaming faces.

Like I'm sixteen years old again, I round the top of the stairwell and head toward Hayley's old bedroom before a high-pitched giggle stops me in my tracks. Through the open door of another room, I spot Iris's daughter, Ella, sitting on the floor beside Dylan. He's got a half-torn pink tutu stretched tightly around his hips, and on his head sits a plastic crown glittering with fake jewels that matches the scepter in his hand.

I go to dart out of view, but it's too late. Dylan makes an exaggerated gasp. "Look, Ella—there's a monster coming out of the forest. Help!" He grabs her arms and pretends to hide his broad shoulders behind her tiny frame, making her squeal and laugh.

Not to brag, but I've always been great with kids. Dropping my weird Dylan-awkwardness for a moment, I suck in a breath, lift my hands into claws, and bound into the room with a loud roar. *Oh my god, Jade, you are certifiable.* Ella laughs her head off.

The embarrassment hits me instantly, but instead of looking at me like I'm a freak, Dylan gives me a smile that makes me stare at him a little too long.

"Have you been sent up to get us?" he asks, tapping his scepter against his knee.

"No, I just came up to grab a sweater."

"Hmm." He folds his arms at me, and heat creeps into my cheeks as his eyes make a slow roam over my body. "So, little Jade Quinn. She got...big." His gaze flashes below my neck for a lightning-fast moment before returning to my eyes.

"Jade got big, and Dylan got...*old*?" I make a face like he's past his prime, when actually, Dylan's grown into a ridiculously attractive man. If tattoos, smirks, and provocative stares are your thing, that is.

A laugh slips out of him. He rests his palms on his outstretched legs, evidently not at all self-conscious about the tutu. "The last time I saw *you* in this house, you had that gigantic bandage over your nose because that brat from little league pitched a softball at your face. I'd wanted to bust that jerk's nose right back, but Dad stopped me."

A tingle rises in my chest at that admission as my fingers instinctively brush my nose.

"Then Hayley tried putting our mom's makeup on it to hide the bruising," Dylan continues, "which escalated into you girls dressing up in Mom's clothes and wearing her lacy bras over your dresses, even though you had nothing to put in them."

Oh. My. God. *That's* what he remembers about me?

"Looks like you do now, though," he murmurs, looking away.

My face catches fire and my brain scrambles for some embarrassing memory about him to make us square. Except all my memories of Dylan seem to revolve around how ridiculously cool he's always been. There has to be *something*. Oh! I know a good one. "Well, since we're taking this fun little trip down memory lane, what about that time you listed your virginity for sale on eBay?"

He groans, covering his face with his palm. "I'm going to kill Hayley for telling you about that."

"Mommy said you shouldn't kill people," Ella says in a singsong voice, dragging a comb through her doll's ratty blonde hair.

I have to stifle my laughter. "She's right, Dylan. You shouldn't kill people."

"Not even when they tell your secrets?" he asks Ella.

She shakes her head. "Nope."

After pinky-promising his niece that he will not murder Hayley, Dylan waves his scepter at me and says, "Did my sister tell you the whole story about the eBay incident? That the only reason I did it was because my parents refused to buy me this expensive bike and told me to raise the money myself?"

She hadn't told me that part. "No. If I'd known that, I would've bid ten cents instead of five."

He hums a laugh. "You didn't bid a thing, you little liar. You were still in pigtails."

"So think of how much five cents actually meant to me."

When his gaze holds mine for a long moment, Nate's warning pushes into my head. *"Stay away from Dylan King. That guy's trouble."*

Why am I standing here talking to Hayley's brother instead of getting that sweater? For some reason, I can't seem to bring myself to leave.

A smirk tugs at my lips. "It's a shame that eBay deleted the listing. With the number of girls who'd have thrown themselves off a bridge for you back then, you could've gotten ten bikes. Hayley called you the Still Springs Heart Slayer. One look from Dylan, and bang—instant death."

I expect a witty comeback or another humiliating story about my past. Instead, the smile falls off Dylan's face, and something shifts in his eyes.

He tugs his bottom lip between two fingers and then angles his body to face Ella, who's trying to force a tiny shoe onto her doll's foot. "When you go downstairs, can you ask Iris to come get Ella?" he says to me. "Tell her the babysitter's tired."

"Yeah, no problem. I was just kidding, by the way," I add for the record.

"Don't fret, Little Jade." He doesn't look at me as he picks up Ella's doll to help her with the second shoe. "I'll see ya around."

The abrupt dismissal makes my throat burn. I swallow tightly and head back toward the hallway, confusion swirling in my chest. I'm halfway out the door when I overhear Ella ask Dylan what "virginity" means. By the time he responds in that deep, smoky voice of his, I'm too far away to hear the explanation.

CHAPTER FIVE

DYLAN

When my best friend from college lost his mom after a long battle with cancer, he'd had to deal with one small house and an ugly dog that never met a floor it didn't rub its ass on.

He and his siblings had been slowly getting rid of her lifetime collection of porcelain houses over the course of her illness. His sister adopted the dog, they donated the rest of her belongings to charity, handed over the keys of the house to a real estate agent, and then washed their hands of the rest.

From the stack of pages listing our parents' assets sitting in the middle of the table, I'm pretty sure my sisters and I are in for a shitshow. Not what you want to wake up to first thing on a Monday morning.

"So you're basically saying we all have to be here every step of the way?" Hayley asks.

It's nice to know I'm not the only one shitting it here.

Miriam, our parents' lawyer, shakes her head. "No, I said that all four of you are listed as executors on your parents' will, which means if you'd like to sell anything, you will all need to sign the paperwork and have it notarized."

"But I'm supposed to go to Greece for a month and Croatia after that," Hayley says in a small voice.

Ah, yes. My sister's soul-searching trip around the Mediterranean that she booked as part of her New Year's resolution for more "self-care."

Iris grips Hayley's leg under the table. "We can discuss all that later."

I may not have grand plans for some European excursion, but I have a life to get back to as well, and you don't hear me whining and moping around.

At least people in this town don't think Hayley's the spawn of Satan.

Part of me thought that maybe, just maybe, Still Springs would've decided to give its small-mindedness a break for a fucking funeral.

But then I overheard two old biddies at the graveside "whispering" loud enough to wake my Mom and Dad in their caskets.

"Hasn't changed a bit," one of them had said to the other, her beady little eyes locked on me.

Which wasn't true at all. When I'd left this place:

My hair had been buzzed.

I'd only had one tattoo.

I'd actually given two shits about people's opinions.

"I heard he deals the drugs now," the other had said.

I've never touched "the drugs" in my life, but no one here would believe that because they're too busy judging me for something that happened when I was eighteen years old.

I hate this fucking town.

Anywhere else in the world, I can be whoever I want.

I don't just come from a wealthy family. I have no tragic past.

I'm just me. Dylan.

Sure, the tattoos put some people off, but I'm okay with that. If they want to be small-minded jackasses, who am I to stop them? If someone really wants to get to know me, they can.

I don't know why Hayley is so upset about having to postpone her trip. At least she still has friends like Jade around. Everyone I knew has either bailed or doesn't talk to me anymore.

Iris and Alex shoot a barrage of questions at our lawyer, and she answers them quickly and concisely.

When Miriam finally leaves Dad's home office, the rest of us sit staring out the window toward the pool.

Hayley is the first to break the silence. "Can we agree not to sell anything until I'm back from Europe?"

Iris thumbs through the gigantic stack of pages in front of her. "We don't have any plans to sell properties at the moment, but that could change once we see what Mom and Dad bought."

I fold my arms and say nothing as my sisters get into it yet again, arguing the best way out of this mess. This is the third time today I've had to listen to them squabble. When they bounce straight to the next topic, I drift off a little. Jade's comments from Saturday night come back to haunt me.

"Hayley called you the Still Springs Heart Slayer. One look from Dylan, and bang—instant death."

She has no idea how true that is. Or, at least, I assume she doesn't. Because if she knew the truth, she probably wouldn't have said a word to me.

"What do you think, Dyl?" Iris asks, bringing me right back.

All three of them stare at me. "I'm up for whatever you all think is best," I say, crossing my fingers that my response makes sense.

Iris and Hayley smile with relief while Alex lifts a quizzical brow.

"You really don't mind staying in town for that long to help with Ella?" she asks.

Oh, shit.

As if my panic is written in Sharpie across my forehead, Iris reaches for my hand. "It'll only be for a few months at most. With Dad gone, I'll be extra busy at work, and without Mom here to watch her..." Iris drifts off, her eyes filling with tears. She runs her fingers under her lashes to clear them. "I have Ella on a waitlist for preschool, but they can't guarantee her a spot until after Christmas. I will interview babysitters if I need to, but I would really rather her be with family, especially after everything that's happened."

Woah, woah, woah. Did she say a few *months*?

Iris gives my hand a squeeze. "You're the only one of us with extra free time and a flexible schedule. With your job, you can work from anywhere."

She says "job" like photography is a cute little hobby I play around with while frolicking in fields of wildflowers. While I have taken plenty of photos in fields of wildflowers, I paid for my apartment with that "hobby."

And what the hell does she mean by extra free time? I wish. I have hundreds of photos to edit from the shoot I did with an aspiring actress a few weeks back. It's not a matter of simply "slapping on a filter," as Alex loves to say. Thinking about the emails piling up in my inbox gives me heart palpitations. If I did this, I'd need to reschedule all my upcoming shoots, which would let down a lot of people. But my sisters don't see that as an inconvenience because "I can work from anywhere."

There's no question that I love my niece. She's probably my favorite person in the world right now. And it really sucks that Mom is gone and can't watch her anymore. But pressing pause on my whole life for a babysitting job? That's too much to ask.

"Iris, I don't know if I can swing it."

Her smile falters. "It'll only be from eight until four, Monday through Thursday. Justin's schedule is crazy, but he's always off on Fridays, and I'm off on weekends."

If I'm watching Ella four days a week, when am I supposed to get my own shit done?

Damn, that sounds selfish. Good thing I didn't say it out loud.

Guilt washes over me like an icy tide. Living so far away means I haven't helped much through the years. Would it really be so bad to hang around until Christmas? The holidays are going to be extra hard without Mom and Dad here. Don't I owe it to my sisters to be there for them since our parents can't?

Iris sits forward and rests her hand on my leg. "Feel free to say no. But Ella loves you *so* much, and I know this would make the transition easier on her."

How the hell am I supposed to say no to that?

For the millionth time, I curse that fucking truck driver who took away our parents. My family clearly needs me, so I'll have to figure something out for my own stuff.

"I'll stay," I decide. "But only until after Christmas."

My spinelessness earns me a hug from all three of them.

What the hell did I just do?

My sisters insist on watching home movies after brunch, but there's no way in hell I want a part of that, so I escape upstairs to the guest room where I usually stay when I'm here. My old room waits right down the hall, and though I've avoided it until now, something makes me walk right past the guest suite to my door, and...wow.

When Mom said she hadn't touched the place, she meant it. My old movie posters are still taped to the wall, the edges curled and the colors faded. The blue bedspread with the matching pillows is the same one I remember. The room isn't dusty, so the cleaners must come in here. Other than the lack of dirty clothes strewn across the carpet, the place looks the same as it did the day I left.

I sink onto the mattress, but before I can flop down, my eyes catch on a thick black book left on my nightstand.

Not a book.

A photo album of pictures I took back in high school. Bonfire nights. Football games. Shots of my entire family at our cabin down by the springs.

So much for not crying today.

I flip through a few more pages until I come across a picture of a strawberry-blonde girl with a hundred and four freckles sprinkled across her nose and cheeks. I know because I'd counted them all.

My hands begin to tremble.

The album lands on the carpet with a thud.

Why did I think it was a good idea to come in here? I'm such a fucking idiot.

I stalk out of the room and slam the door. The family portraits on the wall rattle, but none of them fall. Trying to breathe through the choking panic doesn't do a fucking thing. What else had my therapist suggested? My brain feels like it's melting and I can't think straight. Maybe a cold drink will help.

My legs wobble as I hurry back down the stairs and into the kitchen to pour a glass of filtered water from the fridge.

I gulp it down, eyeing Hayley curled up on the couch in the living room. From the inhuman snores, I assume she's asleep. There's no sign of Alex or Iris. They probably got fed up sitting next to a revving chainsaw.

By the time I finish my water, some of the tension in my throat and chest has subsided.

Until I hear my dad's voice, clear as if he were standing in the next room. "Come on, pickle. You can do it. I'm right here. I'm right here with you."

Every muscle in my body tenses as I move stiffly toward the living room. The home movie still playing on the TV is from some random summer when I was a kid.

Dad's in the pool out back, cheering me on as I try to swim from one side to the other. He's careful to stay within arms reach but doesn't interfere unless he needs to.

I grab the remote and turn the damn thing off.

I may have to stay in town, but I can't be in this house a moment longer.

Where do I go? The cabin? No. Too many memories there. Plus, I'll need to stay close by to help with Ella on Monday. My parents owned half this town. Surely there's an apartment or house or some other place nearby where I can stay.

There's only one way to find out.

Mom and Dad's will and list of assets are still sitting on the desk in the office. I flip through the wad of pages until I find what I'm looking for: an old storefront on Main Street with an upstairs apartment.

Perfect.

I throw some shit into a bag and write a quick note letting Hayley know where I'll be. Then I drag a fuzzy throw over Snoring Beauty and head back upstairs to pack my things. First thing tomorrow, I'm out of here.

CHAPTER SIX

JADE

My yoga instructor, Kayla, catches my eye as I roll up my mat. She makes her way over to me, bringing with her a woody scent of patchouli. *Oh no.*

"You okay today, Jade?" she asks with an unsure smile. "Your body seems a little out of sorts." She squints at my shoulders, but that's not the part of me that's stretched tight with tension.

It's the inside of my gut, which knows I was supposed to pay her invoice a few days ago for this month's classes. But after the pile of bills stamped "overdue" grew babies on my kitchen counter, there was nothing left.

"I'm sorry I haven't paid for this month yet," I blurt in response to her question while bundling my mat under my arm. "It might be a week or so late, but I promise it'll be paid."

"Oh, don't worry, lovely." Her voice is more soothing than the nature soundtrack burbling in the background. "Money is of no consequence; the only wealth is health. But I do offer a variety of payment plans," she's quick to add.

I press my lips together, bottling a ridiculous urge to ask

Kayla if she would accept payment in the form of groceries like we're members of the early civilizations trading animal skins for fish. Plus, it's not like I own the stock at our store. Anything that leaves the shelves has to be accounted for in the books, and Dad would notice if I started giving stuff away.

After getting Kayla's payment plan details, I slip outside into the early morning breeze on Summercrest Street with my chest knotted up. Yoga is the only thing in the world that can get me out of bed at sunrise, but I'm at a point where I can't afford the classes anymore. I'm going to have to go back to free online videos in my living room.

The swampy smell of stale beer spills through the ajar door of The Rocking Horse bar as I step past it on my way to the store. Marjorie gives me a wave through the gap, her other arm making fast glides with her backpack vacuum. She used to clean our store every morning until we couldn't pay her anymore and decided to handle the cleaning ourselves.

Shit, I better motor. I've gotta open up in twenty minutes, and it's probably a dustbin in there.

I round the corner onto Main Street, one hand hooked around my yoga mat and the other digging in my pocket for my keys. I halt at the sight of a tall shape leaning against the brick wall beside the store with his broad back angled away from me and a cell phone pressed to his ear.

What the hell is Hayley's brother doing here?

He pushes his shoulder into the wall, murmuring into the phone while his fingers reach up to tug at his messy strands of hair.

Dylan shifts around and his eyes snap to mine, holding there. I stand frozen solid as if he's a bear that's happened upon my yard, and I can't get inside the house.

Jade Quinn. Move your ass.

I offer him a confused smile as I fumble with my keys and approach the store's faded red door beside him. His eyes stay locked to the side of my face.

"I love you."

The words leave his lips like a husky caress—like he means them with every fiber of his being—and I trip over my own foot and nearly ass-plant onto the pavement.

"Shit, are you okay?" Dylan steps forward to steady me, but I'm upright again. Upright and beet-red from head to toe. "I've gotta go, gorgeous, but I'll see you tomorrow," he says into the phone, and my sluggish morning brain connects the dots. He told *whoever was on the other end of the line* that he loves them. I don't know why it surprises me that he has a girlfriend. Why wouldn't he? He's stupidly handsome and has to be around thirty by now; maybe he's even married, and Hayley just hasn't mentioned it.

"That was Ella," he explains, sliding his phone into his back pocket. "Her mom cut up her banana this morning when she wanted it whole, so she needed some emotional support. Why on earth would anyone take a knife to a banana?"

Ella, his four-year-old niece—that's who he was talking to.

"It's an offense of the highest order," I reply with a chuckle, pushing my key into the lock. "Did you need something at the store?" A little thrill washes through me that this guy came here to buy stuff when his family owns the biggest superstore in the county. *That's why it's called a convenience store, naysayers. Because it's* convenient.

"Nah, I'm waiting for a locksmith." He jerks his chin at the old ice cream store next door. It still hurts to look at the space we were so close to acquiring and expanding into.

The King family snapped it up along with the old Harringtons restaurant beside it. "None of the keys my sister gave me fit the lock," Dylan continues. "Typical Mom and Dad. Bought the place on a whim, tossed the key somewhere, probably never set foot inside. God knows how many fucking roaches are crawling around in there."

What on earth does he plan to do with the store space? It better be something special because that place was my dream. I'd sooner see it stay empty than end up something inconsequential like a storeroom for his rich-boy toys.

He angles his neck toward the road, probably hunting for the locksmith. Around here, that can only be Jerry Saeed, who makes a sloth look supersonic.

"Do you want to come inside and wait there?" I mumble, silently begging Dylan to decline. I've only had one coffee, which means my brain is semi-liquid, and I'm sure this guy already thinks I'm a childish dope.

"Why not, Little Jade?" he says like he heard my thoughts and wants to rub them in. His confident smirk burns a hole into my back as he follows me into the store.

"Early morning yoga session?" he guesses, leaning his elbows against the counter as I slide my mat beneath it.

"What gave it away?" I retort, flicking on all the lights. "Surely not the yoga mat?"

His eyes begin a slow, unapologetic trail across my sports bra and down my leggings. "It was more the outfit." His gaze flicks back to mine. "Sweaty looks good on you."

I glance away with overheated cheeks, wanting those words to come off as sleazy and gross, but for some reason, they don't. They make me want to stand right here in the firing line of Dylan's electric gaze instead of doing what I should—giving the store a quick clean, opening the cash register, and tidying up the shelves.

"You want some coffee?" I ask before remembering the coffee maker crapped itself a few days ago.

"Hell yes. Thank you."

"I only have instant."

He doesn't try to hide his grimace. "Just when I thought this week couldn't get any more depressing. But if that's all you've got, I'm game."

Did he just... Did he just compare his parents' passing away to instant coffee?

I don't know why I find that so refreshing, but it loosens my lungs a little. *Stop being awkward. He's your best friend's brother. Make the man a coffee.*

After offering Dylan a stool, I head into the kitchenette to fix two cups. We sit across from each other at the counter and try not to gag at the watery taste while the weekend dust gathers another layer at our feet.

"Thanks again for coming to the funeral," Dylan says, looking right at me.

"Of course."

Silence builds between us. Normally, the quiet doesn't bother me, but for some reason, this feels really awkward, and I have the overwhelming urge to fill it. "That was a beautiful eulogy you gave."

He glances down. "Thanks."

"That part about your mom and dad always being together was really special."

He sucks his bottom lip between his teeth. "Not something I can relate to, but that was them to a T. Where Mom went, Dad followed. And vice-versa."

He blinks at me over the rim of his cup. "Hayley told me you lost your mom a few years ago."

A blade presses between my ribs. "Yeah. She had cancer."

His compassionate eyes lock on mine, and a moment of understanding shifts between us. When someone you desperately love dies, everything reminds you of them, of the unfathomable prospect of life without that person. Even now, everywhere I turn in the store, I still see Mom cheerfully punching buttons on the cash register or loading fresh stock onto the shelves. Her loss has left a gaping, bottomless hole that will never be filled.

Dylan swallows hard. "I'm sorry. I guess, as that movie goes, life is like a box of chocolates. The best ones always go quickly."

Hold up. I'm pretty sure the line doesn't go like that.

A slow breath passes through his lips. "There's a whole new level of feeling like shit that I never knew existed."

I silently nod, sensing my mind being pulled toward the image of my mother's soft, smiling eyes before I wrench it away. And then I lurch to my feet because if I don't physically move, my eyes might split open.

"Sorry, I've gotta do some cleaning before the customers start coming in," I say, reaching for the broom that's leaning against a stack of delivery boxes.

Dylan gets up quickly and runs his palms down his jeans. "'Course. Thanks for the shithouse coffee."

I blurt a laugh. "Anytime."

The second I say the word, I want to shove it back into my throat. I can't be hanging out with Hayley's older brother. For one, he lives in Austin. The last thing I need is to get attached to someone who's only here for a little while. And despite the flirtatious comments, Dylan King is hardly interested in me.

Plus, there's a reason Hayley rarely comes into this place. Despite our friendship, our family stores are in direct competition, even if mine is David and hers is Goliath. How do I know Dylan's not in here to cozy up to the enemy and conduct secret price checks so that he can undercut us? He's evidently already doing something with the empty store space next door.

"So, what are your plans for next door?" I probe as he scoops up his duffel bag.

"There's an apartment above the old ice cream shop. I'm gonna crash there for a bit. Me and my roach buddies."

My lips fall open. He's going to be *staying* there? For how long? Not that it matters. I just don't need the distraction.

"Something wrong with the house over at the springs?" I ask in a breath.

He looks away and then back at me. "Memories," is all he says.

An orange and red tattoo on his forearm of a burning leaf catches the hazy stream of morning light as he turns for the door.

"Take care of yourself, Jade," he says like he isn't about to basically become my next-door neighbor.

But maybe this is as much as one girl ever gets out of Dylan King. One impotent coffee, one brief conversation, one fleeting moment of his full attention.

One and done.

My phone lights up with a message alert, and Dylan's still close enough to spot the words on the screen: *Nate the Nark.* The nickname will mean nothing to him, but there's only one Nate in this town.

Most people would pretend they didn't notice a message on someone else's phone out of politeness, but Dylan makes no effort to hide his smirk.

"Jade and Nate, sitting in a tree..." he starts.

My face drops down, a frown forming on my brow.

When I brave a look back up, his clear-blue eyes are staring straight at mine. "Make sure he brings the handcuffs," he adds with a quick wink. Before I can reply, he strolls out through the front door and leans back against the wall outside.

Another brazen, inappropriate comment.

So why do my cheeks keep pulling up like they want to smile? Damn cheeks. Traitors, the both of them.

I've still got the words *handcuffs* and *Dylan King* wrapped around each other in my head when Mrs. Horne pushes through the door with her Pomeranian wriggling under one arm. *Here we go.*

"Good morning, Jade," she says, coral-pink lipstick smeared unevenly over her crinkly lips. "I was on my morning walk with Minnie when I thought I should pop in to tell you the good news. I was able to get the pendulum fixed on that old cherry wood clock I was telling you about last week—"

I feel guilty, but I really don't have time for this today.

My gaze catches on Dylan outside, and an idea pops into my mind.

"That sounds fascinating, Mrs. Horne, but do you know what? There was a guy just in here who's really into antique clocks. I think he wants to start his own grandfather clock collection and could use some good advice."

Her painted brows shoot up. "Really?"

"Yeah, he's right outside." I stretch on my stool and point through the front window. "The man out there with the tattoos on his arms. I'm sure he'd love to talk to you. He might pretend he's not interested because he's a bit embarrassed about it, but keep going. I think it'll really help him to hear *every single detail*." I shoot her a wink like we're in on a little secret.

She thanks me and hurries outside before Dylan can leave. I watch them through the window with sheer delight until Latisha, who owns the shoe store, steps in, asking about fresh eggs.

When I glance at the window again, Mrs. Horne is pointing at me. Dylan shoots me a knowing, half-amused stare through the glass that sends a shiver through me. I'm just not sure it's the bad kind.

CHAPTER SEVEN

DYLAN

Everyone is staring at me.

And that's not me being a cocky asshole. The twelve people milling around on the sidewalk, some holding coffees, others clutching purses, are literally gawking right at me as if I'm some sort of exotic fish in an aquarium.

Why can't they pretend I don't exist and talk shit behind my back instead? They probably think I'm here to pull a bank job or something ridiculous like that. My savings account in their precious little bank is probably larger than all their accounts combined. And not all that money came from Mom and Dad.

Seriously. What's with these folks?

I'm actually starting to sweat, and I only packed three shirts in the duffel bag sitting beside me on the sidewalk. I really don't feel like going back to Mom and Dad's anytime soon to do laundry. My therapist taught me how to breathe through shit like this, but she didn't tell me how to breathe when there's no air.

The first bug-eyed local steps up to me and says, "I was so sorry to hear about your parents. They were good people." The emphasis on "they" doesn't go unnoticed. Like she wants me to know that I'm the shitty apple in the bunch.

Newsflash, Karen in the mauve lipstick: I already know.

My brittle smile tightens and so do my hands where they're stuffed into my pockets. *"They* were."

She has the good sense to look embarrassed as she scurries off to her Volvo parked across the street.

A man walking a schnauzer gives me a brusque nod. "Your mom and dad will be missed."

"They sure will." Now, move on and leave me alone.

The next stranger has the nerve to squeeze my bicep. Do I look like I want to be touched right now? "How are you holding up?" she asks.

That's the worst fucking question of them all and the one I get the most.

"I'm shit because both of my parents just died. Thanks for asking," is what I want to say, but I don't. Instead, I give the standard, "I'm fine," because, again, I'm not a complete asshole.

This is my fault for thinking it would be a good idea to move into a place on Main Street.

But I've already texted my sisters to tell them my plans, and called the locksmith, *and* told Jade we'll be neighbors, so my pride won't let me back out now.

Speaking of Jade, thanks to her, my mouth still tastes like revolting coffee, and I've learned way too much about grandfather clocks. At least the lady with the clock obsession didn't ask about Mom and Dad. She seemed lonely, so I let her babble, trying hard to appear interested until she and her dog wandered off toward the park.

A van with the word "Locksmith" hand-painted on the

side finally pulls up. A man in a backward baseball cap climbs out and steps toward me. "Dylan King?"

"That's me."

The people still on the street stand watching like this is more interesting than what's on TV, whispering to each other behind their hands and dragging out their phones. *Run for your lives! Dylan King is moving onto Main Street!*

I've never missed Austin as much as I do right now.

The locksmith pulls out some tools while I stare down at a text on my phone from my therapist saying she's going to call in thirty minutes for a session. I already have enough shit to deal with, but maybe talking to her will help sort out my head.

The sound of an opening door makes me so fucking happy that I can't hide my smile. The man who saved my life slaps a new pair of keys in my palm, followed by a bill I can pay online, and leaves as slowly as he arrived.

I bolt inside the building and kick the door shut before anyone else can bother me. The empty room smells like dust, mildew, and fried food lingering from the old restaurant next door. I really hope it doesn't stink as bad upstairs.

The apartment above the empty store is small, but it'll do for the time being. The mattresses in both bedrooms, on the other hand, need a date with the dump. I pull out my phone to put in an online order from our family's store for one mattress. There's no sense getting two since I won't be having anyone over. The new one won't be as comfy as my bed back home, but at least it won't look like someone pissed all over it and feel like it's made from straw.

Memory foam? Don't mind if I do. The best part is, after a quick call to the store manager, the bed will be delivered by the close of business today.

Now, to get this hovel clean enough to sleep in. I'll need washcloths, sponges, paper towels, a mop, a bucket...

While my mental list continues to grow, I catch a glimpse through the window of a woman wearing bright yellow rubber gloves coming out of The Rocking Horse clutching a hot-pink mop and matching bucket.

Bingo. I practically fall down the stairs in my rush to get to her. When I burst onto the street, she whips around toward me with her mop handle raised, ready to attack.

My hands fly up in front of me. "So sorry. I didn't mean to startle you."

Her brows lift, but the only thing I care about is the way the mop lowers.

"Are you a cleaner?" I ask.

She waves her gloved hand in my face and swings the bucket toward me. "What gave you that idea?"

I tuck my hands into my pockets and shrug. "What can I say? I have a sixth sense about these things. Are you looking for any more jobs? I moved in upstairs and the place is a wreck."

Her gaze falls to the building behind me. "No wonder. No one's rented that place since old Marnie Hill passed."

God, I hope old Marnie Hill didn't "pass" in the apartment. I don't ask, though, because I don't want to know. "Think you can help me out?"

She sets down her mop and bucket and tugs the gloves off her fingers. "How many bedrooms is it?"

"Two. And one bathroom." One disgusting, roach-filled bathroom.

"It'll be expensive."

If she's willing to keep me from having to touch roach carcasses, then money isn't an object. "Name your price."

Her eyes narrow as she considers my question. "Seventy-five dollars."

Is she kidding right now? I pay the cleaning company back in Austin twice that much, and they don't have to deal with suspicious brown stains around the toilet. "Deal."

"You'll have to get some bleach and dusting spray, window cleaner too. And your own mop and bucket." She nudges the pink one with the toe of her shoe. "Sally here doesn't like new dirt."

I have no idea what new dirt is or why she calls her bucket Sally, but *holy shit*. She's going to do the windows too? What did I do in a past life to deserve this small mercy?

"I'll grab it all right now." And would you look at that? There's a store right next door.

I step inside Quinn Brothers for the second time today, and all my blood rushes south when I see Jade bent over a box of—who am I kidding? I'm not looking at what's in that box because I am definitely ogling her perfect ass in those turquoise yoga pants. Fuck me.

No, seriously.

Fuck. Me.

"Did you see me coming, or are you just practicing your downward dog?" I ask.

Jade lets out the cutest little squeak that gets me thinking of some other noises I'd love to hear her make. Not that she and I would ever happen for obvious reasons. Hayley would take a knife to my balls if I went anywhere near her best friend. And since I like my balls right where they are, I force my gaze away.

Jade stands up, and the way the filtered sunlight catches her face makes her look like an angel. If I had my camera, I'd sure as hell be taking a picture.

"You have any bleach?" I ask, trying not to stare at her.

Her lips tip into a sexy little smile. "Why? Is there a dead body up there?" Her hand flies to her mouth. "Oh, shit. Sorry."

Maybe I should be offended about her dead body joke, but it feels kinda nice to make fun of something so shitty. A little "fuck you" to death and all its nasty friends.

"You sound way too excited about the prospect," I say with a chuckle. "Should I be worried about sleeping next door?"

That makes her laugh. She has a nice laugh, a bit husky. "You should always be worried about a woman who owns copious amounts of lime." She waves for me to follow her, and I do my best to keep my eyes off her ass as we meander through packed shelves, but I fail. I fail big time. Those tight curves would fit so nicely in my hands.

She comes to an abrupt stop in front of a shelf stacked with white bottles, and I nearly run into her. I'm so close that her ponytail whips me in the face when she turns around.

"Here's the bleach." She gives one of the gigantic white bottles a pat. "Need anything else?"

It's kinda nice talking to someone who actually knows where products are. At bigger stores, including ours, no one seems to know what the hell's going on. "Cleaning stuff," I reply.

"Anything specific?" she asks, tightening her ponytail.

I have three sisters. A woman tightening her ponytail should not be hot. But when Jade does it, it is. It really is.

"All the cleaning stuff," I say. "I'm dealing with a lot of bodies."

She snaps her fingers and smiles. "Knew it."

Jade loads me up with so many squirt bottles, wipes, and powders that I can't carry them all, even though most of them are tucked inside the red bucket I've decided to name Reginald. "You take cards, right?" I ask, throwing everything on the counter so she can scan the barcodes. I have some cash, but it's back in the apartment.

"Of course we take cards."

I'm not sure why that question bugs her, but from the way she shoves the card reader toward me, she's definitely annoyed.

I pay, and she stuffs everything into brown paper bags with the Quinn Brothers logo stamped on the front. Even with the bags and Reginald, there's still too much for me to carry upstairs. I could make two trips, but for some reason, I hear myself say, "Do you mind helping me bring this up? Save me a trip."

She glances nervously at the door.

"It's really the least you can do after siccing the grandfather cock lady on me."

A loud laugh bursts from her lips. "Grandfather *clock*, Dylan. Not grandfather cock." A blush creeps up her throat and cheeks when she realizes what she said.

Did I tease her just to see if Little Jade would say the word cock? Maybe. Was it worth it? One hundred percent. "Oh, yeah. That makes so much more sense. I got really confused when she started talking about swinging pendulums."

Jade laughs as she hefts Reginald into her arms. "Must be your old man hearing."

I chuckle, but the little rib stings a bit. I'm not *that* much older than she is. Still, I decide to lead the way, mostly because I don't need my "old man eyes" to watch her hips swaying when we head up the stairs to my temporary home. The woman I hired to clean already has the dusty blinds pulled from all the windows and is soaking them in the tub that appears to be free of the carcasses I found earlier.

When she spots Jade, her eyes dart between us, her penciled-in brows lifting all the way to the messy bun at the top of her head.

"Oh, hey, Marjorie." Jade drops Reginald and one of the bags on the linoleum countertop in the kitchenette. "Didn't expect to see you up here."

Marjorie gestures toward me with a yellow-gloved hand. "This handsome young man offered me a job. What's your excuse?"

"I'm just being neighborly. For my new neighbor." Jade's smile appears forced when she glances back at me. "You never need an excuse to help a neighbor."

"Do you want to say neighbor a few more times?" I murmur so that only Jade can hear. Her spine stiffens when my shoulder brushes against hers on my way past.

Marjorie winks. "Mm-hmm."

"We're not together," Jade blurts out. "Tell her, Dylan."

She says that like being with me would be the worst thing in the world. And I get it. Given how this town feels about me, it probably is. But that doesn't stop me from folding my arms over my chest and leaning back against the counter. "You're handling things just fine on your own, neighbor." Consider this payback for the clock lady.

Jade's face turns as red as Reginald.

Marjorie lets out a high-pitched laugh as she noses through the bags and loops a finger through the bleach's handle. "I'm yanking your chain, Jade. I know you and Nate are going steady or whatever the kids are saying these days."

So, Jade *is* seeing that prick. I have to school my features so that I don't grimace. Who in their right mind would want to "go steady" with Nate Williams? That guy is a dick with a capital D. I may not know Jade very well, but she's way too good for him.

"You all set for Fall Fest?" Jade asks Marjorie, clearly trying to change the subject.

How had I forgotten Still Springs' annual fall festival? There are craft fairs, parades, and too many competitions to name. In a few weeks, Main Street will look like Halloween drank too much hot apple cider and threw up everywhere.

"Of course we are. Jack's ordered double the amount of hay as last year." Marjorie turns to me and adds, "For the scarecrows," as if I'm supposed to know what the hell that means.

I smile like I get the joke. "What's Fall Fest without scarecrows?"

"Exactly," Marjorie cackles as she snags a few squirt bottles. "I'd better get back to work before my boss fires me." She winks again and then disappears into the bathroom.

I turn to Jade, who seems to be having a hard time meeting my gaze. "I guess I'll see you around, neighbor."

Her throat colors pink. "I'll see you around."

The moment Jade disappears down the stairs, my phone starts going nuts in my pocket. I consider ignoring the call, but I figure if I'm paying for this session anyway, I may as well answer. I step into the stairwell so the cleaner can't overhear. When the call connects, all I see is the top of a pair of thick glasses, a creased forehead, and a silver bun.

"Hey, Sarah? You have to tilt the screen a bit if you want me to see your face," I say.

"Oh, you don't need to see my face," Sarah replies in her breathy voice, even as she follows my instructions. A bunch of crystals hang in the window directly behind her head, shooting rainbows all over the rust-orange walls. "That better?"

I can't help but smile. My therapist looks nothing like Mom, but something about her calm demeanor and lack of technological skills makes me think of her anyway. "Yeah. It's better."

Sarah pushes her glasses up her nose and gets right down to business. "How are you feeling after the funeral?"

I let out a sigh. "I'm surviving. Being around my sisters helps."

"Have you been doing your breathing exercises?"

"I have."

"And are they helping?"

Hard to tell since I haven't done them. "Yes."

She gives me a coffee-stained smile. "Excellent. Keep practicing any time you're feeling anxious. Have you had any attacks?"

"Nothing I couldn't handle." All things considered, I feel like I'm doing okay.

"Are you still in Maryland?"

"Yeah. And it looks like I will be until Christmas to help with my niece."

She looks up from her notes and blinks at me from over the rim of her glasses, but her expression gives nothing away. "Do you *want* to help out with your niece?"

"It's the least I can do." It's not like I know what to do over at the superstore. Hayley may have already ditched us, but I don't have it in me to do the same.

"That's not what I asked."

Sarah never pulls her punches, something I both admire and loathe about her.

My chest expands with a deep breath. Do I want to help with Ella? I love that kid so much. If Iris and her husband lived anywhere else in the world, I wouldn't be nearly as annoyed about it. It's this place I can't stand. But maybe crossing over that town line had been the worst of it. Maybe the hardest part is over. Maybe it'll only get better from here.

"Yeah. I think I do." I'll figure out the work stuff. I'll need to fly back to Austin to get my computer and cameras, but I can order anything else I need online. It's not like it'll go to waste.

"Then it sounds like you made the right choice for you," Sarah says. "Remember to check in with yourself periodically and that it's okay to change your mind if you feel like it's too much. Boundaries are important in these situations. Have you given any thought to what we talked about before you left?"

Her question is like a shot of anesthetic straight to my heart. "No."

Although her lips purse, she nods her head and moves on.

I know I need to deal with what happened all those years ago, but I have enough shit on my plate right now. I tell myself I'll consider confronting my demons before I leave, even though I know that's a lie.

CHAPTER EIGHT
JADE

Ice-cold lemon gelato glides over my tongue, my moan attracting Nate's eager gaze as he pushes a spoonful of vanilla between his lips.

At ease, Deputy. I'm not trying to seduce you. It's only my tastebuds getting jacked up because I haven't fed them more than grilled cheese and ramen noodles in weeks.

This is what real food tastes like. And it's glorious.

Letting people pay for me has always been a challenge, but Nate insisted when he saw me salivating over the gelato stand. I tip my melting cone toward him. "Thank you for this. Or should I say, *grazie.*"

His lips quirk up. "De nada," he replies, confusing his Spanish with his Italian. I don't know if that's cute or cringe, so I just shake my head with a smile. "Have you ever been to Italy?" he asks.

I stare at him before biting off a laugh. "Are you serious? No, I have never been to Italy. Or Europe. Or even Canada." That requires actual funds.

"Me neither." He smiles, visibly relieved that we have this in common. Because in the hour-and-a-half we've spent eating this Italian fair to the ground, we've discovered that—other than going to the same high school—we're kind of chalk and cheese.

I have a sweet tooth. Nate prefers salty foods.

I love camping, especially down at the springs. Nate despises bugs and doesn't even own a tent.

I enjoy being creeped out by extreme horror movies. Nate thought "The Rocky Horror Picture Show" was scary.

And when a pair of musicians arrived at our table a few minutes ago singing "Quando, Quando, Quando," you couldn't wipe the grin off my face, but Nate turned away with fire-engine-red cheeks like he was the one on show.

I get it. He's a low-key guy. That's not breaking news.

But right now, as he quietly picks at his gelato while I drag my tongue over my own like it's my long-lost boyfriend, I low-key want to set off a firework under this cop's butt just to see what happens.

"So, Officer Williams. Did you always want to chase bad guys for a living?" I lift my brows like that's hot, and he glances down with a fierce blush.

"If you mean working in law enforcement, then absolutely. I enjoy protecting and serving my community. Which mostly involves traffic stops and filling out paperwork. Thankfully, there aren't a lot of 'bad guys' around here." He makes air quotes with his free hand. "Unless you count the guy living next door to you," he mutters, digging harder into his gelato cup.

I sit up a little higher. "What do you mean?"

"Dylan King," he grumbles. "Isn't he staying in the apartment next door to your store?"

"I wouldn't call him a *bad guy*." It's not like I really know Dylan that well, but because he's Hayley's brother, the loyalty I feel to her transfers to him to some degree.

Nate heaves a sigh. "You clearly don't know the full story, and to be honest, I'd sooner not talk about it. But like I said, you should keep your distance." A sudden thought registers in his eyes. "Do you want me to see if I can get him to move out of there? Maybe I can find a technicality, like perhaps the apartment is no longer zoned as—"

"No," I cut in, aghast. "That guy just lost both his parents. You want to evict him from his own apartment?" I sit back a little in my seat, and Nate chases me by stretching his arm across the red and white checkered tablecloth.

"You're right," he says quickly, although the sullen expression hasn't left his face. "Anyway, I don't want to talk about *him*. I want to talk about you." He cocks his head, and while I wouldn't say my stomach flutters, it definitely warms a little.

I bite into the last chunk of my gelato cone. "What do you want to know?"

A blush creeps over his jaw. "Why did you finally decide to go out with me?"

Responses flood my head without warning.

I'm lonely.

I miss my mom. I miss Ruby.

For the first time in my life, I feel like I've drifted out to sea somewhere, and I keep paddling my arms like crazy to get back to shore, but I keep moving further away from where I want to be.

"I'm not sure why now," I reply carefully. I can't tell Nate that I think he's filling some sort of void. "I guess I really like Italian food?"

He laughs, and his arm shifts so close to mine that I can feel the heat coming off his freckled skin. "To be honest, I don't really like Italian, but I like you."

I stifle a snort-laugh. "Sounds like what you like is

cheese," I tease, which he totally deserves for that cute but schmaltzy comment.

His brows gather. "No, I really don't like cheese either. Especially blue cheese. Why would anyone want to eat something that smells like unwashed feet?"

Another chuckle bobs in my throat. "You're really turning me on right now, you know that?"

His eyes bulge. "I am?"

Oh god. Is this guy going to get any of my jokes?

"Yup," I say seriously. "Feet and men in uniform. They're my fetishes. Mmm."

When his brow pinches like he's considering that combination, I rescue him by getting up and tugging on his thick arm beneath his plaid shirt. "Come on, I'm sure there's something left here that we haven't eaten yet."

We weave our way through the spectators lining up at stalls selling everything from homemade pasta sauces to bright yellow bottles of limoncello.

I pick up a pouch of Italian coffee beans and sniff it. Nate may dislike Italian food—*is he the only person on earth who does?*—but I can't get enough of it. "I hope they do this fair every year."

"Things are definitely picking up in this town," he agrees, stepping past an artist painting Renaissance-style couple's portraits, even though they're damn cute and I would've loved one. "The fall festival's gonna be huge this year," he adds. "We're having to bring in extra officers for security."

"Really?"

He nods. "The county's really pushing it. Hey, I thought about you when I read about that magazine article thing in the local paper. Are you going to do it?"

My steps slow. "What magazine article thing?" I barely

have time to keep my house clean or get my hair cut, let alone read the *Still Springs Gazette*.

"Some travel influencer is doing an article for a big magazine about Fall Fest, and she's looking for one local business to feature, which she'll choose at the festival."

"Wow, really?"

"Yeah. At least, I think that's right."

My mind explodes with possibilities as we stroll toward the road that cuts through the center of the fair. I can't imagine our convenience store holding national appeal, but if I ramped up the stock of our local wares that are unique to the town, that could make Quinn Brothers more interesting to this reporter. And it's not like the competition's that stiff; now that the famous Harringtons restaurant has shut down, the best stores in town are the bookstore, the small shop that sells rocks and minerals, and the florist.

If I could turn our convenience store into a boutique of sorts that showcases the finest locally made specialty items that Still Springs has to offer, maybe we could win this feature spot and put our business back on the map, especially for the tourist market.

Nate ducks into a portable restroom, and I wait outside and cling to this glimmer of hope that I haven't felt in months when something firm and warm brushes against me. My face flies up to find Dylan King's ridiculously blue eyes staring down at me.

"Hi, neighbor," he says.

"Hey." I'm sure I've turned crimson.

"Ella, you remember Jade, right...the big monster?" Dylan says as his niece peeks out from his opposite side.

I morph my face into something monster-like, and she giggles, hiding behind her uncle. My eyes lift back up to meet Dylan's gaze, becoming trapped there, when a heavy hand lands on my left shoulder.

"Is everything okay over here?" Nate says firmly, stepping between Dylan and me.

Dylan makes a show of looking over his shoulders. "I don't know, Officer. Have there been some complaints?"

Nate tuts and uses his grip on my shoulder to guide me away from Dylan. But when we all head across the street, the swarm of visitors keeps us pushed together, and the four of us end up standing in front of a photo shoot tent. The tent's backdrop is painted with a colorful scene of the Leaning Tower of Pisa, and a tangle of Italy-themed costumes sits scattered along a table.

"Look! Dress-ups!" Ella cries, bounding into the tent.

The stallholder, a spotty-faced teen, slips lazily off his stool. "It's twenty dollars for a group of four," he says, sounding bored to tears.

"Oh no, we're not together." Nate starts to pull me away.

"Jade! You come too!" Ella says, holding up an Italian Riviera hat that's bigger than she is.

Nate tugs at my elbow while Ella grins at me with a missing front tooth. All my willpower evaporates, and I gently shrug Nate off and head inside the tent. "The monster does as its queen commands," I say, twirling my wrist as I bow.

"Is that okay, Uncle Pickle?" Ella calls out to Dylan, where he's hovering outside the tent, watching me.

"Yeah, is it, *Uncle Pickle?*" I repeat with a smirk.

His cheeks flush—with embarrassment or amusement, I can't tell. "Anything for you, bella," he says to Ella. "Even bad photos taken with a piece of shit camera," he adds under his breath. He tugs out a wad of cash from the back pocket of his jeans and hands a twenty to the stallholder. "Don't worry, Officer, we promise not to break the law," he throws at Nate without looking at him.

Nate stands huffing with his hands on his hips, but when I stick a paper mustache above my lips, smiling at him and then at Dylan, Nate lurches forward. He strides over to the costume table, snatches up a Riviera hat, and flops it on his head.

Ella drapes an Italian flag around her shoulders like a giant cape, and I steal a glance at Dylan while Nate fumbles with one of the fake mustaches. Instead of digging through the costume table, Dylan picks up a gladiator breastplate off the floor and clips it over his T-shirt before slipping a gladiator helmet over his tangle of dirty-blond hair. He tugs down the helmet that should look goofy, but on him, it looks...sexy. I turn away as an image slides into my head of Dylan wearing that breastplate with nothing on underneath, the ridges of his tattooed chest pressing hard against the frame. I flick the unwanted image back out.

For the next few minutes, we pose for hilariously dumb photographs, like the four of us "holding up" the Leaning Tower of Pisa from one side and lifting cardboard signs in the air that say things like "Ciao, Bella!" The entire time, burning tension radiates off Nate's body like a heat signature, especially when Dylan shifts behind me at one point, standing so close that his warm, minty breath fans over the shell of my ear.

The second the teenage photographer drops his camera, Nate tosses down his hat, rips off his mustache, and asks me if we can go.

"I want copies," Dylan calls out to the stall guy, overplaying his excitement. He's obviously trying to piss Nate off, and I don't get the intense hostility between these two. I definitely want copies, so I head over and give the guy my email address before turning back to spot Nate and Dylan in a terse exchange. Dylan's grip tightens on Ella as Nate says something to him with venom in his eyes. *What the actual hell?*

I barely have enough time to remove my mustache and say goodbye before Nate drags me away from this side of the fair and back across the road to the street food.

"Could he have stood any closer to you?" he spits.

"He wasn't standing *that* close," I reply, even though the feeling of Dylan's firm thighs brushing against the curves of my butt is probably never leaving my memory. Besides, I may have come here with Nate, but he's not my boyfriend. I can stand next to whomever I want.

Nate turns to face me, clutching my upper arms to hold me in place. "You don't seem to *get* what I'm saying, Jade. I know you're friends with that guy's sister, but this is not a man you want to get close to, okay? He's fucking dangerous."

"*Nate*," I hiss, glancing around to make sure none of the townspeople are hearing this. "Who says I'm getting close to him? And you seem to forget that I'm here on a date with *you*. Why the big freak out?"

His whole face is a storm cloud. "Because I *know* that guy, and he's a player and a scumbag. If you get together with him, I guarantee that you will regret it, and then you will come crying to me for help. And I'm not going through that shit again."

I switch from being horrified at the assumption that Nate thinks I'm going to jump into bed with my best friend's brother to being confused as hell about what he's going on about.

"What shit? And what do you mean *again*?" I say in a

lowered voice. Whatever it is must be bad for Nate to get this riled up.

His brow scrunches, and he glances around before pulling me behind one of the food trucks to where no one's within earshot. "Dylan King killed my cousin, Miranda," he says, a flash of pain hitting his eyes.

My lips fall open. "What?"

Every inch of him tightens. "I was a little kid when it all happened, but Miranda and I were pretty close... We saw each other most Sundays for family lunch. I remember when she told me that she had a new boyfriend, and I'll never forget how happy she looked. She brought Dylan to Sunday lunch, but she and her stepdad had a huge fight about it, and she didn't come back for weeks. Miranda stopped going to basketball and debate, and her grades slipped because that asshole got her hooked on opiates.

"Then, out of the blue, she turned up looking all skinny and sad, with these sunken, empty eyes because Dylan broke up with her. To be honest, I was ecstatic. I thought that would be the end of it, and I'd finally get my cousin back. But that turned out to be the last family lunch she ever came to. Then, one day, the phone rang in the middle of the night." His forehead drops as his voice splinters, and I reach to fold my fingers around his forearm. "Miranda was found dead in some random house outside town. She'd OD'd on a whole cocktail of opiates." Nate thumb-points over his shoulder. "Drugs that *fucker* got her hooked on in the first place. Dylan didn't even take an ounce of responsibility for what happened to her. Honestly, he's lucky I don't shove my fist so far down his throat that he chokes on his own shit. I get why he came back for the funeral, but I *don't* get why the fuck he's still in town. I can't even look at him."

"Oh, Nate." My voice comes out as a soft whisper. "I'm so sorry. I didn't know."

He glues his gaze to the dirt beneath our shoes, and I step forward to wrap my arms around his shoulders, sensing him stiffen before he finally relaxes into me.

As we stand there hugging, it's not Nate but a different person who clouds my thoughts, haunting them.

I've been so nice and carefree with Dylan these past few days, not knowing any of this. Yes, he's my best friend's brother. Yes, he just lost his parents in a horrible accident.

But if Nate is right, what Dylan did to that girl is unforgivable. No wonder Hayley has never brought any of this up. She probably didn't want me to know.

I squeeze Nate a little tighter and turn my head into his shoulder. If what I just heard is true, Dylan King is bad news, and the sooner he leaves Still Springs, the better.

CHAPTER NINE

DYLAN

I can't sleep with my eyes open. Believe me, I've tried. But it sure would be handy to have that skill right about now. Because listening to my sister Alex's girlfriend, Libby, drone on and on about business this, and markups that, and cost-analysis or whatever the shit she just said makes me want to press snooze on the whole world and sleep for a month.

I hadn't planned on being roped into this today, but here we are, hanging out in the back office of Kings superstore. And the shit thing is, I can't even leave because I rode here with Alex. I'm supposed to be babysitting Ella, but Iris called early this morning to say my niece was running a fever and needed to go to the pediatrician.

I offered to take her, but Iris had been pretty insistent that I should hang out with Alex and Libby instead since the three of us hardly ever get the chance. I thought we could go for lunch or a hike down at the springs, but instead, I'm staring at numbers on charts, pretending I know what they mean.

Dad and Mom were always hands-on with their businesses, which was great for them because they both had degrees in management and marketing and years of experience. My liberal arts degree, however, means jack shit in this world.

The four other people in the room nod like bobblehead dolls as Libby clicks through to the next slide. When we finish up here, I have a date with Lightroom and Photoshop. The new enlarger and cheap daylight tank I ordered should arrive tomorrow. There's plenty of shit to photograph around here, plus the evenings kinda drag without anyone to hang out with.

Libby moves on to a chart with a bunch of numbers, most of them red. Man, she has a sweet mohawk. I always wanted to be able to pull off a mohawk. Tried it once in middle school. Did not go well.

Focus, Dylan.

From what I gather, this store isn't hitting its third-quarter targets.

"So, the store isn't doing well?" I say in an effort to be somewhat engaging.

Everyone turns toward me in unison.

Libby's smile screams "placating" as she shakes her head. "With a recession on the horizon, no one is doing well. But we're prepared for the impact of an economic downturn. I'm in the process of renegotiating with some of our suppliers regarding discounts on some staple goods that should significantly increase our profit margins. If we can dump some of our surplus stock that doesn't sell as well, we should be looking at a nice increase over the last quarter."

She may as well be speaking Latin, for all I understand. But I nod anyway. "That's good?"

"It's very good. And we're hoping the influx of

customers for Fall Fest will kick off the Christmas season with a bang."

"Christmas isn't for another three months."

For some reason, that makes everyone in the office laugh.

"Dylan, Dylan, Dylan. Christmas is already here."

Last I checked, it was only September, but whatever. I guess the "planning" mentality meant always looking forward instead of being in the moment. I've always preferred the latter. It's probably why I love photography so much. Capturing fleeting moments in time and saving them forever.

The meeting ends without me contributing anything beyond my presence. Everyone else sticks around for coffee and donuts from the break room, but I'm not one for idle chit-chat, so I head straight for the exit.

I'm about to reach for the doorknob when Libby calls me back.

Thankfully, she's on her own and knows better than to ask me how I'm doing. "You gotta sec?" she asks. "Alex wanted me to talk to you about something."

"Sure. What's up?"

She runs a hand down the shaved side of her head. "I'm not sure if you've heard, but Sunny Gillespie is going to be doing a feature on Still Springs."

The name doesn't sound familiar, but then again, sometimes my family forgets I haven't lived here in years. "Should I know who that is?"

Laughing, she drags her phone out of her pocket and opens her Instagram account. A moment later, I'm staring at a petite brunette with doe-eyes and a megawatt smile that belongs in a toothpaste commercial.

"Recognize her now?" Libby asks.

"Sure don't."

"Sunny Gillespie," she repeats.

"Oh yeah, Sunny Gillespie."

"So you do remember her."

"Nope."

That earns me a punch in the arm. "You are such a cad sometimes."

I shrug because she isn't wrong.

Libby closes her eyes and pinches the bridge of her nose, exhaling an exasperated sigh. "I can't believe I'm about to say this," she mutters under her breath before looking back at me. "Sunny-D."

Now *that* rings a bell. And the nickname hadn't been Sunny-D, but rather Sunny Double-D...for obvious reasons. I glance back at the photo. "I remember her now. She's cute." She's also definitely had some work done.

"Hell yeah, she's cute." Libby slips her phone back into her pocket. "And she used to have a huge thing for you back in high school."

"She did, huh?" No surprise there. I was kinda a big deal back then. Which isn't really anything worth bragging about, considering we were in *Shit* Springs.

"Yeah. So, Alex and I were thinking that you could work your voodoo magic and convince Sunny to give us the spread."

I deadpan, "You want me to whore myself out for a magazine article?"

Her face pales and she starts shaking her head, looking over her shoulder like someone's going to tell her she's a shitty person for suggesting something so unethical. "God, no. That's not what I meant at all—"

"No worries, Lib. I'll do it."

She blows out a relieved breath. "You will?"

"Sure. Why not?" It's not like I have anything better to do that day. My sisters won't let me hole up in my apartment. I can show Sunny around town, take her for some food, and do whatever else is required of me. As long as the locals point their rude stares in other directions, I'm good.

Libby says she'll organize the details, and I high-tail it out of the office before anyone else can corner me. On my way through the warehouse, a few of the workers wave, but thankfully, no one tries to strike up a conversation.

Once I'm back in the store, I check my phone and find a text from Iris. Ella has an ear infection, so I'm off the hook for babysitting tomorrow too. When you're sick, you want your mom. Simple as that. I can totally relate. I got food poisoning once, and Mom flew all the way to Texas to take care of me.

My chest starts to tighten. I'm not gonna break down here. No, sir. Operation distraction engaged.

My stomach rumbles. Food sounds like the perfect distraction.

I meander through the towering shelves of cereal to an endcap display of frosted cookies that look damn good. I grab a box and continue on to the next aisle where, low and behold, I run into my very cute neighbor.

I haven't seen Jade since crashing her date with the biggest asshole on the east coast. Had I done that on purpose? Hell no. Had I loved every second of watching that prick squirm? You betcha.

I'd gone down to Quinn Brothers this morning for milk, but Jade hadn't been there yet. Which left me wondering if she came home last night or if she'd stayed with Robocop.

Not that it matters. If short, rotund dickheads are her type, she's found her perfect match.

Jade has a container of locally made chutney in one

hand and her phone in the other. I hear the telltale click of a camera and can't help but wonder why she wants a picture of chutney.

"What do we have here?" I say, sidling up next to her.

Jade shrieks and the phone flies out of her hand, landing at my feet. She presses a palm to her chest, her face turning the same shade of pink as her sweater. There are no yoga pants today, but the tightly fitting jeans are a decent consolation prize.

"Holy shit, Dylan. You scared me."

"Why? Thinking about shoplifting?" I bend down at the same time she does, but I get to her phone first.

"Of course not." She wiggles her fingers at me. "May I have that back, please?"

Maybe it makes me a dick, but I have this overwhelming urge to swipe through her pictures. The angles are basic, and she's been using the flash, so there's a glare on everything. And would you look at that? She doesn't have only one photograph of chutney, she has a whole gallery full of random condiments and jams, as well as candles and their price tags.

Now, I may not be very knowledgeable about business, but I can only think of one reason the owner of a rival store would be taking pictures of our prices. "You're a spy, aren't you?"

"Don't be ridiculous." She swipes for the phone, but I turn at the last second and block her with my shoulder. "Can I please have it back, Dylan?"

"Mmm...no." I keep flicking through her camera roll. Toilet paper. Milk. Baggies. Firestarters. "Jade Quinn!" I gasp. "What are you doing taking pictures of yourself in a lacy red bra?" I joke.

A lady with a wild perm stops her cart to give us a disapproving *tsk*.

Jade's face is now the color of said imaginary red bra. Great. Now I can't seem to get the thought of her shirtless out of my head.

"Dammit, Dylan!" Jade grabs for the phone I'm holding out of reach. Short of climbing me like a ladder, she's not getting this back.

I finally get to the end of the products to find a selfie of Jade and Robocop from last night's fair. For some reason, I really, really want to delete it. She looks so fucking happy, and I can't figure out why. "What do you see in this guy? He looks like a red panda."

Her lips purse. "Nate is nice."

"I bet he is," I mutter, handing back her phone. "Nice" is one adjective I've never heard attached to my name. Not that I care what people think of me. "What're you doing after you get finished spying?"

She stuffs the phone back into her purse. "I'm *not* spying."

"Yeah. Okay. You have plans after this or what, Pink Panther?"

"I'm going back to the store."

"Perfect. I'll meet you out front." I still need to pay for my snack even though my last name is on the building.

Jade runs along after me, her purse swinging against her thigh. "Hold on. What do you mean you'll meet me out front?"

Isn't it obvious? "I need a ride back to my apartment, and you're going to give me one."

"Why would I want to do that?"

"Because you're *nice*."

I walk off to pay for my cookies and sit on a bench outside the store, waiting for Jade to finish spying. I'm not sure if I should be concerned about the fact that she's taking pictures of products and prices, but I figure it can't be that bad.

A young woman wearing hiking boots and jean shorts that barely peek from beneath her oversized hoodie saunters by, her gaze cutting to me as she smiles. I don't know who she is, but I smile back because apparently girls like "nice" guys, and smiling seems like the "nice" thing to do. The sliding doors glide open, but instead of going inside, the woman turns around and comes back toward me.

Her shorts ride a little higher on her tanned thighs when she sinks onto the bench beside me. "Hey."

I smile and pretend like I want to talk to this stranger because it's *nice*. "Hello."

She pushes her gold aviators up onto her forehead and doesn't try to hide the fact that she is one hundred percent checking me out. "What do you have there?" Not sure if she's nodding toward my dick or the cookie box resting on my thighs.

Better to be safe than sorry. I hold up one of my cookies and take a bite. Okay. These are seriously delicious. If Jade doesn't hurry, I'm going to end up eating all of them and needing to run back inside to grab another box for later.

"Any good?" the woman asks.

I flip open the lid and extend the box toward her. "See for yourself."

She fishes out a cookie and slips it between her glossy pink lips. Her eyes flutter closed, and her head falls back, kinda like that scene from *When Harry Met Sally*. "Mmm... so good," she moans.

I'm pretty sure she's trying to be seductive, but it's not

working. The crumbs sticking to her lip gloss aren't helping either.

"My name's Cindi, with an 'i'," she says. "What's yours?"

"Dylan. With a 'y'."

That makes her smile. "You live around here, Dylan?"

"I do for now." I should probably tell her she has multi-colored sprinkles caught between her teeth, but I'm not really sure if that's going to embarrass her or not. Hayley would want to know, but Iris definitely wouldn't.

"A few girlfriends and I are staying in a cabin down by the springs for a couple of weeks," she says around another bite. "If you're looking for a good time, you should swing by."

"Maybe I will."

A throat clears behind my new friend. I look up to find Jade scowling down at us, her furrowed gaze darting between Cindi and me. Cindi glances over her shoulder but doesn't seem the least bit fazed.

"I'm leaving," Jade clips.

"Sounds good. I'll meet you at the car." I get Cindi-with-an-i's number before carrying my delicious cookies over to Jade's white Honda Civic. She's already inside with the engine running and the air on full blast. I close the vents on my side and adjust the seat so my knees aren't up against the dashboard. Whoever sat here before me must've been a shrimp. Probably Robocop.

Jade shifts into reverse and backs out of the parking spot without so much as a glance in my direction. "Who was that?" she asks, shifting into drive.

"Cindi with an 'i'."

Jade snorts. "Of course."

"What's wrong? You have something against girls named Cindi?"

"Nope." She pops the "p" but says no more.

Sublime's "What I Got" comes on the radio—great fucking song, by the way. I turn it up, sit back, and watch the world pass by. It's been so mild lately that the leaves have only begun to change. It won't be long before they're at the height of their beauty, right in time for the fall festival. Maybe I'll fit in a hike or two to get some shots down by the springs.

Jade's knuckles turn white from how tightly she's gripping the wheel.

"Do you need me to drive?" I offer.

Her green eyes flicker to me before returning to the road. "No. Why?"

"Because you're strangling the steering wheel like it owes you money."

Her grip loosens, but her shoulders remain up around her ears. I've known Jade forever; she practically lived at our house growing up, so I'm not sure why she's acting so off today. Yesterday, she seemed as relaxed as ever, joking around with Ella and me.

Maybe she's mad about me stealing her phone. Sometimes, I forget that people don't always feel the same way about me as I do about them. Jade's always been like a little sister who I never see, but a lot of time has passed since I used to throw her and Hayley into our pool, and that obviously isn't the case for her.

"Look, if you're annoyed about me stealing your phone, I apologize. I shouldn't have snooped through your snoopy photos."

Her eyes narrow on the road. "I don't care about you taking my phone."

"Was it the bra comment? Is that why you're mad?"

"I'm not mad about the bra comment."

Definitely mad about the bra comment. I can only think of one thing to fix this. The smell of sugar and vanilla sweetens the air when I throw open the box on my lap. "Want a cookie? They're amazing."

"No, I don't want a cookie." Her eyes bounce down to the box before returning to the road.

"Suit yourself." No cookie for her means more for me. I close the lid and stare at her profile. She doesn't look at me until we reach the stoplight on the outskirts of town. Seeing her like this makes my stomach sink. Maybe there's something else going on, something that has nothing to do with me. "Are you okay, Jade?"

"I'm fine."

Uh oh...

Thanks to my sisters, I can read between the lines of those two fateful words. She's pissed about something but is not quite ready to discuss what it is. It's only a matter of time before she boils over.

Jade parallel parks between an old Bronco and a black pickup, then shifts the car to park. "Look, I don't want to be insensitive. I know you just lost your parents, and you're Hayley's brother, but I don't really think we should be friends."

Okay. This is completely out of left field. "Why not?"

Her mouth opens and shuts a few times before the words tumble out. "You have a...reputation. And I don't think being seen with you is going to be good for business." She presses her lips together, her cheeks turning crimson.

My chest clenches up. So *that's* what this is about? My fucking "reputation." That little weasel must've been filling her head with shit. Fuck that. If she wants to judge me without having the full story like everyone else, then who am I to stop her?

I throw open the car door but don't climb out right away. Instead, I turn toward Jade—who still isn't looking at me. "For some reason, I thought you were different from the other assholes in this town," I mumble. "I really should've known better." I slam the door and escape, realizing that sticking around this place has been a big mistake.

CHAPTER TEN

JADE

I hit 'send' on my email to Magnolia Sloane, the eccentric clay sculptor who lives on the outskirts of town, before drawing a line through her name on my notepad.

Seven down, four to go.

So far, I've found eleven local artists and creators who'll hopefully be interested in stocking their arts and crafts at the store for us to sell on commission. The tricky part will be getting enough stock in before the magazine reporter arrives in town for Fall Fest.

A moment of panic grips my throat, but I fight it off with a gulp of watery coffee. I can do this. I nearly pulled off a business merger that only came undone because of reasons I couldn't have prevented. My eyes dart up to Mom's face on the wall, and I use her soft smile as encouragement. *I'm gonna win this glossy feature spread, and I'm gonna make it my bitch. Oops, sorry, Mom.*

A giant shadow falls over the window, accompanied by the screech of worn brake pads. I huff with irritation as a massive delivery truck pulls up outside for the sixth time this week, blocking the store from the Main Street traffic.

Only a few months ago, I had our shop signs repainted fire-engine red to catch the eyes of visitors driving through the center of town. And now this delivery dude keeps blocking the signs *and* the shop with his monster truck before disappearing into Dylan's apartment next door. And if it's not him, it's the continuous cycle of food delivery trucks and tradespeople's vans. Because apparently, being born with a silver spoon in your mouth means you don't ever have to cook anything or fix your own leaky taps.

Maybe I'm being too hard on Dylan. I didn't like how he looked at me in the car the other day after I fumbled my words and told him he has a "reputation." Even if that's true, one thing I've learned from what happened to Ruby this summer is that there are always two sides to every story. People think they know stuff, but sometimes they don't know shit.

I lean sideways on my stool and crane my neck to see what the delivery guy's dropping off to Dylan this time. All I can make out is another giant cardboard box that looks like it contains something heavy. Honestly, what is all that shit he's ordering?

I tap my computer to life to check my emails, chewing the inside of my cheek. None of the artists have replied yet—which is of no surprise given the pace of this town—but there's a new message sitting in the store's inbox from the bank. My gut tightens with dread, and I consider burning the computer to the ground before I suck in a breath and open the email.

> This is a formal notification that you are in default of your obligation to make payments on your commercial loan...

Shit. Before Mom got sick, she and Dad took out a large

loan for the shop to make some crucial and expensive upgrades. They found her cancer soon after, and everything started to go downhill. I hurriedly scan the rest of the letter, my breath hitching at the final paragraph.

> Unless the total amount in arrears is received within 90 days, we will have no choice but to begin the foreclosure process on your property.

I slam the laptop shut, my palm trembling against the metal casing as I sit frozen solid. Can they actually do that? Surely, Mom and Dad didn't put the store up as collateral? I grip my stomach and force myself to take a run of deep breaths.

It's okay. You're only behind on three months of payments. You can talk to Dad...you can talk to Ruby...you can figure this out.

But the last thing I want is to bring Ruby into this. She'll feel a million times worse than she already does about the merger falling apart. We've discussed selling Grandma's house, but Grandma refuses. She's convinced she's going to get better and move out of the nursing home as soon as possible. Besides, what's happening with the store isn't Grandma's fault. There has to be another way.

I'll talk to Dad. Maybe we can borrow some more money through his home loan—just to cover the next few payments and catch up on what we owe.

The uncomfortable thought of having to ask Dad to do that makes me flip open my laptop again. I *need* to get that magazine spread, whatever the cost. Emailing a few local craftspeople isn't enough—I have to do more, to be proactive, like I was taught in business school.

Perhaps I can contact the Fall Fest journalist in advance

and organize a phone call to butter her up. According to the *Gazette*, her name is Sunny Gillespie and she grew up in Still Springs, which explains why a reporter of her caliber is doing a feature on this tiny town.

Her Instagram looks like a luxury travel magazine in itself, her grid filled with images of her doing yoga in the aqua shallows of the Maldives or standing atop a New Zealand mountain with her arms stretched in a V-shape. The fact that I'm supposed to impress this woman is a joke for the stand-up stage.

I send her a message, but given she's got more than three million followers, there's a good chance she won't see it. I could reach out to her through her assistant at the magazine, but I've tried to contact journalists before and for much smaller publications. It's like sending an email into a black hole.

I click back to her social media, when my eye snags on a follower we have in common: @HayHay_NYC.

Of course the glamorous, jet-setting Hayley would know who Sunny Gillespie is. They also both live in New York City, so maybe they're even friends!

I find Hayley's number in my recently dialed calls and tap her name. When I called to check on her yesterday, she'd just landed in Crete.

Hayley answers on the second ring. "Still keeping tabs on me?" she says warmly.

I smile. "Always. How are you doing?"

The bounce in her tone disappears as she fills me in on another sightseeing day spent fighting off tears at everything that reminded her of her parents: an ice cream cone flavor, a patterned style of dress, a piece of art her dad would've loved.

We chat quietly for a bit while someone comes into the

store to browse—ugh—before I ask Hayley if she knows Sunny Gillespie. My chest sinks when she tells me that she knows who she is, but they've never met in person.

"I think she was in Dylan's year at school," Hayley adds.

"Oh, right."

"How's your new next-door neighbor, anyway?" Hayley asks. "Dyl's been a bit hard to pin down lately. Has he been behaving himself?"

I dig my thumb into the old scratch on the wood counter where I carved the words "I love Mommy" when I was little. "What do you mean?"

"Oh, I don't know. Love the boy to bits, but sometimes he can be a bit of a ratbag. Especially when he's upset and emotional."

So I've heard.

"My dear brother tends to leave a wreckage of broken hearts everywhere he goes," Hayley continues before making a knowing laugh. "I've already said a little prayer for the ladies of Still Springs. You're lucky you're my best friend, so you've got protection. He knows I'd kill him if he ever tried to touch you."

My throat thickens strangely at those words, but I manage to force a smile into the phone. "Of course not. *Ew,*" I add purely for effect. "Besides, I'm with Nate."

"The Nark," she finishes.

"I've stopped calling him that." Given how much I let Nate kiss my face off in his car the other night, I thought it best to put the high school nickname to rest. He'd wanted to come inside the house, and it's not like I wasn't tempted, but I'd kind of wanted to get *into* a pair of soft, cozy pajamas more than I'd wanted to strip out of something. So, I'd sent Nate home with probably a horrendous case of blue balls.

After Hayley and I hang up, I consider heading next

door to ask Dylan if he's kept in touch with Sunny, but I don't want him to know how desperate I am for this article. Not when he eats dollar bills for breakfast and—for all I know—has Sunny already etched into his long list of conquests. No thanks.

I decide to at least attempt to contact Sunny through her assistant when another shadow shrouds the store in darkness.

My face flies up to meet a different truck blocking the storefront, this one marked "All Class Tiling."

Oh, for fuck's sake. Tiling takes *hours*. If Dylan is having his bathroom remodeled, his damn tiler can park somewhere else.

I lurch up off my stool and push through the front door onto the pavement, but the tiler's already headed into the building, leaving the front door ajar. I quickly flip the sign to "Back Soon" and lock up the store before bounding over and giving the door a few knocks. When they go unanswered, I step inside the musty space, calling out, "Hello?"

A bearded guy in a pair of worn khaki shorts and a polo-necked shirt sticks his head out from behind the old wall partition. "Can I help you?" he says, giving my chest a long look.

I cross my arms over myself. "Is Dylan here?"

"I think he's upstairs. He told me to let myself in."

I glance around at the randomly stacked boxes and the weird pieces of equipment I've never seen before. I turn back to the tiler. "If you're doing some work here, do you mind moving your truck into the alley around the back?"

"Why?"

"Because you're blocking my storefront and my signage, and I rely on those to attract customers."

He uses the tape measure he's holding to scratch his

butt cheek. "Look, love, the door to the alley's boarded up, so it's gonna be a giant pain in my ass to bring in the tiles from around the back. If you want me to move, you're gonna have to talk to the boss."

"The boss?"

He jerks his chin at the side door leading to the apartment upstairs.

With a sigh, I stalk through the door and up the stairs, looking for the all-important *boss*.

A nervous churn takes over my stomach as I reach the top step, halting at the sight of a very bare, very tattooed, very male back facing me from an open doorway. *Holy shit*. Dylan stands rubbing his hair with a towel, the action drawing out the broad ridges of muscle that are almost entirely inked with stunning, intricate drawings. *Oh my*. My gaze brushes over an iris flower, a star constellation, a compass... He spins around, and his eyes flash wide when they meet mine.

"Jade," he says as my gaze drops to the dark ink drawn over his pecs and toned stomach before he reaches for a T-shirt and throws it over his head. For once, he's not using the opportunity to flirt and tease. In fact, he looks caught off-guard. "What are you doing here?" he says, stepping out into the narrow hallway and running his fingers through his hair. "Another round of spying, Pink Panther? Or are you here to call me an asshole again?"

My eyes narrow. "I never called you that. In fact, you called *me* one, if I recall."

He pushes his tongue into his cheek. "No. I called the other people in the town assholes, *if I recall*. This place is like the mothership for assholes. Everywhere you turn...oh, look! There's an asshole."

"Stop saying asshole."

A laugh slips out of him before that pissed-off look returns to his face that was there the last time I saw him. "To what do I owe the pleasure, then?" he asks.

I shift on my feet as his eyes trail over my face before moving down the blonde braid falling over my shoulder.

"Um, I'm just wondering if your tiling guy can move his truck. He said to ask you."

"Why? Do you own the street outside?"

"*No,* but I do own a business that relies on foot traffic and people driving past to see the store and its signs. Which they can't do if a giant truck is blocking it for hours on end."

Dylan folds his thick arms. "He's just measuring up today for a new floor Iris wants to put in and bringing in some tiles. He won't be long, but I'll make sure he doesn't screw around." His gaze rakes down and up my body. "Is that all? I was just about to head out."

To meet Cindi with an "i"? pops into my head out of nowhere.

"What are you doing with all that stuff downstairs?" I blurt instead, not sure why my feet are refusing to move. "All the deliveries…that weird thing that looks like a microscope."

The corner of his mouth twitches. "Maybe if you're nice to me, I'll show you."

My brows lift. "*Nice* to you?"

He runs a hand over his jaw like he's trying to figure out what to do with me, and my eyes zero in on the black letters decorating his knuckles.

"Yeah, nice to me. But you can't bring that jackass you're seeing with you," Dylan adds. "That guy's disqualified from every fucking thing in my life."

"Nate's not a *jackass.*"

"Debatable. Actually, no. Fact."

I shake my head with a bemused laugh, looking away.

Dylan's fingers slide into the pockets of his jeans. His voice slips a little. "That sanctimonious asshole been telling you things about me?" He mutes just the word "asshole," miming it instead. I have to work really hard not to smile, which would not be appropriate when he's being unkind to Nate.

When I don't reply, Dylan leans closer and lowers his voice, sending shivers racing down my spine. "Don't believe everything you hear, Little Jade."

"Stop calling me that," I snap. "I'm twenty-three years old."

"Such a big girl," he replies, the husk in his tone making the back of my neck heat up, even though I know he's only being a smart-ass.

While I can't say I hate having this flirtatious side of him back, I take a step away, but not before catching a nice whiff of men's soap. "Look, I'd appreciate it if you'd ask your army of minions and delivery people—or whoever they all are—to park elsewhere if they're going to stay a while."

"Yes, ma'am."

I go to leave, but something compels me to turn my attention back on him.

"About what Nate told me..."

Dylan's whole face tightens, and I have no idea where I'm going with this, but I think there's a part of me that wants to know what happened from Dylan's side of the fence. To make sure that I'm not missing something important about the tragedy that befell Nate's cousin. The slightly haunted look in Dylan's eyes makes me clam up, though, and I realize it's absolutely none of my business.

He's probably waiting for me to finish, but when I don't say anything, he heaves a sigh. "Whatever Nate Williams says means fuck all to me. I stopped giving a shit about people's opinions when you were still in pigtails, *Little Jade*." Dylan makes a big show of checking his watch.

I can take a hint. "Thanks for being so helpful," I mutter sarcastically before heading back down the stairs.

For the rest of the afternoon, I fill my hours restocking the shelves and organizing a store visit with two of the artisans who replied to my email, but my mind is all knotted up.

"My dear brother tends to leave a wreckage of broken hearts everywhere he goes."

I don't know why those words are clinging to my brain.

I drop onto my stool, staring at the window display but seeing only the unsettling, guarded hurt in Dylan's eyes when I brought up Nate's cousin. I shake off a stupid wish that he'd opened up to me about it. Why the hell would he? We barely know each other. And why do I even care when I'm dating Nate?

After the sun sinks from view and I change the window sign to "Closed," I turn around and rest my back against the wall, still seeing those long, tattooed fingers. Before I can think, I reach up to the back of my neck and imagine what they might feel like cupping the soft skin there. I imagine him brushing his knuckles down the side of my face before catching my jaw firmly in his hand and tugging my mouth forward.

Oh boy.

Oh no.

You are not *allowed to like him. Not now, not* ever.

Not only is Dylan a walking red flag, but Hayley would flip out.

Plus, after what Nate told me, I'm meant to hate the guy... aren't I?

I give myself a mental slap before giving Mom's picture

a couple of goodnight pats, locking up, and strolling down the street to my car. As I walk past the building next door, I promise myself I won't look up at Dylan's window and see if his light is on.

Three steps later, my eyes dart upward. There's a soft glow of light shining from his living room, but there are no cars parked out the front. No sign of any Cindis with an "i."

God, why am I even thinking about that?

I up my pace and bound away with a guilty feeling gnawing at my gut. But somewhere even deeper inside it, in a place I can't reach, there's a nervous thrill building that I can't seem to switch off.

CHAPTER ELEVEN

DYLAN

I fucked up.

Those words keep running through my mind the entire drive over to my parents' house for yet another family meeting. The only reason I agreed to it is because Ella is going to be there, and I haven't seen her since she got sick a few days ago. Iris assured me she's right as rain now, so Ella and I will be hanging out all day tomorrow. I can't wait. I've missed not seeing that little monster.

Alex twists the dial on the radio, muting Kurt Cobain's soulful voice. "Why are you in a mood?" she asks.

"I'm not."

She snorts. "Clearly."

I don't know why it pisses me off so much that Jade's opinion of me is the same as everyone else's. It shouldn't matter, but for some reason it does. And today would've been the perfect opportunity to tell her the truth about what really happened instead of letting that fuckwit she's dating control the narrative. But what did I do instead?

I basically told her to fuck off.

My therapist would say I'm avoiding the issue. What's

so wrong with that? If I saw a gigantic crocodile in the middle of the road, I'd sure as hell avoid it too. And talking about this hurts a lot worse than a big-ass reptile with the world's strongest bite.

Alex pulls into Mom and Dad's gravel driveway, and like every other time I've come here since the accident, I expect to see them waiting on the stoop, but there's no one there. That is until the front door flies open and a tiny human comes barreling out, catching my legs the moment I climb out of the car and squeezing with all her might.

"Uncle Pickle! I've missed you so, so, *sooo* much."

"I missed you too, monster."

This kid is seriously the coolest person in the world. The only way to release myself from her stronghold is to tickle her under the arms. She knows it too. The moment I do, she squeals and takes off back into the house. I dutifully chase after her, nearly ramming into Iris on my way into the kitchen, where Ella's sparkly pink shoes peek out from beneath the fluttering curtains.

Turns out she's as bad at hide-and-seek as her mother. "Has anyone seen Ella?" I say. "I heard she's been too sick to play."

Iris closes the door behind Alex. "Nope. Haven't seen her in days. I've been thinking about sending out a search party."

"Call the police. No. The FBI! No. The president!"

A high-pitched giggle emerges from the vibrating curtains before Ella pops her head out and grins. "I'm right here, you ninny."

What is she, a ninety-year-old grandma? Who the hell says ninny? "Hey! Who are you calling a ninny?"

"Ella, what did Daddy say about calling people names?" Iris chides.

I scoop up my niece and whisper in her ear, "Your daddy is a ninny."

She slaps both of her hands over her mouth to stifle her laughter.

Iris pulls out her phone to FaceTime Hayley, who picks up on the first ring. "Can we make this quick?" she shouts over the techno music pulsing in the background. "I can't hear a thing."

"That's no problem," Iris says. "First, I want to talk about the race."

How had I forgotten about the mud race? Saturday morning, before the Fall Fest parade, teams have to slog through cold, wet muck; hurdle over barriers; climb shit; and do a heap of other stuff in order to get their names added to a plaque down at city hall.

"We need one more teammate to compete," she goes on.

My sisters turn toward me, their eyes wide and pleading. Even Hayley pulls a guilt-trip face over the shot glass in her hand.

This is what always happens. They don't do this shit over the phone because they know I can't resist their onslaught of puppy-dog eyes and pouty mouths. *Dammit.*

I'm about to say, "No fucking way," when I remember the little girl doing frontward rolls in the living room. Instead, I go with, "Not happening."

"We need four people," Iris pleads, clasping her hands beneath her chin like she used to when she wanted to ride my bicycle. Guess what happened when I finally let her? She crashed the thing.

I gesture toward the computer screen. "I'm sure Hayley's willing to come back and run. Aren't you, Buttons?"

The computer glitches, and her look of abject horror

gets stuck on the screen.

Alex shakes her head. "Very funny. Unfortunately, at least two team members need to be men, which is total bullshit, but those are the rules."

"Doesn't Justin have any friends?" I ask Iris.

"They're already on their own teams."

Sarah would tell me to close my eyes and decide whether this opportunity makes me expand or contract. Expand means go for it. And I feel hella-contracted when I think of all those people watching me, talking about me...

But since not participating will let my sisters down, I ignore my instincts, drop my head, and utter, "Fine," under my breath.

Iris promptly withdraws a neon pink monstrosity from a paper bag on the counter and hands it to me. *Contract. Contract. Contract.*

"I'm not wearing this." No fucking way am I going to be caught dead in a T-shirt that says: "Welcome to the KINGdom."

Alex nudges my shoulder. "Come on, Dyl. Dad came up with these himself."

Why does that not surprise me? His jokes were always so terrible. A sharp pain moves through my chest. I'd give anything to hear him tell one right now so I could roll my eyes and ask how someone like me came from such a dork. "Still not wearing it."

Iris returns the shirt to the bag with a huff. My therapist would high-five me for standing my ground on this. Boundaries and all that shit.

Someone shouts in the background of Hayley's call. She twists to wave at whoever it is and then says, "Guys, I'm so sorry, but I gotta go." Before we can say goodbye, the screen cuts to black.

"Is that everything?" I ask Iris, still wondering why we couldn't have done this on a call.

Trading a look with Alex, Iris sighs and tucks a blonde curl behind her ear. "No, but I don't want to talk about the rest without Hayley. Let me go potty, and I'll bring you back to town."

"Potty" goes right up there with "jammies" in the list of words I find myself saying thanks to the tiny demon running circles around Dad's ratty old chair. If I squint my eyes, I swear I can see him sitting there, remote in hand, watching *The Curse of Oak Island*.

When tears start to well in my eyes, I turn my back before my sisters can ask me what's wrong. "You take your time in the potty, Iris. I'm going to drive myself." I'm sick and tired of being driven around like Miss Fucking Daisy. Also, the last thing I want is to end up having to ask my neighbor to drive me anywhere again. Talk about awkward.

Damn, now that I'm thinking about Jade, I can't stop. Usually, I'm not a fan of women encroaching on my space unless it's for a little adult-time fun, but having Jade in the apartment had been kinda nice. Probably because I'm so used to her being around from when we were younger.

Too bad that's all over now, given she wants nothing to do with me. I definitely need my own mode of transportation.

Dad always used to hang his keys on this corny key-shaped piece of wood with hooks that we got him one Father's Day. Sure enough, I find what I'm looking for right where he left it.

I slip the key off the hook and squeeze it tight. It feels all kinds of strange taking the thing without asking him first. I can almost hear him now: "You break it, you buy it."

Such a dork.

Inside the garage, Dad's 1965 Shelby GT350 peeks out from beneath a gray tarp. He and Mom used to drive it in the Fall Fest parade. Past that is his 1964 Pontiac GTO. Either one would probably be a more responsible choice since I'm in charge of Ella, but I'm only interested in one vehicle: His 1959 Triumph Bonneville.

This bike is the reason I fell in love with two wheels instead of four. It's not the rarest motorcycle or the most expensive, but I fucking adore this thing. He used to take me out on it to check out the changing leaves every fall growing up, then we'd cruise down Main Street and swing by Harringtons for a bite to eat.

I remember seeing Jade and her sister playing around in the window display on more than one occasion.

It's been nice getting to reconnect with Jade. She reminds me of better times. When I'm around her, every part of me expands...and I mean *every* part.

Then, Nate had to go and tell her a bullshit version of the truth and take away the one person in Still Springs who I don't mind talking to outside my family.

I give my head a quick shake. Jade is the last girl I should be thinking about right now, and the moment I get back to my apartment, I know I'll be fixating on Jade. Unless I replace her with someone else.

Time to pull out my phone and bring up the number I scored easily the other day, shooting Cindi with an "i" a message.

Before I kick-start the bike, my phone pings.

Not only is Cindi up for a visit, but she sent the address too.

Whoever built this cabin down by the springs must've really loved cedar. I can smell the fragrant wood all the way from the stone driveway. All the windows are lit up like beacons in the night, but I can't see anything inside, thanks to the closed blinds.

I leave the helmet on the seat and jog up the bowed stairs to the wrap-around porch. Before I can raise my hand to knock, the door flies open and a bouncy brunette who smells like liquor and roses gives me a blinding smile. "You must be the Dylan we've heard so much about," she says, her gaze making an unabashed sweep from my head to my boots.

I'm not really sure what she would've heard about me since I barely spoke to her friend, but I decide to play along. "That's me."

Cindi slips beneath this woman's arm to give me a hug. "Hey, you." Her lips brush my cheek, warm and a little sticky from her lip gloss. "I'm glad you texted. I got so sad when I didn't hear from you. Come on in. I want you to meet the girls." She grips my fingers and drags me past the woman who answered the door. "You've already met Marsha, and this is Tory."

She gestures toward a woman with dark eyes who's sitting on the couch.

Marsha drops down beside Tory while Cindi leads me over to an olive-green recliner. A bottle of gin and a half-empty two-liter of tonic waits on the low coffee table beside three glasses. Some muted reality TV show flickers across the TV mounted above the fireplace.

"You want a drink?" Cindi asks me.

"Nah. I'm good."

She bends over the table, presumably to make herself a drink, flashing me the top of her neon pink thong. For some reason, my body has zero reaction to the sight, and I usually love catching an eyeful of thong.

With the glass clasped between her manicured fingers, Cindi drops right into my lap. "You sure about that?" She shoves the glass beneath my nose. *Holy shit.* Pretty sure she forgot the tonic.

"Positive." I don't want to get stuck out here with no way home and end up having to call one of my sisters to pick me up. Their judgment is the last thing I need right now. They can cope with their grief in their own way, and I'll handle mine.

From over Cindi's shoulder, Tory's soft brown eyes eat me up like I'm a thick slice of chocolate cake. "Sooo, Dylan, what do you do?"

I can't tell if she's slurring or trying to be seductive. If it's the latter, she misses the mark. "I'm a photographer."

"That's so hot," Cindi murmurs, playing with my hair as she sips from her glass.

"So hot," Marsha agrees while Tory bobs her head.

"OMG, Marsha! You should show him your Insta." Cindi turns to me. "She's so talented. Like, *so* talented."

"So talented," Tory parrots.

"You guys! I'm not going to show him my Insta."

Thank god because I have no desire whatsoever to see her "Insta." If I had a dollar for every person who wanted to show me shit pictures they've taken after they find out what I do, I wouldn't need my trust fund.

Time to switch to a different topic. "So, what brings you ladies to Still Springs?"

Marsha lets out a long sigh that makes it seem like she's about to say something incredibly insightful. "We're all so jaded from the whole dating scene down state, ya know?"

All so jade*d...*

A woman with blazing green eyes flickers through my mind. I force her right back out and paste on a smile.

"So we decided to get away from our usual haunts," Marsha adds, somehow without taking a breath. "My parents always used to bring me to Fall Fest, so I suggested that, and here we are."

"Here you are," I echo, matching her excited tone.

"And the day we arrived, I met *you*," Cindi croons. "It's like fate."

"Just like fate," I agree, even though this had nothing to do with fate but with me not wanting to go home and dwell on how shitty I treated the woman I'm definitely not thinking about.

Cindi peers at me through glassy blue eyes. "I *really* think you should have a drink."

"I'm good."

"I'm sure you are." She winks as she tilts her glass toward my lips. "Come on. For me? Pretty please?"

Short of kicking her off my lap, I really don't have much of a choice if I don't want liquid all over my shirt. So I take a dutiful sip; the gin burns my throat the whole way down.

"Good, right? I like sharing." When Cindi's lips graze my jaw, the other two giggle.

Marsha links her fingers with Tory's and gives the woman's knuckles a lingering kiss, her eyes still on me. "We're all really good at sharing."

Ohhhh-kay. This is not how I expected tonight to go. I thought maybe I'd get off with Cindi with an "i", but a foursome? It's like I stepped into my own personal porno.

Normally, I'd be up for just about anything. But it's like my dick has gone into hibernation. There's a beautiful woman sitting on my lap and two more making out on the couch beside me, but nothing is happening downstairs. Not even a fucking twitch.

"So, I've been wondering," Cindi breathes heavily against my ear. "Are you a dirty boy? Because you sure do look like one."

Her question makes my entire being contract. "Showered before I got here, actually."

She smiles against my cheek as her hand snakes down my stomach to my unimpressed dick. "You know what I mean."

Why do people insist on equating enjoying sex with being "dirty"? Isn't the purpose of sex to enjoy it? Technically, I guess it's to procreate, but orgasms wouldn't exist if we weren't meant to have a shitload of fun while we're doing it.

"Loosen up. Let's have some fun," Cindi says before her mouth finds its way to mine. I allow her tongue's assault, but I can't help imagining what it'd be like to have Jade in her skin-tight yoga pants sitting on my lap instead...thighs spread, her perfect body grinding against mine until we're both ready to peel off our clothes and get lost in each other.

I bet Jade wouldn't try to choke me with her tongue. Or maybe she would, and I'd like it. But Cindi with an "i" isn't doing it for me tonight. Which makes no fucking sense. This is why I came here. This is what I do. Why isn't my body cooperating?

When Cindi finally comes up for air, I take the drink tilted precariously toward my lap and set it on the coffee table. She shifts so that she's straddling me, and I hold her there a second just in case...

Nope. Still nothing happening downstairs.

"I hate to disappoint, but I've gotta head out." I help Cindi relocate to the chair's arm before pushing to my feet.

Marsha and Tory take a break from groping each other to throw matching pouts my way. "But you just got here."

"Yeah, you just got here," Cindi whines, looking so forlorn that I almost feel bad for leaving. But not bad enough to stick around.

"Yeah, sorry. I forgot I had to do something tonight. Maybe I'll see you at Fall Fest." With that, I slip out the door, climb back on my bike, and get the hell out of dodge.

I have every intention of going straight home, except Jade is stuck inside my head and I can't get her out. Maybe I should go see her instead.

Yeah, right. I can't do that. Hayley would murder me. Jade probably wouldn't let me in the door anyway, not after the way I acted earlier.

Then again, Jade is *nice*, so maybe she'd give me a chance to explain. That sounds a heck of a lot better than sitting around an empty apartment all by myself.

I roll to a stop at the intersection, one road leading to Main Street, the other to Jade's place. I overheard her tell Hayley that she's staying at her grandma's. I still remember having to drop Jade off there after sleepovers.

I brace my boot on the road, and the bike tilts slightly beneath me.

To Jade or not to Jade? That is the question.

Am I going to get any sleep if I head home with my head more tangled than Ella's yo-yo string? Nope. And a man my age needs his beauty sleep. I guess there's really only one choice left to make.

Before I know it, I'm pulling into a driveway that leads to a little brick rancher. Jade's white Civic is parked out front.

When she answers the door in a pair of lacy shorts beneath a thin Rob Zombie T-shirt, my hibernating dick decides it's time to rise and shine. Man, am I glad I came over tonight.

"Dylan. What are you..." She clears her throat, throwing frantic glances at the empty street. "What are you doing here?"

"I was an"—I mime the word "asshole"—"to you earlier, and I've come to apologize." *I also really like that T-shirt you're wearing. How'd you feel about taking it off?*

The taken-aback look on her face is warranted. I'm as surprised as she is that I'm even here, saying these words.

"Um, okay. Do you want to come in?" she asks.

The warmth in my chest expands. "Sure."

When the door closes behind me, she beelines for the living room to pause The Exorcist. What's she doing watching that shit all by herself this late at night? I wouldn't be able to sleep. "Want anything to drink?" she asks, heading for the fridge.

I can't take my eyes off the curves of her ass rounding out her shorts, which is a thousand times sexier than Cindi's neon thong.

This isn't good.

It's so not good.

And having a drink here isn't a good idea either because drunk Dylan tends to forget things like the fact that he shouldn't be checking out his baby sister's best friend. Sober Dylan knows better...

Mostly.

I force my eyes toward the pot of ramen steaming on the stove. "No, thanks," I reply about the drink.

"Suit yourself." Jade carries a bottle of light beer over to the couch and drops down, tucking one leg beneath her and the other so that her chin is resting on her knee.

Is she trying to look as cute as hell or is this her natural pose?

Expectant green eyes wait patiently for me to sit next to her.

I'm about to ask what Dickhead Williams told her about me when I realize that'll only piss me off more. Instead, I decide to go back to the beginning. "I started going out with Miranda Williams at the beginning of my senior year."

Jade's eyes widen, and her ponytail sways when she shakes her head. "Oh, Dylan. You don't have to tell me."

"I know I don't. But I want you to know my side of the story." Scratch that. I *need* her to know. I don't really understand why the fuck that is, but I do. I slide my clammy hands down my jeans and inhale a shaky breath. "Miranda was my first girlfriend. Technically, she's been my only girlfriend." Which is kinda pathetic when you think about it. "Anyway, her home life was shit, so she spent a lot of time at my parents' place. Everyone loved her, and she latched onto them more than she ever did to me."

A slight wrinkle appears between Jade's brows.

"One Friday night, Miranda called me saying she fell down the stairs and thought she may have broken her arm. She refused to call an ambulance, so I picked her up from her house and drove her to the ER. Since she wasn't eighteen yet, the doctors called her parents. Her stepdad came in fuming, swearing at me like her getting hurt was my fault." I'd wanted to knock his teeth out for talking to me like that, but that's neither here nor there.

"The staff threatened to call the police," I continue, "but he calmed down. Miranda got this pink cast on her arm, and I was the first to sign it." I took up all the space on the front of that thing, drawing hearts and shit like a lovesick idiot. "But the next Monday, she showed up at school without a cast, acting like it never fucking happened, wearing long sleeves and refusing to show anyone her arm.

"They'd given her some heavy painkillers, and I didn't even realize you could get hooked on that shit until a few months later when I caught her taking pills at lunch. She told me they were prescription, so it was fine." Only it wasn't fine. Not by a long shot. "By the time I learned the truth, it was too late. I tried to get her to find help, but she kept insisting that she didn't have a problem. Then she started getting these panic attacks about me breaking up with her when I went to college. I didn't intend to end things, but it was like she was determined to push me away. Everything kinda snowballed from there. She'd break up with me, then come to my house crying and begging me to take her back. I wasn't sleeping at all—could barely keep my eyes open in class. Eventually, I couldn't take it anymore and broke up with her. Needless to say, she didn't take it well."

Miranda keyed my car, left threatening voicemails—even went so far as to break Hayley's window with a rock, mistaking it for mine. Thankfully, my baby sister had been at a sleepover at—you guessed it—Jade's house. I don't tell Jade any of that, though, because this is hard enough to relive without dragging Miranda's name through the mud.

After the whole window incident, Mom and Dad stepped in. "My parents helped me file a restraining order," I say to Jade, leaving out that I felt like the biggest asshole for doing it. "I thought that was the end of things until I got a call from a blocked number on a random Tuesday night. Miranda was completely drunk or high...maybe both? I don't know. But she could barely speak." I'd changed my number at that point, so I wasn't sure how she got hold of it. "She asked if we could talk, but I didn't think that was a good idea, so I said no. The next day, she tried to call again, but I didn't answer. The following morning, Mom called to tell me Miranda had overdosed."

Jade sucks in a breath, her knuckles turning white where she grips the unopened beer.

"I still wonder if she would've survived if I'd told her yes." *Every fucking night.*

"Oh, Dylan..." Jade's hand finds mine, her soft palm soothing and warm.

The contact may be casual and light, but fuck does it feel good. I repress the urge to lace my fingers with hers and hold on tight. I can't remember the last time I held hands with someone besides my niece. Jade's thumb traces over the rose on the back of my hand—the one I got for Mom when I turned eighteen. My heart beats a little harder; my gaze finds her mouth and clings there.

Jade's phone suddenly blasts to life on the table, and our hands quickly separate. She silences the call almost immediately, but it's too late. I've already seen the name *Nate* flashing across the screen.

It's the wake-up call I need to stand up from the couch. *What the fuck am I doing?* "So anyway, that's my sob story," I say.

Jade scrambles to her feet. "Wait. You don't have to go."

"I really do." Otherwise, I'm going to guzzle that beer she's holding on to for dear life and then try to drown myself in her delicate hands, pouty lips, and emerald eyes.

"Hasta la vista, Jadie." I do this stupid-as-hell salute thing and return to the night, telling myself this was a mistake. But it's hard to believe that when my heart feels lighter than it has in years.

CHAPTER TWELVE

JADE

I SWEEP MY GAZE OVER THE FESTIVALGOERS MILLING past the towering pumpkin displays and homemade scarecrow sculptures, searching for one face in particular. But there's no sign of a petite brunette clutching a reporter's notepad, which is no surprise given the size of the crowd. Nate wasn't wrong. The county must've pumped a bunch of new marketing dollars into Fall Fest this year.

As I turn back toward the Quinn Brothers booth, a figure I'd know anywhere catches my eye. My lips pull up at the waist-length black hair and the smitten smile as Ruby wraps her arms around the neck of a blushing pilot.

Aww, bless. Still all over each other like puppies. My smile widens as I edge my way through the spectators toward the lovebirds who arrived in town last night.

"Who let you two in? *Security!*" I joke as I round on Ruby and Flynn. They quickly untangle, and Ruby flings her arms around me, even though we all had breakfast together this morning at my place.

"You been feeding this fair steroids behind our backs, Jade?" Flynn asks with a smirk, stroking Ruby's shoulder.

I laugh. "I know. It's gargantuan, right?"

"Look out world, Still Springs just joined the map. Maybe I'll start doing regular flights here for my boss."

I snort. "Let's manage our expectations, shall we?"

Ruby's still giving me that lit-up look she has when she hasn't seen me for ages. "Any sign of that reporter yet?" she asks, knowing it's my mission of the day.

"Not yet." I press a hand to my hip while scanning the crowd again. "But I've got the booth set up over there with some colorful mosaic jewelry, these fantastically gruesome clay sculptures, and some painted bowls I just got in, so hopefully, she comes past."

"She will." Ruby slips an arm through mine as the three of us stroll over to the Quinn Brothers booth, where Dad's making a face at the sculptures of misshapen heads with no eyes and screaming mouths. A laugh bubbles out of me. I sure didn't get my fondness for horror from Dad.

Flynn strides over to shake Dad's hand. Ruby hangs back and watches them with a dopey smile. A twinge of envy tugs in my chest over what she's found with Flynn. But if it can only be one of us, I'm glad it's her.

I lean against a wooden pole wrapped with fairy lights and cross my arms. "Look at you with the candy eyes."

She catches her face between her palms. "I'm so in love, it's ridiculous. You might need to slap me out of it."

"Hell no. You're both way too adorable for that. And it's so good to see you happy."

She tilts her head, giving me the same assessing look she did this morning. "Thanks. And you're okay? Dad said things still aren't great at the store."

I respond with a nonchalant wave of my hand. "All is under control, captain. You know Dad, such a drama queen."

I try to smile, but my throat locks as a thought pounds through my head. *Liar. Always pretending everything is okay so that other people won't feel bad. So that* you *won't feel bad for not being able to find a way to save the store that your mom left for you. Sweep it under the rug, like you always do, Jade. Sweep, sweep, sweep.*

Ruby nudges my knee with hers. "Anything I can do? I could come back and—"

"*No.*" No way in hell am I letting my sister leave her new job and life with Flynn after everything she went through. I clutch her wrists, staring into her eyes. "I'm telling you, it's fine. We'll be okay."

She smiles with relief. "Great. So how's it all going with..." Her cheeks redden as she glances past my shoulder. "Nate!"

I spin to find the deputy sheriff on approach, dressed in a red plaid shirt, brown leather boots, and a bandana tied around his neck. He looks like one of the scarecrows come to life.

Ruby points a finger at him, smiling. "Are you in one of the shows today?"

"No," he replies without further comment before stepping forward to kiss my cheek. He shakes Ruby's hand like she's a colleague, and they exchange a few moments of stiff small talk while I run my eyes over Nate's profile.

I'm so not *in love, it's ridiculous.*

Which is fine. Nate and I have only been dating for a little while. But shouldn't I feel *something* by now? Something more than mostly tolerating his company and his kisses? He's nice enough, but he's also kind of...bland.

His hazel eyes gleam at me like he feels the opposite. "Would you like to walk around the festival?"

Actually, no. I'd rather do anything but. "Oh, thanks, but I've gotta mind the booth with Dad."

"Your dad can't handle a booth on his own?"

My brows come together. "No, he can't. He's got a bad back, and that reporter is coming by, remember? And I need for her to—"

Ruby steps forward. "I'll mind the booth, Jade. You go have some fun with Nate."

"No way. You only just got back to town." The last thing she probably wants to do is work.

Her fingers gently brush my arm. "You've done so much for the store these past few months, so it's my turn to do something. Besides, it'll give me a chance to spend some time with Dad. Flynn's parents are around here somewhere, so he'll be happy to hang with them for a bit. Plus, we've got all of tomorrow. Don't forget the mud race." We both groan but know there's no getting out of it. I usually enjoy games, but ones of the less slimy variety.

"Thank you, Ruby," Nate says, taking my fingers and tugging me up the street.

I reluctantly let him lead me away from the booth that I worked so hard to set up while calling out for Ruby to please call me if the reporter comes by.

I search for Sunny Gillespie's face everywhere while Nate and I stroll past haybales spiked with maple-shaped signs and red-and-gold flags flapping from iron lamp posts, his fingers threaded with mine. I want to enjoy the festival and try to connect with Nate, but I feel like someone's tied my gut into knots. I've spent this past week distracting myself from the shop troubles and the bounced loan payments by trawling Pinterest for festival booth ideas that might impress Sunny. The late nights paid off because our booth is an undeniable standout beside the florist's wilting displays and the rock shop's plastic tubs of stones and minerals. Our booth looks like it's been professionally styled, with rustic, upturned crates hosting blooms of dried flowers and strung-up olden-day photographs of Still Springs hanging from wires. But if things don't go well today, and the reporter misses our booth...

"Are you okay?" Nate squeezes my fingers. "You seem distracted."

I sigh. "I guess I feel like I should be working instead of wandering around doing nothing."

His hand loosens in mine. "I didn't realize that being with me counted as nothing."

"It's not," I reply quickly. "I didn't mean it like that. I just really want to talk to this reporter, and there are about a billion people at this festival, so I'm worried I won't catch her."

"There aren't even a billion people in America." He smiles like he's sorry for me that I didn't know that.

I shake my head and decide not to bother explaining that I didn't mean it literally.

Nate stops and places his hands on my shoulders. "Why don't I buy you a funnel cake?"

My ears prick up like a puppy's. "With extra whipped cream and strawberries?"

He frowns intently. "I'm not sure they'll allow extra toppings, but we can ask."

I breathe a light laugh, and we head over to the food tents and order two delicious-smelling funnel cakes, balancing them on paper plates and finding a spot near the stage area to stand and eat.

Two bites in, Nate and I jump at the ear-piercing squeal of a microphone feeding back through speakers.

"Sorry about that," the town mayor, Julia Pappas, says

into the mic. "Hello, Still Spriiiings!" she calls out like a rockstar greeting Madison Square Garden.

A couple of muttered greetings sound around us as a few spectators gather.

"It's time for the Third Annual Still Springs Fall Fest Talent Show!" the mayor announces. I grimace around my funnel cake. Given the quality of the talent show's acts last year, I suspect its days are numbered.

Mayor Pappas pulls out a crumpled piece of paper from her pocket. "Everybody put your hands together for Frank Goldsmith!"

Frank, a close friend of Ruby's ex, steps up to the microphone and snaps it off its stand. He nods at the long-haired teen behind the sound desk, and a moment later, the song "Baby Got Back (I Like Big Butts)" assaults the air. I hold my hand over my mouth with horror while Frank mimes to the track, complete with rapper-style hand waves.

When the song is mercifully over, I shoot Nate a smirk. "Your turn. Which song are you gonna mime? 'Too Many Dicks (On the Dance Floor)'?"

He barks a laugh like that's way funnier than it is and bends to press a lingering kiss against the nape of my neck. My skin breaks out in goosebumps, and not in a good way.

"Should we go?" he suggests, smacking his lips like I taste better than his funnel cake. "We can check out the hayrides?"

Before I can reply, a tiny, musical voice shouts from behind me. "Look, Uncle Pickle. That man has a puppet!"

Dylan's niece, Ella, scampers right past me toward where Mr. Chen is hovering on the side of the stage, clutching a ventriloquist dummy. *Mr. Chen! You're a dark horse.* The dummy's eyes roll back in its head as it hangs upside down. Looks like the start of an excellent horror film.

Dylan casually strides in a few feet away, and my stomach flips over. He crouches beside Ella to say something in her ear, but the second he stands back up, his eyes fly straight to mine. My cheeks heat, and our gazes cling together for a long moment before he returns his attention to Ella.

"Oh, *shit*," Nate grumbles when he spots Dylan. He takes hold of my arm. "Let's go."

"No, wait." My feet suddenly feel rooted to the spot. "Maybe we should see one more act. It looks like it's Mr. Chen and his dummy."

Nate shakes his head. "I'm ready for a hayride."

"And I'm ready to stay here." I unhook my arm from his grip.

He huffs but doesn't push me again to leave. Instead, he stands with his arms crossed, scowling at the stage.

The truth is, I'm hardly on the edge of my seat with anticipation over Mr. Chen and his puppet show. But this is the first time I've run into Dylan since he turned up at my house and said all that stuff about Nate's cousin, and I've been kind of itching to see him ever since. He'd left so quickly when Nate called that I hadn't even had a chance to respond to what he'd told me. To thank him for trusting me with something so personal and private. To ask him the reason he'd wanted me to know. Is it because I'm close to Hayley?

I know he's still staying next door to the store because his motorcycle has been parked down the street, but he hasn't come into the shop to buy anything all week. Is he avoiding me because he's embarrassed about opening up like that?

"Honestly, why can't that guy just fuck off out of town,"

Nate mutters, shooting dagger eyes at Dylan behind his back.

Enough is enough. I frown at Nate. "That guy is my best friend's brother, so you might want to tone it down a notch."

His jaw falls open. "Are you kidding me?" He leans closer, speaking through his teeth. "You've already forgotten everything I told you about him? About what he did to Miranda?"

"Of course not." My tone softens because I can see how badly Nate is still hurting over his cousin. "But are you really sure you have the full story about what happened? Because Dylan told me that—"

"Dylan told you what?" Nate's cheeks whiten. "What the hell are you talking about?"

I glance back at Dylan, relieved to find him standing far enough away that he can't possibly hear this. He and Ella are watching the ventriloquist show; I can see Mr. Chen's mouth moving from here every time the puppet speaks.

"I can't believe you," Nate spits before I can answer. "I told you in confidence about what that deadbeat did to my cousin, and you've been *talking* to him about it."

Tension chews up the air between us as we watch Mr. Chen try to get his dummy to perform a magic trick, but all the cards collapse onto the ground.

"I didn't tell Dylan what you told me," I say carefully. "In fact, he did most of the talking. But if I'm honest, his story wasn't exactly the same as yours."

Nate's fingers tighten at his side. "Oh, yeah? How so?"

"He said that he never gave your cousin any drugs." Repeating Dylan's words to Nate makes me feel strangely disloyal, but I can't let Nate continue slandering the guy if he has some wrong information here. It's exactly what happened to Ruby with her ex: the whole town believed the worst of her without knowing the true story. And while Nate was Miranda's cousin, Dylan was the one directly involved in this situation. He was there.

"Dylan said that your cousin got hooked on painkillers when she went to hospital with a broken arm," I continue shakily. "That he tried to help her, but he couldn't. That she—"

Nate expels a harsh breath and shoots me a disgusted look. "And you believed all his bullshit?"

"I didn't see any reason not to."

Either Dylan is the world's greatest actor and con artist, which is admittedly possible, or he was telling the truth. There were too many raw emotions scrawled over his face that night he shared this with me. Dylan's story was also full of detail, whereas Nate's was more like piecing bits together and taking the word of Miranda's stepdad, who clearly had it out for Dylan from the start.

Nate bites hard into his bottom lip. "This is gonna be a problem for me, Jade. A very big problem. In fact, if you're going to be my girlfriend, then you're going to have to stay away from that prick. And that is not a request. You want to be with me? You don't talk to him anymore. End of story."

I blink at Nate, my eyes running over his agitated face.

But I don't *want to be with you. I wish I did because it would be...simple. Easy.*

But sometimes simple and easy don't cut it.

"Yeah, I think it *is* the end of the story," I say, feeling genuinely disappointed. "This isn't working for me, Nate. I'm sorry."

He flinches like I slapped him. "Are you serious? You're ending this because of that fucking loser?"

Anger builds in my chest. "He's not a fucking *loser*. If you just try talking to him about this—"

"Oh, fuck off," Nate snaps. "And fuck you, Jade." He dumps his plastic plate onto the ground, sending remnants of whipped cream splattering across my tennis shoes before he storms off.

I watch him go with my mouth hanging open, registering that this is the first time in my life that I've ever been told to F-off. Talk about a milestone. It doesn't feel great, so I twist back to the stage, my eyes burning. When I've composed myself, I brave another glance at Dylan and Ella, finding Hayley's brother standing alone. He's craning his neck, watching Ella with the group of children huddled in front of the stage. They're laughing at one of the high school kids attempting to stack a tower of tin cans.

A war breaks out within me to either leave this shitshow of a talent contest or walk right up to Dylan and say hi. To be the one person in this town who doesn't believe everything that's said about him, and to give him the time of day.

He turns his head, and our gazes catch, my cheeks heating. *Ugh, he caught me staring.*

He looks past my shoulder like he's wondering where Nate went. When our eyes find each other's again, he gives me a half-smile that steals some of the breath from my chest. I smile back, and we take a step toward each other before a small, shapely woman brushes right past me and latches onto Dylan's forearm.

"Dylan?" she says with a blindingly beautiful smile. Holy shit, that's Sunny Gillespie.

Dylan shoots her that same sexy smirk he just gave me. A sharp feeling pinches my throat, and it presses harder when he reaches an arm around Sunny's waist and pulls her in for a hug like they know each other.

I force my eyes to the stage, my mind whirring. *That. Is. Sunny. Gillespie. Go and introduce yourself, Jade!*

But the reporter's still clinging to Dylan like a vine, now standing on her tiptoes and molding her body to his. His gaze flickers to mine over her shoulder, and I quickly look away.

My hands need something to do, so I pull out my phone to check if Ruby's called. But of course she hasn't because the reporter's standing right in front of me, gripping Dylan's arm and bringing it closer to her nose like she's appreciating the artwork.

I pretend to type into my phone and listen hard so I can hear bits of their conversation.

"...Heard about your mom and dad..." Sunny says.

"...Rather not talk about it..."

"...Here to do a big feature on the town..."

"...Heard that. My sisters would love for us to have some involvement..."

"...Perfect, I'm looking for one local business to feature..." she says, and the earth falls out from under me.

No, no, no! The Kings don't need the exposure. They don't even have a booth at this festival—she *can't* pick them over us.

My fingers quiver as I slide my phone into my back pocket, contemplating whether I should just bound over there and crash Sunny and Dylan's little reunion, even if that makes me look desperate.

A trio of giggling young women push past me, nearly knocking me on my butt. They make a beeline for Dylan, interrupting him with Sunny the way I should have. It takes me a second to place one of them as Cindi with an "i," and I'm not sure who the other two are, but all three are looking at Dylan like they're ready to devour him for dessert. Make that the four of them.

As I watch Dylan engulfed by beautiful women—those who either haven't heard about or don't care about his reputation—the message rings loud and clear.

I'm not special to him just because he told me a sad story about his past. He's a flirt...a player...a good time. He told me himself: he hasn't had a girlfriend since high school.

Ugh, why am I even thinking about this? He's Hayley's brother!

Not even Sunny Gillepsie is worth the humiliation of striding over there and making it appear like I'm groupie number five. Plus, it's pretty apparent which business she's going to choose for her article.

With my jaw grinding, I turn around and stride as far away from the talent show stage as I can get.

CHAPTER THIRTEEN

DYLAN

I don't consider myself a jealous person. But for some reason, seeing Nate fucking Williams put his mouth on Jade's neck earlier made me want to put my fist in his weasley face. And I know that makes me the biggest hypocrite on the planet because I am literally surrounded by women right now, but here we are.

I'm also not thrilled about the way Sunny keeps hanging onto my arm, but I don't want to embarrass her by shaking free. Cindi doesn't seem to mind in the slightest, lifting to her toes and pressing a glossy, sticky kiss to my cheek. Probably because she's so good at "sharing."

"I was hoping I'd run into you," Cindi says while her friends grin at me from over her shoulder, wiggling their fingers in a weird sort of wave. "We're going out tonight and I really think you should come." Her gaze travels over to Sunny. "You can even bring your friend if you want."

Telling Cindi a flat-out no will undoubtedly lead to her trying to change my mind, so I go with something more neutral. "We'll see."

Thankfully, Ella saves me from having to interact

beyond that by bounding over like a miniature superhero and demanding boardwalk fries.

The women coo over my niece, but Ella doesn't appear impressed as she laces her chubby hands with mine and tugs me toward the food trucks. "Sorry, ladies. I've gotta get this monster some food before she eats me," I say over my shoulder.

Ella chomps her teeth and growls low in her throat.

With my hand occupied in case Sunny gets any ideas, the reporter drifts along next to me. Every so often, she pulls a notebook from the back of her tight jeans and jots something down or takes a picture with her phone. We chat a little while we wait in line at the fry truck, and I buy Ella and Sunny fries. We then head back through the buzzing crowd toward Main Street, where the bulk of the vendors are set up.

There are more crafts in the high school gymnasium, and tonight is the battle of the bands at the football field. When I was younger, my friends and I used to spend Friday night down at the cabin getting roaring drunk and show up to the parade with raging hangovers.

Sunny glances up at me with a smile as bright as her name. "After all these years, who would've thought I'd be strolling down the streets of Still Springs with Dylan King?"

"Crazy, right?" I laugh, but it sounds forced. Reminiscing with a woman I barely remember isn't something I care to do, so I steer our conversation back to the present. "So, what made you want to do an article on Still Springs?" Seems to me there are a gazillion topics more interesting than this place.

She doesn't think about her response for very long. "With everything going on in the world, people want feel-good stories now more than ever. Plus, anything about fall usually gets a ton of hits, and small towns are trending. I told my editor all about our wholesome little fall festival, and she was immediately on board." She sweeps her gaze from the candy apple and kettle corn stand down to the antique store's gigantic half-price sale sign. "Although it doesn't seem so little anymore."

She can say that again. There are people everywhere. And while it's a great infusion of cash into the local economy, all these crowds make me want to go straight back to the apartment and hide until everyone's gone. I know it doesn't make sense because I live in a city, but this is different because half of these faces I recognize. And from the glowers and glares, I know they recognize me too.

Ella hands me her greasy paper cup, and I pop the few crunchy fries at the bottom into my mouth before throwing it into the trash. "Well, your community appreciates it," I say to Sunny. My sisters are still going nuts over the news, and I've heard a few folks up at the store talking about the article as well. When nothing exciting happens, I suppose this sort of shit is newsworthy.

"I hope so. A national spread is nothing to be sniffed at."

I'm sorry, but that's the fourth time since this morning that she's said the word "spread," and every time she does, my mind dives right into the gutter.

Ella asks me to buy her a bunch of rocks from a vendor, and of course, she has to have the hot-pink bag to put them in.

"Your niece is adorable." Sunny ruffles Ella's pigtails. The little beast twists around to glare and growl at Sunny. I have to bite back my laughter.

"Yeah, she is." And she knows she has me wrapped around her pink-tipped fingers. "Hey, do you mind if we swing by my place for a minute?"

"Trying to bring me home on a first date?" Sunny says with a *tsk* and a playful slap on my arm.

Hearing the word "date" makes me break out in a cold sweat. "I actually need to get Ella back to her mom." The talent(less) show put me a little behind schedule, not to mention all the trinkets we've bought, like the shiny rocks, a blinking tiara and matching wand, and a cross-eyed wooden doll.

"No need to look so scandalized. It was obviously a joke," Sunny laughs, and I immediately relax.

The moment we round the corner, Ella darts through the crowd to where her mom and dad are waiting in front of my apartment. I'm about to follow her when my gaze snags on a familiar profile.

My feet remain glued to the sidewalk as the middle-aged woman with strawberry-blonde hair slowly turns toward me. All the air in my lungs escapes, and I'm suddenly an eighteen-year-old kid who just got one of the worst calls of his life.

Miranda Williams had always been a dead ringer for her mom, and now all I can see is Miranda's smile and sparkling eyes and—*shit*.

"Dylan?"

I hear Sunny, but she sounds so far away, and why is it so fucking warm in October? Five minutes ago there was a breeze, but now there's no breeze, and where the hell is the breeze? Miranda's mom begins to walk my way, but she mustn't see me because she's still smiling, and *fuck*, she looks so much like Miranda it's like I'm seeing a fucking ghost.

By some miracle, my legs finally unlock. I bolt between booths, duck behind a scarecrow staked into a hay bale, and crouch in a narrow alley.

What was it that Sarah always said to do?

I tug on my T-shirt collar and force myself to take a breath, counting to three on the inhale, then pushing the air back out through my lips to the count of four. Colors. I need to think of stuff that's blue.

Okay...um....the sky, that's blue.

The scarecrow's plaid shirt. The bottle cap over by the other wall. My jeans. With each item I find during my solo game of I Spy, my heart beats a little slower.

By the time I'm breathing normally, my legs have turned completely numb.

Sarah has been pushing me to visit Miranda's mom in order to put my past behind me once and for all, but if today is any indication, I won't be going anywhere near my ex-girlfriend's family. Miranda may have been gone for twelve years, but these wounds are still bleeding and I'm not sure they'll ever stop.

Eventually, I stand up and peer into the crowd, searching for Miranda's mom, but she must've moved on. *Thank god*. I slip back out of the alley, but my heart is still skipping around in my chest, like Ella when she's playing hopscotch. I paste on a smile and move toward my sisters and Sunny, who appears oblivious to my meltdown.

Alex gives me a nod, and Iris thanks me for taking Ella this morning so they could get caught up at the store.

I glimpse Jade at the stall outside Quinn Brothers. She's with a young woman with black hair, who's smiling and chatting to some customers. I vaguely remember Jade's sister Ruby. The two of them couldn't look any more different, but they both have the same warm smiles that seem to hold nothing back.

Just seeing Jade makes the tightness in my chest loosen a little bit more.

Her eyes connect with mine for a brief moment before returning to the sour-faced woman inspecting a creepy piece of pottery. Not really your usual stock for a convenience store, but it seems to be bringing in the customers. People are lined up down the street for Jade's stall. I scan the customers for one face in particular but find no one familiar.

I still haven't spoken to Jade since showing up to her house uninvited. Not sure why I thought she'd come by and see me after I told her my deepest, darkest secrets. Two days ago, I nearly called out to her when I saw her locking up the store, but then I spotted the police cruiser parked outside and decided to leave it. Accidentally running into Nate Williams is bad enough. I'm not about to do it on purpose.

Sunny claps her hand beneath her chin and does this bouncy thing on her toes like Ella does when she needs to pee. "Oh my gosh. Quinn Brothers! I used to love going there when I was little. It hasn't changed at all. Does Archie Quinn still own it?" she asks, whipping out that notebook again.

"I think so, but his daughter Jade runs the place," I say, my heart rate finally getting back to normal. "They have just about everything you need if you're staying in town." I fish my keys from my pocket, needing a minute to collect myself, maybe grab a glass of water, or lock myself inside and hide for the rest of the day. "I'm going to run upstairs. I'll just be a sec."

Sunny doesn't get the hint and follows me inside, talking about her memories of eating at Harringtons and getting ice cream here. She glances toward the sheets of plastic hanging over the back windows but doesn't ask why they're there or about the plans for this place. Upstairs, I grab my old Pentax camera from my room and a leather harness so I won't have to carry a bag.

Sunny, who's followed me up, turns in a circle, taking in the stark space with a smile inching along her lips. "Wow, Dylan. Your place has so much personality."

If I had any plans to stay in Still Springs, I probably would have paid someone to paint the white walls, but as it stands, this apartment will be a blank canvas for the next tenant as soon as I leave. After the contractors finish tiling the bathroom, Iris plans to flip the place for a decent profit. "I have a condo in Austin. This is only temporary."

"Austin is a great city. I love it there." She smiles like she expects an invitation from me to visit, but she's barking up the wrong tree.

"Yeah, it is. You ready to go back out?"

The way she purses her lips and glances at my bedroom door makes me think she's about to suggest something, but then she nods and follows me back down to the street.

After a quick recon to ensure I'm not going to run into any more ghosts from my past, I pop the lens cap off my camera and adjust the settings so that the sun peeking through the heavy clouds doesn't wash everything out.

The best part of being on this side of a camera is that everyone who sees you seems to stop and actually smile.

Like the group of rowdy teens in soccer jerseys. Not a scowl or a judgmental stare in sight.

"I forgot you were a photographer," Sunny remarks when I kneel down to take a picture of a little girl about Ella's age whose ice cream has melted all over her hands, careful not to get her face in the frame for privacy.

I shrug and say, "It pays the bills." It also calms me when I'm feeling anxious. There's something comforting about being able to hide behind a lens, almost like you're invisible. Yeah, people see the camera, but they're rarely looking at the person holding it.

Without thinking, my gaze travels back to the Quinn Brothers booth. Muted sunlight catches Jade's gorgeous face just right, and I snap a picture. The way she and her dad laugh leaves my chest aching.

I wish I would've come home more after moving to Austin—even attended this stupid festival the last few years Dad asked me to. While the looks and whispers definitely still piss me off, they don't get to me quite as much as they did when I was younger.

I hate that I let all the judgmental assholes in town keep me away for so long.

CHAPTER FOURTEEN

DYLAN

Sunny and I meander aimlessly, and I take pictures while she chats to locals and voice-notes herself with her phone. Every so often, I think I glimpse Miranda's mom, but it turns out to be someone else.

When the sun begins to sink below the horizon, the crowd thins as everyone heads over to the Battle of the Bands or the Fiddle Contest up at the state park.

"You want to grab a drink?" Sunny asks.

Nope, sure don't.

Still, I concede with a, "Why not." My sisters won't be impressed if they find out I turned her down. Besides, I don't have any other plans, and maybe a drink would help burn away some of the lingering tension in my chest.

"Oh! Let's go to The Rocking Horse," Sunny says. "I haven't been there in years."

Kill me now. "Let's do it." At least it's within spitting distance of my apartment, meaning I can leave any time I want.

The moment we step inside the packed bar, Sunny lets out this screeching squeal that has everyone within earshot swiveling on stools and craning their necks to stare at us. A woman who looks vaguely familiar makes the same god-awful sound and tackles Sunny into one of the high-top tables.

"You dirty little slut! You never told me you were coming home!" the newcomer shouts over the karaoke singer's ear-piercing rendition of "Girls Just Wanna Have Fun."

"It was a last-minute thing," Sunny says, tugging me closer by the sleeve. "Carrie, you remember Dylan King."

The woman's eyes widen behind her horn-rimmed glasses as her gaze sweeps from my head to my boots. "Do I ever."

"Good to see you again, Carrie," I offer, even though I have no clue how she knows me. "Can I get you ladies a drink?"

"Vodka and tonic for me," Sunny says, turning to her friend.

Carrie raises her bulbous glass. "Gin and tonic for me. Thanks, handsome."

I turn my back and immediately hear them whispering my name and squealing some more. I guess I should be flattered, and maybe I would be if the blonde woman in dark denim and a white sweater that hangs off one shoulder leaning against the bar didn't steal all my attention.

The end of Jade's ponytail sweeps between her bare shoulder blades. I scan the bar for her short-ass boyfriend, but he's nowhere to be found. Can't say I'm sad about it. Maybe I'll get lucky and leave before he shows up.

I shoulder my way between two guys who look way too young to be here and sidle up next to Jade. "Hey."

Her green-eyed gaze flicks toward me, and I'm transfixed. "Oh, hi, Dylan." I don't miss the way her eyes seem to linger on my arms where they're folded atop the bar. "Didn't expect to see you here."

"Believe me, this is the last place on earth I want to be."

Her lips flatten. "Then why did you come?"

I nod toward where Sunny and her friend have taken up residence at the table near the door. Jade's shoulders tighten. If I didn't know better, I'd say she looks jealous. But I do know better.

Speaking of jealous…

"Where's the boyfriend?" I ask.

Jade's chin lifts. "I'm pretty sure he stopped being my boyfriend the moment he told me to fuck off."

My brow scrunches. "He did *what*?" As if I didn't already hate the prick enough. "Why would he say something like that to you?" I tell myself I'm only pissed off because this girl is like a sister to Hayley and, by extension, a sister to me, but I'm not so sure that's true.

Jade shrugs her shoulders. "Doesn't matter."

Like hell it doesn't. Did his parents not teach him basic fucking manners? No woman deserves to be spoken to like that, least of all Jade.

"So, you and the reporter, huh?" she asks with a tilt of her head toward Sunny.

Now it's my turn to shrug. "My sisters asked me to show her around."

Jade looks away and mutters under her breath, "Like you guys need more money."

What does money have to do with anything? I'm about to ask what she meant by that little comment when she turns back to me and steps closer. With the way her eyes burn right into mine, Sunny and her article are the last things on my mind.

"Did they tell you to have drinks with her tonight, too?"

Jade asks, lifting a brow as her perfect pink lips close around her straw, and she takes a deep drag of the cocktail in her hand.

Do I immediately fantasize about the way those lips would look wrapped around my dick? I'd love to say no, but that would be a lie. My voice comes out a little gruff when I respond. "What can I say? I like to go above and beyond for the ladies."

"I bet you do," she murmurs.

If my voice is gravel, Jade's is all smoke.

And I don't know what the fuck to do with it. What has Jade's doppelganger done with the woman who's been more reserved than not, and why is she standing so close to me that I can smell the cherries in her glass?

"Little Jade. Are you drunk?" Her eyes are clear, not bloodshot or glassy. And she doesn't seem to be unsteady in those wedge heels that make her legs look long enough to grip my hips nicely. But there's no way she'd say what she just did sober.

She holds up a finger. "Buzzed, yes. But not drunk."

"Are you on your own?" Or is she on a date with one of the countless guys checking out her ass right now? Seriously, they want to get their eyes up where they belong before I introduce their faces to my boot.

"Yeah. Ruby and Flynn left a little bit ago," Jade says.

"And you didn't want to go with them?"

"Nah. I wanted to stay here and drown my sorrows."

"What sorrows are those?"

She squints her eyes and shrugs.

The bartender finally comes over to me, and I order Sunny and her friend a drink. I then get myself a beer and hand over my credit card to open a tab, offering to pay for another drink for Jade. She protests, but not much, eventually ordering a cocktail I've never heard of before.

The thought of leaving Jade to go back to Sunny makes my chest feel lined with lead. It doesn't help that the two guys in trucker hats over at the pool table are checking out Jade's tits in that sweater. I have a feeling the moment I step aside, those two are going to swoop right in. So, instead, I lean an elbow on the bar and say, "You want to drown those sorrows with a shot?"

There's defiance in her eyes when she smiles. "Only if you take one too."

This is a terrible, awful idea, which, of course means I'm all for it. "Order two, and I'll be right back."

I drop Sunny's drinks over to where she and her friend are sitting.

"Thank you, Dylan," they say in unison.

Before I can head back to Jade, Sunny catches my arm. "Where do you think you're going?"

"I met a friend over at the bar."

She glances over my shoulder, her brow furrowing as she lifts her drink to her lips. "Promise you'll be right back?"

"Yeah. I want to hear all about what you're up to these days," Carrie adds.

I give Sunny's hand a pat and make a promise I have no intention of keeping. Maybe that makes me a shitty guy, but I'm not too worried about it because that fucker in a backwards hat just nudged his friend and tipped his chin toward Jade. And now he's sauntering toward where she's waiting for me.

Not tonight, jackass.

I beeline for the bar, slotting into the space in front of Jade before Hathead can get a look in. I can feel his glower drilling into the side of my head, but I don't spare him a glance. Two shot glasses wait on the sticky bar, filled with layers of dark and light alcohol and topped with whipped cream.

The cream leaks onto my fingers when I pick up the glass. "What's this?" Smells like almonds and coffee.

Jade's lips lift. "A blowjob."

I nearly drop the fucking drink before I recover, and I know that I shouldn't say what's on the tip of my tongue, but I can't help myself. "Better not let Hayley find out you're giving me a blowjob."

Jade snorts and downs the shot in one go. I do the same, and holy shit, that's sweet. I chase the drink with a swig of beer. Doesn't help.

"How are those sorrows?" I ask.

Jade makes a face. "Still there."

"Would another blow job fix it?" *Always helps me.*

Her green eyes sparkle with mischief. "There's only one way to find out."

I twist toward the bartender and order another round.

"Your fan club must be getting impatient," Jade says with a quick glance at where I left Sunny and her friend.

"I don't care." Right now, there's only one woman who has my attention. My eyes can't help but trace the lines of her collarbone, and I imagine what it would be like to have my tongue do the same.

Two shots land in front of us, startling me out of thoughts I should not be having about Hayley's best friend.

Thankfully, Jade seems none the wiser, saluting me with her drink.

This one's a little easier to take, although I swear I can feel the liquid hit my stomach with a splash. I swap the glass for my beer and tilt the top toward my partner in crime. "Feeling better yet?"

Her nose scrunches as she considers. Fuck, she looks cute when she does that. "A little."

Two more it is. I gesture for the bartender to keep them coming. Jade rests an elbow against the bar and chases the straw around her drink, eventually capturing it between her lips. Her gaze drops to my arms. "I've always wanted a tattoo," she says like it's some deep, dark confession.

"Oh, yeah?"

Golden strands from her ponytail slip over her shoulder when she nods. "Apart from something for my mom, I go back and forth between a vine entwined with a snake or a skull covered in flowers."

Either one would look so fucking hot on her. "Where would you want it?"

"I can't decide." Her brows arch. "Any suggestions?"

My hand tightens around my beer. I drink what's left of it as I consider exactly where on her tight body I'd kill to find either one. "Let's see. You could get it here." Jade's breath hitches when I trace a finger down the side of her ribcage. "But that spot hurts like a sonofabitch." My finger halts at the top of her jeans. "Or right here." My palm grazes over the point where her thigh meets her hip. I can imagine Jade in a string bikini, with a tattoo stretching across that patch of sun-kissed skin. My dick can imagine it too.

Jade's gaze falls to where two shots wait on the bar. When did the bartender drop these off? I pull back and lift my shot for a toast. "To getting drunk with Jade Quinn."

She taps her glass against mine, her face and neck flushed all over. We finish those, but a tiny dollop of whipped cream clings to her lips. I know there's a joke in there somewhere, but my brain doesn't seem to be working because all I can think about is how much I want to lick it off.

Instead, I decide to err on the side of caution and gently brush my thumb across her pillowy bottom lip instead. But then I slip the tip of my thumb inside my mouth and lick *that* off, so it kinda comes full circle.

Jade's warm breath whispers across my neck. I don't remember closing the distance between us and really should step away, but I don't, and neither does she.

After another shot, there's so much sugar swimming in my stomach that I'm close to hurling all over the already sticky floor. "I never thought I'd say this, but I'm kinda sick of blowjobs."

Jade's eyes make an unabashed sweep down to the front of my jeans before returning to my face. "That's too bad."

Oh, shit. She did not just say that. "Stop that right now."

I didn't think it was possible, but her lips look even prettier when they're smirking. "Stop what?"

"You know what." If her gaze was to drift south right now, she'd realize exactly what that heated look does to me.

"Oh!" Jade punches my arm and it fucking hurts. Damn, she's strong. "Do you know what we should do?"

Go back to my place and drown our sorrows naked? "No, what?"

Whatever is in her head makes her giggle like Ella when she's had too much candy and soda. I have a sneaking suspicion that Jade is a little more tipsy than buzzed. Especially when she snorts and says, "Let's send a pic to Hayley."

Personally, I like my plan better.

But you know what? If Jade wants a picture, she deserves a picture.

I throw my arm around Jade's shoulders and press my

face against hers to fit into the tight frame. We both smile as she taps the button. The picture is grainy as hell and one of my eyes looks a bit wonky, but I ask her to text it to me, too, because why not? I already have that goofy one of us in costumes from the Italian fair that I may have Photo-shopped a certain dickhead out of. May as well add to my collection.

Jade's teeth drag along her bottom lip, and I get the crazy urge to capture her cheeks in my hands and do the same thing. But that's drunk Dylan talking, and he'll be gone in the morning.

"I would, but I don't have your number," she says.

I gesture toward the phone clenched in her fist. She unlocks it so that I can text the picture to myself. While I'm at it, I go ahead and add myself as a new contact just for fun. And then I see the string of messages from her shit-head ex-boyfriend and decide to make a little tweak there as well.

My phone buzzes, and when I drag the handset out of my pocket, Jade's message isn't the only one there.

> **HAYLEY**
>
> What's your arm doing around my best friend?

I type a quick reply.

> What's your nose doing in my business?

> She's not your business.

Maybe I want to make Jade my business. But I don't type that because hearing my sister's opinions will only ruin my night, and as much as I had dreaded coming in here, tonight has been fun.

I glance up from my screen to find Jade watching me through wide eyes. "That Cindi-with an 'i'?" she asks.

Interesting that she remembers Cindi's name. I file that away for sober Dylan to sort out. "Hayley with a 'y', actually."

Her eyes widen. "What's she saying?"

"She's telling me to stop getting blowjobs from her best friend."

Giggling, Jade orders two more, and while we wait, I ask if she's planning on running in the mud race tomorrow.

She lets out a loud groan and slaps her palm against her forehead. "Shit."

I'm not looking forward to the event either, but that seems like an overly dramatic reaction.

"I've been so busy trying to get the stall ready that I completely forgot about the stupid race." Her head falls onto the bar and she moans again. "Why the hell did I ask Nate to be on our team?"

Now the reaction makes sense. "Kick him off."

Look at me, five—or is it six?—shots deep and still problem-solving. Boom.

"Where am I going to find another guy on such short notice?" Jade asks. "Plus, I haven't been able to tell Dad yet how much of an ass Nate turned out to be. He was so excited that I was dating a cop." She blinks at me from beneath her lashes. "Are you running?"

"Afraid so." But right now, I really wish I wasn't because as much as I hate exercising, doing so to help Jade sounds almost tolerable.

"It'll be fine," she murmurs, to herself or me—it's hard to tell.

I have a feeling the moment that douche comes near Jade, he's going to start groveling and saying he's sorry, and she seems like the kind of woman to forgive him even though he doesn't deserve it.

My brow tightens with that thought before a cool hand slips around my elbow. I turn to find Sunny smiling at me. "I'm going to head out," she says, ignoring Jade completely. "See you tomorrow?"

"Sure."

Jade hiccups and sticks out a wobbly hand. "Hi, I'm Jade. From the Quinn Brothers store around the corner." Sunny pauses before giving Jade a limp handshake. Sunny's eyes dart to mine while Jade begins rattling off a sales spiel about her shop and those weird-ass head sculpture things she was selling today. I can tell she's getting nowhere with Sunny, and she's kind of slurring, so I gently fold my fingers around her forearm. Jade stops speaking instantly and looks at me.

"I think we're all done with work for the day, aren't we?" I say gently.

"At least, *I* thought we were," Sunny mutters before asking Jade for her store's website. I'll bet my bike outside that Sunny is only being mildly polite and has zero intention of looking it up.

"Website? Oh, we're building one at the moment," Jade replies, flushing pink like that's a load of shit. She offers to email Sunny the URL when it's up, but Sunny says that's not necessary.

She quickly thanks Jade and turns her back on her. "A convenience store for a national feature spread?" Sunny whispers to me. "Is she serious?"

A defensive feeling surges through me, but before I can say anything, Sunny presses a wet kiss to my cheek. I don't miss how Jade rolls her eyes as Sunny saunters away.

"I think that's my cue to go home," Jade says. "Thanks

for the drinks." She stuffs her phone into her purse and starts for the door. I close out my tab as quickly as possible, leave a big fat tip, and catch up to her outside as she heads toward her store.

"You have an apartment in the back that I don't know about?" I ask, lingering like a creep and telling myself it's only because I want to make sure she doesn't end up passed out on the sidewalk.

Her keys jingle in her hands as she tries one, then the other. "Don't you worry about me, old man. This isn't the first time I've crashed here. I'm a seasoned pro."

Why does she insist on calling me old man? I'm not *that* old. "Yeah, but where do you crash, exactly?"

"The office floor is surprisingly comfortable."

She can't be serious. "You're not sleeping on a floor."

"No?" She props her hands on her hips and stares me down, probably trying to be intimidating, but she looks so fucking cute that it makes me want to eat her up. "Where am I sleeping then?"

I fold my arms over my chest and give her my best smile, the one that has gotten me into a lot of trouble through the years. Which is fitting for this particular scenario because what I'm about to say could get us both into trouble if my sister finds out. "I hear that your sexy neighbor has a nice new bed."

Her wide eyes flicker to my apartment next door before returning to me. "Thanks for the offer, but I'm not into casual sex."

For some reason, her assumption that I'm only into booty calls and one-night stands pisses me off, even though she's not exactly wrong. Which is why there's a bit of a bite to my tone when I respond. "That's great to hear because I'm not really into screwing my baby sister's drunk friends."

Jade doesn't even have the good sense to look scandalized. "Good."

"Good." I drag my keys from my pocket and start for the door. "Are you coming or what?"

Her footsteps shuffle behind me, the scent of her perfume driving me a little wild. I hold open the door, and once she's brushed past me, I lock it and head for the stairs. Up in my apartment, I flick on the lights and throw my keys on the linoleum countertop. Jade bends to undo the straps on her shoes, offering me the perfect view of the lacy pink bra beneath her sweater. I force my gaze away and try not to think about how full and perky her tits look as I start for my bedroom, stopping at the door. She squeezes past where I've halted, looking around at the mostly bare space but saying nothing.

I brace my hands against the doorframe to keep from following her. "I'm using the guest room for work, so you can have my bed."

Her head whips toward me. "Where are you sleeping?"

"The couch."

"I can sleep on the couch."

"Not happening. Just don't tell anyone you spent the night in my bed, or your reputation will never recover."

I can feel her eyes on me as I retreat to the living room and drop onto the couch, my back already aching.

CHAPTER FIFTEEN

JADE

I wake up with my tongue glued to the roof of my mouth. Blinking hazily, I turn to face the peach glow of sunlight streaming through unfamiliar blinds before sitting up with a start. *Where the hell am I?*

I scan the unadorned walls, the rattan ceiling light, the gray comforter billowing around me. Memories of last night pour into my head like an avalanche. Drinking at The Rocking Horse. Doing shots with Dylan King. I gasp and tug the sheets up to my chin.

I'm in Dylan's apartment...in his *bed*!

I peek out at the bedroom door that's still shut, finding no indication that he came into this room last night or attempted to remove any of the underwear I still have on. *No, Jade, he wasn't trying to hit on you; he just didn't want you to sleep on the floor of the store.*

Embarrassment crawls up my neck at the realization that he must think I'm some kind of hooch hound who spends my Friday nights getting so plastered that I can't drive. *Ugh*, that's not me at all. I'd planned to head home right after Ruby and Flynn left, but then Dylan had strolled in like a motorcycle magazine model and offered to buy me a drink, deleting that entire plan from my mind. And apparently, I'm as bad as Cindi with an "i" because I distinctly remember flirting with him all night.

Mortified, I bury my face in the comforter. I don't know why I'd imagined his bed would smell like stale beer or cigarettes. I've never even seen him smoke. But all I can smell on his sheets is that musky men's soap that may or may not haunt my dreams.

I need to stop smelling Dylan and get the hell out of here.

I kick out of the bed and throw on my sweater and jeans like the man in question might burst in at any moment. After hurriedly making the bed, I inch out into the hallway, relieved to spot my purse sitting on the kitchen counter. I tip-toe past the living room, freezing at the sight of the tall shape stretched out across the couch.

Dylan's laying on his back with one of his arms resting across his stomach that rises and falls with the even rhythm of sleep. He's shirtless, and my gaze slowly roams over the intricate artwork decorating his torso before trailing down to the black boxer briefs sitting low on his hips, the underwear disappearing beneath a knitted throw blanket.

I swallow hard, allowing the truth to slide into my head without fighting it.

He's so sexy.

My purse erupts with noise at twelve thousand decibels, and I lurch to snatch it off the counter before running so fast down the stairs that I nearly skid at the bottom.

I bury my purse in my chest to smother the ringing until I burst outside onto the pavement, finding Ruby's name flashing on the screen.

"Hey," I say breathlessly.

"Morning. Just checking in to see if you got home okay last night."

I rub my eyes and head past the deserted stalls lined along Main Street toward my car, ducking my head like I'm doing the walk of shame.

"Actually, I didn't go home," I mumble. "I..." *Don't lie to Ruby.* "I stayed at the apartment next door because I didn't want to drive. All good."

I can picture my sister's lips falling open. "You mean where Hayley's brother is staying?"

"The very same."

She turns silent as I pull out my car key and quickly unlock the door before I freeze my butt off.

"*Jade,*" Ruby warns.

"Nothing happened, I swear. It's not like that. We had a few drinks, and he felt bad when I said I'd sleep at the store, so he offered to let me crash. In separate rooms, of course."

"Phew. There are so many reasons why I wouldn't want you hooking up with that guy."

My brows pull together. "And what are those?"

"Well, the fact that he's Hayley's brother, and he's also a lot older than you. Then there's some not-nice stuff I've heard about him."

"Yeah, well, I've heard those things too, and I think a lot of it is bullshit, to be honest."

Ruby goes quiet.

I yawn, acknowledging how horrendous my mood is without coffee and with a pounding headache. "Sorry. How about we ditch the mud run and have a nice brunch somewhere with free refills instead?" I offer groggily.

She chuckles. "In my dreams, sister. You know it's good promo for the store. See you there in an hour."

I have just enough time to drive home, shower, and change into the Quinn Brothers T-shirt and black shorts combo that I chose for our team. The hangover from last night throbs in my temples as I stand at the bathroom mirror and attempt to give myself a head massage.

My phone lights up on the vanity with a message, and my brow scrunches at the name on the screen.

> **SHITHEAD**
>
> Are you at the mud run yet? Is it okay if we meet up to talk about yesterday?

Who the heck is *Shithead?*

Then I remember Dylan entering his number into my phone last night. I know he's self-deprecating, but calling himself "Shithead" is going a bit far, isn't it?

My stomach dips when I read his question again. Do I *want* to meet up with him to discuss last night's dangerous flirtations and fall back under the spell of that take-my-pants-off smile?

Hell yes.

But that's a form of torture I don't need.

> I'm still at home, sorry, running late
>
> Blame it on the guy who forced me to do shots last night

> What the hell??? What guy? Are you OK?
>
> If you give me his name, I'll run a check. See if he has any priors.

I stare at the message before it slots into place. This isn't Dylan, it's Nate.

Dylan was playing with my phone last night. *Sneaky bastard.* I bite away a smile while hurriedly typing back to Nate.

> I was just kidding
>
> But I won't get there early enough to talk, sorry
>
> See you there

I toss my phone back onto the counter, still salty at Nate over how he spoke to me yesterday. I really have no interest in trying to salvage this thing between us or even hearing what he has to say. He lost me at "Fuck you."

I STEP OVER THE SMALL FENCE SURROUNDING THE local park, which has been transformed into what looks like a military obstacle course from hell. I don't know how they're going to get rid of all this mud that's been poured in to create a soggy track of physical challenges, which disappears into the wooded area that's hiding goodness knows what horrors.

Silently thanking my painkillers for being so good to me, I weave my way through the small crowd of competitors, finding Ruby and Flynn lingering near the starting line. I shoot them a wave before Nate steps into my path, his lips turned down, his eyes red, his cheeks pale.

"What's wrong?" I say on a breath. *Oh god, who died now?*

"I'm so sorry, Jade."

"For what?"

My gut twists as Nate reaches for my arm. "For yesterday."

I let out a long breath. "Oh jeez, from the look on your face, I thought something really terrible happened."

Actual tears spring to Nate's eyes. "It did. You broke up with me. I never thought I'd feel this way. I didn't sleep at all last night."

I glance impatiently over his shoulder to where Ruby's gripping Flynn's bicep while she stretches out her quads. "Nate, we weren't technically in a relationship yet," I remind him. "And we have to go start the race. Sorry, but this isn't the right time to talk about this."

I edge past him, and he trails me like a lost dog over to Ruby and Flynn. The four of us discuss the race, though Nate's only plan seems to be making regretful eyes at me.

All four contestants on each team have to cross the finish line, but individual times are recorded and calculated to determine the winning team. So, rather than stick together, we each need to complete the course as fast as we can. Ruby hands out wristbands displaying our team's number, and she and I attach each other's while Flynn helps Nate with his.

"How's it all going?" she asks me under her breath, subtly jerking her head at Nate. Last night at the bar, I'd told her all about our fight and Nate's F-bomb.

"He apologized and wants to talk," I whisper. "I think he wants us to keep being a thing."

She makes a face, and a laugh slips through my lips. Going out with Nate was worth a shot, but Ruby knows as well as I do that this thing is dead in the water.

If only Nate would get the memo. He shuffles close to me while we wait for the race to begin, murmuring an invitation to go get some hot apple cider afterward. I tell him that I plan to spend the rest of the day with Ruby, taking a small step sideways. *Please get out of my space.*

A flash of neon pink fabric catches my eye as another team steps up to the starting area a few feet away. My stomach swoops when I realize it's Dylan and his family, who are wearing pink shirts that say: "Welcome to the KINGdom."

I stifle a laugh, but not before registering that Dylan's totally pulling his off. He's wearing black basketball shorts beneath the pink, and my eyes give his muscled legs a slow once-over, lingering on the tattoo of a compass rose that's wrapped around the back of one calf.

I feel bad that I haven't thanked him yet for letting me hijack his bed last night. My eyes dip away, then back to him again, wondering if he'll notice me, but he's leaning over one of his sisters, attaching her wristband.

"Jade!" Ruby says. "Didn't you hear them say we're about to go? You ready?"

"It's doubtful." I turn my attention to the grubby trail stretched out beyond the starting line, readying my feet and leaning forward. "Godspeed," I say to my teammates, and a second later, the horn blasts.

I push forward, instantly tangled up in a moving mass of bodies that feels like an accident waiting to happen. Up ahead, I spot Iris King and her husband charging forward, but I can't see Dylan in the whir of bodies. I quickly lose sight of Ruby and Flynn, too, but I can feel Nate breathing down my neck from behind like a freaking ghost haunting me. I up my pace, even though I know I could never outrun him.

I keep going, relieved to find mostly dry ground in this section, my feet switching between running and leaping over tires and hay bales. It's not so bad.

That is until the path twists left into the forest, and the first mud pit emerges in a clearing beyond a cluster of maple trees. People are squealing and groaning as they push over a sloppy hill of dirt and sink into waist-deep mud, wading through the sludge toward the next soggy mound.

"Need some help?" Nate says gruffly beside me, and my hangover spikes.

"No thanks, I'm fine." I give him a sidelong glance. "In fact, you go on ahead. You heard what Ruby said—we need to all make our best times. And you're a cop, so you should really come in first."

"Are you sure?" He looks ahead at where Ruby's clutching onto Flynn in the mud bath as they plow forward.

"*Yes.* Go, go, go. This vile activity might actually be worth it if we win something." One of the prizes is a free write-up in the local newspaper, although that pales in comparison to what was on offer with Sunny.

Nate nods curtly and takes off ahead, sliding up and over the mud hill with ease, but the display of brawn doesn't do anything for me.

I'm now dragging the chain for our team, so I launch myself forward and sink my hands into the sludge, finding my way over the hill and into the muck on the other side. My teeth clench as I trudge through the freezing cold slime, passing a few familiar faces before reaching the end and climbing out of the pit.

The next challenge is a stretch of rope suspended horizontally over a long trough of mud, and I summon all my strength and haul myself along without dropping into the brown bath below.

After that is a one-mile run through the woods, and just as I'm nearly dried off, the back of my calf seizes up with a painful cramp.

"Ow, ow, ow!" I grip the throbbing muscle and hobble off the track so I don't get mowed down by other runners. My legs stretch out over a flat rock as I catch my breath and dig my knuckles into my pinched calf. If I hadn't had to stop doing yoga classes and exercising my muscles, this wouldn't have happened.

It takes several minutes for the cramp to ease, and I hurry back onto the track, annoyed about letting down my teammates. The number of runners has thinned out by now, but as I near the end of the trail, someone pants my name behind me.

I spin to find Dylan heading toward me while giving his sister Alex a piggyback.

"Oh no, what happened?" I ask.

Alex shakes her head at herself. "I think I sprained my ankle back near that rope thing. Lucky Dyl was here to rescue me."

"You carried her that whole way?" I say to Dylan, twisting to study the endless track behind us.

Sweat drips off his brow, drawing wavy lines through the mud painted on his cheeks. "Didn't have a choice. They've blocked people going back in the other direction." He adjusts his grip on his sister, and I try not to ogle his flexing biceps. "What's your excuse for being such a slacker?"

"I got a bad cramp. Maybe we're all too out of shape to do this."

He laughs as his eyes trail over my body. "You okay?"

"Yeah, I'm fine. You guys go ahead. Or do you want help?" I step forward. His back must be killing him.

Dylan glances at the gigantic climbing wall up ahead and then back at me. "Nah, we'll be fine. I'm gonna cut through those trees over there."

Alex apologizes to him again, and I try not to wince at the sight of her swollen ankle turning blue beneath the streaks of mud.

Dylan gives me a quick smile that makes me feel like I've been running too hard again before tightening his grip on Alex. I watch him carry her off through the trees like some sort of fantasy knight with tattoos and a pink T-shirt.

After slapping myself back into action, I decide against cheating by following them through the trees. I don't want to get my whole team disqualified. My leg feels recovered now, so I hurry forward and heft my way up the wall using the ropes and grips. It looked easy enough from a distance, but up close, the wall is high and steep and coated in slippery mud. I keep losing my grip and falling back into the mud pool below.

"Someone save me from this nightmare!" I cry out to no one before making four more attempts. With a victory squeal, I finally launch myself up onto the top of the wall, collapsing onto my elbows.

On the other side sits a mud slide that disappears into a mucky brown bath. I'm beyond over this hell, but the only way out is down. I flop my legs over the edge and lean forward, my gaze snagging on Dylan standing at the bottom with his arms crossed like he's waiting for the big show.

"Well?" he calls out when I don't move. "Are you waiting for me to come up there and carry you?"

That mental image makes my pulse jump and sets me off kilter. I fling my arms out to stop myself from falling and looking stupid, but all that does is topple me over the edge. I tumble forward into a gush of air, my arms and legs flailing before a *whoosh* sound slaps my ears and cold, slimy liquid crashes over me like a tsunami.

I find my balance and gasp as I stand up in a pool of sludge, mud pouring off my hair, my face, my arms...

"Holy shit, are you okay?" Dylan says although I can't see him.

I wipe gunk out of my eyes before his fingers gently clutch my forearm, turning me to look at him. Dylan's standing beside me in the mud pool, his expression caught somewhere between concerned and amused.

"Don't look at me like that," I say, licking dirt off my lips. "You didn't have to do that stupid wall thing. You probably pushed Alex over just so you'd have an excuse not to."

He turns his ear to me. "Sorry, what was that you just said? I couldn't understand you with all that shit on your face."

Oh, he wants to tease me, does he? I dig my fingers into the mud still caked inside my palm and toss it at him.

Mud splatters across his face. Dylan inhales with shock and turns his gaze on me. When he bends to collect a good fistful of the brown ooze with his lips curling up, I lurch forward before he can launch it, giving his chest a shove with both hands. He flies backward and ass-plants in the mud. I snort-laugh, holding the back of my hand to my lips.

"Oh, you wanna go with me, Little Jade?" he taunts, rising back onto his feet like the Creature From the Black Lagoon.

"I can take you, *Gramps*."

He swipes his whole arm through the liquid in my direction until it splashes all over me. I scream through a laugh and spin around, realizing there are only a few more climbers left struggling over the wall.

"You are such a troublemaker," I accuse before turning back to Dylan and shoving both my hands through the mucky water, over and over, splashing him repeatedly as I move closer. He snaps a hand out and takes hold of my shirt, twisting me around so that I'm facing away from him.

My butt slides right up against his groin, which I can feel all too well beneath his thin athletic shorts, and my laugh turns into a gasp. We both still, and I can hear Dylan's breaths shorten behind me before he quickly digs into the mud and pastes it down my hair like he's icing a cake.

I squeal and turn back around, finding his sky-blue eyes burning into mine.

I meet his stare before dropping my gaze to his mud-splattered legs and clothes. "You're filthy," I tease.

"You have no idea," he returns, something in his tone making my heart pound harder.

I let my gaze trail down and up Dylan's body, the soaked fabric clinging to his muscles everywhere. And I mean *everywhere*. My eyes lift back to his, an electric current firing between us. "Filthy looks good on you."

He inhales sharply and steps forward, his palm folding around my hip and searing heat into my skin. He brings his lips to my ear, his breath washing over my skin. "It looks even better on you. And it's driving me fucking crazy." He tightens his grip on my hip, his breaths uneven against my ear. "I want to peel off what's left of those clothes and take you into the shower with me."

I expel a hard breath and turn into him, my lips almost brushing his neck. But I halt there, feeling the wall between us that cannot be breached. "Dylan, we can't."

He drops his forehead, the tips of his hair caressing my face. "I know," he says. "Fuck."

He lets go of my hip and moves to step away, but I reach out and grab the hem of his T-shirt, holding him in place. I give him a tug, and he follows me without resisting, through the mud and over to the edge of the climbing wall. His eyes gaze into mine before slipping to my mouth, making my pulse skyrocket. I know I need to stop this, so I lean forward and hook my leg around his calf, tripping him over. *Hah, I win.*

He tumbles backward with a stunned laugh, but not before reaching out and pulling me down with him. We slam down together on the shallow edge of the mud pool, with Dylan splayed out on his back while I crash over the top of him. His arms lock around my back, and our slick bodies slide together like two mud wrestlers, my thigh pushing between his legs.

Neither of us lets go. We lay there holding each other through panting breaths, my face buried in his neck. Even through the mud, he smells so damn *good,* and I can't help but tighten my arms around him, the action drawing a sigh from the back of his throat.

My best friend's face flashes in my mind, making me loosen my grip while Dylan's palms skate up and down my lower back.

"Hayley," I warn against his skin, and Dylan groans.

"Don't say that name," he says in my ear. When his hips tilt up a little, pressing into mine, I have to bite my lip to stop myself from moaning. "Say my name instead," he whispers.

I search for a breath that I can't seem to catch. *"Dylan,"* I murmur with a needy ache.

He growls and turns his face into me, his lips brushing my jaw with a shiver of invisible sparks. He presses his full mouth to a part of my skin that's not covered with mud, holding his lips there and breathing against me, and my fingers glide up his shoulder and weave into his hair.

His lips begin to move against my neck, lighting little fires beneath my skin as he holds my jaw in place so that he can trace his mouth over the skin beneath my ear. When his tongue makes a tentative stroke against my neck and then comes back in for more, I turn my head and crash my lips to his, catching his groan in my mouth as I cradle his face.

His fingers bite into my waist, and he pulls me harder against him as I lose all sense of where we are and mold my mouth to his, pressing our tongues together. A rough moan rumbles from his throat as we explore each other's mouths in a deep, hungry kiss that isn't only wild and raw... it's dizzying and dreamlike. It feels like *bliss*. If this is how Dylan King kisses every girl, no wonder he leaves a wreckage of broken hearts everywhere he goes.

That thought empties a bucket of cold water over me.

I don't want casual.

I don't want to be just another broken heart.

I go to pull back, but he sits up on his elbows, chasing my mouth, and I get sucked right back into the euphoria, wrapping our tongues together with a gasp.

"What the fuck?" barks a deep voice.

Dylan and I lurch apart, my head snapping up to meet Nate standing several feet away, glaring down at us with his jaw agape.

CHAPTER SIXTEEN

DYLAN

Well, fuck me sideways. Jade Quinn kisses exactly how I imagined she would. All soft lips and quiet mewls and exactly enough greedy tongue to make me lose my mind.

The asshole who just interrupted us is still growling from somewhere behind us.

Jade practically falls off me, and I have to have a serious chat with myself to keep from pulling her right back. I twist my head, meeting the narrowed gaze of a pissed-off little shithead who looks like I just fucked his mom.

"Are you kidding me right now, Jade?" Robocop grinds out, his hands clenched into fists like he wants nothing more than to kill me and bury my body right here in the mud.

Jade shrinks away from me like we just did something wrong. Which, I guess if we take Hayley's opinion into consideration, we did. But we're two consenting adults who kissed. Not a big deal.

"I need to talk to you," Shithead seethes at Jade, barely sparing me a glance.

Which is probably a good thing considering that if he

looked down right now, he'd see how hard my dick is. The mud squelches as Jade stumbles to her feet. I adjust myself as best I can before following her.

Jade glances over at me, her cheeks pink beneath her mud-freckles.

"Do you *want* to talk to him?" I ask, keeping my voice low.

Before she can respond, Shrimpy answers for her. "Of course she wants to talk to me! Up until yesterday, she was my fucking girlfriend."

I turn my back to him, creating a barrier between the little prick and the beautiful woman with wide, worried eyes. "Jade? Do you want to talk to him?" I ask again.

She shakes her head, and that's all I need to know. I twist around to where Deputy Douchbag bristles on the bank. If he doesn't stop breathing so hard, he's gonna pop a blood vessel. "She says she doesn't want to talk to you."

"Who the hell asked you?"

"Shhh, the grown-ups are talking," I cut back, turning to Jade.

Robocop lurches forward, and I meet his onrush with a step of my own. His heels dig into the mud as he stops himself from doing something really stupid.

"Maybe if you calm down, that'll change," I say to him. "But until you do, you may as well take your own advice and fuck off." I don't know how forgiving Jade is. If it were me, I'd never speak to the guy again, but I don't have to live in this town.

Deputy Dickwad angles his gaze past me to stare at Jade. "I just want to make things right between us. I know I screwed up yesterday, but you don't have to throw yourself at the first piece of trash that comes along just to make me jealous."

My jaw grinds at "piece of trash," but for Jade's sake, I put my response to that on ice.

Jade huffs a sigh. "I'm not trying to make you jealous, Nate."

"You expect me to believe you actually like the narcissistic asshole who murdered my cousin?"

A sharpness invades my chest. I may be a lot of things, and I've made more than my fair share of mistakes and bad decisions, but I did *not* fucking murder anyone. "You know, it's kinda scary that someone meant to serve and protect this town is so fucking stupid," I say.

The little guy steps up, his chest all puffed and heaving. Too bad I'm down in the muck and still taller than him. "What'd you say, King?"

I hate that my voice doesn't come out as strong as it should. "Maybe you should read the fucking police reports before spreading shit that isn't true." There are plenty of them where Miranda Williams and her family are concerned.

"Maybe you should—"

"Nate!" Jade interjects. "You need to go. *Now*."

My throat and chest are so tight that it's almost impossible to drag in my next breath.

Nate mutters a few more "fucks" before stomping away.

The dry muck running up Jade's forearm cracks when she reaches for my arm. "Sorry about that. I didn't mean to drag you into my drama."

Her warmth finds its way into my bones, easing some of the tension in my chest. The longer I stare at her, the easier it is to breathe. I slip free of her hold, taking her hand instead. A blush finds her cheeks, and her fingers curl around mine as we both climb out of the pit. I try not to think about how good her hand feels or the way my stomach nosedives when she licks her lips.

I hate that she's apologizing right now for something that isn't her fault. "The only thing you dragged me into was that mud pit," I say. "And if I'm being honest, I kinda wish you'd do it again so we could pick up where we left off."

The spark returns to her eyes as she peers up at me through thick lashes. "Oh yeah?"

My free hand falls to her slippery hip. "Yeah."

"Hey, Jade!" a woman shouts. "Everything okay?"

Jade drops my hand like it's on fire as her sister jogs toward us.

"I sent Nate to go find you, but now he's disappeared too." Ruby's eyes flit between us while Jade puts a little more distance between our muddy bodies.

"Hey. Yeah, sorry," Jade says. "I got stuck in the mud, and Dylan helped me out."

It shouldn't bother me that Jade's treating me like I'm some dirty little secret. But the subtle rejection stings. Heaven forbid she admit to having anything to do with the *infamous* Dylan King.

Ruby eyes me with what I'm pretty sure is suspicion. "That was nice of him."

I shrug and smile. "What can I say? Every once in a while, I'm nice. See you around, Jade."

Jade doesn't spare me so much as a glance. "Yeah. See you around."

With a weird hollowness in my chest, I cut through the colorful forest to where the teams that finished the race are celebrating in the parking lot with beers and cheers. Everyone is thrilled, it seems, but my sisters. Iris and Alex look like they've been run over by a bus. Not one smile in the bunch.

"Geez, ladies. Who died?"

Tears spring to Iris's eyes and she rubs her nose with a dirty hand, leaving a muddy mustache on her upper lip that I hope no one tells her about before I can take a picture for blackmail purposes. "Not funny, Pickle."

I sink next to where she's sitting on the tailgate of her husband's pickup truck and give her shoulder a nudge. "Come on. Lighten up. We'll get our names on the plaque next year."

"We?" Alex perks up from the truck bed, a massive ice pack strapped to her ankle, her foot a grapey shade of purple. "You mean you'll run with us again?"

"Why not? I'd hate for this town to think of me as anything but a winner."

That makes them laugh, but there's sadness laced through it.

"Oh, hey," Iris says, nudging me back. "Speaking of winners. Sunny wasn't sure if you got her message this morning, so she texted and said she'll meet you at your apartment before the parade."

Shit. I had seen Sunny's message this morning, but I'd been a little too preoccupied with making breakfast for my unexpected guest to respond. Unfortunately, when I knocked on my bedroom door, I found the bed made and no sign of Jade. Usually, that sort of thing would be a relief, but it kinda felt like she'd regretted staying over, even though nothing happened between us. Apart from when she just kissed me as if her life depended on it, that is. The back of my neck heats at the memory, until I remember she ditched me the moment her sister came close.

Why do women have to be so fucking confusing?

"That's fine," I say about Sunny, ready for the day to be over already.

I glance across the parking lot to where Jade and Ruby stand chatting with Ruby's boyfriend, catching the youngest Quinn looking in my direction. When I offer her a smile, she tenses up and turns away.

So fucking confusing.

AFTER THE RACE, I HEAD BACK TO MY PLACE TO shower before meeting Sunny outside on Main Street for the parade. When the first float comes around the corner, my gaze finds Jade's braid. Looks like she's showered and changed as well. Bet she smells like heaven. I wait for her to turn and acknowledge me, but she doesn't even glance my way. Part of me expects her "tough guy" boyfriend to show up—sorry, *ex*-boyfriend—but there's thankfully been no sign of him so far.

Sunny suggests walking around to the bank for a more elevated view, but I convince her to stay here, purely so I can see how Jade reacts when she sees me again. For the next hour, Sunny and I make small talk, and I snap a few photos. Jade doesn't turn around once.

After the final float carrying the high school football team passes through, everyone packs up their coolers and folding camping chairs for the mass exodus toward the town parking lot.

I expect Sunny to follow them, but instead, she loops her arm through mine and asks if I'll go with her to the fire hall, where the last of the official festival events are taking place. What I really want to do is follow Jade into Quinn Brothers and ask if she's been thinking about our kiss as much as I have. Instead, I remind myself that I promised my sisters I'd keep the reporter wooed and tow my charge up the hill along with everyone else.

Country music crackles through the fire station speakers. A bunch of thick logs are set in the driveway in front of the empty bays while men in different shades of flannel line up at a registration table for the wood-chopping competition. That's right. Wood choppin'.

This must be something new because I don't remember this being a thing way back when. Dad would've gotten a kick out of it. I can imagine him wearing a shirt that said "I heart wood" on it or something equally ridiculous, oblivious to the double entendre.

Sunny squeezes my bicep, her French-tipped nails digging into my arm. "Oh my gosh. This is the best thing ever. You should sign up!"

It'll be a cold day in hell before I stand in front of these people and chop a piece of wood. Running that mud race was bad enough. "I'm gonna pass." My body still isn't right after sleeping on the couch, and hauling Alex to the medical tent earlier didn't help matters.

Sunny purses her cherry-red lips in a pout that has zero impact. Over her head, my stomach flips when I spot Jade weaving through the crowd with her sister until they halt at the far side of the blocked-off area. I'm about to steer Sunny closer when Jade's fun little ex comes up behind her. She turns to face him, her expression not nearly as pissed off as it should be.

If someone spoke to me the way Nate had to her, he'd be getting a full-on death glare, not a cute little frown. Surely she's not going to forgive him, is she? Not that it's any of my business who Jade wants to go out with. Except it kinda is, though, since my tongue was tangled with hers a few hours ago.

"Come on, Dylan. Please? For me?" Sunny bats her lashes like that's going to sway me.

Robocop steps away from Jade to join the end of the registration line.

And for some reason, I feel like chopping some fucking wood. "Yeah. Okay. I'll be right back."

Sunny giggles and wishes me good luck, but I'm already pushing through the crowd and lining up right behind my new best friend.

Shithead Williams's smile vanishes the second he sees me. "The fuck are you doing here?"

My lips lift. "Chopping wood. You?"

"Look. I don't know what game you're playing, but you need to back the hell off. I'm not going to let you ruin Jade the way you ruined Miranda."

We both take a step toward the table. "I guess that's up to Jade."

The way his shoulders hunch around his ears makes him look a bit like Quasimodo.

The woman sitting behind the table beams up at him. "Oh, hey, Officer Williams. Back to claim your title?"

Fucking lovely. I didn't realize Deputy Douchebag actually knew what he was doing with this. I can only hope that the few times I helped my dad chop wood down at the cabin come in handy so I don't make a complete fool out of myself.

"Sure am, Lucy," he replies, but his smarmy smile is pointed at me. She gives him a number to pin to his red and black flannel shirt.

Nate moves to take up a position beside one of the logs and snatches a pair of leather gloves from his back pocket.

Shit. Everyone has gloves. Everyone but me.

"Name?" the smiley young woman asks from the other side of the table.

"Dylan King."

Her brow furrows as she jots down my name and hands me a number. Lucky me: I'm in the spot right beside my new best friend. The only plus side is that I'm close to the barrier, and Jade is standing on the other side. Sunny whoops and shouts, "Go Dylan!", reliving her cheerleader glory days. Jade's head whips toward Sunny before returning to me, her brows pinched and her lips pursed.

Lips I wouldn't mind feeling pressed against mine again, only minus the interruption.

The sun breaks through the heavy layer of clouds that has lingered all day. I peel off my leather jacket and hang it over the barrier right in front of Jade. Then, I lean so close that her little gasp of air fans against my cheek. "If I win, do I get another kiss?" I ask under my breath so that only she can hear.

The flushed red cheeks are a really good look on her. "I don't want your mega-fan to get jealous," she murmurs back.

Oh, please. Sunny isn't a mega-fan. She's only hanging out with me because my sisters organized it. "That's not an answer."

Jade bites her bottom lip, leaving behind a cute little indentation. "You're not going to win."

"Then I guess you have nothing to worry about."

One of the announcers calls all of the contestants to their positions.

I cock my head and gaze into her eyes. "Yes or no, Jade?"

She holds my stare, and one side of her mouth turns up a touch. "Okay."

When I return to my spot, fighting away a smile, my bestie looks like he's about to chop me in half instead of the log laid out in front of him. I grip the handle of the ax and heave it over my shoulder, testing its weight. It's heavier than it looks, which doesn't bode well for my shoulders.

The first person to cut their log in half wins the grand prize. Seems simple enough. Every other contestant has a pretty focused expression on their face, so maybe this isn't going to be a walk in the park. The bell sounds and I take my first swing, realizing I may not win that kiss after all.

This is nothing like splitting logs for a fire. This takes precision and power and endurance that I don't fucking have. You know what I do have? Enough hatred for the sneery asshole beside me to keep chopping until I can feel the skin of my palms melting off. Do I stop when my hands are more blister than skin? Hell fucking no. I keep going, swinging again and again, until my arms feel like wet noodles and sweat burns my eyes.

Knowing the champ isn't much further along spurs me on. I begin knocking away at the opposite side until the log resembles an hourglass. Fuck me, this is hard. As much as I hate to do it, I let my ax down for a second to wipe my eyes with the hem of my shirt.

Catching Jade's gaze skimming across my abdomen gives me the strength I need to lift the ax in my crying hands and keep going. The crowd's cheering builds to my right, where some burly asshole with shoulders so big he has no neck is hammering away, bits of wood flying around him.

A few more hits are all it takes for my arms to start trembling. Shithead curses when he realizes how close I am to finishing, his own ax swinging haphazardly in front of him.

Four more swipes, and I hear the telltale crack. *Holy shit*, the top half of my log slams onto the pavement.

The crowd falls silent, and all the other contestants freeze, some with axes in midair, all of them staring slack-jawed at me. It's so quiet that I can hear the sweat dripping off my forehead splatter onto the concrete. My arms tremble, and my heart hammers as I stare down at that broken hunk of wood.

Shithead Williams lets out a feral growl and chucks his ax to the ground, narrowly missing my foot. He stomps out of the ring like a toddler who didn't get his way.

"L-looks like we have a winner!" the announcer stutters, clearly as stunned as everybody else, as he carries his microphone over to my station to inspect my work.

Blood drips down my hands, and it'll be a long-ass time before I'm able to jerk off again, but the spark in Jade's eyes makes all the pain worthwhile.

CHAPTER SEVENTEEN

JADE

I won't deny that watching Dylan King hack a chunk of wood into two pieces was the X-rated fantasy I didn't know I needed. He was all muscle and sweat and determination as he split that log to bits, and I might've drooled a little.

The possibility that my promise to kiss him if he won was what drove him to wield that ax like Thor is almost enough to make me forget what happened before that. *Almost.* Because two entire milliseconds might've passed between when Dylan and I panted into each other's mouths in that mud pond and him gluing himself to another woman. And not just any woman—the one I was meant to spend time with to help the store from being seized by the bank.

I don't know why I even agreed to the kiss after seeing him with Sunny today. He put me on the spot with his seductive smirk and persuasive stare. But the truth is that I'm pissed off. Which is why when the wood-chopping judge holds up Dylan's trembling arm to declare him the winner, I let my bashful smile fade, back away from the barrier, then edge through the cheering onlookers to find Ruby.

The second I spot her sitting with Dad on a bench over near the town park, I practically become airborne as I race toward the people who aren't a danger to my heart.

Dad is sitting forward, elbows to thighs, and Ruby's softly rubbing his lower back.

"Everything okay?" I ask, frowning.

Dad winces. "Back's not doing good."

"Told you not to do the samba show," I joke, and Ruby chuckles. I sit on Dad's other side and gently tap his knee. "I was worried all this festival stuff wouldn't be good for your back. You should rest up at home."

Ruby's sympathetic eyes dart to me. "My thoughts exactly. Flynn's already gone to get the car and bring it as close as possible. We'll take Dad home."

I want to offer to go with them, but I can't. Someone has to pack up our booth now that the festival's over and get everything back inside the store and prepped for tomorrow. A wave of tiredness makes my shoulders slump, but I force the foggy feeling away. "I'll come over to Dad's later when I've packed everything up."

Ruby passes me a grateful smile. "I'll make Mom's spaghetti for dinner. And instead of leaving with us, I'm sure Flynn wouldn't mind helping you pack the booth down."

"No, don't be silly, I've got it. It's no big deal."

"Okay," Ruby replies, her tone unsure. "But will you text me if you want one of us to come back?"

"Roger that."

Remembering that Ruby's going to be taking off back home tomorrow sends a sharp sting to my eyes, and I hide it by jumping to my feet. "Better get over to the booth," I say brightly. "There's probably a queue from here to DC of folks wanting to buy those screaming-head sculptures that secretly want to kill us all. It's a damn shame I can't keep them for myself."

Dad's laugh turns into another wince of pain, and I bend to give his weathered forehead a kiss. "Love you, champ."

"I love you too."

I point at Ruby. "You're still a gray area. Might love you, might only like you... I haven't decided yet."

Smiling, she gives my butt a playful whack as I step past her. Before disappearing down the hill, I call out for her to please let me know if anything changes with Dad.

I pace down Second and turn onto Main, groaning under my breath at the Pinterest-perfect booth that I now have to tear down by myself. After staring at the tangle of shop wares, rustic décor, and fairy lights with my hands on my hips, I decide to begin with the upturned produce crates holding vases of dried flowers.

I'm carefully filling one of the crates with the flowers when my phone chimes from my back pocket. When I dig it out, the name on the screen confuses me for a second before my stomach dips hard.

> SEXY NEIGHBOR
> I'm owed a kiss

I consider ignoring him for all of four seconds but then type out a reply. So much for kicking Dylan out of my head or giving him lip about Sunny.

> I'm flattered, but I have a rule against kissing old ladies

> Making fun of my age again, Little Jade? 🫥

>> Isn't this my neighbor, Mrs. Felton?

I snort-laugh at that.

> Is she sexy?

>> Can't say she's my type, but if she's yours, I ain't judging 🐺

> Nope. I'd describe my type as cute and blonde.

> Likes to kiss me when I'm filthy.

I turn hot all over, and I know I should stop giving my attention to this smooth operator who breaks hearts like cheap umbrellas, but my fingers keep typing. Stupid, dumb fingers.

>> How did you even get my number, Gramps?

> I texted it to myself that night in the bar when we took that adorable pic

I note that he doesn't say "pic *for Hayley*" because that would be a warning shot I'm pretty sure neither of us wants to hear right now. Before I can reply, Dylan sends another message.

> Are you mad I texted myself your number?
> You gonna get Robocop to arrest me?

>> Now there's an idea...

> Knew you'd take any excuse to get me into a pair of handcuffs

> Nah, prison orange isn't your color

> You're right... green is my color

I gaze at the handset, my mind making all sorts of leaps between that comment and the fact that Jade is a shade of green and I have green eyes. *Chill. He probably looks good in green and knows it.*

> Don't think I don't notice you changing the subject

> I'm owed a kiss. I earned it fair and square

"Jade."

My head whips up to meet Nate's glum face and hunched shoulders. I shove my phone into my back pocket. "Yes?" I ask, unable to hide my irritation that he's here, interrupting me, *again*.

"Can we talk about earlier?" he asks in a wounded voice.

"Earlier?"

"I still can't believe you kissed that prick."

"*Nate*." A knot of frustration forms in my chest. "Please let it go. It's none of your business. You and I aren't together anymore."

"I know." He huffs and shakes his head. "I get it. You want a break."

"No, not a break. I'm happy to be friends, but the dating part is over. I'm sorry." Jeez, we dated for five minutes and this guy's acting like it's the separation of the century.

"Fine," he replies through his teeth. "If you want to

degrade yourself by sleeping with that dirty-dick loser, knock yourself out. But don't say I didn't warn you when you get an STD. Because, believe me, he'll screw anything that walks."

My lips purse tightly as I give Nate a fed-up stare, deciding not to point out how offensive that last sentence was to me, not just Dylan.

"Thanks for the heads up," I reply flippantly, refusing to let Nate see me rattled over this. "I gotta pack up here, so... sayonara."

I push past him to begin unclipping olden-day photographs from the display despite having been halfway through a different task. I take down four photos before glancing over my shoulder, relieved to see the deputy sheriff long gone. *God, what a fucking bully.*

Even though I abandoned Dylan in the middle of our text chat, I leave my phone inside my pocket. Nate may have a horrible way of putting things, but that doesn't mean there isn't an ounce of truth to what he said. Even if Dylan didn't have a reputation for being a skirt-chasing playboy, he's still my best friend's brother. The thought of having to tell Hayley that we kissed clogs my stomach with dread.

I force myself to focus, and an hour later, I've got most things packed away when the gentle crunch of footsteps approaches behind me. Locals have been milling past all afternoon, but now that dusk has fallen, most people have gone home.

Somehow, I know it's him before I even turn around. But when I do, I'm still not ready for the onslaught of clear-blue eyes that sparkle when he smiles. Heaven help me, I need one of those Three Stooges-style face slaps.

"You didn't answer my text," Dylan says casually, clutching something wrapped in paper.

"What text? Sorry, I was...packing up the booth."

"Saw that through the window. I sent a message asking if you wanted something to eat. When you didn't reply, I made an executive decision." He holds out the burrito, and I accept it from his fingers. "I was going to offer to help you pack up after picking this up for you, but you work fast." His impressed gaze roams over the empty booth.

"Thanks," is all I can get out before I shove half the burrito in my mouth because, holy moly, I'm starving. Ruby won't be happy if I turn up for her dinner with a full stomach, but if I'm honest, my sister is far from a master chef. This thing, however, tastes like heaven.

Dylan's lips curl up as he watches me take a few more bites before he tilts his head at the shelving with an offer in his eyes. I nod and watch him begin to disassemble the shelves, even though his arms must be half dead after all that ax swinging. Thirty seconds of standing on the sidelines is all it takes before I lurch forward to take over, not wanting Dylan to have to handle my responsibilities. But he insists on helping, and together, we get the rest of the booth packed away in record time.

I hold open the front door of the store while Dylan carries the heavy stuff inside, then trail him into the storeroom to help set the shelving against the wall. When we're done, he clutches his right bicep over his white T-shirt, massaging it with his fingers.

I pout through my smile. "I'm surprised those arms are still attached."

"Let's not jump to conclusions," he replies, and I laugh.

For a few endless breaths, we stand in the storeroom and watch each other.

"I worked *very* hard to chop that wood," he eventually says, like a little boy who's done something good.

"You did."

He takes a tentative step closer. "I thought there was a prize at the end, but I didn't get it."

I frown. "Damn. That doesn't sound fair."

He continues to move slowly toward me, the air between us thickening along with my throat. "If you think I'm going to try and pressure you into kissing me because we made a deal, that's not gonna happen."

Disappointment filters into my chest, but I keep my expression light. "No? Changed your mind?"

"Far from it." His palms land on either side of my shoulders against the brick wall, trapping all the air in my lungs. "But I'm not in the habit of forcing myself on women, and I've decided that kissing you is a lot more fun when you want it as badly as I do."

The spot between my legs tingles with warmth, and I arch my back a little, curling toward him. "I didn't say I don't want it. But what I want and what's good for me are two different things."

He releases one hand from the wall to brush a wayward wisp of hair off my face. "You think I'm not good for you?"

It feels like an awkward time to bring up Sunny *or* Dylan's dating history, so I go with the other reason. "Hayley wouldn't like this, and you know it."

His cheeks color a fraction, but he doesn't release me from his cage that smells sublime. "You let me worry about Hayley," he says quietly.

That's not quite enough to quash my anxiety, but I become distracted by the way his gaze burns a trail down my cheek, across my mouth, and back up to my eyes. "Kiss me, Jade."

My lips part, and my heart beats faster. "I thought you weren't going to try and talk me into it."

Keeping one hand braced against the wall, his other gently curls around my jaw. He lowers his lips closer to mine, his breath soft and minty. "I don't think I need to. I think you want to kiss me just as much as I want you to."

I tilt toward him even more, the tops of my thighs pressing against the bottoms of his. I reduce what's left of the space between our lips until it's almost nonexistent, speaking against his mouth. "I think you're right."

Heat flares in his eyes.

I know I shouldn't be doing this, which is why it's only going to happen once more.

Just one more taste.

My tongue comes out and makes a soft stroke over his bottom lip, the surprise move drawing a deep rumble from his throat as his grip on my jaw tightens. His mouth comes down hard on mine, the back of my head pressing against the wall as our tongues catch and drag in a rough, sexy-as-hell kiss that sucks all the strength from my knees.

"You taste so fucking good," he says hotly against my mouth. "Every time I see you, all I can think about is bending you over."

I moan and nearly collapse as he crushes our mouths back together, his strong thigh pushing between my legs and forcing my feet further apart. His rock-solid length rubs firmly against my core through our clothes, making me gasp as he groans into my mouth.

"Dylan," I warn through my teeth as his lips fall to my neck, making me shudder when he runs his tongue over my skin.

"Do you want me to stop?" he breathes near my ear.

I should.

"No," I whimper, and he growls and wraps my braid around his fingers, using it to tug my mouth back to his. His tongue drags against mine as his hips push intently against my own, his dick so thick and large that my eyes almost roll back in my head.

"You want this?" he says throatily, grinding against me.

The room is a fireball, and I have to press my palms to the wall behind me to stop myself from touching him. "We can't."

Those words make him loosen his hold on me, and I instantly mourn the loss of contact when his hips release mine. I quickly take hold of his back and run my palms down the ridges of muscle, stopping him from leaving. It takes all the willpower I have not to glide my hands over his perfect ass or palm the thick mound straining the front of his jeans. The temptation to undo his zipper and hike his jeans halfway down his thighs has my breaths haggard, but I find my resolve and untie myself from him, stepping sideways. I honestly can't believe I have the strength to shut this thing down. *I'm superwoman.*

With me gone, Dylan's forehead drops into the crook of his arm that's still held against the wall, and one blue eye peeks out at me.

"I really have to get going," I say with a great deal of reluctance. "But I hope you liked your prize." I suck my bottom lip between my teeth for effect.

Dylan gives my mouth a hungry stare before pushing off the wall with a lamenting sigh. "You know, I heard there's a wood-chopping convention in the next county—"

"Shhh." I laugh and give his arm a light shove, careful not to exacerbate his pain. "You should go and rest those arms."

"Oh, I don't know how much rest this right arm's gonna get tonight."

Holy shit, if he's talking about jerking off because of me... because of this...

Before I can let that vision suck me back into the danger zone, I shakily open the storage door and let Dylan walk out first. I've still got a few containers to put away, so I tell him goodnight in the lonely chill of the empty store space, thanking him again for the burrito and his help.

Dylan gives me a tight-lipped smile before disappearing out the door, and I push away a ridiculous feeling of disappointment that he didn't try to kiss me goodnight. I made perfectly clear that I didn't want things to go any further, so why on earth would he do that? I've become a head-case.

Before I can do something idiotic like find an excuse to tap on his door and undo my restraint that's hanging on by a thread, I whip out my phone and text Ruby that I'm on my way home.

CHAPTER EIGHTEEN

DYLAN

I can still taste her.

The memory of it consumes me as I idly rub my thumb across my lower lip. Not only did I kiss Jade twice in one day, I fucking loved every second of it. I would've done more than kiss her if she'd been up for it. Too bad she shut us down because she would've looked like my wet dream bent over that counter in the store.

I had to relieve myself in the shower last night and again this morning because of that mental image. My poor, blistered hand is not impressed.

Ella's screech cuts through thoughts I definitely shouldn't be having while I'm sitting on a bench at the town playground. "Uncle Pickle! Watch this!"

"I'm watching!" I call back. Time to focus on yet another perfect descent from the twisty green slide. This time, she has her hands up in the air like she's on a roller coaster.

Her pigtails bob and swing as she jogs over to me, her sparkly pink shoes kicking up wood chips as she goes. "Did you see?"

This kid reminds me so much of me when I was little. Maybe it was a first-born thing or a result of being the only boy, but I couldn't get enough of Dad's attention. "Look at me" were probably my first words. God, I miss him and Mom. What I wouldn't give to be heading over to their place after this for a hot cup of coffee and a chat about the next vehicle Dad wants to buy.

"Sure did," I say, swallowing the lump in my throat. "You know what you should try next?"

Her eyes turn as round as saucers. "What?"

"Backwards."

Her spaghetti-stained lips lift into a grin and she's off, back on her favorite piece of equipment in this park. Not that there's much of a choice when there's only that twisty slide, four swings, a merry-go-round, monkey bars—my hands ache at the thought—and a seesaw that's been here since I was little and makes more noise than an iron headboard in an orgy.

As Ella climbs the stairs to the top of the slide, my mind drifts back to yesterday. I stretch my weary arms toward the thick carpet of gray clouds looming in the sky. A light breeze drifts across my face, reminding me of the way Jade's whispered words had done the same.

"What I want and what's good for me are two different things."

Hearing Jade say that made me feel kinda shitty, even though she's probably right in thinking I'm not good for her. I'll be leaving Still Springs in a couple of months, and once I'm gone, I don't know when I'll be back.

Ella waves from the top of the slide, and I lift my hand to return the gesture. My triceps weep from the movement.

My chest turns heavy at the thought of not getting to spend as much time with the little daredevil flying backward down the slide. Being around my sisters has also been nice, even though we've mostly been hanging out at the notary signing papers or reminiscing about Mom and Dad.

Would it be so bad to stay in town a little longer? I'm getting enough work done here, and I have to travel for most of my shoots anyway. Ella will be starting kindergarten next fall, and Iris won't need me after that.

What am I thinking? After almost running into Miranda's mom, it's clear that I can't stay *here*.

Besides, Hayley would *not* be impressed if she found out I've been kissing her best friend.

Or would she?

I mean, Hayley loves me, and she definitely loves Jade. Maybe once she got used to the idea, she would love that her two favorite people are hanging out together. There's only one way to find out.

Ella bounds over to the lowest swing and positions the rubber sling across her stomach so she can rear back and make herself "fly." Her arms shoot out as she swings back and forth. Watching her makes my stomach a bit queasy.

I pull out my phone to dial my youngest sister's number when her name magically appears on the screen. How fortuitous.

I answer with a smile. "Hey, Buttons. I was about to call you. How's the Med?"

"Don't you 'Hey Buttons' me, Dylan King."

Her sharp tone has me snapping to attention.

"Do you know who just messaged me out of the fucking blue?"

"I bet you're going to tell me."

"Nate Williams."

I catch my forehead in my hand. Isn't that fantastic? Honestly, that guy needs to get a hobby. "Oh, yeah? And what did the fabulous Officer Williams have to say?" I ask even though I already know.

"Only that he caught you and Jade making out at the race yesterday."

So much for easing her into the idea. *Fucking Nate.* "I can explain."

Can I, though? Even I don't know what this thing is between Jade and me.

"Oh, no. You're not going to talk your way out of this one," Hayley says firmly. "I don't care how bored you are; you're not to go near her again."

Bored? I'm not fucking *bored*. If anything, I'm busier than I ever was before. It just so happens that, despite being busy, I find myself wanting to carve out time to spend with my neighbor. Like last night. I should've been editing, and instead, I went down and helped Jade with her booth.

I've taken a lot of shit from my sisters over the years, and most of it I deserved. But I'm a grown-ass man, and Jade is a grown-ass woman, and if we want to get naked and do grown-ass things, there's nothing my baby sister can do about it.

Hayley's ragged breaths rattle through the speaker. I settle back on the bench and wait for what's coming. Because it's clear from her muttered curse that she's far from finished.

"Jade is a good person," Hayley says.

No shit. That's probably why I'm into her. She's one of the only people in this town who hasn't looked at me like I'm a piece of shit stuck to the sidewalk. "And I'm not?"

For some reason, that makes her snort. "Come on. We both know what you do to girls."

My head shakes as I tilt it to the sky. She makes it sound like I'm a serial killer. Yeah, I don't have the best track record with women, but I like to think what happened with Miranda is a good reason for not letting anyone get too close. In saying that, things feel different with Jade. Hell, she's the only person outside my family and my therapist who I've talked to about Miranda. And if that's not significant, I don't know what is.

"When's the last time you went on an actual date?" Hayley presses.

"I don't see what that has to do with—"

"When?"

My teeth grind together so hard my jaw aches. "It doesn't matter."

"*When?*"

She knows fucking when. "Twelve years ago."

"Exactly. And Jade isn't looking for what you have to offer."

Funny. She seemed pretty into "what I have to offer" last night. Better keep that to myself, though. "You don't speak for her."

"Well, I do now," Hayley argues. "Because I'm invoking King's Code."

What. The. Hell?

In thirty years, I've only invoked King's Code once: when I told Hayley I would disown her if she started dating one of my old high school "friends." Not because I didn't want to see her happy, but because Johnny McDonald was a complete and total asshole. The one time he'd visited me in college, he'd shown me pictures of his girlfriend's tits. That's right. His *girlfriend's*—a girl he claimed to love.

I haven't been in love in a long-ass time, but there's no way in hell I would let some other guy see naked photos of the girl I'm sleeping with. And if Johnny dated my baby sister and showed pics of her to anyone else, I would have been obligated to kill him, and then I would have ended up in jail, and our parents would have been devastated, and it would've been a whole thing.

That situation had warranted King's Code.

This one, however, does not.

Ella's back on the slide, but when she waves at me this time, I can't even bring myself to lift my arm.

"Did you hear me, Dylan?" Hayley snaps.

"I heard you." Kinda hard not to when she's basically shouting.

She grumbles something under her breath and then says, "I've gotta go."

Before I can say goodbye, the line goes dead.

I grip my phone with both hands, somehow resisting the urge to chuck the damn thing across the playground.

King's fucking Code.

Our family code leaves no wiggle room in situations like this. My sisters have invoked it way more often than I ever have. The purpose has always been to keep each other safe.

This doesn't feel like Hayley is trying to keep me safe, though—or Jade for that matter. This feels like my sister throwing a tantrum because her best friend wants to play with someone else.

None of it would bother me if Jade wasn't the only person in this town—apart from my sisters—who I look forward to seeing. That's not a profession of love by any means, but it's something. Normally, after spending a few hours with a woman, I'm ready to bolt.

That's not the case with Jade.

Every time I run into her, I find myself searching for reasons to linger. Like with the photos at the Italian fair and the stupid wood-chopping competition. Even the mud race.

After carrying Alex to the medics, I didn't need to go back and check on Jade. But I did.

I gave up a foursome to confess my deepest, darkest secrets to the woman, for fuck's sake.

And now, thanks to my sister, I can't even go near her.

By the time we get back to the apartment, Iris is waiting for us outside, only she isn't watching Ella and me stroll down Main Street. She's staring up at the Quinn Brothers sign and tapping her lips like she does when she's lost in thought.

"Mommy!" Ella squeals and launches herself at my sister.

Iris whirls around and gives Ella the biggest smile. "There's my girl." She bends down to scoop up her daughter and squeeze her tight. "How was your day with Uncle Pickle?"

"The best. He let me go down the slide backward!"

When Iris lifts her brow at me, all I can do is shrug. "What? I did it when I was little."

"Mom said you used to eat crayons too. Are you going to let her do that as well?"

First, I was, like, three. And I wanted to see if the colors tasted differently. They didn't.

"I wanna eat crayons!" Ella chimes in.

I give her pigtail a tug. "No, you don't. They taste really, really bad."

Iris's keys jingle when she pulls them from her pocket to unlock the door to her car.

That's when I notice a folded piece of pink paper on my motorcycle's windshield. When I open it up, my brows draw together. A fucking ticket for parking too far away from the curb even though I'm as close as everyone else on the street? I know exactly who wrote this bullshit before I scan down to Nate Williams's chicken-scratch signature at the bottom.

I ball the ticket in my fist. It'll be a cold day in hell before I pay this fine.

"This is a great location," Iris murmurs, dragging back my attention. "Three empty storefronts right beside each other would be such a waste."

I stuff the ticket into my back pocket, still seething. "Maybe you should ask Ella for counting lessons. There are only two empty storefronts." My apartment and the old Harringtons restaurant.

She pushes off the car and nudges me with her elbow. "Not for long."

Something in her tone makes my sore shoulders tense up. My gaze flickers to Jade's store before falling on the brick building a few doors down from Harringtons. "Is Brenda O'Malley selling the bookstore?"

Iris shakes her head.

That means... "Quinn Brothers is closing?" Jade hasn't mentioned anything about giving up the store. Not that we're close friends and talk about that sort of stuff. Still, something that big surely would've come up in conversation, right? The store seems so important to her.

"A little bird told me they're behind on loan payments," Iris says. "If we make an offer now, we could own all three."

This is what our family does. Buys and sells property; builds businesses. And we make money hand over fist doing it. But something about this idea feels wrong.

Quinn Brothers is a staple in this town. According to the sign, the place has been open for almost a century.

Iris grabs my bicep and shakes it so hard that tears prick the backs of my eyes. "This could actually work, Dyl. Dad always dreamed of having a store in town, but none of the buildings were big enough. We'd reach the tourist market when they come to the springs and catch all the foot traffic from the farmers market on weekends."

I never knew Dad wanted to open a Kings in town. He always seemed content with the larger locations outside Still Springs.

Maybe Jade would be happy to have a decent offer on the store. If it's true that she's not able to make the loan payments, she might be thrilled to have the trouble taken off her hands.

There's only one person who can answer that question —Jade Quinn. Unfortunately, though, King's Code forbids unnecessary interactions.

Thinking about Jade's store being under that much strain makes me feel guilty for the text I got earlier from Sunny confirming that she wants to feature Kings in her article. "Hey, sis. Before you go, do you mind giving Sunny a call for a quote or two? I can text you her number." I really don't have anything to say to the woman.

"Yeah, no problem."

"Oh, and you might mention Quinn Brothers. Sunny asked me about using some of the photos I took from Fall Fest, and there are a few really good ones of this place that I'd love her to include."

Although Iris gives me a strange look, she agrees to mention the store.

After she thanks me again for watching Ella, she hops into the car and clips Ella into her car seat. When Iris drives away, I'm left standing here, not-*not* staring through the glass, hoping for a glimpse of my cute neighbor.

I love my baby sister, but right now, I kinda want to tell Hayley to take the code and shove it.

Hayley's just being protective of Jade because she thinks I'm going to hurt her—I get that. But I don't have any plans to hurt Jade. As long as she knows I'm leaving town, I don't see why we can't hang out together. We can be grown up about this thing between us—whatever *it* is—and see what happens.

I drag my thumb along my lower lip, reliving the incredible feeling of Jade's soft mouth on mine.

Hayley has a problem with me not going on dates with women, huh? I squint up at the Quinn Brothers sign.

Maybe it's time to go on a fucking date.

CHAPTER NINETEEN

JADE

The Burner triplets and their mom whip out of the store's front door like a tornado changing course, leaving me to assess the devastation. A wearied sigh escapes me as I crouch to pick up dropped candy bars, gummy bears, and cookie packets, carefully restacking them back on the shelf.

The bell attached to the door jingles again, and my stomach twists with anticipation as I head back up aisle four, wondering if it'll be him this time. The *him* I should definitely not be thinking about twenty-four-seven, but my brain doesn't seem to want to comply with that ruling. Three whole days have passed since Dylan and I made out like rabid animals against the storeroom wall, and I still can't think about his mouth against mine without losing my breath.

I step around the milk fridge, my chest sinking when, instead of seeing Dylan, I'm met with a stack of cardboard boxes dumped inside the store entrance rather than around the back like I asked. Through the window, I catch a glimpse of a delivery van screeching away.

"Thanks, man. Very helpful," I mutter while

inspecting the packing slip taped to the top box. *Ooh.* These are the decorative mugs I ordered from a regional homewares wholesaler. One thing I figured out during my stalking session at Kings was that I can't tap into the homewares market by only selling expensive items handcrafted by local artists. I should mix them in with some cheaper stuff that still has that artisan look, so there's something available for every budget. And our pottery drew a decent crowd at Fall Fest. *Step aside, Einstein. The genius is at work.*

I wrap my arms around the top box and groan as I heft it into the storeroom while trying not to end up injured and bedridden like poor Dad. Nerves prickle my skin when I remember that today is his appointment with a spine specialist after his urgent MRI scan earlier this week. My aunt Jackie drove Dad to the clinic so I could stay and watch the store. We can't afford to close right now, even for a day, and we certainly can't afford casual staff.

By the time I've got the fourth delivery box stacked against the storeroom wall, sweat is beading on my forehead despite it being forty degrees outside.

I switch off the heating for a few minutes to cool down and drag my box cutter along the seam of the top box. When I peel back the flaps and peer inside, my jaw falls open. "No!" I dig through the sharp jumble of broken porcelain, careful not to cut myself.

I could return the mugs, but—*shit, shit, shit.* When I ordered them, I checked a disclaimer that said the supplier takes no responsibility for third-party delivery breakages. But their own delivery quote was so criminally expensive that I ended up booking my own courier.

My jaw clenches as I march back to the front counter with the delivery slip so I can call the reckless driver and blast him for costing me hundreds of dollars. He's going to have to cover this.

I snatch up my phone, finding a missed call from Dad. My fingertips shake as I dial his number.

"Hey, Dad. How'd it go?"

His long pause makes my breath lodge in my throat. "Thankfully, it's nothing sinister, *but* I have three herniated discs, which the doc described as 'very severe'."

"Oh no."

"Oh, yes." I can tell Dad's forcing a smile, but there's a heaviness to his voice. "And that's not all, love. Usually, they'd begin with non-invasive treatments, but given the severity of my symptoms and the fact that I can barely walk, the doc has suggested surgery."

My chest clamps. "*Surgery?* Are you sure?"

"Unless I'm losing my hearing as well as my mobility, I'm sure, sweetheart."

My brow tightens as the front door swings open and a couple who look like posh out-of-towners wander in. The man immediately begins speaking to me while Dad's still mumbling dates and timelines in my ear, so I hold my finger up at the customer with an apologetic smile. The man gives me a hard frown.

"Sorry, Dad, we have a customer. I'll call you a bit later, okay?" The man in front of me glances at his blingy watch.

"Sure, love," Dad replies. "I'll give Ruby a call and let her know."

I hang up and paint a welcoming smile on my face, even though I want to tell this crabby customer to take a hike so I can burst into tears.

My dad has to have *spine surgery*. What kind of risks are involved? How much pain will he be in? What will the recovery be like? How much will this all *cost*?

"Did you hear me, girl?" the man in front of me snaps.

"Sorry," I reply with a little head-shake. "What was it you asked?"

"Can you tell me where the grocery store is that's about twenty minutes out of town? I believe it's called Crowns."

"Kings, darling." His wife comes up beside him, adjusting her silk scarf. "Can you give us directions to the *Kings* grocery store, please?"

I turn my gaze to her, resisting the urge to glare. "We sell groceries right here." I lift my upturned palm like a game show assistant. "What can I get you?"

She furrows her brow at the small crates of apples and bananas sitting behind me. "Oh, we're looking for a much bigger and *fresher* selection. Come on, darling." She gives the man's elbow a tug. "We'll ask someone from that lovely bookstore down the street." As she leads her husband out, she shivers, muttering something about the shop being an ice box.

Oh damn, I forgot to turn the heating back on. Fighting off another wave of panic about Dad, I head over to the furnace keypad and tap the On/Off button, but nothing happens. No light, no sound, no sign of life. I push my thumb in harder, but the thing's gone totally dead.

I groan and tip my face to the ceiling. "Anything else?!" I whine to the universe. While keeping an ear out for customers, I head into the office and dig through a filing cabinet of old documents, hunting for the furnace manual, but of course, the moment I actually need it, it's nowhere to be seen. My next idea is to call the manufacturer. I find their number on Google, but apparently, they don't have a single person at hand to answer the phone, so I leave a terse voicemail. *This day.*

It takes another twenty minutes of tidying up the

shelves for me to work up the courage to open the other three boxes of mugs. Each one is a total wreck like the first. I honestly can't bear the cost of this. Not with the overdue loan payments, the growing mountain of bills, and now Dad's surgery... How on earth are we meant to cover all this?!

I'm hunched over the storeroom floor, gulping choked breaths, when the front door jingles open.

Get up, Jade. You have a customer.

Except I can't move.

I can't get my legs to work.

I can't even find any air to breathe.

"Hellooo?" A deep, familiar voice grows closer in time with his footsteps. It sounds like Dylan is checking each aisle before he steps through the storeroom door. "Jade?"

He quickly paces closer and crouches in front of me. "What's wrong? Are you all right?"

I lift my face and blink into his wide eyes, searching for words that won't form in my dried throat.

"Jade," Dylan repeats.

"I'm..." I press my palm to my chest. "I can't..."

"You can't what? You can't breathe?" He collects my clammy hands in his, his strong fingers closing over mine.

When I nod, he shifts around to sit beside me, releasing one of my hands to lay his palm on my upper back. "Is it asthma? An allergy? Should I call—"

I shake my head. "I'm just..." I expel a shuddery breath through my lips. "I think I'm... I think I'm freaking out."

Dylan's hand scores lines up and down my back. "Okay, that I can work with. My therapist always tells me to inhale slowly, counting to three, then breathe out on the count of four." He gives me an encouraging nod, and we perform the action together, breathing in deeply for three and out for four. After a minute or so of doing it, the world begins to sharpen again, and my lungs loosen in my chest.

"I think I'm okay," I whisper, glancing at where Dylan's fingers are still softly folded around mine. "I feel better. Thank you."

"No problem."

Reluctantly, I let go of his hand and shakily climb to my feet. After a few more breaths to steady myself, I leave the storeroom with my face on fire. Dylan finally turned up, and I was keeled over like a hysteric, which is so not me. I reach the counter and turn around, finding him watching me with his fingers lightly brushing up and down the back of his neck. My eyes fall on the string of buttons tattooed down the muscled underside of one arm.

"You okay?" he asks in an uncertain tone.

"Yeah." I clear my throat. "I feel fine now."

His eyes don't leave mine. "You just had a panic attack."

"I'm not sure it was—"

"I get them too, Jade. So, if you act like there's something wrong with having a big old freak-out when life is being a bitch, I might get offended."

A long, heavy sigh streams out of me as I rest my hip against the counter. "I'm having a really stressful day," I admit. "But I'm working through it."

His eyes continue to search my face before he says, "It's freezing in here. Did you turn the heat down?"

"The furnace stopped working today. I have no idea why."

"That's too bad." His gaze clings to mine. "You want me to warm you up?"

Heat streaks up the back of my neck. "*Dylan.*"

A throaty chuckle slips out of him. "I'm just kidding."

"Is there something you came in to buy?" I ask, instantly

regretting the subtle push for him to finish up here and get going. But he does look so utterly warm and inviting, and if I let him wrap his strong arms around me right now, I'm not sure I'd ever let go.

Instead of answering my question, his gaze shifts to my laptop on the counter, where I was working on our new online store before the Burners came in. Sunny gave me the idea for Quinn Brothers Online when she asked for our website. To increase our revenue streams, we need to be able to sell stuff to locals who are immobile or sick, or when the weather's horrendous and no one wants to come out and shop. Kings has offered a home delivery service since it opened—it's time we got out of the dark ages and did the same.

"Are you building a website?" Dylan asks, stepping toward the computer.

"I am. Apparently, the internet is becoming a thing now. We're also thinking of getting a transistor radio and maybe one of those stick phones where you hold the receiver up to your mouth."

He chuckles, but a flash of horror strikes me when he takes a closer look at the site that looks like amateur-hour beside the King's professionally built website.

"Did you take these pics?" He squints at the product images I snapped with my phone.

"Sure did. You want to license them? Enter them into one of those Nat Geo competitions? I think that toilet roll portrait could really sweep the board this year."

He throws me one of his crooked smiles that's so damn sexy I have to look away. Someone should thoroughly kiss that lethal weapon right off his face.

Dylan turns to rest his back against the counter, folding his arms. "So, you're doing all this yourself, huh?"

"All this?"

"Managing the store, building the website, taking the photos, fixing the furnace, making the shit coffee... all by your sweet self."

The way he's looking at me—like he can see the burning ball of pressure living behind my chest wall—has my gaze scattering. "I'm good at multitasking."

When I glance back at Dylan, he locks me in a silent staring competition. "What can I do to help?" he asks softly.

A bewildered laugh gathers in my throat because I have no idea what to say to that other than... "Nothing. I've got it all covered. But thanks. And I'll remember—three breaths in, four breaths out."

I force a smile because I can't think of anything more mortifying than one of the multimillionaire Kings knowing that my tiny, second-rate store can't make ends meet.

"Actually, I did come in here to buy something," Dylan says, suddenly pushing off the counter.

"Cool." *So, it wasn't to see me then.* "What is it you need?"

He grabs the shopping cart with the squeaky wheel and pushes it down the first aisle, tossing in random items. I don't want to crowd him like a stalker, so I inch back to my stool and begin absently clicking buttons on my laptop until Dylan reappears, his cart loaded up with groceries. I run my gaze over the fancy laundry detergent that hardly anyone buys, the giant jars of pickled olives, the Belgian chocolate boxes, the frozen organic berry bars... This haul is going to cost him a fortune.

"Your store running low on stock or something?" I ask suspiciously, swiping each item across the counter until they beep.

He fishes his wallet out of his back pocket. "Nah, it's

just easier to get it all here." He reaches for one of Magnolia Sloane's gruesome clay sculptures and plonks it before me. "Plus, we don't sell these, and I've always wanted one."

He's gotta be bluffing, but I keep a straight face and bag up the distorted head while he bites away a smile.

I consider offering to help him carry his mountain of bags next door, but the last thing I need is to end up alone with Dylan in his apartment. Especially after he obviously just bought all this stuff to help boost our sales for the day. If I follow him next door, there's at least a seventy-five percent chance I'll try to climb him like a tree and burrow my nose into that heavenly spot in the crook of his neck.

Instead, I watch Dylan slide his wallet back into his pocket, trying to kick the stupid hearts out of my eyes. "*Oh, there was one other thing I came in here for,*" he says.

"Yeah?"

"Have dinner with me."

"What?"

"I know we can't have a date-date," he adds quickly, "but we can have a friend-date. You like food; *I* like food. Maybe we can do food together. Given we're friendly neighbors and all."

If only there's some way to will my blush away and play it cool, but I'm sure I've turned as red as a tomato.

"Something out of town, so it's just us with no spies or stickybeaks?" Dylan adds, leaning his forearms against the counter so we're at eye-level. It takes a Herculean effort not to swoon.

"Something out of town could work," I murmur.

His smile lights up his eyes. "When?"

"Sunday?" I *know* I shouldn't be agreeing to this, but my damn lips won't stop moving. Selfish, silly lips. "We close early on Sunday."

"Perfect."

Loading up a million shopping bags on his arms and looking too adorable for words, he gives me one more smile before he turns to leave. "Sunday night it is, *friend*."

"See you then, *pal*."

Oh boy.

Three in, four out.

CHAPTER TWENTY

DYLAN

"Come again?"

I'm pretty sure Sarah heard me the first two times I said the words. Still, she's getting up there in years, so I repeat myself. "I said I'm going out to dinner with Jade." If I ever get off this video session, that is. My therapist and I have already been chatting for the last forty minutes, mostly about my parents. Not exactly your typical pre-date psych-up, but since this isn't your typical date, I figure it doesn't matter.

She pushes her glasses up the bridge of her nose. "You're going on a date with your neighbor?" she says slowly as if she's still processing. Look at me, using one of her favorite buzzwords.

"No. We're going to dinner as friends." I know that this thing with Jade can't go anywhere, and I'd all but talked myself out of asking her on a date. But then she looked so damn frazzled in the store the other day; I wanted to get her out of that place and show her a good time. Two friends having food and a bit of fun. Nothing less, nothing more.

Out of the blue, Sarah says, "You must love pickled olives."

Not what I was expecting to come out of her mouth. "I hate them, actually." My answer is out before I realize the reason for her random comment. In the corner of my screen, the mammoth jars I bought from Jade's store the other day are clearly visible on my counter beside the ugly misshapen-head sculpture that I'm, admittedly, starting to grow fond of.

A lot of people seem to come and go out of Quinn Brothers empty-handed. If Jade's business is in as much trouble as my sister believes, she needs sales. And after finding her mid-panic attack, it's clear she needs help. So, I decided to do just that by buying the priciest products on the shelves. The laundry detergent I picked up smells like heaven. The berry bars I got were pretty good, too, and Ella likes to sneak the chocolate when she thinks I'm not looking. But those vile olives were a mistake that don't fit in any of my cupboards. They're certainly not going anywhere near my stomach.

A slow, knowing smile inches along Sarah's lips. I can practically see her putting two and two together.

Neighbor is cute and owns a store.

Dylan buys products he doesn't need to help neighbor.

Dylan asks neighbor out to dinner.

Dylan claims that neighbor and he are just friends.

Dylan is a damn liar.

"Are you interested in your neighbor romantically?" Sarah asks.

To be honest, my feelings are a fucking disaster when it comes to Jade Quinn. Am I attracted to her? Sure. I'd have to be dead not to be. Would I fuck her against a wall into next Tuesday if given the chance? Absolutely.

But then there's this protectiveness that seeps in as well, as evidenced by those olives and the fact that I've spent the last few days trying to figure out how to tell her the photos she took for the website are shit and convince her to let me take them instead.

The only women I usually feel protective over are in my family, so that makes this incredibly confusing and complicated.

I drum my fingers against the wooden table, ready to put this line of questioning to bed. "Does it really matter? I'm leaving town soon, and she's Hayley's best friend." Besides, Sarah doesn't think I'll be able to fully commit to anyone if I don't process and work through all the shit that happened with Miranda. Which apparently includes a visit to my ex's mother. And since I have no plans to do that…

"Have you asked Jade what she's looking for in a romantic relationship?" Sarah asks.

I don't need to. Jade has commitment flowing through her veins. Just look at how she's clinging to that sinking ship of a store. My fingers tap a little harder as my chest draws tight.

When I don't immediately respond, Sarah hits me with another doozy. "How do you feel about letting your youngest sister dictate who you date?"

Damn, I wish she'd pull her punches just this once. "She's only trying to protect Jade."

"From what?"

"From me." Obviously.

"I see." Sarah's lips purse the way they always do when she disagrees with something, but since I'm paying her to listen, she can't come right out and say it. "Do you plan on lying to Jade about your intentions?"

Technically, I already did the moment I said we'd be going out as "friends."

"Are you going to disrespect her or treat her poorly?" Sarah goes on.

"Of course not."

"Then why does your sister's opinion on this situation matter more than yours or Jade's?"

Sarah must be an only child if she doesn't realize the line I'm crossing here. A line I have a feeling I'd cross again and again if it made Jade smile the way she did when I asked her to dinner.

Before I can answer, I catch a glimpse of the clock above the stove. Shit, I gotta get going. "Sorry, I have to run. Thanks for the chat, Sarah."

"Think about what I said, Dylan." She winks and adds, "And enjoy your *date*."

The screen goes black before I can correct her.

I grab my leather jacket from the back of the chair and slip my arms into the sleeves on my way out the door. I guess I should ask Jade what she's looking for from me before I assume she's hearing wedding bells. I should also definitely remind her that I'm heading back to Austin soon, just in case.

If we both go into this with our eyes wide open, no one gets hurt. Right?

When I hit the bottom of the stairs, I fish my keys out of my pocket. The moment my boot crosses the threshold, it lands on a brown paper sack. Whatever's inside the bag squishes like Ella's playdough. *Not* what you want ground into the carpet.

I bend down to pick it up. The stench that assaults my nose makes me gag. Is that—*shit*?

I'm not being metaphorical, either.

Someone left a bag of shit on my fucking doorstep.

I scan my bike's windshield for tickets signed by a certain jackass officer.

None today, thank god. Although, right now, I'd rather pay a fine than deal with shit on my boot. For all the hate I get around here, no one seems to despise me quite as much as Jade's ex, so I assume the "present" is from him. What sort of grown-ass man leaves shit on someone's stoop? If only I could prove Nate Williams was the culprit.

I slip out of my black leather boot to keep from tracking shit everywhere and hold the bag away from my nose as I carry it out to the public trash can at the corner. Then I head back inside to clean my boot and wash my hands, cursing the little prick the entire time. Now I'm going to be late picking up Jade, and I hate being late.

This has gone on long enough. First thing tomorrow, I'm calling my lawyer to see if there's anything I can do about the harassment, and then look into getting cameras installed outside. I refuse to live the next couple of months looking over my shoulder because a little piss ant thinks I stole his girlfriend. Next time Officer Williams wants to leave me a present, I'm going to catch him red-handed.

I'm still irritated as hell by the time I pull into Jade's driveway, but the moment her front door swings open, all the tension inside me uncoils. Still sitting on my bike, I tug off my helmet to get a clear view of the way her hair curls in soft waves against her cream-colored sweater. The high black boots over her tight jeans reach almost to her knees. I know I'm staring, but the only thought in my head is, "Let's skip dinner, go inside, and strip out of these clothes." And that can't happen... can it?

King's Code. Remember the code.

Jade's smile warms her face. "You're late."

Grimacing, I curse Nate for the hundredth time. "Sorry. I had some unexpected shit to deal with." To keep my hands busy, I stand up and lift the seat to unhook the spare helmet while Jade locks her front door. When she reaches me, the faint vanilla of her perfume tickles the back of my tongue.

I hold out the helmet. "I have this, but we can take your car if you don't want to mess up your hair."

"Are you kidding me?" She snags the helmet right out of my hand. "I've been dying to ride that since I saw it on Main Street."

"We're still talking about the bike, right?" I say with a wink, sinking back onto the seat.

Her throaty laugh ties my insides in knots. But it's nothing compared to the feeling of Jade bracing her hands on my shoulders and throwing a leg over the bike like she's done this a thousand times, or the sheer torture of her toned thighs gripping me tight and her breasts glued to my back as she holds onto my waist.

I'm in big fucking trouble.

OFF THE HIGHWAY SITS A SMALL ITALIAN DINER THAT my parents used to love. The squatty brick building with red, white, and green awnings stretched over the windows doesn't look like much, but the owner is from Verona, and his food is as good as, if not better than, any of the places I've eaten in Italy. The last time I came here was with Mom and Dad for their anniversary.

I considered not bringing Jade here for that very reason, but Sarah suggested that it might be healing for me to go to places like this and allow myself to "sit in" my memories.

Which basically feels like being stripped naked and thrown on a bed of hot coals.

Jade squeezes my shoulder when I indicate and turn into the parking lot. It's so subtle that I'm not even sure she realizes she's doing it. But her touch reminds me that I'm not alone, making it a little easier to breathe.

The moment I pull into a parking space, I inhale a few deep breaths while tears prick my eyes. Only when I'm sure none of them are going to fall do I remove my helmet.

Hopefully, I'm right in pegging Jade as a fellow Italian lover. She had been at that fair, after all.

With Deputy Douchebag.

A little moment of jealousy that I'm not used to feeling pinches my throat. What did she ever see in that guy?

She removes her helmet and sets it on the seat so she can flip over her hair and run her fingers through her curls. Whatever shampoo or hairspray voodoo she's used hits me like a punch in the face, and all of a sudden, I'm not sad anymore.

I adjust myself in my jeans.

Definitely not sad.

When she stands back up, her hair looks as perfect as it did before. And Jade Quinn might be the sexiest woman I've ever seen. All soft curves and don't-mess-with-me eyes.

She peers up at the sign with a smile curling her lips. "Would you believe that I've lived here my whole life and I've never been here before?"

"No?"

She lifts a slender shoulder in a casual shrug. "I'm so busy with the store that it feels like I never go anywhere."

I manage to reach the door before she does so I can hold it open for her. Friends do that for each other, right? "Where would you go if you didn't have the store?"

She pauses for a second before saying, "That's a good question."

It's one she doesn't get to answer because the server steps through the swinging kitchen door and grabs two menus, rattling off tonight's specials as she brings us to a table by the window. There are fake red and white carnations sitting in a bud vase beside the red pepper flakes. Not exactly romantic, which is a good thing.

Jade nibbles her lower lip in the most distracting way as she flicks through the menu's plastic pages. "What's good?"

I don't even have to glance over the listings to answer. "The lobster tagliatelle."

Her brows get this little wrinkle between them when she slides her finger over to the price.

"Order whatever you want," I say. "My treat."

The slight shimmer on her eyelids makes her green eyes pop when she glances up at me. "I can pay for my own food."

"And my poor, dead mother would turn over in her grave if I let you."

Jade's eyes widen a fraction as her gaze falls to her menu. Too soon to play the dead mom card? Maybe. But the fact of the matter is, I'd rather lick the bottom of my boot than let her pay for her meal, even though it's nice knowing that she didn't agree to come with me because of what I can buy for her.

When the server comes back over and Jade orders the lobster, I have to force a delighted smile off my face. I tell the server to make it two and tack on a bottle of my parents' favorite wine because why not? I can only have one glass since I'm driving, but you can't come into this place and not get the Sangiovese. Pretty sure that's some sort of cardinal sin.

Once we're alone again with nothing but the hum of the other couples sharing quiet conversations and the soft instrumental music drifting through the restaurant, I ask Jade her plans for the week. She starts listing all the things she has to do at the store, and it seems like a lot for one person. Too much, really. Panic attack-inducing for sure. Iris's questions about Quinn Brothers filter into my mind.

The server drops off a bread basket, and as we each slather butter over our rolls, I decide now's as good a time as any to broach the topic of selling the store.

"Can I ask you something?"

Jade leans back in her chair, a smirk hinting at her glossed lips. "Since you're buying me lobster, I suppose I'll allow it."

"Have you ever thought about selling the store?"

She blinks at me with a stunned look. "Why would you ask me that?"

"Just curious. You're so busy… you said you were really stressed… it makes me wonder if you feel like it's all worth it."

"It is," she clips. "But I don't really want to talk about the store. It's kinda nice not to have to think about it for a change."

Makes sense.

Wonder if she'd be up for talking about that mud race we never finished? I'm not sure I'll ever forgive Robocop for interrupting our first kiss. Has he tried to get in touch with her since Fall Fest? He'd be an idiot if he hadn't. "So, have you heard from Officer Williams lately?" I ask with a sudden sting in my throat.

The corners of Jade's lips lift. "Since this isn't a date, you probably shouldn't ask me questions about my ex."

Way to avoid the question. "Don't friends talk about the people they've dated?" I tease.

She tilts her head at me. "Are we really friends, Dylan? Or are we casual acquaintances sharing food?"

"We're definitely friends." I have more history with Jade than anyone other than my family. Ancient history, sure, but history all the same.

She folds her arms over the front of her sweater, making my gaze slip down to her chest and linger there. My body tingles from the memory of her pressed up against me. On the bike. In her store. In the mud.

"Oh yeah?" Jade drawls. "When's my birthday, *friend*?"

She and Hayley were born around the same time. Mom always got a sneaky gift for Jade at Hayley's parties, and Hayley was born in... "May."

Her eyes expand.

Fucking nailed it. Now to remember the exact day and really impress her because that's a totally normal thing to want to do with your friends. "The twenty-third?"

She shakes her head. "Twenty-fifth."

Damn. "A for effort?"

Her lips twitch. "B plus."

"I'll take it." Then, because I can't help myself, I ask, "When's mine?"

"March twenty-fourth."

My brows pull up. Wow, she's spot-on. Interesting...

Almost as interesting as the fact that her cheeks have turned as red as that plastic carnation sitting between us. Little Jade remembers my birthday. That really shouldn't matter at all, but for some reason, I kinda love it.

The server returns with two wine glasses and holds out the bottle for me to read the label. I nod, but instead of waiting for her to pour a sample, I ask her to uncork the bottle and leave it.

When she does, I fill our glasses, Jade's a little more than mine, while she sits back and watches. Her fingers clasp the delicate stem and twists the glass back and forth.

I lift my glass toward hers and wait for her to do the same. "Here's looking at you, pet."

Her eyes flash to mine, and her blush deepens as our glasses clink together. "I'm pretty sure it's 'kid.' Here's looking at you, *kid*."

"If you say so." I shrug, not caring either way when we have more important things to talk about than movie quotes. "Deny it all you want, *kid*, but we are friends who know each other's birthdays and occasionally make out."

Her glass pauses at her lips for a moment. "I wouldn't call twice occasionally," she murmurs over the rim.

For some reason, my mouth thinks it's a good idea to say, "Then I guess we'll have to fix that, won't we?"

CHAPTER TWENTY-ONE

JADE

Dylan's eyes burn a trail into mine over the table, my pulse jumping higher.

He looks hungry. And not for lobster tagliatelle.

His gaze drifts south, settling on my mouth before dragging back up to my eyes. It's a constant physical challenge not to fall under this sexy man's spell and dismiss the warnings.

"My dear brother leaves a wreckage of broken hearts wherever he goes."

"What are you thinking so hard about?" Dylan asks, his fingertips grazing the stem of his wine glass. My eyes catch on the letters tattooed over his knuckles. Instead of answering, I reach out and take his hand, unlocking his fingers so I can read the upturned word.

M O R E

My eyes lift to his. "More what?"

He places his other hand in front of me, spreading open his fingers.

L O V E, I read upside down.

The server steps in with two steaming, aromatic plates of lobster pasta, and we break apart.

After she leaves, I dig my fork into a juicy chunk of lobster. "*Love more.* You're a romantic."

"You sound surprised."

"Come on, we both know you're not a one-woman man," I say teasingly, but there's a hint of serious undertone.

Dylan covers his mouth as he chews. "Says who?"

"Says Hayley," I want to reply, but uttering that name would dump a bucket of ice over this checkered tablecloth, so I revert to my safe place of being a smart-ass.

"Says the STD clinic?" I giggle against my wine glass, making it one hundred percent clear that I'm only messing with him.

Dylan shoots me a pretend scowl before suddenly digging into his pocket and pulling out his phone.

"I was *kidding*," I say emphatically, but Dylan casually thumbs through his phone, then slides the handset toward me.

"Clean as a whistle," he says, shooting me a victory smirk while I figure out what I'm looking at. It's some sort of digital medical report that lists a run of sexually transmitted diseases, the words "*not detected*" printed beside each one. The date next to Dylan's name at the top is recent.

Oh god. Good one, Jade.

"Don't I feel like an asshole right now," I mumble with flaming cheeks while returning the phone to Dylan. But when I brave a look at him, he's still smiling.

"It's all good," he says. "You're not the first to make that assumption."

I lean forward. "I really was kidding."

"Yeah, yeah." Dylan genuinely looks unbothered, and I'm not sure what to make of that. It can't be a good thing if he's become completely desensitized to people making these sorts of judgments about him.

"So, you didn't answer my question earlier," he says, lifting his glass and exposing a strip of corded forearm beneath his rolled-up shirt. "If you didn't have the store to think about, where would you go if you could go anywhere?"

I tilt my face to the ceiling. After putting all my effort —*and* my money—into the store, it's not something I've thought too much about.

"Italy would be amazing," I decide. "That's super high on my list, and I've always wanted to go to Isla de las Muñecas in Mexico."

"Isla de where?"

"The Island of the Dolls. According to a legend, a little girl once drowned there, so a man who lived on the island hung up hundreds of old dolls as a tribute, and then he ended up drowning too. Apparently, all the dolls are now possessed."

Dylan lowers his fork. "Jade, what the fuck? Why would you want to go there?"

I chuckle and shrug a shoulder. "I love scary stuff. I also really want to check out The Amityville House on Long Island and a bunch of other haunted houses from horror movies. Transylvania would be pretty cool to visit, too."

He shakes his head, but his eyes sparkle as they catch on my thin, silver bracelet of tiny skulls linked together. "You must really get into Halloween."

"Is there any other holiday?"

He smirks and cuts into his lobster. "Noted, my friend."

That "f" word puts an abrupt end to the conversation, and we both chew in silence for a few moments.

"So, *Austin's* not on your list of places to visit, then,"

Dylan eventually says. He narrows his gaze at me, but it's all show.

I fake a frown. "Why would I go there? What could I possibly want to see in Austin that would ever interest me?"

He hums a laugh. "Harsh. The possessed death-dolls of Mexico are top of the list, though."

We smile at each other, and I let the wine relax me enough to appreciate where I am and who I'm with. This sure beats doing Sunday evening inventory at the store.

"Speaking of Austin, when are you going back?" I ask, an emptiness invading my chest at the thought of him leaving.

Dylan glances down at his plate, taking a second to answer. "I promised to help Iris until Christmas."

I nod, feeling the high that I've been on tonight slowly collapsing. But maybe Dylan moving across the country soon is just what I need. I can't be tempted to keep kissing my best friend's brother if he isn't dangled right in front of me.

Dylan's gaze travels over my face like he's wondering what I'm thinking, so I reach for a different topic that's also on my mind.

"Can I ask you a question?" I begin.

"Depends on what it is. I'm not comfortable discussing my personal life with people who consider Death Island an ideal holiday destination."

Chuckling, I circle my forefinger around the rim of my wine glass. "Why did you ask me about selling the store? Don't tell me the Kings are secretly plotting to buy it."

I'm mostly kidding, but the serious look that clouds his eyes makes my stomach drop.

"I asked because I can't help but notice it's just *you* in

there all the time," Dylan says, clearly trying to be delicate. "Your sister's moved away, your dad doesn't seem to be around much, and I guess it seems like a shit-ton of work for one person. I can't imagine the returns are all that high for a small convenience store, and...I dunno." He lifts a shoulder. "You're still young and have your whole life ahead of you. Is it all really worth it?"

My eyes burn a little as I blink at him, wondering why that question hits so hard.

Is it all really worth it?

"I don't want to offend you," he adds quickly. "I know your store's been in your family for ages, and believe it or not, that's not something I know much about. I've never had anything to do with my parents' businesses."

Sexy Dylan is hard enough to resist. Sweet, honest Dylan is almost too appealing to endure. "I'm not offended. And you're right, it's a shit-ton of work," I admit. "When Ruby left, I thought I'd have Dad around a bit longer to help me figure out how to make the store more profitable, but he hasn't been well lately."

Dylan's brow pinches. "What do you mean?"

"He has back problems. He needs to have surgery, but then, hopefully, he'll be good."

"Surgery? Shit, Jade. I'm sorry to hear that."

"Yeah, thanks." Unease prickles up my neck as the conversation veers closer to uncomfortable territory. I just let it slip that the store's been struggling to make a profit, and that's information I really didn't want the eldest member of the King empire to know.

When I look back at Dylan, I find him eyeing me. "I think you and I are a lot alike," he says.

In what world? "Yeah? How's that?"

"You're passionate about the things you love. Not afraid to go after what you want." Something catches alight in his eyes that sends a spiral of warmth up my spine. "And we've both lost people we can never replace."

Pain twists inside me at the reference to my mother. "Yeah."

I go to ask Dylan how he's coping with the loss of both his parents—still an unfathomable thought to me—but the server sweeps back in to clear our plates. "Would you like dessert?" she asks, handing us two menus. I'm so full from the pasta that I give Dylan a glance to see how he's feeling.

"All dinner and no dessert makes Jade a dull girl," he warns jokingly.

I cover my mouth so that I don't laugh.

Chuckling, he peers into his dessert menu. "I'll have the tiramisu," he tells the server, and I order the same because, as full as I am, I can't turn down dessert.

Dylan pours me a second glass of wine, and I decide not to return to the heavy topic of loss. Instead, the conversation shifts to our few shared memories of when we were young, what we did after college, and a lot about Dylan's photography. I'm clueless about cameras, but the excitement that dances in his eyes when he talks about composition and lighting and something called the rule of thirds makes me want to know everything. He tells me that sometimes it gets him down what camera phones have done to the photography industry, but then he'll snap a perfect shot and remember why he can't give it up.

Fifty minutes later, the dessert plates have long been cleared, and the server is hovering nearby.

I lightly pat my stomach, looking around the nearly empty restaurant. "Should we go? That was *amazing*. Thank you."

"Of course. Anytime." Dylan clears his throat and waves at the server, who bounds over with the payment machine. He whips out a platinum credit card and pays the bill before we head outside to his bike parked around the side of the restaurant.

"So where to now?" I ask because I don't feel like being taken home yet.

Something that looks like relief washes through his gaze. "Tough choice. There are so many good options in Still Springs."

I chuckle at his sarcasm. We both know The Rocking Horse will be open, but there's a high risk of running into someone we know there, and I really don't feel like sharing him.

Dylan jerks his head at the bike. "How about I take you for a ride?"

My giggle sends a confused frown to his brow. "Is that your usual line, Casanova? *How about I take you for a ride?*" I do my best low-voice, smooth-guy impersonation.

"Oh, you don't like my pick-up line?"

"It's cheesier than cheese pizza."

He meets my stare, the both of us trying not to smile. "I can do better than that."

"Yeah? Give me your best line." I fold my arms at him. "Actually, no. Give me your worst." That feels safer than him taking a genuine shot at charming the pants off me. It'll probably work.

Dylan runs a hand up the back of his mussed hair before amusement fills his eyes. "A girl at this bar in Austin once said to me: Excuse me, are you a bank loan? Because you've got *my* interest."

A spark of jealousy flares in my chest, but I hide it with a snort-laugh. "Cute."

He nudges the tip of my shoe with his. "What about you? I bet you've heard a hundred shitty pick-up lines."

I don't even have to think about this one. "So, are you going to show me your tits after this or what?"

Dylan nearly chokes. "That's a joke."

"Wish it was."

"Someone actually said that to you? As a pick-up line?"

"Yup." My lips pop on the "p." "The Rocking Horse, circa graduation year. I tossed my drink in the guy's face."

Dylan's eyes make one of those slow, unabashed slides down my body. He then steps right up to me and brings the heat of his breath to my ear. "So, are you gonna show me your tits after this or what?"

He recoils with a smirk like he's expecting me to whack him. But that's not my style.

With my back facing the restaurant, I glance at the empty highway, then lift the base of my sweater all the way to my neck. Cold air rushes over my cleavage, but all I feel is the heat pouring from Dylan's gaze as his eyes run over the bare skin bulging from my lacy white bra.

"*Fuck,* Jade," he says in a gravelly breath as I drop my shirt back down, feeling victorious but trembling all over.

"So, are you gonna take me for that ride?" I ask.

Every sentence now feels laced with innuendo, and the situation isn't helped when Dylan hands me the spare helmet before bringing his lips close to my ear again. "I could ride with you *all night long,*" he says, and heat pools between my legs, making my thighs press together.

Dylan climbs onto the bike and waits for me to slide in behind him, my thighs clinging tightly to his and my fingers lacing over his taut stomach.

He kick-starts the bike, and we zoom off the main highway and up through the forest-lined, winding roads of the state park. Adrenaline blazes through me as the bike tilts and accelerates, a smile fused to my cheeks, and my body wrapped around Dylan's to keep warm. After what feels like the most exhilarating hour of my life, he pulls over near the exit leading to the town, his gloved hand landing on my thigh.

We lift our visors, and he twists around, my gaze drinking in his gleaming blue eyes. "How are you doing back there?" he asks, his voice a little muffled by the helmet.

"I'm good. That was awesome."

I can't see his mouth, but I can tell he's smiling. "You want me to take you home?"

"Not unless you want to."

His thumb strokes back and forth over my thigh. "Not at all."

I have no idea what to propose other than the dreaded Rocking Horse. I could invite Dylan over to my place to hang out, but that could sound like I'm propositioning him. Plus, I've got nothing in my cupboards except rice crackers and ramen. Unless...

"Why don't you show me that secret project you've been working on at your apartment?" I suggest nervously. "Have I been *nice* enough to see it?"

His eyes move back and forth between my own before he glances away with a deep inhale. We both know that going to his apartment is just as risky as him coming to my place. But the offer's now been made, and I decide not to take it back. I *want* to see what he's been working on.

Dylan catches the base of my helmet between his fingers like he's giving my chin an affectionate squeeze. "You've been more than nice."

"Okay then," I say a little breathlessly. "Show me what you've been cooking up in that mystery lab."

"Yes, ma'am."

He twists back around, flips his visor down, and covers one of my hands with his. His gloved fingers thread through mine, and I give his hand a light squeeze before the bike rumbles back to life, and he has to let go.

CHAPTER TWENTY-TWO

DYLAN

I THROW MY KEYS AND WALLET ONTO THE COUNTER before kicking off my boots. The whole ride back to town was torture with a capital T. I deserve a medal for keeping focused on the road instead of the way Jade's warm body was glued to the back of mine.

The last thing I expected from tonight was to bring her back to my place, but the idea of appeasing her curiosity about what I've been working on was too good to pass up. Plus, I'm not ready to say goodnight. Dinner was amazing; I loved every minute of getting to know the woman Jade has grown up to become. The eyeful of her chest she gifted me after dessert wasn't so bad either. Turns out that Jade has a bit of a wild side, and I am totally here for it.

She unzips her high boots and sets them next to mine. When her eyes snag on the black revolving door leading to the second bedroom, which I had installed to keep out the light, her head tilts, and those honeyed waves slip off her shoulders. "It's a kinky sex dungeon, isn't it."

I almost laugh but manage to keep my composure as I

step inside the door, give her my best "It-could-be-a-kinky-sex-dungeon" smile, and say, "Want to find out?"

And fuck if it doesn't feel good when she files through the tight space beside me without hesitation. Her soft hair tickles my chin, her light vanilla scent wrapping around my nose. Our chests brush when we both exhale at the same time. *This woman's gonna be the death of me.*

I rotate the door until we're encased in total darkness and chemical-laced air assaults my senses.

Jade's soft breath dances across the side of my neck. "This doesn't smell like a sex dungeon."

"How would you know?"

She chuckles. "I guess I should've said this doesn't smell like *my* sex dungeon."

Great. Now all I can think about is Jade in a leather thong, black stilettos, and nipple clamps with a whip in her hand. Ignoring the rush of blood down south, I slide my hand along the smooth wall to the light switch and give it a flick. The safety bulb coating the room in a blood-red glow doesn't help with the whole "sex dungeon" fantasy either.

"It's a darkroom," she whispers, turning in a slow circle to gaze up at the photographs hanging on the clotheslines suspended from the walls. Most of the images are from Fall Fest, but I have a few from a recent shoot in Austin, and there are a couple of Mom and Dad from an old roll of film I found at their place.

I've never been nervous about people seeing my work, even in its rawest stage, but something about having Jade here makes me feel strangely vulnerable.

"Disappointed?" I ask.

She laughs as she tilts a photograph of Main Street toward her. "Only a little."

Note to self: Turn Harringtons restaurant next door into a sex dungeon ASAP.

She moves on to the photo of the little girl with the melted ice cream, probably my second favorite from that roll. "I didn't realize people still use darkrooms," Jade says.

Shooting digitally does make more sense than doing it this way, but I love the nostalgia of having a darkroom and the rush of excitement when you finally develop the negatives. It was probably a waste of money installing the door since I'm leaving in a few months, but I can take it with me when I go.

"I edit most of my pictures in Photoshop like the rest of the world, but still shoot in black and white with my 35mm camera whenever I can," I explain. "There's something thrilling about having to wait to see if you got the shot versus the instant gratification of digital photography."

She glances at me from over her shoulder. "So you're not into instant gratification?"

What is it with all the innuendos tonight? Is she trying to kill me? My gaze lingers on her plush mouth before I drag my eyes back to hers. "I never said that. But I can be patient and don't mind working for it."

Her smile broadens. "Good to know."

"You want to give it a go?"

"I assume you mean print a picture," she says with a laugh.

"I mean whatever you think I mean." We could turn this into a sex dungeon instead if that's what she wants. I have a tie in my bedroom, and she has wrists made for tying up.

"I'd love to print a picture," Jade says. "What do I do?"

So that's a no on the dungeon? I shake away my lingering lewd thoughts and focus on photography because that sounds like *so* much more fun than peeling away every piece of her clothing under these red lights.

I'm kind of sorry that I don't have any film to develop, so I'd have an excuse to turn off the lights and fumble around "looking" for what I need, finding Jade's body instead. All that's left now is printing. Since I already have the aperture and time settings figured out for this roll, all the tedious steps are out of the way.

"First, you'll need some paper." I pull out an 8 x 10 from the black container that's meant to keep light from reaching the photosensitive sheets and hand it to Jade. "Put this on the enlarger's baseboard right there."

"I assume the enlarger is this fancy microscope thing?" she asks, taking the paper from me.

"You assume correct, Little Jade."

After shooting me a cute scowl for that nickname, she follows my instructions and waits while I hold the negative up to the light to find the perfect photo. *Bingo.* I slide the negative in place and wait to hear what Jade has to say when she sees it.

"Fifteen seconds of exposure should be perfect." I point to the red switch on the side. "Press that when I say go." I get the timer ready and count down from three.

When I give the cue, Jade presses the button and the enlarger bursts to life, projecting the close-up photo I took of her at her festival booth, smiling at a customer. It's not one of those fake smiles either—the ones where you can tell people are saying "cheese." Jade looks genuinely happy, her eyes crinkly and sparkling as she clutches one of those hideous sculptures.

She gasps. "When did you take this?"

"Fall Fest, when you weren't looking." I glance at the timer. "Okay, turn it off in three, two, one…"

The white light shuts off, leaving us bathed in red once more.

"Now, put the paper in the developer there and tilt the tray back and forth. Gently, or else you'll—"

Jade rocks the plastic tray filled with liquid. She curses when a bunch of it spills over the edge onto the newspaper-covered table.

"Or else you'll slop it all over," I mutter with a laugh.

She winces. "Sorry."

"It's not a big deal." That's what the newspaper is for.

The image slowly comes to life, the contrast between the bright sky and the dark sweater Jade wore that day crisp and clear.

"How long does it stay in this?" she asks.

"Almost done." After a minute, I tell her to use the tongs to lift the photograph and let it drip for a few seconds before doing the same with the stop bath. After ten seconds in there, it's on to the fixer for another minute.

"That's it?" she asks, smoothing her hands down her jeans as she smiles down at the photo beneath the liquid.

"You don't sound impressed."

She throws a look over her shoulder that I can't quite read. "Should I be?"

Hell yes, she should. This takes time and practice and trial and error and heaps of patience. Maybe I should've walked her through how to create a test strip and change the contrast.

The timer lets out a cheerful ding.

"Now what?" she asks.

"Now we wash." I use the tongs to slide the photo into the final tray beneath the hose connected to the bathroom sink through a hole in the wall.

"How long till it's done?"

"Ten minutes should be enough time." Then we'll hang it up and wait for it to dry like the rest of these photos.

Jade reaches over me and types ten minutes into the timer. Her hypnotic eyes find mine. "In case we get distracted," she says.

I really like how this woman thinks. I step forward from behind her and place my hands on either side of the table, caging her in and trying to ignore how perfect her ass feels against my swelling dick as I gather her hair aside to expose the column of her neck. "I've been distracted all night," I confess, running my nose down the warm, smooth skin of her neck that tastes like the vanilla icing on the cookies I'm obsessed with from the store.

She leans back, her head landing on my shoulder. "Me too."

The way her breathing hitches makes me want to do terrible, sinful things to this woman. Instead, I make do with kissing right below her ear, where her perfume clings.

"This is a really bad idea," Jade breathes.

"The worst." My finger slips beneath the neck of her sweater to trace her collarbone. "You like bad ideas, Jade?" I know I sure do.

She's bathed in a dull-red glow, like even the room itself is warning us to stop, but stopping is the last thing on my mind. I need to know that Jade feels the same. That she understands what this means for both of us.

"Hayley warned me not to touch you." And yet here I am, touching her anyway. "Said she'd disown me if I do." Even if we only steal this one night together, the consequences may follow us into tomorrow. I'm willing to risk it, but is she? I don't want Jade to lose her best friend over me, but I also know I'm not strong enough to walk away on my own.

"Tell me you want me to touch you anyway," I continue, my breaths turning shallow.

Get lost or get lost in each other.

The choice is hers.

Jade bites her bottom lip as her fingertips trace the word "love" inked on my hand. I tell myself it's a coincidence; that my hand is right there by her thigh, so of course she's going to reach for it, but my heart still stutters when she lifts my fingers to her lips and presses a kiss to my knuckles. "I don't want to hurt Hayley, but this...tonight...is about you and me. No one else." Her eyes tilt up to meet mine, and her smile knocks the breath out of my lungs.

She lowers my hand between her thighs, and it is game fucking on.

My heart thunders against my ribs, ready to burst from my chest. I run my tongue along the sensitive skin where her neck meets her shoulder while working my thumb along the seam of her jeans, searching for—

She gasps and presses her ass into me.

Searching for *that*.

My other hand finds her breast, and the word "more" tattooed there has never been as accurate because that's what I'm desperate for: *More*.

I work my fingers in slow, steady circles, but her stiff jeans have got to go. Jade whimpers when I stop, but practically purrs in my ear when I reach for her waistband. With a pop and a zip, I peel those tight jeans down to her knees.

Her white silk and lace panties match the bra I already know she's wearing beneath her sweater. I plan on taking that off next until a patch of wetness at her center steals all my focus. She moans when I press my thumb against the damp silk, and her head tips back against my shoulder.

It's not enough. I still need more. And from the way

Jade's back arches, she looks like she needs more too. I draw her panties aside so I can see her pussy, bare and glistening, and drag my fingers through her slick folds to her clit. "Look at you. Fucking soaked." And I've barely touched her. "I can't wait to see what a mess we make together."

Her eyes are closed where her head rests on my shoulder, and that won't do at all. "Eyes open, baby. I want you to watch me touch you." To remember how I made her feel, even when I'm gone.

When her lashes flutter open, I slip a finger inside utter perfection. So tight and so fucking wet. Each stroke brings more of her weight against my body, like her legs are ready to give out.

I curl my finger and flick my thumb over her clit, eliciting another moan. "Like that?" I manage to breathe.

"Yes." She reaches back to grip me outside my jeans. My hips thrust into her palm on instinct.

She rides my hand, and I commit to memory what she likes, how hard her hips grind, so I'll know what to do when I'm fucking her. "My hand looks good down there, doesn't it, baby?"

"So good."

"You know what'd look even better?" She hums in response. "My tongue."

Jade's whimper is all the confirmation I need to withdraw my fingers, spin her around, and yank those jeans to the floor where they belong. I lift her up onto the table and drop to my knees. When I push her thighs further apart, there's no resistance, and she opens wide for me.

I glance up to make sure she wants this as much as I do, finding her fevered gaze glued to me and her teeth sinking into her bottom lip.

I don't know who I have to thank for this, but as soon as

my tongue swipes through her center, I'm thanking everyone. Jade for giving me a chance. My sister for being far, far away. That asshole who asked to see her tits because that shitty pickup line is what led us here. Hell, even Fuckhead Williams for screwing up so badly.

I tongue Jade's swollen clit, working hard and fast while telling my impatient dick to take a chill pill. I don't know if this one taste is all I'll get, but if it is, I'll be jerking off to this memory for years to come.

Jade's fingers tangle in my hair, dragging me harder against her until my tongue is buried so deep it may never escape. My name on her lips is the sweetest fucking sound I've ever heard, but the desperate, broken noise she makes when her pussy clenches around my tongue is a pretty close second.

I lap up every drop of her before standing on trembling legs and bracing my hands against the table on either side of Jade's still-spread thighs. When the timer at her back dings, she starts to giggle.

"Good thing you set that," I rasp. "I was *very* distracted."

I remove the photograph from the water tray and carefully hang it on the line, taking a few seconds to catch my breath, so my thrashing heart doesn't explode. Jade has other ideas because the moment our eyes meet, she's tugging my shirt over my head and clawing at the buttons on my jeans. "These come off. *Now*."

Far be it for me to disappoint. I drop my pants, but leave on my black boxer briefs to give her another chance to change her mind. When she reaches for the waistband, I step away.

I give the hem on her sweater a tug. "You first, greedy girl." With a smirk, she lifts her arms over her head. Up and off it comes, and I'm staring at Jade's tits for the second time tonight. The way her dusky nipples peek from behind the lace makes my mouth water. I slip a finger beneath the edge to tease the pebbled tip, my dick getting harder with each swipe.

One strap falls down, and I decide to help the other. With a twist and a flick of the clasp at the back, her bra falls away. I cup her in both palms before running my thumbs back and forth over her nipples, watching them grow harder in the red light.

Speaking of harder, my dick is like stone.

Jade slides off the table and traces the constellations on my ribs down to the swallow inked at the cut of my hip. What can I say? Not all my tattoos are winners.

She takes my hard length into her fist and says, "I knew you'd be huge."

I run my nose down the slender column of her throat to her collarbone. "Oh yeah? Been thinking a lot about my dick, huh? It's okay, my dick's been thinking about you too."

She laughs, spreading her legs wider to accommodate my hips. "Has it?"

"Those tight yoga pants you wear drive us both insane."

When she rubs my tip over her slick entrance, tension ratchets up my spine. "I need to get a—" *Fuck.* What's the word I'm looking for? A... a... *Come on, brain, you're better than this; I know you're starved of blood right now, but—* "condom."

"I'm clean," Jade whispers. "I got tested a few months ago and haven't been with anyone since."

She and Robocop didn't fuck? That makes me so happy I could sing, and I can't carry a fucking tune. I've also already shown her my test results...

Holy shit. I've never gone bareback with anyone. Are we really going to do this?

"Are you on birth control?" I ask.

"I have an IUD," she replies with a coy smile, her grip on me tightening as she eases the tip inside her body.

My hips punch forward, burying my dick to the hilt, and my eyes practically roll back in my head. *Fuck* she feels so fucking good. Jade gasps; her nails bite into my shoulders. I want to give her time to adjust, but my body has other ideas. I pull out slowly and then ease back inside. Her heels dig so hard into the base of my spine that it feels like I'm going to have a bruise.

"Harder," she whispers against my ear.

My body obliges Jade's every request. *Harder. Faster. More.* Losing myself a little more with each thrust.

I need to slow down.

I need to be everywhere at once.

I need *more*.

Our bodies collide over and over. Tension coils at the base of my spine.

Jade rakes her nails down my arms, and I seriously consider having the streaks she leaves behind tattooed so I'll never forget this moment.

"Yes, Dylan. Don't stop," she cries, head thrown back, red light highlighting her cheekbones.

I don't plan to.

I slip a hand between us to play with her clit, rubbing and flicking until she's coming apart in my arms.

My gaze moves between her desire-filled eyes and the way her tits bounce with every buck of my hips. When my balls start to tighten, I pull out at the last second and fist my dick, stroking fast as black spots invade my vision.

"Get on your knees and push your tits together."

Jade drops down with a smirk, cupping her tits and lifting them up like the most perfect offering. Two more strokes and I spill across her perky breasts, my cum dripping down the hardened peaks.

Holy shit.

That was…unexpected.

"Where's my camera?" I rasp, only half teasing.

"Don't even think about it," she laughs.

I tell her not to move and leave the darkroom to grab her a wet cloth from the bathroom. But when I catch my smiling reflection in the mirror above the sink, reality starts to set in. My heart begins to pound in my ears.

I just did the one thing I promised I wouldn't do.

I fucked my little sister's best friend.

And I really hope I get to do it again.

CHAPTER TWENTY-THREE

JADE

Grocery orders fill the laptop screen in front of me, but all I can see is his handsome face bathed in red light, his eyes foggy with desire, his teeth clamping down on his bottom lip as he slams hard into me.

Heat washes up my back, and I wrestle my attention back onto the first run of online orders that came in over the weekend. I should've come into the store yesterday evening and packed them all up, ready to deliver early this morning.

Except, last night, I completely lost my mind and had sex with my best friend's brother on his darkroom table before taking off right afterward like a freak.

What I'd *wanted* to do was wrap my arms around Dylan's still-trembling neck and ask him to take me into his bedroom so we could do it all over again. I'd wanted to fall asleep against his chest and wake up running my fingers over every swirl of ink on his body. I'd wanted to make pancakes that morning and smear maple syrup across his thoroughly kissed lips with the back of my spoon before licking it off.

But instead of doing any of that, I'd stamped a kiss to

Dylan's cheek and mumbled a useless excuse about having to go do stuff at the store.

"You're kidding, right?" Dylan says, looking deliciously disheveled and definitely confused.

"Afraid not. I have things to do before opening tomorrow. We've got the website running now, so we might have some orders."

"Jade." He reaches for my hand, still shirtless but back in his jeans.

I step backward. "It's all good. I probably should've mentioned earlier that I still had to drop into the store tonight."

"Can I help with whatever you've gotta do that's so urgent?"

"No, don't worry, it's late."

He looks at me for a long moment before saying, "If you shoot me a text when you're done, I'll give you a ride home."

"Okay. Thanks. I'll see you a bit later."

I hadn't texted Dylan.

I hadn't even gone into the store.

Instead, I'd done something that I hadn't done since I was eighteen.

I'd walked home. All three miles. Because the moment Dylan had tugged up his jeans and the hot lust burning through my body had cooled a touch, reality had slapped me hard in the face.

Hayley's warnings.

Nate's warnings.

Dylan's announcement that he's moving back to Austin after Christmas.

I'd escaped down the stairs of his apartment and hurried right past the store in the direction of home, unable to stop shivering. I'd gone and done the one thing I'd sworn I wouldn't. I'd let Dylan inside my body, inside my heart. I'm not a wham-bam-thank-you-ma'am kind of person. I don't do casual sex and darkroom hook-ups. When it comes to relationships, I dream about a long-term partner, and a couple of adorably messy kids, and a house in Still Springs with a white picket fence. But Dylan's made more than clear that he's not into girlfriends or long-term commitments. He looks for a different kind of happy ending to me.

I'd remembered all this the second he buttoned up his jeans, so fleeing his apartment was a defensive move. A preemptive strike. Because I couldn't have handled him asking if he could drop me home right after getting what he wanted. Or worse—inviting me to stay the night out of obligation so my feelings didn't get hurt. *No thanks.*

That's why I left, and now I feel like total shit. I can't even enjoy this small spike in business from our online orders, which I know we're lucky to have. Even with the new homewares and artworks I've been bringing in and the extra takings during Fall Fest, our sales are still at dismal levels.

With cement in my chest, I click on the first online order before my phone chimes from my purse. My mind shoots straight to Dylan, and I nearly spill the contents of my bag while trying to dig out the handset, but it's Ruby's name blinking on the screen.

"Hey," I say.

"Are you okay?" she asks right away. "You sound flat."

"I'm all right."

"No, you're not."

A deep breath drags between my lips. "Something happened last night."

"What something?"

I stare at the order on my screen, still seeing glimpses of

that darkroom...of a tattooed chest leaning over me, imprisoning me with mind-bending pleasure. Holding all of this in is starting to feel unbearable. "I went out for dinner with Hayley's brother. And then..."

"Oh, god."

"Not helping, Ruby."

She clears her throat. "Sorry. Go on."

It takes me a few breaths to admit the words aloud. "We slept together."

"Oh, Jade."

I can almost see Ruby clutching her brow. "I know. But I feel like we had to get it out of our system. You know he's been living next door, and there's an attraction there."

She sighs. "Does Hayley know?"

My breath stutters. "No." *God,* Dylan had brought Hayley up last night and given me an open invitation to shut things down between us before they escalated. I didn't want to do anything behind Hayley's back, but Dylan had been pressed up against me, all sexy smirk and ignited eyes, and I'd caved like a house of cards. I'd wanted him so badly that I lost all self-control.

"You haven't done anything wrong," Ruby says. "Hayley might not like it, but she'll come round." She inhales deeply. "I can't say I'm not a bit worried about some of the stuff I've heard about Dylan. But Flynn came with some pretty big red flags, and you always supported my feelings for him. So, if Dylan makes you happy, that's good enough for me."

I smile sadly. "Thanks, sis. But even without the Hayley stuff, he's going back to Austin soon, so this has to be a one-time thing."

"Okay. I just don't want you to get hurt."

A jab of pain pierces my chest. *Too late.* I've given Dylan a part of myself that I can never take back.

"So, how's Dad?" I ask, keen on a change of subject. Ruby had the day off work today, so she met Dad and my aunt in DC, where he's seeing one of the country's top spine specialists.

"That's actually why I'm calling. The clinic had a cancellation, so he's already seen the doctor."

My lips fall open. "And you let me ramble on about my stupid love life? What happened?"

The shift in Ruby's tone makes my stomach tense. "So much for hoping the doc would say it's not as bad as we thought. It's actually worse. Dad definitely needs the surgery, and it'll be a more complicated and longer recovery than we thought."

My palm flies to my chest. "Oh no. Where is he now?"

"He just went in for some more tests. He asked me to call and update you, but he'll ring you later. He's in good spirits, but I think we have to face facts that he's probably not going to be able to come back to work. So, we have to decide what to do about the store because you can't do it all on your own."

"Yes, I can."

"*Jade.*"

My gaze rakes over the orders I still need to package up and deliver today, the unpacked boxes stacked beside the storeroom door, the Sunday inventory sheet I haven't filled out yet, and the specials pricing tags that still need to be arranged. *Three breaths in, four breaths out.* "I'll figure it out. Just give me a bit of time."

We both turn silent before saying a reluctant goodbye, the conversation clearly left unfinished.

I wouldn't dream of asking Ruby to give up her new life

to move back here and work at the store again, which leaves only one option: We catch up on our overdue loan payments and begin making enough profit to hire a casual staff member. Until then, I need to knuckle down and get everything done on my own. While the online ordering system has added to the massive workload, it'll boost our revenue, so it's got to be a step in the right direction.

After Latisha comes in to buy a single loaf of bread and a carton of milk, I print out the four online orders and begin packing the groceries into empty boxes.

Just after eleven, Rosie Perandez calls, complaining that she hasn't received her order yet. I assure her it'll be there soon, estimating that I'll need to close the store for thirty minutes and hurriedly make the deliveries.

At twelve-thirty, the furnace that was fixed last week conks out again, and I spend twenty-five minutes on hold with the repair company while shoving the specials prices into their slots.

Ten minutes before one, Mrs. Horne wanders in with her Pomeranian circling her clicking cane. *Perfect.*

"Jade, I have wonderful news." Mrs. Horne's smile reveals a stripe of peach lipstick across her teeth. "I bid in something called an 'online auction' last night on an early nineteenth-century Danish clock. My young neighbor helped me with the computer part, but I managed it, and I made the winning bid! The longcase clock is mine and is being shipped to me as we speak."

"Wow, that's great." I offer her a genuinely proud smile, but on the inside, my brain is screaming.

I don't have time for this, Mrs. Horne.

I don't have time to get these orders packed and delivered on schedule.

I don't have time to put out the rest of the special tags and unpack the new stock.

I don't have time to figure out how to meet our overdue loan payments.

I don't even have time to go to the damn bathroom.

Mrs. Horne beams until the sides of her eyes sport more lines than a map. "Did I ever tell you why I love grandfather clocks so much, Jade?"

Just say yes. I suck in a bracing breath of air. "I don't think you did."

"Well, of course, they are remarkable machines. Not only mesmerizing in design, but they are exceedingly accurate timepieces. My mother had a clock in every room of the house. She had a terrible sense of time, and she needed them to avoid being late for things." A tinge of sorrow enters her cloudy-blue eyes. "They remind me of her, you see. The clocks. Every tick is like her heartbeat; every chime, the sweet tinkle of her laugh."

I blink back at Mrs. Horne, stunned into silence. I knew she was lonely, but I hadn't realized any of that might have to do with her missing her own mother. Especially someone of her age.

What, Jade? You thought that one day you'd get old enough that you'd forget your mom existed? That you'd stop waiting for her to be the one to walk into the store whenever the bell jingles, ready to wrap you in a ticklish hug that smells like peppermint tea?

A burning feeling builds behind my eyes. "Mrs. Horne, that's...that's really beautiful."

Her wrinkled lips curl up. "Thank you. It's rather silly once I hear myself say it. My mother was certainly no clock —quite the opposite."

I swallow the lump in my throat. "Do you think Minnie

would like some water?" I dart a glance at the little dog who's stretched out on the floor, panting.

"Oh yes, please."

I push off the counter and fetch a bowl of water. Minnie laps up a few gulps before Mrs. Horne leads her out the front door without—you guessed it—buying a thing.

After I return the bowl to the kitchenette, I sit on my stool and gaze up at the framed photo of Mom and Dad until their faces turn blurry.

A minute later, I'm wiping my eyes when Mrs. Perandez calls again about her order. I apologize before hanging a "Closed" sign in the window and dashing down the street to my car. I drive it up to the front of the store and nearly throw my back out while hefting delivery boxes into the trunk. They don't all fit, so I end up making two trips from the store to make the four deliveries.

When I get back, the store's been shut for more than an hour, and I curse the possibility of having missed customers. I'll have to come up with a better system for fulfilling orders outside of opening hours because, right now, we can't afford to pay a delivery driver.

I still need to put out the new stock that was delivered this morning, but I'm exhausted and starving, so I snatch a bread roll out of the bakery bin and scarf it down before slumping over the counter with my face in my arms. *Just a teeny-tiny sleep. Two minutes, tops.*

I sink into the bliss of silence before the front door blasts open, the bell clanging loudly.

I jerk up on my stool to find a chubby, four-year-old face blinking up at me. My eyes flash wide and dart to Dylan, who's hovering a few feet behind his niece in a black T-shirt and gray jeans. My stomach fizzes wildly. *He looks too good.*

"Sorry, hi," I blurt awkwardly, rubbing my eyes. "I think I fell asleep."

Dylan's lips tilt up, but the usual brightness in his eyes has vanished. "Ella said she saw you carrying boxes through the window. We thought we could come and help after lunch."

"I can make a BIG castle with the boxes," Ella says with her arms stretched wide, glittery pink bangles jangling from her tiny wrists.

"Well, that would be *very* helpful," I reply, getting off my stool and rounding the counter so I can crouch to her eye level. "But don't you have something more fun you want to do?"

She shakes her head, her pigtails bouncing. "I want to work at a shop."

"You do? Well, that *is* a very important job." I can feel Dylan's eyes on me, so I stifle my awkwardness over last night by standing up and blurting an icebreaker.

"And what can I get you?" I ask him. "Sorry, we're fresh out of walking sticks and incontinence pads."

One side of his mouth quirks up. "Bad jokes are still in stock, though, I see."

"Oh yeah, you can always get those in here."

A low laugh hums in his throat, but there's still no mirth in his eyes. "Delivery day?" He upnods at the giant stack of cardboard sitting beside the counter.

"Just some new stock that arrived this morning."

His gaze returns to mine. "Do you normally just put it out on the shelves?"

"Yeah, but I haven't had time yet." A yawn rises in my throat, and I cover it with my hand.

Dylan's gaze trails over my face before he drops down to one knee in front of Ella. "You wanna put the new things away with me, monster? We can count how many things we each put on the shelf, and whoever gets the highest number wins. But we have to make sure everything goes in the right spot."

She nods hard. "Yes! I'm gonna win! I'm gonna beat you, Uncle Pickle!"

Dylan offers me a tight-lipped smile as he gets up and guides Ella over to the boxes. He flips open the top one, and they carefully begin unpacking cartons of herbal tea like employees.

What is happening right now? It's not like I don't appreciate the help, but why is he here?

The three elderly men who play bridge at The Rocking Horse shuffle through the door, so I turn my attention to them while Dylan and Ella shift around in the aisles, murmuring to each other. When I overhear Dylan telling Ella that she's up to number twenty-two and he's still stuck on twelve, a smile hits my cheeks that I can't help.

When I step into aisle two to put away a hot sauce that one of the old guys left on the counter, my gaze collides with Dylan's. He tenses up, glancing away. At some point between now and last night, flirty, smirky, sexy Dylan has been replaced with someone much more serious-faced and guarded. Dread filters into my stomach at the thought that it's because we had sex and now he doesn't want to know me. But he's here, helping in the store for reasons I don't understand. Is he ticked off because I said I'd let him give me a ride home last night, then ghosted him?

The second that thought arrives in my mind, it refuses to leave. What I did was for self-preservation, but it was also rude. I know that. I should at least apologize...maybe try to explain.

When I spot Ella kneeling at the far end of the aisle,

slowly and carefully setting pastel-colored boxes of herbal tea onto the empty shelf, I seize my chance.

I walk up to Dylan, who's putting out jars of coffee, speaking under my breath. "Can I talk to you?"

He continues to stare at the shelf. "Sure. You want to text me, or..."

Okay, I deserved that.

I take hold of his arm and gently tug him out of Ella's earshot, although we can still see her. I move in front of Dylan so his gaze falls on mine.

I inhale a deep breath. "I wanted to say something about last night."

A line appears across his brow.

"I'm sorry I left so quickly. And I'm sorry I didn't text you to take me home."

My heart thumps harder as his eyes search mine. "Did you sleep here? Or did you call your buddy Nate?"

"Nate? Of course not. No, I walked home."

His jaw pulses. "You *walked*?"

"I felt like some air."

A look of hurt eclipses his face. "So, you decided it was better to walk home late at night, which isn't fucking safe, rather than torture yourself with a few more minutes of my company."

"Dylan." My brow scrunches. "Don't be like that. I really did have stuff to do at the store, and I was planning to text you, but then..." I swallow hard.

"Then what? You decided that what we did was a mistake? That it wasn't fun after all?"

My heart picks up its pace as I gaze up at him, wishing he meant that the way it almost sounded. But that word he used...

"Of course it was fun," I say. "But that's the problem. That's what this is to you: *Fun*."

His brows lift. "Since when is fun a bad thing?"

"It's bad if we've done something behind Hayley's back—totally ignored her wishes—if it's for no more than a bit of fun."

"You know what? I think it's time you stop using Hayley as an excuse." He paces right up to me, his breath hot and trembling against my face. I don't feel like pushing him away. I feel like grabbing his shirt and yanking his mouth to mine, but I resist. "You and I are adults," Dylan says, staring into my eyes. "We can do whatever the hell we want. And Hayley might not like it, but she'll get over it."

"Get over *what*?" I find myself whispering. "A bit of fun? Because that's not enough for me." I hate how needy I sound, but it's exactly what I am right now. I need to know if I'm just another name on Dylan King's long list of conquests. I didn't expect him to want even a second kiss from me, let alone this. It makes no sense.

His hand falls to my waist, his fingers clutching the slip of bare skin beneath my shirt as he brings his lips to my ear. "I'm going to forgive you for making me feel like total shit when you left me last night. I'm going to forgive you for making me wait up way too late for your text that never fucking came. I'm going to forgive you for making me think about you right until I fell asleep and the second I woke up." His fingers tighten around me. "I'm going to forgive you for making me want you *so fucking bad* when I feel like you're already done with me. I'm going to forgive you for all that because I know why you did it." He swallows hard, his Adam's apple bobbing. "You're doing what everyone else does and assuming the worst of me."

I bring my arms around his back, dragging him so close

that his thighs brush against mine and his nose grazes over my ear. "I'm sorry," I say, breathing him in. "That's not true. I don't think the worst of you."

He turns his face into the side of my neck. "Yeah, you do. But that's okay because, to tell you the truth, I think I am the worst man for you."

CHAPTER TWENTY-FOUR

DYLAN

"And then she just left," I say to my therapist. "Can you believe that?"

I had some of the hottest sex of my life with Jade, made her come twice, and she still walked out like it was nothing. Makes no fucking sense. Had she not wanted more? I sure as hell had. I'd wanted her to hang out afterward so we could talk, sleep nestled together in my bed, and then wake up next to me. Hell, I'd even wanted to have breakfast with the woman. Dangerous thoughts, I know. That's why I called Sarah first thing the next day. Unfortunately, she didn't answer.

Thank god she called me back this morning.

She taps her manicured nails against her knee as she blinks at me from the other side of the camera. "Did Jade say why she left?"

I sit back in my chair and run her through our conversation at the store for what feels like the millionth time.

"That's what this is to you... fun."
"...that's not enough for me."
"What is this?"

"She thinks I'm only interested in her for a bit of fun."

Sarah's glasses slip down the bridge of her nose until she pushes them back to where they belong. "Is she right?"

Good question. I rub a hand down the back of my neck. "I don't know."

Part of me wishes Jade and I had never reconnected, and that she'd go back to being the little blonde kid who used to tag along with my baby sister.

The other part of me stares out the window that looks over Main Street when I should be editing photos, hoping for a glimpse of Jade. That part also keeps checking my phone for a text and wonders if it would be psychotic to dump all my cleaning products down the sink so that I have an excuse to buy a fresh lot from the store next door.

"Do you think that's something you should figure out?" Sarah asks.

Probably. But I don't know where to start. Women have come and gone, and I've always been happy to see them go. This time, though, I'm not so sure that's the case.

"It sounds like Jade is looking for more," Sarah continues. "If you aren't willing to give her what she needs, you need to let her find someone who will."

Someone like Officer Shithead.

My teeth clench so hard that my jaw aches.

When Jade didn't text me after she left, I nearly lost my mind thinking something had happened to her. And yeah, I may have gone downstairs to check the store like a stalker. She didn't answer when I knocked, and I considered texting to make sure she was okay, but I stopped myself because it felt an awful lot like she was avoiding me. Then I started wondering if she'd called Deputy Douchebag for a ride home. The thought of Jade going back to him after she's been with me makes me madder than the stack of tickets, the bag of shit, and every single judgmental asshole in this town combined.

My gaze makes its way to the darkroom door as I rub idly at my healing hands.

If it's not Nate Williams, it'll be someone else. Apart from my family, Jade is the only good thing in Still Springs, and I'm hardly the only one who's noticed. I saw those guys at the bar checking her out a few weeks back. It's only a matter of time before she's with someone else. Someone *nice*.

Too bad I'm not looking for a girlfriend. God, could you imagine me and Jade strolling around Main Street, holding hands? Actually...that doesn't sound half bad. I'd treat her a lot better than Officer Shithead did.

What am I thinking?

I don't want to go down that road again. And Jade couldn't get away fast enough, so I'm pretty sure she's done with me.

Sarah pushes up the sleeve of her sweater to check her gold watch. "Looks like we're almost out of time. I have an opening on Friday at four. Do you want me to pop in your name?"

"Sure." That gives me a few days to figure some things out.

We say goodbye and end the call. I open my laptop, determined to get a bit of work done before Ella arrives, but I end up staring at the Lightroom icon, thinking about my neighbor instead.

I think about the dark circles beneath her eyes when I saw her yesterday and the paleness of her cheeks. The fact that she fell asleep sitting at the register.

Jade is the only one working at that store. I can't imagine how exhausting it must be to put in such long hours without help, and keeping a place like that going doesn't end when the sign on the door says "Closed."

As hurt as I was about her leaving the other night, I still had to make sure she was all right and that she wasn't heading for another panic attack. And if that's not telling, I don't know what is. Normally, I'd be relieved to not have to deal with a woman being clingy, but I would've happily let Jade cling to me like a fucking leech if she wanted.

A heavy knock reverberates from downstairs. I close my laptop and bound down the stairs only to find no one waiting outside.

My smile falters as I search the ground for suspicious brown paper bags. Nothing. I'm about to close the door when Ella and Iris leap out from behind the large blue mailbox on the sidewalk.

"Surprise!" my niece shouts. The blood-red lipstick smeared around her mouth has smudged onto her teeth, making her look like a tiny, deranged vampire. "Did we scare you, Uncle Pickle?" she asks.

I deadpan, "So much. I think I peed my pants."

That makes her giggle and check to see if I'm lying or not.

Iris throws her eyes to the heavens before heaving a bedazzled wheelie bag of god-knows-what from the car. Ella snaps open the handle and drags it along the sidewalk, away from my apartment.

"Where are you headed, Joker? My place is this way."

"I wanna go scare Jade."

My gaze flits to the "Open" sign hanging in the Quinn Brother's front door. Strange. They aren't supposed to open for another twenty-five minutes.

Ignoring the way Iris's brows lift, I open my door wider and motion Ella inside. "Not today, kiddo."

I still need to figure out what I'm going to say to Jade the next time we meet. I haven't seen her since Ella interrupted our hug and demanded to be let into it. And since my niece's bladder is the size of a penny, she'd announced that she had to pee, so we left without getting to finish stocking the shelves.

Should I play it cool and pretend like nothing happened? That doesn't feel right, but maybe it's for the best. If Jade already regrets being with me, the worst thing I can do is bring it up again. Unless *she* wants to bring it up. Then that's another story.

Although Ella doesn't look happy about my plans, she steers her bag over to me and leaves it on the stoop. I nearly throw my back out when I lift the damn thing. What's she got in here? A bunch of rocks? Wouldn't put it past her. That kid has a thing for gravel.

Up in my apartment, Iris drops onto one of the kitchen chairs with a heavy sigh while Ella flops on the floor right in front of the couch and unzips her bag. Holy shit, that's a lot of makeup. I have a feeling I'm going to look like a painted lady by noon.

"Coffee?" I ask my sister.

Her ponytail swings when she shakes her head. "Just water, thanks."

I grab a glass from the cupboard and fill it from the fridge. When I set the glass down, she immediately brings it to her face and presses it to her cheek. "You okay, sis?"

Her eyes sink shut. "I'm fine. Just a little queasy."

Ella lines up lipsticks and nail polishes in a rainbow of colors along the edge of the coffee table. "What are we gonna do today?" she asks.

"You tell me."

The doll she withdraws from her bag looks like something out of a horror movie. Jade loves horror movies. Halloween is this coming weekend. I wonder if she'll dress as something sexy or scary? Does she have any plans for Halloween night?

I shove those thoughts aside. We aren't a thing, and we never can be.

Seriously, though. Ella's doll is only a head and shoulders and...hands? What the fuck? The blonde hair is half chopped, there's only one eye, and someone—or something—has chewed on the fingers of its right hand. It's the stuff of nightmares that makes me think of that island Jade told me about. The one with the possessed dolls. This thing belongs there.

Ella's face lights up. "Let's help Jade at the store again!"

Iris chokes on her water. Probably should've mentioned that I helped a competitor yesterday. *Whoops*.

"Uncle Pickle?" Ella grabs a tube of lipstick and begins smearing it in circles over the doll's cheeks. "Is Jade your girlfriend?"

A nervous tremor tenses my stomach. "No, monster, we're just friends."

Iris is silent for way too long. I can almost hear the gears in her mind turning as she taps her fingernail against the glass. "Have you talked to your *friend* about Quinn Brothers?" she eventually asks. "Is she interested in selling?"

My brow lines. "That's something you'll have to ask Jade."

Iris's lips lift into a slow smile. "Maybe I'll ask Hayley instead. You know, since they're *best friends*."

Man, she's vicious today. She looks like she wants to say more, but then her eyes widen, and she clutches the strap on her purse still slung over her arm. "Can I use your bathroom?"

"No, I'm going to make you pee on the street."

"I saw a dog pee on a street before," Ella chimes in, now terrorizing the doll with sky-blue eyeshadow.

Iris rolls her eyes but doesn't wait for my permission. The bathroom door slams shut, and I nearly sink onto the ground with relief. That is until she opens the door a few minutes later and I catch the tears in her eyes.

When I ask what's wrong, she glances over at Ella before turning back to me and whispering, "I'm pregnant."

My lips fall open. That explains the mood swings today. Wow. Baby number two. I didn't even realize that Iris and Justin were trying. "Congrats. That's great." When Iris nods but doesn't smile, I add, "Right?"

Her voice breaks. "This baby won't know Mom or Dad. Even Ella is going to forget them."

My chest twists. Fuck. She's right. This kid won't know Mom's infectious laugh or Dad's terrible jokes. We won't have any pictures of them holding the new baby at the hospital or videos of them singing off-key at the first birthday party. That's the trouble with losing someone you love. No matter how much you strive to keep their memory alive, those memories in your head aren't transferable. You can tell all the stories you want, but it'll never be the same as them being here.

I wrap my arms around my sister, my own eyes burning with tears when she buries her head in my shoulder. "We won't forget," I promise.

"Yeah, but you won't be around."

She's right. I'm leaving after Christmas, and I have no plans to come back. But I'll have to, won't I? Iris doesn't like to fly, and with two kids and Justin's crazy work schedule, she won't have much time to come visit in Austin.

For a moment, I let myself consider alternative options.

Consider...staying.

I could get a bigger place here that would be a hell of a lot cheaper than my condo in Austin. I could help Iris with Ella and the new baby if she's stuck. Traveling for shoots wouldn't be that hard. I could see Jade...and the prick she ends up with. Somebody nice and respectable. An accountant or a bank manager, or a guy named Steve who works at the DMV.

Maybe I don't want to stay.

Iris's shaky breath fans against my cheek as she pulls away and smooths a hand down her stomach. "I need to get to work. Don't tell anyone, okay? We're keeping it in the family until I get through the first trimester."

"Yeah, no problem. Congratulations, sis."

She gives me a tearful smile and a wobbly "Thanks" before leaving me alone with a little monster, a possessed doll, and a lot of thinking left to do.

Ella keeps picking up bottles of nail polish, frowning, and putting them back, only to choose a different color. My legs are going numb from the way I'm sitting cross-legged beside her on the rug, but I'm afraid to move in case she remembers she has other makeup. I'm cool with the polish she smeared on my nails, but I don't think I can pull off lipstick.

Ella lets out a frustrated groan. "None of these go with her dress."

I don't point out that the doll I've "lovingly" named Lady-Fingers isn't wearing a dress. "What color do you need?"

She purses her lips as she fastens yet another barrette

into the doll's hair. I already have two in my hair as well, but it's kind of nice having the front strands out of my eyes.

"I need green," she says.

If I had a car, I'd suggest running to Kings, but since I don't... "Want to see if Jade has any green?"

Ella is up and at the door before I can haul myself to my feet. Her tutu bounces up and down as she dances with excitement. My stomach buzzes with nerves the whole way to the store and doesn't stop until the bell above the door chimes and Jade glances up. Our gazes connect, and my breath stalls in my lungs.

God, she's beautiful.

"Hi, Jade!" Ella waves with both her hands. "Do you have nail polish?"

"Sure do. Aisle four."

"Hey! *I'm* four!" Ella announces before disappearing without another word.

When Jade's gaze drops to my fingers, her smile blooms. "Nice nails."

I hold up both hands for her to admire. "Thanks. My stylist says they bring out my eyes." Not sure what that means since they're hot-pink and sparkly. Jade's smile widens, and I find it hard to tear my eyes away.

Her brows lift. "And the barrettes?"

Shit. I forgot about the damn barrettes. I swipe them out of my hair and stuff them into my pocket.

"Uncle Pickle! Jade has green!" Ella calls from the aisle.

"Grab it quick before someone comes in and takes it," I shout back.

Jade leans forward on her stool and braces her elbows against the counter. "Okay, I've been dying to ask: Why does she call you Uncle Pickle?"

My cheeks heat, and I briefly consider making up some

story to save myself the embarrassment of the truth, but then I get a better idea. "I'll tell you if you answer something for me first."

Her brow pinches. "What's that?"

"Yesterday, you asked me what *this* is." I gesture between us. "I want to know what *you* think it is."

She freezes, her eyes widening and her cheeks flushing red. Then, she pushes upright and splays her hands on the countertop. Her shoulders rise and fall with a heavy sigh. "If you want the truth, Dylan, I think I'm just another notch on your bedpost."

I feel my face tighten. Well, isn't that a kick to the groin? No wonder she ran away.

Ella pops her head out to ask if she can buy some candy. I tell her to get whatever she wants, even though Iris is going to kill me for it later. Once Ella disappears, I turn back to Jade and swipe my clammy hands down my jeans. "And if I say you're not?"

Her head tilts. "I'm not sure I'd believe you."

After what she's probably heard from Hayley, I'm not sure I blame her. "Let's say, for argument's sake, you did believe me. What would happen then?"

She purses her lips as she considers. "*If* I believed you, I would be waiting for you to ask me out again, which you would do right away because you couldn't wait another minute."

I do want to ask Jade out again. And not just to hook up. Don't get me wrong, I'd gladly fuck her sideways again if given the chance, but I also wouldn't mind bringing her to dinner and a movie or for a night away to my family's cabin down at the springs.

I open my mouth to tell her as much, when Jade blurts, "Now you have to tell me about Uncle Pickle."

I guess that's the end of that conversation.

"When Iris was little, she used to call me 'Dyl'. Like, dill pickle. And since I was the only boy in a house of girls..." I can't believe I'm about to say this out loud to the girl I'm trying to impress. "They thought I had a pickle between my legs." I've tried telling my sisters not to call me that, but they overruled me like usual. Now I will forever be known as "Uncle Pickle."

Although Jade laughs, her eyes seem sad. "That's the best story I've heard all day."

"And I expect you to take it to the grave."

Ella skids around the corner with her arms stuffed with candy, nail polish, and a plunger. I'm too scared to ask about the last thing, so I keep my questions to myself and drag out my wallet while Jade rings the items into the register. With our random assortment tucked into a Quinn Brothers bag, we thank Jade and head out onto the street.

Ella gives my hand a squeeze. "I like her lots."

A harsh fall breeze slaps my cheeks. "So do I, monster."

That's why I drag out my phone and type out a text.

> I can't wait another minute. Go out with me again?

I watch through the window as Jade picks up her phone from the counter. Her eyes widen and then her lips lift into the most breathtaking smile as her thumbs fly across the screen. My phone buzzes, and my heart leaps when I read her reply.

> PINK PANTHER
> When?

CHAPTER TWENTY-FIVE

JADE

Tiny, spooky characters jockey for position in the store's entryway, pushing and elbowing to get to the bowls of trick-or-treat candy I've set out on the counter.

"All right, one at a time there, Dracula," I tell a tiny vampire with blood dripping from his lips and a fistful of chocolate bars poking through his chubby fingers. A mini Wednesday Addams shoulder-checks him out of the way. "Careful, Wednesday," I add with a smile. The girl's mom leads her outside with an apologetic head-shake.

The Burner triplets bust through the door, looking adorable and definitely squeezable in ketchup, mustard, and relish costumes. They frantically gouge through the candy, spilling half of it all over the floor.

When I crouch to pick up the treats, my ridiculously short skirt rides up, and I give it a sharp tug back down. After telling Dylan about the Island of the Dolls in Mexico, I'd decided to order a creepy doll costume for Halloween, which looked deliciously ghoulish on the website. But when the package arrived, out fell a blue gingham dress with a three-inch wind-up key poking from the back, thigh-high white stockings with frilled edges, and two blue hair bows. Before setting up the shop tonight for trick-or-treaters, I'd ripped a few tears in the stockings and smeared some dirt down the front of the dress, trying to make myself less cutesy and more freaky. I'd then painted my face with doll makeup and weaved two braids in my hair, clipping the bows to the ends.

"You look great, Jade," Mrs. Burner says with a smile before wrangling her wriggly condiments out the door. My eyes trail after her, searching for a face I haven't caught sight of yet. I have no idea what kind of costume a guy like Dylan would wear to Halloween. He seems low-key enough to throw on a long-haired wig and label himself a rock star, tatts already included. Or maybe he's more the obscure pop culture type who'd turn up as a random album cover character that no one's heard of.

The list of possibilities grows in my head as I greet each teeny terror that comes through the door until a tall witch with long green hair makes me do a double-take.

"Hey, Iris," I say with a grin, my stomach swooping when Dylan steps in behind her with Ella.

Ohhh... oh my. My gaze tears down and up his black SWAT uniform that hugs his arms and legs in all the right places. His hands are covered with fingerless black gloves, and a pair of dark sunglasses sits up on his head, pushing back his messy hair. He looks lethal, all right. Lethally *hot*.

"Wow," Dylan murmurs as his eyes move over me the same way.

"I'm supposed to be a creepy doll," I explain. "But it's a bit more Dorothy from *The Wizard of Oz*. You know, if Dorothy had an OnlyFans."

His throaty chuckle reaches right into my stomach, but

Ella snags my attention when she leaps forward, her Little Red Riding Hood cloak bouncing off her pigtails.

I step past the counter and crouch to her eye level. "I'm sorry, Red Riding Hood, I don't have any cake today for Grandma."

Her eyes grow wide. "The wolf ate Grandma."

My hand flies to my chest. "That's terrible. I'm so sorry."

"She tasted like bones and blood."

I can't help but laugh, relieved when Iris and Dylan join in.

"Come on, monster," Dylan says, laying a hand on his niece's shoulder. "You better get some candy before that Piglet we saw back there catches up. Pigs are notorious greedy guts."

Ella hurriedly fills the remaining space in her little woven basket while Dylan returns his gaze to me. "I'll see you at The Rocking Horse later?" he confirms under his breath while Iris leads Ella outside.

"Yes, Officer," I reply, and something alights in his eyes.

He quickly steps forward to take hold of my elbow. "Don't do that to me," he whispers. "Especially in *that* outfit."

I have to take a deep breath so I don't overheat. As he weaves his way out past the line-up of kids, I tilt sideways to fully appreciate how good his ass looks in those black pants.

"BOO!" shouts a croaky voice that nearly sends me out of my skin.

I stare down at the three-foot ghost blinking up at me, his plastic pumpkin bucket overflowing with candy. "Okay, Casper. You better make some room in there for the good stuff."

An hour later, I've closed up the store, and I'm making my way to The Rocking Horse with goosebumps on my arms from the chill and nerves churning up my stomach.

When I step inside the bar adorned with cobwebs, skeletons, and bats, the song "Disturbia" by Rihanna floods my ears. Same as every year, the place is packed with locals in freaky fancy dress, hoping to take home the "best costume" award and a free case of beer. I weave through the crowd, hunting for my date. Just thinking about him sends a pang of want to my stomach that's stronger than any I've ever felt.

I'm really not sure what to do about it.

I've always felt certain about most things in life, but when it comes to Dylan King, I feel like I'm sailing through uncharted waters. I don't know if I'm going to stumble upon an island paradise or sink to the bottom of the ocean.

"Jade?"

I spin around to find Nate squinting at my face like he can't quite figure out if it's really me. *Oh, come on, man, I'm not that unrecognizable.*

"How'd you guess?" I deadpan.

"I think it's the hair," he replies seriously. Nate's dressed as a pirate in what I'm pretty sure is the exact same costume he wore last year.

"So, you're Dorothy?" he guesses, lifting his beer bottle to his lips.

I make a wrong-answer buzzer sound. "I'm a creepy doll." I twist my back to him so he can see the key.

A young guy dressed as a skeleton bumps my shoulder when he stumbles past, balancing three beers. He apologizes and continues on, and Nate shakes his head after him. "It's not even nine, and the village idiots are already half-tanked. Did that guy look twenty-one to you? They better be checking IDs at the bar." He frowns at the bartenders.

"I'm sure they are. Especially with the deputy sheriff here."

Nate's cheeks open into a smile like I just gave him the biggest compliment of his life.

"Anyway, speaking of the bar," I mumble, "I'm gonna go get a drink."

"I'll get it," he cuts in, stepping forward. "What are you having? A champagne for the lady?"

A large hand flattens over my upper back, and I instinctively turn into the firm body that steps close behind me. "Hi," Dylan says near my ear, smelling like that lush soap he uses and sending a warm shiver of goosebumps across my neck.

"Oh, man, seriously?" Nate scoffs. "You came as *me*?"

Dylan laughs out loud. "Bit of a difference between a special tactical unit and a small town sheriff. Oops, my bad. I meant to say *deputy* sheriff."

Nate grits out an angry sound, and I step between them before real blood is spilled on Halloween.

I look up at Dylan through my false doll lashes. "Should we go get drinks?"

"Yeah, Nate needs to catch up with all his friends." He waves an arm at the empty space around the pirate, whose brows bunch tightly together.

I can't help but feel bad for Nate, but then I remind myself how much of a douche he's been to me with his quick temper and acid tongue. If he was nicer to be around, maybe we could've been friends. I force my focus back on my date, who leads me toward the bar with a protective hand fused to my back.

I rest my elbows against the bar and run my eyes over Dylan's sexy uniform while he orders us two Bloody Mary cocktails. His feet are encased with thick black boots and a baton swings from the belt of his padded vest.

Standing on my toes, I bring my lips close to his ear. "Is that a baton in your pocket, Officer, or are you just happy to see me?"

He turns his head, his electric-blue eyes locking on mine. "Oh, I'm very happy to see you." He leans closer as my cheeks flush warm. "Are we doing bad pick-up lines again? Because I've got one." He runs his gaze down the length of me, lowering his voice. "Hey, baby-doll. You gonna let me play with you?" Heat licks up my spine at the hunger in his gaze.

While the bartender pours our cocktails, Dylan's fingers fold around the key that's poking from my back. "Is this how I turn you on?" he asks with a gleam in his eye. He gives the key a little tug, using it to maneuver me even closer to him. "Yeah, I think we could play some interesting games with this."

The bartender pushes the two cocktails toward us in the nick of time. My burning attraction to Dylan—especially in that thirst trap of a uniform—almost has me sweating, but I don't want tonight to be only about that. And he may have had a similar thought because he puts a little distance between us and carries our cocktails over to a pair of empty stools beside the jukebox.

"Do they still do that 'best costume' competition here?" he asks as I settle beside him.

"Oh, yeah. Who do you think is gonna take home the blue ribbon tonight?"

"The sexy doll."

I smile at him over the rim of my glass. "*Creepy* doll."

He gives me a contrary smile and sweeps his gaze over the room. "That guy has a good chance." He tips his glass at the man wearing a business suit suspended high over his shoulders so it looks like he's clutching his own head. "Or Nate Williams," Dylan adds with a straight face. "I mean, being a pirate on Halloween is so fucking original. How did he even get the idea—it's so left field."

I knock my knee against his, smiling. "Don't be an asshole."

His eyes expand. "Now, *that* would've been the perfect outfit for him. A giant asshole. He wouldn't even have to bother with a costume."

I cackle into my drink. I really don't want to talk about Nate, so I shoot for a subject change. "All right, what's your favorite horror movie?"

He blows through his lips. "I feel like I have to get this right because you're alarmingly obsessed with creepy shit. I can't say something lame like *Scream 4*."

My lips turn up. "You can say whatever you want."

He thinks. "*Jaws*."

"*Jaws* isn't a horror movie."

"It's about a man-eating shark who swallows a little kid playing at the beach. I was pretty fucking horrified when I first saw it."

"It's actually a thriller. Try again."

"Fine, *The Shining*. I sneaked downstairs once when Dad was watching it, and it freaked me the hell out when that psycho said: 'Johnny's here!'"

He's too adorable, but I have to laugh. "Um, the line's actually, 'Here's Johnny!'"

Confusion clouds Dylan's eyes. "You sure?"

I can't stop smiling or staring at him as I nod.

"So, what's your favorite horror movie?" he asks.

"I'd have to say the original *Texas Chainsaw Massacre*. It's disturbing as hell, so obviously, I adore it."

He shakes his head but can't seem to pull his eyes off me. "Biggest fear?"

"Ooh, tough one." Losing what's left of my family would rank number one, and a fear of failure is something I've always struggled with, but those topics seem a bit heavy, so I go with "Confined spaces. Being buried alive would be my worst nightmare. And you?"

"Clowns. I just saw Pennywise walk in, and now I might have to cut and run."

I turn and catch a glimpse of the famous clown character with wild red hair lining up at the bar on the other side of the room.

I twist back to Dylan and grin. "Note to self: Dress as a clown next year for Halloween."

"Not if I'm your date," he retorts with a smirk.

A wave of nerves hits me over the fact that we both just referenced being here in twelve months—together. I swallow tightly, and Dylan clears his throat.

"Halloween-themed tattoo that you would get," he says, introducing a new question to the mix.

"Hmm. Something like this one. I noticed it in your darkroom."

I lean so close that our legs press together and lay my palm over his inner thigh, where I spotted a cool tattoo of a skull and roses while he was pounding into me. He widens his legs a touch, and my breath catches in my throat.

"Yeah, you liked that, did you?" he says, my fingers slipping a little closer to something that definitely isn't a tattoo.

My heart pounds faster as Dylan's eyes roam over my

face, hovering on my lips, before his gaze flickers to something behind me. "Oh, fuck no."

I twist to see the Pennywise clown heading straight for us like a scene from a horror movie, its plastic mask frozen into a toothy smile as it sidesteps people drinking and dancing.

I know that Dylan's not actually afraid of this five-foot-eight person in a clown costume, but he grabs my waist and pulls me onto his lap with my back facing him, my doll-key pressing against his abdomen. I squeal and shift my legs sideways across his thick thighs, his arms folding around my front as he turns his nose into my neck.

"Way to distract me from my fear. This dress should be illegal," he says roughly, slipping one hand beneath the side of my skirt and running it high up my thigh. His fingertips graze the edge of my panties, and a needy sigh slips out of me. I lock my hooded gaze on Pennywise, who's now stopped still and is staring right at us. *Okay, I admit, that clown is creepy.*

I lean into Dylan's shoulder, the protruding key making my back arch. "I think Pennywise likes to watch."

I can feel Dylan's smoky gaze looking down over my shoulder at the tight swells of my breasts straining against my dress. "Let's give him a show then," he says, clutching my jaw and steering my face to his.

His warm mouth lands on mine, and my lips part instantly, welcoming his tongue as it sweeps into my mouth. I'm not usually an exhibitionist, but it feels kinda hot having this costumed stranger watch us make out with a helpless urgency like we've been craving this. Dylan's palms grip my face as I twist toward him, seeking more of his intoxicating taste. A moan wells up in his throat, and I swallow it down. "You taste so good, baby," he breaths against my lips.

"Oh my god, are you fucking *serious*?" cries a familiar voice.

Dylan and I gasp in unison and jerk apart as the clown rips the mask off its head.

Hayley stands gaping at us, her eyes wide with horror.

CHAPTER TWENTY-SIX

DYLAN

It's a good thing the "Monster Mash" is blaring through the speakers, otherwise everyone in this bar would be staring instead of just the painted faces closest to us. "Hayley, you need to calm down," I warn under my breath so that only she can hear.

From the way her chin jerks back, you'd swear I slapped her. "Don't you dare tell me to calm down."

Okay, shrieking banshee is not a good look on my baby sister. "You're causing a scene." And that's saying a lot, considering there are two rag dolls making out on the dance floor and a woman in a skin-tight catsuit is leading around a man dressed like a dog on a leash.

Hayley's hand flies to her ruffled collar before she points a gloved finger in my face. "*I'm* the one causing the scene? You're trying to bang my *best friend* in the middle of a fucking bar."

Good thing Hayley didn't accidentally walk in on us in the darkroom the other day. My stomach twists into knots when I glance over my shoulder and find a line of silver tears along Jade's extra-long fake lashes. I don't give a shit how pissed my sister is; she doesn't get to speak about Jade like that. Should I have touched or kissed her so brazenly in the heart of the town's rumor mill? In hindsight, probably not. But I couldn't help myself, and from the way Jade had kissed me back, she seemed pretty into it as well.

Jade clears her throat. "Hayley, I—"

Hayley cuts her off. "I, what? I'm screwing your brother and didn't think to tell you about it? Just like you never told me about the little kiss you two shared at Fall Fest? What the hell, Jade?"

"That's enough," I say before more hateful words can spew from my sister's mouth. "We're not doing this here. You can come to my place if you want to have an adult discussion."

Hayley's eyes flash with anger. "Fine."

I turn back to Jade and give her shoulders a squeeze. "Are you okay?"

She nods and wipes her eyes with her fingertips, smudging her doll makeup. "I'm sorry."

"For what? Making me crazy about you?"

A small smile lifts the corner of her lips. "Obviously not. I just hate that she found out like this. I wanted to tell her in person, but I didn't know how, and... I just wish I'd known she'd be here."

"I still would've had a hard time keeping my hands to myself," I reply honestly.

Jade's lips rise a little more, and I feel like I should be wearing some shining armor and riding a white steed. From the way Hayley is glowering, I could probably use an extra layer of protection. "Do you want to come up to my place?" I ask Jade. "Or would you rather stay here?" Jade's been looking forward to tonight for a while, and I'd hate for her to cut the night short because of my sister and her drama.

Jade glances over my shoulder, but Hayley's already stomping for the exit. "We should probably get this over with."

Thank fuck. I really don't want to deal with Hayley on my own. Not that I can't handle my sister, but Jade deserves a chance to speak for herself, and I don't want her to have to do that without me by her side. But first... I snag our Bloody Marys, hand Jade hers, and clink our glasses together. "Bottoms up."

We finish our cocktails at the same time, leave the empty glasses on the table, and start for the door. I reach back and take Jade's hand, leading her between skeletons, witches, and werewolves out onto the street, where Hayley is pacing like a feral clown in a cage. My worst nightmare on so many levels.

Hayley comes to a halt beneath the iron streetlight, her gaze falling to our joined hands. Jade tries to pull away, but I don't let her. We have nothing to be ashamed of, and the sooner my sister realizes that, the better.

I don't let go of Jade's fingers until we reach my front door and I'm forced to fish my keys from my pocket.

The red pom-poms on Hayley's oversized shoes flop around with each stomp up the stairs. When we finally reach my apartment, Hayley stalks to the coffee table before whipping toward us. I position myself so that Jade is at my back in case my sister decides to go full possessed-clown and start ripping flesh with her teeth.

She opens her mouth, but before she can say a word, I hold up my hand. Now she looks like she wants to bite it clean off. "Before you say whatever it is that will undoubtedly piss me off, you owe Jade an apology. She's been working her ass off at the store and was really looking forward to blowing off some steam tonight. She got all dolled up,"—*pun absolutely intended*—"and then you ruined her favorite holiday with your dramatics."

"I know it's her favorite holiday, asshole. That's why I'm here. I was going to surprise her, but I guess she surprised me instead."

"Hayley," Jade says, firmer this time. "I'm really sorry that you found out like this, but—"

Hayley cuts across to me as if Jade hadn't even spoken. "Where do you get off, acting like you know her better than I do?" she says to me. "She's been my best friend for twelve fucking years."

Is this how she treats her "friends?" Not letting them say a word to defend themselves, even though they shouldn't *have* to defend themselves in the first place? I wait a beat to see if Jade wants to jump in again, but she seems content to glare at my sister.

"And yet she didn't feel like she could tell you that we're dating," I point out.

"Oh, please. You aren't *dating*." Hayley lifts to her toes to throw over my shoulder, "He's only trying to get into your pants, Jade."

Jade's shoulders stiffen, and I'd like to say that mine don't, but that's a lie.

Hayley's hands fly to her mouth, her gaze bouncing between us. "Dylan, no. Tell me you didn't break the code."

So much for letting her down gently. "Hayley—"

"I can't believe you," she hisses.

I'm not sure what to say, so I keep quiet. Better to let her get it all out without interruption before she starts accusing me of mansplaining or some other bullshit.

She jabs her gloved finger into my arm. "I told you not to go near her."

"This isn't just on Dylan." Jade braves my sister's wrath

when she reaches for my hand. I give her fingers a squeeze. "We both went into this with open eyes."

Hayley's head whips toward Jade. "Oh, don't worry. I'll get to you."

"Don't talk to her like that." I don't care if she's severely jet-lagged or possessed by some malicious clown spirit—she needs to watch her tone.

Jade steps forward, and her hand lands on my chest. "I've got this. Hayley, if you can't calm down and talk to us with the respect we both deserve, then you should leave."

Hayley blows out a breath, but when she speaks again, she's lost some of the bitchiness. "How many times have you told me that your dream is to get married, have kids, and live in Still Springs forever?" she asks Jade. "What happened to finding someone who wants the same things? Because let me tell you, my brother is *not* that guy."

Excuse me? "You don't know what kind of guy I am." Yeah, she's my sister, but we haven't lived in the same state for over a decade.

"No?" Hayley's eyes narrow into slits, and I'd honestly rather she put the mask back on. "I know you're the kind of guy who has threesomes in Venice and Berlin. Who sleeps with a different girl every night you're in London. You can't even remember their names half the time."

I try to swallow past the sudden rock in my throat, but it's not happening. I don't dare glance at Jade for fear of seeing the look of horror on her face.

"Do you want to talk about all the models you've photographed and then fucked?" Hayley goes on.

My head's starting to spin, and my palms are leakier than my bathroom sink. Why the hell did I think it'd be a good idea to tell my sister about all the shit I've done in the past? Jade's not going to want to come near me now—and for good reason.

I've been the worst kind of man—one who doesn't commit, whose bedpost has so many notches it looks like it's been chewed by rabid beavers. I may not be acting like that right now, but a few months ago...yeah. I was that guy.

Jade's hand slips from mine, and I don't even try to hold on.

She steps in front of me, ready to bolt out of the apartment, and—

"Get out," Jade snaps.

Wait a minute. Did she just tell my sister to—

"I mean it, Hayley," Jade says. "I love you, but you're out of line coming in here and acting like this."

Hayley's jaw falls open, but instead of waiting around to find whatever words she seems to be searching for, she whirls around and stomps down the stairs. A second later, the door to the street bangs shut.

"Fuck." I drive my hands through my hair. "I'm..." What the hell am I supposed to say? "I'm so sorry," I say to Jade's back. I should've insisted that she stay at the bar so she didn't have to deal with my sister's tantrum. And after all that shit Hayley said, there's no way she's going to stick around.

Jade turns to face me, and I find myself holding my breath as I watch a single tear slip between her false lashes. She quickly dashes it away. "I can't believe—"

Shit. Here it comes.

I manage to draw in a shaky breath.

"—she spoke to you like that," Jade finishes.

Hold on here. Jade's not mad at *me*? She's mad at *Hayley*? And I thought my stomach couldn't sink any lower. I don't want them throwing away twelve years of friendship over me. I'm really not worth it. "She's just trying to protect you."

Jade sniffles and swipes her cheeks with her fingertips. Her green eyes lock with mine. "That's funny. It felt like you were the one protecting me, not her."

She's right. More importantly, she's not running away when she has every reason to. "Everything Hayley said is true. I'm..." What am I even trying to say? It's not like I can defend my actions. Jade deserves to know exactly what I've done in the past. "If you want to leave, I understand."

Her lips press together. "Do you want me to go?"

"I want you to stay." It scares me just how much.

"Then I stay."

This woman. She keeps on surprising me. "You know what, Jade Quinn? Something tells me I have a thing for you."

She steps forward, and her gaze slips to the front of my black trousers. "You mean the baton in your pocket, Officer?"

Heat blazes up my spine. "Let me rephrase that: I have *two* things for you. One I know exactly what to do with, the other... I'm still trying to figure it out."

She opens her mouth, presumably to respond, but a yawn escapes instead.

"You're tired." It's not a question. The woman has been burning the wick at both ends; she's probably ready to fall over.

"I don't know what I am."

"Want me to take you home?"

The way she blinks up at me through her lashes sends my heart into overdrive. And let's just say the blood pumping through my veins isn't going to my brain. "I'd rather stay here," she says with a mischievous tilt to her lips.

Having Jade stay would certainly turn this night around. "Are you planning on running away in the morning?" That shit really hurt.

The blue bows at the ends of her braids swing when she shakes her head.

Looks like Jade and I are having a sleepover. God, I hope there's a pillow fight.

She slips out of her heels and saunters toward the bathroom. "You have any washcloths?" she throws over her shoulder. "I need to scrub off this face paint."

"Yeah. They're under the sink."

She comes out a few minutes later, fresh-faced and pink-cheeked. "I've changed my mind. I need to go."

"Wrong. You should stay."

A flush creeps up her neck to her jaw. "I just started my period."

Well, that's a bummer. On the plus side, at least there won't be any little Dylans or tiny Jades running around the place in nine months. "Contrary to what my sister says, I'm not only interested in getting in your pants. Your company is tolerable too."

She smiles through a blush and seems to mull it over before saying, "Let me run down to the store and grab a few things."

"And have you ditch me again? Fat chance, doll." I gesture toward her purse on the counter. "Give me the keys and tell me what you need." When she doesn't move, I click my fingers impatiently. "Do I need to turn that key in your back to get you going? I have three sisters. It's hardly the first time I've had to buy stuff for someone's period. Do you want pads or tampons?"

Her eyes are wide and unsure. "Um...tampons, please."

"What size?" That's right. I know they come in sizes,

thanks to Iris bitching about what having Ella has done to her body.

"Regular is fine. And if you could grab my backpack from the office, that would be great." She tugs on the hem of her skirt. "This will scream 'walk of shame' tomorrow."

I'm not sure what Jade has in her backpack, but it probably isn't something to sleep in. I pop into my room to grab my favorite Indian Motorcycle T-shirt and a pair of athletic shorts that are a bit small for me. "Here. You can change into these if you want." I trade the clothes for the keys and head downstairs and out into the brisk night, immediately regretting not throwing on a jacket. My breath comes out in white puffs as I fumble for the correct key. Eventually, I get inside Quinn Brothers and flip on the lights. I find the tampons easily enough and grab a toothbrush as well. Then I head back into the office to grab Jade's bag.

Bag in hand, I leave some cash on the register. Would you look at that? There's still some candy left over. My sisters are always saying they can't get enough chocolate when they're pmsing, so I grab the bowl as well. I'm about to lock up, when the entrance door flies open and Deputy Douchebag strolls in. Actually, since he's dressed as a pirate, that name doesn't quite fit. Let's go with Captain Cockblock.

When he sees me, he stiffens. "You're not Jade." His eye that's not concealed beneath an eyepatch narrows on the items clutched in my hand. "Are you stealing those?"

I roll my eyes. "No. I left money on the register."

He stalks toward me, his hand falling to the pocket of his silky genie pants. Out comes a pair of silver handcuffs.

You've gotta be fucking kidding me. "Since when do pirates carry handcuffs?"

"Since now," he grinds through clenched teeth. "I've

always known you were bad news, but this is low, even for you. Seducing my girl so you can rob her store. Turn around and put your hands behind your back, asshole."

This is not happening. "Something wrong with your eyes?" I say, holding up the stuff in my hand. "If I was going to rob the place, I'd hardly be hitting the toothbrushes and tampons. Jade gave me the keys."

"I said turn around."

This guy is ridiculous. I shift everything in my hands to the crook of my left arm so I can fish my phone from my pocket, determined to clear this up once and for all.

Nate whips a fucking taser from his other pocket and points the damn thing at me. "Freeze!"

"Seriously?"

"I said to put your hands behind your back."

He sounds frantic enough to actually shoot me with the thing, so I give in and set everything I'm carrying on the ground. Next thing I know, my wrists are being pulled behind my back, and I'm standing in the middle of Quinn Brothers wearing a set of metal bracelets.

Captain Cockblock keeps the taser aimed at me as he dials his cell phone. "Jade? It's Nate Williams. I need you to come down to your store right away."

I guess this is happening.

Two minutes later, Jade bursts through the door in my shorts and slippers that are way too big for her and my leather jacket zipped to her chin. Her eyes expand when they land on me.

"Hey, baby," I say to her.

"Dylan—what happened?"

Nate steps between us. "After you disappeared from The Rocking Horse, I came in to see if you were here and all right. I caught this perp trespassing and stealing. He claims you gave him your keys."

Jade gapes at him. "That's because I did give him my keys! Get those handcuffs off him, Nate."

"Not until—"

"*Nate*, if you don't take off those handcuffs right now, I'm going to charge *you* with trespassing."

The prick takes forever unlocking the cuffs, but he looks pretty chastised, so I decide not to be a total ass and keep the nasty comments on the tip of my tongue to myself. Jade snatches up her stuff and grabs my hand.

When Nate sees our fingers threaded together, he stalks out of the store with a childish huff and slams the door.

I almost feel bad for him. Almost.

Jade apologizes the whole way back to my apartment, even though none of this is her fault. When she steps into the bathroom with her things, I go into my room, toe off my boots, and change out of my costume.

By the time Jade comes in, I'm three chocolate bars deep and seriously considering a fourth. That is until I see her standing at the foot of the bed in my clothes. When I gave her that shirt to wear, I hadn't really thought ahead. It's white and thin as hell, and I can one hundred percent see her nipples through the soft fabric.

"You did this on purpose, didn't you?" she says, gesturing to her chest.

I shake my head. "No, but I'm really fucking glad I did." What a happy accident.

She rolls her eyes and settles herself on the bed beside me. I nudge the bowl of chocolate closer to her to keep myself from eating any more. "I just brushed my teeth," she says, "so I really shouldn't." She bites into her bottom lip. "Thanks for that, by the way. It was really thoughtful."

"I'm happy you can benefit from my obsession with shoplifting toothbrushes." I nod at the chocolate. "Go on, it's Halloween."

"Oh, fine." She picks up a Butterfinger and tears open the package. A moan escapes her throat when she takes the first bite. Note to self: Buy more Butterfingers.

"Are you feeling okay?" I ask.

"Yeah, I'm good. My cramps aren't too bad tonight."

That's something, at least. Alex used to have to sleep with a heating pad when she was on her period. "You know what I hear works great for cramps?"

Jade covers her mouth as she chews. "No, what?"

"Orgasms."

The bite she took must go down the wrong tube because she begins coughing and sputtering. I grab the glass she left on the nightstand and thrust it toward her.

"You're an idiot," she croaks after a drink. "I thought you were serious."

"I am serious. Look it up." And if she still doesn't believe me, I'd be more than willing to do a little experiment if she's up for it.

"Oh my god." She gives my shoulder a hard shove, and I fall back onto the pillow.

"Just saying...the offer's there."

She's still laughing as she sets the wrapper and bowl aside, curling up next to me with her hands clasped beneath her cheek. "You aren't anything like I thought you'd be."

Not sure if that's a good or bad thing. "How'd you think I'd be?"

"Cooler."

"I'm sorry. Did you not see my SWAT uniform?" I was the coolest guy in that bar by a long shot.

Her gaze slips to my mouth as she scoots closer. "That

was pretty cool," she murmurs, tracing the black rose tattoo on the inside of my bicep. "But I think I prefer you out of it."

I know exactly what she means. As hot as Jade looked in that doll costume, I much prefer her in my bed, wearing my T-shirt. The hem lifts ever so slightly, revealing a stretch of tanned stomach that's begging for my touch.

"*And* I just got arrested," I add. "I'm a total badass."

"You *almost* got arrested...by a pirate."

She has a point.

I wrap my hands around Jade's hips and pull her even closer so I can breathe her in. She tucks her head beneath my chin and snuggles into my chest. It's been a long time since I've fallen asleep with a woman in my arms...and I really fucking love it.

JADE DOESN'T STOP ALL WEEK. ON MONDAY, SHE GETS so busy that she forgets to eat. Who does that? Not me. Food is priority number one. Or at least it used to be before I met Jade.

Ella and I drop by Quinn Brothers on Tuesday with peanut butter and jelly sandwiches that my niece made all by herself. The half-packed boxes everywhere tell me that the store's online orders have gotten out of hand, not that I say that to Jade. She gets excited each time a new one comes through, but I'm more focused on the way the circles beneath her dulled eyes are getting gradually darker.

Jade stays in her office until midnight on Wednesday.

On Thursday, I bribe her with takeout to have a break, but she goes right back to work the moment she sets down her chopsticks.

My next idea is to offer to run the deliveries for her, but she refuses my help. The only thing she'll let me do is sit behind the register because I can edit photos while I'm on my ass. Ella isn't feeling well after insisting on three portions of mac and cheese, so she nods off in Jade's office while Jade's out making deliveries and I'm manning the register out front. I should probably run back to make sure Ella hasn't puked. That was a lot of cheese for one little kid.

On my way into the office, my phone buzzes with yet another message from Alex.

> Family meeting tomorrow at 6pm
>
> Be there

A "please" wouldn't go astray, although Alex has never been one for pleasantries. She's been setting meetings all week. Iris has been felled by morning sickness, so Justin has dropped Ella over every morning. I haven't heard a peep from Hayley since Halloween. I have a feeling this "family meeting" is really an excuse for an ambush.

> Can't make it tomorrow
>
> Sorry

Alex texts right back, but I shove my phone in my pocket and head into the office, where Ella's snoring away on the floor with her hands tucked beneath her chubby cheek. Damn, this kid is cute. I'm going to miss her if I go back to Austin. Things are also going so well with Jade; I kinda hate giving that up too. Sure, we could try the long-distance thing, but does that ever work?

The front door's jingling bell drags me out of my head. I slap on a smile and hurry back out front to greet the customer. My smile vanishes when I nearly trip over a woman with a long blonde ponytail who's collapsed in the middle of the floor. A woman that—

"Jade?" I run around the counter to kneel beside her. "*Jade!*"

She's not responding. Why isn't she responding? I shake her shoulder and call her name again, but only silence answers.

CHAPTER TWENTY-SEVEN

JADE

My eyes slowly peel open, the aroma of coffee drifting over my nose and rousing my senses. Blinking groggily, I make out a pattern of dark beams of wood stretched across a white cathedral-style ceiling.

I turn my head, my disoriented gaze catching up to my surroundings. A basket of wood set beside a stone fireplace. An enormous flatscreen TV mounted above it. A plush leather armchair draped with a knitted blanket. I'm in some sort of luxurious cabin that's beautifully decorated in shades of wood and soft grays. The only thing I recognize is—

"Dylan." My voice comes out croaky.

His head whips toward me from an open-plan kitchen, his lips splitting into a smile. "You're up."

Not technically correct, since I'm lying on the world's most comfortable couch, but I am awake.

A run of hazy memories drifts into my vision like a slideshow.

Dylan shaking me awake on the floor of the store.

A sleepy ride to the hospital with Dylan behind the wheel of my car.

A crowded waiting room, nurses and doctors, sharp needles and blood tests, a quick phone call with Ruby, and a middle-of-the-night diagnosis of "exhaustion."

After that, Dylan had spoken to the doctor in hushed tones and taken me home, except I woke up...

"Where am I?" I ask scratchily, sitting up on my elbows as Dylan places a steaming mug of coffee on the glass table beside me.

"My cabin. Actually, it's my family's, but I use it the most. Hayley never took you here?"

"No. She did tell me you guys owned a cabin near the springs, but you know Hayley."

"Likes galleries and martinis, hates insects and silence?" he replies with a wry smile before gently lifting my feet under the blanket so he can sit beside me. He settles my legs over his thighs, and a flurry of sleeping butterflies awakens in my stomach.

I force my eyes off his handsome face to give the spacious yet cozy room another glance. Through the patio doors, the strip of sky over the oak trees is painted with the peach hue of dawn. Dylan did tell me he was a morning person, whereas I tend to start my days erring on the side of homicidal. But right now, through the tiredness, I feel strangely...content.

"Do you remember passing out last night before I took you to the hospital?" Dylan asks, a line appearing between his brows.

"I don't remember fainting, but I remember feeling really dizzy." So dizzy that I couldn't stop myself from falling. I'm really lucky I didn't get a concussion. "Like the doctor said, I was just really, really tired, but it'll get better."

Dylan gives my lower leg a squeeze through the blanket. "The doc also said you need to rest for at least a week. But on the way back to your place last night, you started on about going to the store in the morning, so I kind of took charge. I spoke to Ruby, who was all for it."

"Took charge?"

He upnods at our surroundings. "Bringing you here. Because to be honest, Jade, that job is making you sick, and I really don't feel like losing my fucking mind when I find you passed out again or worse."

I sit up a little higher. "But we can't close the store. We've got bills to pay, and we're behind on all of them. My dad can't possibly—"

"Ruby's coming back today to run things while you're staying here."

My lips fall open. "No."

He shakes his head. "Doctor's orders. *And* Ruby's—her running the store this week was her idea. She's also gonna come by later today and visit you. She doesn't know about us, by the way; I didn't know if you'd want me to tell her. I said I was offering the place to you because it's empty and quiet, and you're Hayley's friend. I can make myself scarce when Ruby visits."

He chews the inside of his cheek as his words sink into my head. "*She doesn't know about* us, *by the way.*"

Is there an *us*?

That thought is eclipsed by another. I can't stay here for a whole week while Ruby leaves behind her job, her home, and her boyfriend to work at the place she left behind for a good reason.

"Dylan, I really appreciate all this," I begin, "but I can't do that to Ruby. She's got Flynn, and—"

"Flynn's coming back too. Ruby said he's got the week off flying, so it's all good."

My exhausted head falls back against the striped cushions. Right now, I don't even have the energy to argue. "Maybe I can stay here for a bit. Just a day or two."

A smile hints at his mouth. "And maybe I can do things to entice you to stay longer."

I raise a brow. *"Things?"*

The strokes of his palm over my legs become a little firmer. "Make you gourmet meals...let you have free reign over the TV...give you full-body oil massages."

"Now you're talking," I say with a weak smirk.

Our flushed gazes cling tightly together for a long moment before he sits forward to push the coffee mug toward me. "All in good time, heathen. Think you're up to drinking that first?"

"Shit yes." I edge my way up into a sitting position and reach for the coffee. "Come to me, baby."

Dylan stays true to his word about everything. For several days, he makes all my meals, lets me have free run of the TV, and only leaves the cabin to get groceries or when Ruby and Flynn visit. He sleeps with one arm draped over me in the master bedroom, but he makes no other moves to touch me—insisting I rest, which is *not* what I would have expected from this guy at all.

Is this how Dylan behaves with all the girls he has flings with? Lures them into a honeypot of attentive sweetness and criminally sexy smiles before one day slipping on his helmet and riding off into the sunset, never to be heard from again?

I'm not ready to face the answer to that question. All I

know is that I like being around him. Even when he's outside taking endless photos of toadstools clinging to tree trunks and random squirrels darting around the forest while I'm glued to the couch watching trash TV, all I feel is... calm.

This isn't like me.

I'm usually go-go-go, an energizer bunny who's permanently charged. Sure, it did take a while for me to settle my thoughts here at first and to stop panicking about the store and Ruby, but Dylan was right—I needed to give my mind and my body a rest.

I also can't deny that I like the stillness here. I like the view of the fall leaves outside and the grassy trail leading down to the springs. I like the wild, earthy smells of the trees and the whistles and calls of the birds. I seem to have passed out at the store and woken up in some sort of dream world where, for the first time in my life, I actually want to do nothing and let someone take care of me.

A specific someone who's looking a little too good in that white T-shirt, his inked bicep bulging as he fiddles with the dials of a camera on the kitchen counter.

The mindless reality TV episode I was watching begins to fade away as a sharp ache of longing stirs in my belly. How can I have spent this many days in Dylan's company and not even kissed him yet? I mean, *look* at those lips. As if he heard my thoughts, he bites down on his bottom one as he focuses on his camera. *What a freaking tease*.

"Whatcha doing over there?" I ask.

"It's a bit dark in here, so I'm adjusting the ISO."

"Want to test it out on me?"

I'm hardly dressed for a photo shoot in my sweatpants and pale blue shirt, but Dylan's lips kick up. "Absolutely.

It's impossible to take a bad shot of you, so you're good for my fragile ego."

He carries the camera over to me and holds it up to his eye. His fingers cradle the lens and twist it, which is way sexier than I'm sure he realizes.

I fiddle with my hair while he takes a few snaps, draping my long braid over my shoulder as I try for a relaxed smile.

"So fucking gorgeous," he says, gazing at the photo he just took in the camera screen. My chest warms at his words.

"Can I take one of you?" I ask.

He lets out half a laugh. "I'm not really a front-of-camera kind of guy."

"I strongly refute that claim." I make sure he sees my up-and-down look. "You are *very much* a front-of-camera kind of guy."

"Is that so?" He hands me the camera.

"Jeez, it's heavier than I thought." I peer through the lens and take a few shots of him looking mildly embarrassed and excessively attractive.

"Now *that* is a perfect shot." I hold the camera screen up so he can see himself with his fingers gripping the pockets of his sweatpants, his shoulders filling out his T-shirt.

Although he smiles, he snatches back the camera. "It's my turn again." He directs me to lie back on the couch with one arm folded behind my head like I'm posing for a Calvin Klein ad.

"Who gave you permission to be that sexy?" he murmurs as he clicks.

"What about this?" I ask, pulling my shirt right over my head until I'm left only in my bra. I link my fingers behind my neck, arching my back. "Does this look good?"

Dylan hums his approval from behind the camera. He then shoots me a look like I'm being naughty, but I'm completely aware of that.

"Is this better?" I continue, peeling down one strap of my sports bra.

Dylan swallows tightly. "Looks a little uneven."

"How about now?" I tug down the other strap, and now it's his breaths that are uneven. Dylan's usually so cool and in control; seeing him react like this is kind of a rush. While keeping my gaze locked on his, I keep pulling at the fabric until my bare breasts pop out, one by one.

He inhales sharply. "*Fuck,* Jade."

"Come here?" I murmur.

Dylan sets the camera on the glass table and reaches me in one stride. His palms find my lower back and he lifts me up, turns us both around, and sits down so that I'm straddling him over the couch.

Like he's starved for me, he lowers his mouth to my breast and closes his lips tightly around my nipple. I tilt my head back and moan softly as he circles me with his tongue. He shifts his mouth back and forth between both sides of my chest, trying to taste all of me. The incredible sensation makes me claw at his thick strands of hair before I grab a fistful and yank his hungry mouth up to mine. *I'm in control now*.

He sighs as our tongues wind together in a desperate kiss, like we've been holding back for days and have finally found some relief.

"Baby, what are you doing to me?" Dylan breathes against my mouth, and I roll my hips against him, grinding into his rock-solid erection. He groans and thrusts up against me through our clothes, over and over, like he's having sex with me through the fabric.

"*Fuck,* I want you so bad," he says through his teeth, each drive of his hips drawing another moan from my lips. "I want you everywhere...all the time...in every. Fucking. Room. In. This. Fucking. House." Each word is another thrust, and my body's burning so hot that I'm sure I'm about to combust.

"Have me," I say in a gasp. "Have me any way you want."

Dylan hauls me off his thighs before guiding me onto my back and kicking the blanket away. He brings his lips to my stomach, above where the bra is still looped around me, and drags his tongue up the center of my cleavage before returning his hot mouth to my nipples. With a needy sound, he grabs the sports bra and tugs it up over my head before reaching for the waistband of my sweatpants.

"This okay?" he asks, and I nod vigorously before he hikes the cotton down my legs. Once he's got them off, he peels my soaked panties right off and brings them up to his nose, inhaling deeply with heavy eyes. *Oh, wow.*

Dylan tosses my underwear aside and gazes down at me. When he glides a hand down his stomach and grips his bulging dick through his sweatpants, my whole body crackles with heat.

"Can you open up for me, baby?" he asks, stroking himself over the material.

Holy shit, okay. I swallow hard and let one thigh drop open, wrenching a groan from Dylan's throat. "I wish you could see how good you look," he says before kneeling in front of me. "I could eat you for every meal." A second later, his tongue connects with my core, a sigh of pleasure tipping my head back as Dylan makes a ravenous sound against me. He pushes my thighs up and back, opening me up so he can burrow his tongue inside me before swirling it over my clit.

He continues to work his mouth on me, and a storm of pleasure begins to build between my legs until it suddenly explodes with a thousand lightning strikes, making me cry out and writhe against Dylan's relentless tongue.

"You liked that, baby?" he asks, kissing the inside of my thighs and up my stomach before his lips land on my neck. "Not as much as I did."

After we maul each other's mouths with another frenzied kiss, he turns me over, wraps his arms around my torso, and pulls me up so that my back is resting against his thumping chest. His thickness rubs against my behind, drawing a heady sigh from my throat. I reach back to grip him through his pants before I tug at the waistband and sink my hand inside. A groan drifts out of him as I pull out his full length.

"See how hard you make me?" He pants against my cheek as I stroke him up and down. "I'm gonna fucking burst for you."

We breathe haggardly against each other's lips as I work him up and down, his fingers finding my core and sliding inside. After we feel each other everywhere for a few breathless minutes, Dylan gently guides me off him. He gets back up and hikes his shirt over his head, my hungry gaze drinking in his toned chest before he hauls his pants down his thighs and sits back down on the sofa.

Desire sparkles in his eyes as he taps the inside of his thigh. I practically lunge at him, climbing over his legs and straddling him. His gaze falls to the swollen skin between my parted legs.

"So pretty and perfect," he says, running his fingertips through my core. He then lines up his tip with my opening and pushes inside.

My vision fogs, and my temperature climbs to a million

degrees as all-consuming pleasure grips me everywhere. "*Dylan,*" I gasp, bracing a hand against his chest as he punches his hips up, sealing me with his full length before drawing out again.

"Look at you, taking all of me. I want to feel all of you too," he rasps, sinking all the way inside again before dragging out. I grip his shoulders tightly while his movements turn faster and harder, his palms imprisoning my thighs, holding me in place. All concepts of time and space disappear as he continues to fill me, hard and deep, wringing every drop of pleasure from my bones. He then lifts me up and guides me around so that my back falls against his chest. The living room swims in my vision.

"That's it. Good girl. Fuck me," he coaxes as he drives up into me, my body meeting his with each thrust.

The intense euphoria almost becomes too much to bear until Dylan brings his lips to my ear. "You gonna come on me?" he asks in an aching voice, his thumb moving to flicker over my clit. "Please, baby. I need it."

Another explosion erupts within me, raining lava over my insides as I cry out and collapse against him. Dylan folds his arms around me and hums a sound of appreciation into my neck while I catch my breath.

He's still inside me, hard as stone, and I begin to gyrate my hips, loving the broken groan that scrapes out of his throat. "Is that good?" I ask. He nods against my cheek, like he can barely hold himself up. "What about this?" I whisper, grinding my body down as hard as I can before rising all the way up and sinking back down again. The pleasure cells in my body begin to quickly refill, and within seconds, we're both moaning again as I push his thighs wider apart and ride him hard until he rasps out a sexy groan and collapses against me, his breaths ragged against my neck.

Dylan shifts around to fall back against the couch, pulling me down with him and wrapping both arms tightly around me. He deposits a run of soft kisses into the nape of my neck as I lie encased inside the warmest, loveliest, safest cradle I could imagine.

Neither of us lets go for a long time.

CHAPTER TWENTY-EIGHT
DYLAN

Jade curls deeper into my embrace, tucking her head beneath my chin. *Right where she belongs.* We should probably get off the couch and put our clothes back on, but neither of us seems too pushed. I'm not thinking of going for another round—don't get me wrong, if Jade's hand falls in any way from where it's pressed to my chest, my body is more than ready to go. But as I draw invisible circles on her bare shoulder, my mind drifts to what pushed her into this position in the first place.

The Quinn Brothers store.

She's so determined to make the place work when there are much easier ways to make money. Her commitment is commendable, but at some point, she's got to know when to throw in the towel. And if passing out on the floor from exhaustion isn't that cue to either get some help or close up shop, I don't know what is.

"Can I ask you something?" I say quietly in case she's dozing.

Her hair tickles my chin when she nods. "Sure."

"Why do you push yourself so hard?" A building and some stock hardly seem worth her health.

After a moment, she says, "The store is my family's legacy. My grandpa and his brother opened it way back when, and then my mom and dad took over. They spent more time there than at home—we all did. " Her soft sigh fans across my collarbone. "The store was supposed to be for Ruby and me, but it was never my sister's dream."

"But it's yours?" I ask, still trying to make sense of Jade's need to keep a sinking ship afloat. I understand legacy and commitment to family, but at some point, doesn't she get to choose what she wants instead of living out someone else's expectations?

I'm sure some part of my dad had been disappointed that Hayley and I decided not to go into "the family business," but he always respected our decisions and never made us feel guilty. I'm sure Jade's dad would be the same.

"It used to be. But lately, it feels like I don't have time to dream," she murmurs, reaching around my torso to tuck her hands beneath my back.

Everyone deserves to dream a dream that's all their own. And if Jade wants to reclaim this one, who am I to say she's wrong? "So, how do we save the store?"

She lifts her head to stare at me through wide eyes as her brow bunches. "I'm sorry, but did you say 'we'?"

Has this past week not proven to her that I'm in this? I tuck a strand of hair behind her ear so that I can see her gorgeous face. "I can't have you collapsing again. It really put me out."

"Oh, it did, did it?"

"Very much. I had so many plans this week."

She stamps a kiss on my smiling lips like she can't seem

to help herself, and it feels so fucking good. She then props her chin on her fist and rests her fist on my chest.

"Let's see..." She does this cute squinty thing with her eyes as she clicks her tongue. "The website," she says after a few beats. "I think that's how I—"

"We."

"I mean *we* save this place. Sales are coming through in droves."

That's something, at least. Quinn Brothers may be ten years behind the rest of the world, but it shouldn't take much to catch them up. "Think of how many more sales you'll get when you let me take the photos for your website." I can get all the stuff I need to set up a proper studio and have decent product shots loaded up by the end of the week.

Her mouth turns down. "Dylan..."

"Jade..." I mimic.

"If I get too many online orders, there's no way to deliver them all without closing the store. And with no other employees—"

"*I* can work at the store." Running the register is straightforward enough, and I like to think I'm a smart guy and can figure out the rest.

"I can't ask you to do that."

"You didn't. I volunteered. It'd be no hassle at all. I could bring down my computer and edit from there." Sure, it'd be a bit distracting, but nothing I can't handle. Besides, Ella loves the store. She can help too.

Jade's teeth scrape her bottom lip, but there's a spark in her eyes that I haven't seen all week. "I can't pay you."

"All I want is your company. But if you'd like to throw in the occasional sexual favor, I promise not to complain."

She breathes a light laugh. "Aren't you sweet?" She

slowly walks her fingers down my chest to my abdomen.

I roll her onto my lap, and she lets out the cutest squeal when her legs fall to either side of my hips. "Not as sweet as you," I murmur against her throat, letting my hands slide north to cup her—

A knock at the front door interrupts my devious plans. When Jade's sister calls her name, Jade launches off me like a rocket ship in Cape Canaveral. She scrambles around, throwing on clothes and tossing my shirt and sweatpants at me.

Guess it's time to get dressed. These boxer briefs and sweats aren't going to do a thing to hide a raging hard-on, but I put them on as quickly as possible. Jade's gaze that keeps dropping to my tented sweats isn't helping matters. "Stop looking at it," I hiss under my breath, adjusting myself as best I can.

"But it's so impressive," she whispers back with a coy smile.

I drop onto the couch with a laugh and throw a pillow over my lap.

Jade swings open the door. All I can see of Jade's sister is a head of dark hair and a flash of blue sweater.

"Ruby, hi." A blush blooms across Jade's cheeks as her eyes dart to me before she clears the frog from her throat. "What're you doing here?"

"Checking on you." Ruby throws an arm around Jade's neck, drawing her in for a quick hug. "Feeling better?" Her mouth tilts down when she pulls back and scans Jade from head to toe. "You're looking a little flushed."

"I'm feeling a lot better."

Ruby casts a wary glance in my direction. "Are you going to invite me in, or—"

"Oh, yeah. Sorry. Come in." Jade opens the door wider

so Ruby can step inside. Before I can offer a greeting, Jade says, "Dylan was just leaving."

I was?

Jade grabs her car keys from the hook inside the door and tosses them at me. They land on the pillow with a jingle, and that's when I realize: Jade *still* doesn't want Ruby to know about us. Talk about a boner killer.

The revelation really shouldn't bother me; I told her it was up to her when or even if she told her sister, but after everything that's happened, I thought maybe she wouldn't still be ashamed of being with me.

My heart twists in my chest.

Looks like I'm wrong.

Not wanting to make things more awkward than they already are, I clutch the keys and stand to give Jade's sister a wave. "Hey, Ruby. Perfect timing. I was just headed out." I can feel Jade looking at me when I slip on my shoes, but I don't spare her a glance in case Ruby catches me staring for too long. My jaw pops as I cross the wide wrap-around porch and take the three steps down to the winding flagstone path.

I'm not mad; I get why she doesn't want Ruby to know. I'm just disappointed.

Really fucking disappointed.

A harsh wind whips through the creaking pines that stretch toward a gray sky. Should've probably grabbed my coat on the way out. Too late now. No way am I going back in there when I feel like this.

"Dylan?" Jade calls. "Dylan, wait up."

Talking is the last thing I feel like doing, so I keep going. We can talk about this later and set some ground rules or whatever shit she wants, like who we're allowed to tell: My family. And who we're not: Everyone else.

Jade catches up to me right when I slide into the driver's seat.

"I'm sorry about acting so weird," she says, pink-cheeked and a little out of breath.

Great. Now I feel like shit for making her come all this way. I give her my best smile. "Fear not. You're hardly the first girl who wants me to be her dirty little secret."

She catches the door when I try to close it. "I don't feel like that, Dylan." Her gaze darts to the cabin, and the stain on her cheeks deepens. "Ruby knows that you and I have hooked up."

"Wonderful. I'm sure she's thrilled."

And there it is, another frown confirming my suspicions. Instead of trying to deny it, Jade asks where I'm going. I could head back to the apartment and get some shit done, but that doesn't hold any appeal.

There's a whole thread of texts from my sisters asking me to come to Mom and Dad's. I'm already in a shit mood, so maybe I'll get that over with. "I need to go to a family meeting."

"Oh..." Her shoulders sink. "Will Hayley be there?"

"Probably."

"Do me a favor? Ask her to call me? I haven't heard from her since she rang to see if I was okay."

I tell her I will, and we say our goodbyes. As I pull out of the long driveway, I notice Jade watching me from the porch. I've already promised to help her with the store—and I'm going to. But my reasons for sticking around after Christmas are feeling awfully one-sided right now.

The more time I spend with Jade, the more I care about her. Which is a feeling I'm not used to and have no fucking clue what to do with. All I know is that it's going to hurt like hell if she decides in the end that I'm not worth the hassle.

I walk into my parents' place to face three scowling women. I'd expected Hayley to be angry, but not Iris or Alex.

"Nice of you to finally join us," Iris clips.

I take no offense at her snippy tone. She is pregnant, after all, and Ella's had the chicken pox, which must've been pretty scary for everyone.

I'm about to apologize until my therapist's voice drifts into my ear. Why should I apologize when I've done nothing wrong, and I *don't* feel sorry? "I've been busy," I say instead.

"I'm sure you have," Alex mutters from where she's leaning with her hip against the island.

Beside her, Hayley watches me through narrowed eyes. I wait for her snide remark, but she says nothing. And I thought she was scary on Halloween. This silence is much worse.

It's probably best to keep that marble slab between me and my sisters, so I take a seat at the dining table instead of joining them at the island. "What's this meeting about?"

Iris glances at Alex first and then Hayley before leveling me with an even stare. "We need to talk about the house."

"What house?" Mom and Dad had places in Florida and Arizona, and a few overseas as well. But when Alex glances around the kitchen, I have a sinking feeling they're not referring to the others. "*This* house?"

The three of them nod, but it's Alex who says, "There's no point holding onto the place if no one's going to live in it. We're not in any rush, but it'll make it easier if we sign the documents now so that when the time comes to put it on the market, we're not under pressure to all be here at the same time." She pushes a stack of papers with a pen on top across the counter.

"But we don't want to sell it." This is our family home. We all grew up here. Why does no one else seem to care about any of that?

"Maybe Dylan will move in. He seems to have gotten pretty comfortable in Still Springs," Hayley mutters.

Iris seems to perk up. "Oh, yes. I want to talk to you about Jade."

Here we go…

"We're getting ready to make an offer on the store, but I need to know if she and her dad are open to selling. If we acquire Quinn Brothers, we could have a new Kings open by next summer when the tourists start pouring into town."

I expected a dressing down about King's Code, not a conversation about Jade's store. Now that I know it's Jade's goal to make it work, I can't let my family buy the place, even if our dad did dream of having a location in the center of Still Springs. He isn't here anymore, but Jade is. Whether I stay in Still Springs or not, this is the least I can do for her.

"I don't think we should make an offer at all," I say.

Iris and Alex trade confused glances, but Hayley holds my stare, her neutral expression giving nothing away.

"Why not?" Iris and Alex ask in unison.

"Because Jade isn't interested in selling."

"She may not be, but I keep hearing that the store's always empty and that they're behind on their accounts. We're not trying to kick her out, Dylan. We're trying to help her."

That may be the case, but we're not going to "help" unless Jade specifically asks for it. "No offers unless Jade changes her mind. Okay?"

"Geez. Don't get your panties in a bunch," Alex murmurs.

Now, back to our parents' house. I take a deep breath. "I don't think we should even think about selling this house."

Iris's head drops into her hands. "Dylan..."

"I'm trying to figure some shit out, okay? Give me a week or two and we can circle back. Please?" If I decide to stay, I'm going to need more space than the apartment on Main Street. And maybe Jade is right to surround herself in a place where she spent so much time with her family. I have a lot of good memories in this house—we all do. It would be a shame to give those away.

"Two weeks," Iris agrees. Alex nods, but Hayley's still a statue.

The two of them grab the papers from the counter and disappear down the hallway into Dad's office. Hayley doesn't move, and neither do I.

This has gone on long enough.

I miss my baby sister, and Jade clearly misses her too. Hayley's had enough time to pout or process or whatever the hell she needs to do.

I get up from my chair and cross to the island to brace my hands on the marble countertop and stare directly into the eyes of the beast. "Call Jade."

My sister's sneer sends a shiver down my spine. "She doesn't seem to care what I have to say, so what's the point?"

"I never thought you'd be so petty."

"And I never thought you'd break our family code."

"Dad created the code to help us look out for each other. Telling me not to date Jade wasn't to keep me safe. You were being selfish."

"I was trying to save my friend!" she snaps. "You're going to ruin her, and I'll be the one picking up the pieces when you leave. Excuse me for wanting to save her the heartache."

A few months ago, maybe I would've agreed with Hayley, but now? I close my eyes and inhale deeply, once, twice. By the third breath, I don't exactly feel calm, but I do feel steady enough to tell Hayley the truth. "What if I'm not going to ruin her? She's all I can think about."

Hayley sighs and shakes her head. "How long is that going to last, Dyl? Jade isn't a hit-it-and-quit-it kind of girl."

"I know that."

"So, what? Are you going to stay in Still Springs? Because she's never wanted to live anywhere else."

"I don't know. Maybe." There are worse places in the world to live than Still Springs. I think I can really help Jade with the store, I'd love to be around for Iris when the new baby comes, and I'd get to hang out with Ella whenever I want.

Hayley's chin jerks back. "You're serious."

"Hell yes, I'm serious." The words fly out before I can stop them and...*holy shit*. They're true. I'm so fucking serious about Jade it's scary. That's why her not telling Ruby about us hurts so much.

I'm one step away from being all in, and it feels like Jade's one step away from being all out.

Hayley purses her lips and studies me for the longest time before letting out a heavy sigh. "Well, then...I guess I was wrong. And I'm sorry."

I finally walk around to the other side of the island and wrap my sister in a hug. "I'm sorry too, Buttons."

Her hands come around my back, and she squeezes me tight. "Don't hurt her, Pickle."

I don't plan on hurting Jade. But that doesn't mean she won't hurt me.

CHAPTER TWENTY-NINE

JADE

WHILE GRIPPING MY TOOTHBRUSH WITH ONE HAND, I use my other to reach for my ringing phone, silently hoping it's Dylan. Coming back to Grandma's house yesterday didn't bring me the relief I thought it would. While I am anxious to get back to the store, I already miss the quiet peace of being at the springs...the total lack of responsibility...the sweet intimacy of sharing a space with *him*.

But the name flashing on the screen makes my brush pause inside my mouth and my eyes widen. I hurriedly spit and grab a hand towel to wipe toothpaste off my mouth before picking up the call.

"Hayley... Hi." My gut draws tight. I'm not sure how I feel about Hayley right now. Yes, I should've told her right away that I'd been seeing her brother, but her intense reaction to it has left a bitter taste in my mouth.

"I'm so sorry to call you this early," she says, "but I'm outside your door and you're not answering. Are you home, or have you left already?"

"No. Shit, sorry. I'm in the bathroom and didn't hear the door. I'll be right there." I hang up, then dash down the carpeted hallway to the front door, taking a deep breath before flinging it open.

Hayley hovers on the concrete porch with a designer tote bag hanging from one shoulder and a sheepish crease between her eyes. Behind her, the faint wail of a siren cuts through the melodic chirps of birds fluttering through the orangey leaves of the maple trees.

"Got time for a quick chat?" she asks before swallowing hard.

"Sure." I open the door wider, and she steps past me, bringing a whiff of fruity perfume. Normally, we'd go in for a hug, but not this time. Instead, I trail Hayley into the living room, glancing at my watch. I planned to head into Quinn Brothers early today. Ruby told me that the store was practically dead while I was away, apart from the online orders, but I need something to distract my brain from thinking about Dylan. After our awkward exchange about Ruby at the cabin, he'd come back later that night, but he hadn't raised the topic again, and neither had I. I hadn't wanted to admit to him that I'm nervous to tell Ruby I'm falling for the only guy she's ever warned me against. He'd then know how I feel about him, and what if he doesn't feel the same? How mortifying would that be?

We hadn't even slept together that night, and the following morning, I woke to find him gone, along with his camera and bike. That left me feeling icky, like he didn't want to be around me anymore but was too polite to say so. Which is fair enough; I'm not his girlfriend, and I'd taken up more than enough of his time. So, I packed up my things, wrote him a thank you note, and drove home. Ruby insisted on working one last day at the store, so I spent most of yesterday with Dad, going over his hospital admission forms and watching old Seinfeld reruns with him at his house.

Dylan and I have texted a few times, but it's been stilted. Hence the need to divert my brain from overthinking all this.

Hayley clears her throat, stealing back my attention. She leans forward from the adjacent floral couch to cup my knee. "I'm sorry, babe," she says, remorse crowding her features. "I was going to call you yesterday and say this, but then I decided I wanted to do it in person." She lets out a trembling breath. "I said some out-of-line things to you and Dylan on Halloween night, and I can own that. I was a complete bitch, and I'm sorry."

This is the Hayley I know and love. My chest softens. "It's okay. I'm sorry that I didn't tell you about Dylan and me. I honestly had no intention of dating your brother, but it kind of just...happened."

Hayley glances down with a sigh. "I might've been a bit too forceful about the whole thing. I mean...is it weird thinking about you guys together? Definitely. Am I envious at the thought of you liking him more than you do me? Of course."

"That won't happen." I have more than enough room in my heart to love Hayley *and* her... That unexpected thought train makes my stomach flip hard. I don't love Dylan...do I?

"*But,*" Hayley adds, "do I think the two of you looked beyond adorable together?" She rolls her eyes. "Okay, yes. And you might find this hard to believe, but the biggest reason I was so against it was because I didn't want *you* to get hurt, Jade."

My insides knot up. "I know." Her subtle reminder that Dylan "leaves a wreckage of broken hearts wherever he goes" is what I need to hear, as painful as it is. But I also knew that going in, and the ugly truth is that it's too late to save me now. I'm already in deep enough to become another piece of that wreckage, but when Dylan tells me he's leaving for Austin and that we should "stay in touch," I'll face the firing squad with my head held high. I chose to have a fling with him rather than nothing at all, and whether that was the right decision or not, it's too late to change it.

"I love you so much," Hayley says, and I lift off the couch to pull her into a hug, repeating those words back to her. After we break apart, she digs through her tote bag and pulls out a copy of *Luxe Travel USA*. "I also brought this as a bit of a peace offering," she says, handing me the glossy magazine. "Sunny Gillespie's article just came out about Fall Fest, and I thought you might want to see it."

"Oh, wow. Of course." My thumb whips through the pages until I land on the four-page spread about our town. A little rock grows in my throat when I spot the giant photo of the Kings superstore. Why would Hayley consider this a peace offering? She must know I would have killed to have had this media coverage for Quinn Brothers.

She sits forward, her elbows digging into her thighs. "Read it."

I inhale deeply and begin scanning the words. The rock in my throat loosens when I realize that Iris did the interview on behalf of the King family. She's a natural at this sort of thing, and her comments are smart and insightful. When my eyes trail the text over to the third page, a little gasp leaves my lips when I see two beautifully sunlit photos of the Quinn Brothers booth from Fall Fest. In one of them, I'm talking to a customer while holding up one of Magnolia Sloane's ghoulish head sculptures.

"Dylan took those," Hayley says as I trace my fingers over the images. "He sent them to Sunny, and they're obviously great, so she put them in. And that's not all." Hayley leans closer to tap the next page. "Read the first few paragraphs there."

I read where she's pointing, and my eyes grow wide at the long write-up about the Quinn Brothers store. Iris talks not only about our wide variety of groceries and supplies but also about our unique local homewares, crafts, and artworks. It's more than a mention—it's a sales pitch.

My eyes fly to Hayley's. "Iris did all this?"

She smiles. "If I'm honest, it was Dylan's idea. But it was a great one, and we all agreed. Iris actually suggested to Sunny that she interview you for that part, but she was too close to her deadline."

My smile inches wider, and warmth moves up my chest. *It was Dylan's idea.*

Could that man be any more wonderful? If I hadn't already fallen for him, my heart wouldn't have a chance. And he hadn't said a word to me about any of this. He hasn't looked for praise or boasted; he just silently made sure to take care of me the way he has since we reconnected.

Hayley stands up with a smile. "I know you're probably in a rush to get to the store, so I'll get out of your hair."

She's right. I really need to get going, but I hate saying goodbye so quickly. I set the magazine on the coffee table and jump up beside her. "How long are you in town? Maybe we could grab dinner tonight?"

"Absolutely. I'll be here for a few more days." She steps forward for a hug, and I meet her halfway, holding on tight. Against my hair, she says. "I know things between us have been strained, but I really wish you would've told me how bad things were at the store."

My brows gather as I pull away. "What do you mean?"

A look of confusion tightens her face like she doesn't

understand why I'm not spilling every single detail. I would've told Hayley eventually, but I wanted it to be on my own terms. "Aren't you guys struggling to make ends meet?" she asks.

My heart begins to pound. "Did Dylan tell you that?"

She shakes her head. "No, Iris did."

Iris? "You guys have been talking about my store?"

Hayley struggles to reply, which sets my mind racing. What else did Dylan tell them? What must they think of me? My gaze lands on that magazine. Did Iris say all those nice things out of pity? Do they pity me? The thought of Dylan telling his sisters all about the sorry state of my store makes me sick to my stomach. Why would he do that?

Dylan has asked me before if we would ever consider selling…

The Kings already own the two buildings next door…

It all clicks.

Dylan told me that his sisters asked him to escort Sunny around town to get that article.

Is he doing the same thing with *me* to try and get the store?

No. That's insane. I hate that the thought even crossed my mind.

But as I glance back at my friend whose surname is *King*, the more I wonder… "Are you guys conspiring to buy out Quinn Brothers?" I ask.

Hayley's face pales, and I suck in a sharp breath.

Before I can ask more questions, my phone buzzes from the glass table, and my furrowed gaze darts to the notification. After scanning the first few words from Nate, I snatch up the handset.

> **SHITHEAD**
>
> I'm at work and just heard about the fire! Are you ok??
>
> Tell me you're at home or at your dad's…

"Fire? What fire?" I gasp.

Hayley's brow lines. "Is everything okay?" She moves beside me to read the text, her wide-eyed gaze flying back to mine. "What's on fire?"

My heart jumps into my throat, and I can barely get the words out. Because there can be only one thing Nate's talking about.

"The store."

⁂

Hayley's car screeches down Summercrest, neither of us saying anything as my heart thumps out of my chest. The choking smell of smoke filters into the car despite the windows being shut, and the moment Hayley makes a left on Main, an impossible scene appears like something out of my worst nightmares.

A giant fire engine sits behind four police cars with their blue and red lights flashing. Firefighters in coats and helmets scurry around, some pointing thick fire hoses at the building engulfed in flames. A building that's… *Oh god.* Furious flames lash through the windows of the Quinn Brothers store, the glass blown out and shattered all over the sidewalk. The red front door is completely gone, like it's been eaten by the blaze. Frightening pops and cracks explode from the half-collapsed roof. There's smoke everywhere, and the sky is painted black.

The second Hayley pulls over, I throw open the car

door and jump out. Intense heat slaps my cheeks, and the ashy taste of smoke coats my tongue.

"Jade!" Hayley shouts from behind me, but I barely hear her as I rush past a gathering of locals toward the inferno.

"No..." My eyes fill up, creating a blurred image of orange and black; flames fighting smoke. A nearby firefighter turns and flings out a gloved hand, waving at me to stay back because the revving of the fire engine hose is so loud that we can't speak.

"No, no, *no!*" I think I scream before dropping to my knees beside the cordoned-off area, clutching my head. Flurries of ash flakes fly past my shoulders, chased by sparks of orange embers.

Hayley runs up beside me and crouches, stretching an arm around my back. "I'm so sorry," she says over and over as I stare at my entire world being swallowed alive by a burning monster.

Dylan... My pulse spikes as I search the building next to the store. It doesn't look like the fire has spread to it, and a firefighter is pointing a hose at his apartment to keep it soaking wet.

Still, I scramble to my feet. *"Dylan!"* I cry up at his window like a madwoman, my thighs hitting police tape.

Hayley's palm lands on my back. "He's okay; he's at Iris's. He stayed there last night because Ella wanted a sleepover. I already sent him a message."

The closest firefighter takes a few steps over to me. "It's okay, ma'am. The whole street's already been evacuated," she reassures, her cheeks blackened from soot. "No one's been hurt."

"That's my store," I gasp, pointing at Quinn Brothers.

"It is?" Her helmet swings toward a handful of police

officers who I don't recognize, then back to me. "I'm very sorry to hear it, lovey. Those officers will wanna talk to you; I'll bring 'em over."

"What happened?" I ask in a desperate tone. "What caused this?"

Her thick, gloved hand curls around my shoulder. "We don't know yet. Are you all right, lovey?"

I shake my head, fighting for breath, but I can't find any. My legs buckle again, and I sink to the pavement. I need to call Dad. And Ruby. And Dylan.

Above my head, I hear the firefighter and Hayley talking about me, exchanging the word "shock" several times, but I can't piece together what they're saying. I can't piece together any of this. Maybe it's not my store and I'm mixed up. Maybe it's a dream. Maybe the fire isn't that bad, and we'll only lose the front door. Maybe...

"Jade, we should go," Hayley suggests somberly, dropping onto her butt beside me. "Maybe you shouldn't watch this."

I shake my head. "I need to call my dad."

"Your dad knows," cuts in a familiar voice, and I glance up to find Nate staring down at me in his police uniform. Despite the radio crackling loudly from his shoulder, he must've heard what I just said.

"Dad knows?" I reply in a confused breath.

Nate nods, turning down the volume on his radio. "He's registered as the owner of the business, so when we got the call at the station, I phoned him right away. He said he didn't have any way of getting here because he's unwell, but he was going to call you."

"Shit, I haven't looked at my phone since I got your message."

Hayley hands me my phone, and I glance at the handset, finding multiple missed calls from Dad, Ruby, and Dylan. Tears swim in my eyes.

Nate bends to give my shoulder a squeeze. "We're gonna figure out what happened, Jade."

"Thank you," is all I say before he climbs under the police tape and marches over to the other cops.

A fierce ache stretches my chest as I turn my gaze back to the store. It still looks like a scene ripped out of hell, but the flames are a little smaller, and I think the firefighters might be getting the blaze under control. I need to call Dad and Ruby back, but the thought of hearing their voices makes me want to be sick all over the pavement. *I can't believe this is happening.*

While Hayley stretches her neck to assess the growing crowd of onlookers, I finally work up the courage to call Dad back. We spend most of the call with him breathing heavily down the line while I cry. He tries to reassure me that "Everything happens for a reason," and "The store is insured, so we don't have to worry about money," but his words fall flat against my ears. I don't think there's anything that could be said right now to make me feel better. My family's legacy—everything I've worked for—is *literally* going up in flames.

After we hang up, I dial Ruby's number. The second she answers, my eyes break open and more tears gush out.

"It's okay," she says gently, but she's sniffling too. "It's not your fault. We're going to figure this out. Flynn just flew to New York this morning for work, but I'm going to be there soon."

"I don't think you should come," I sob into the phone. "The store, it looks…it looks so bad. It's gone, Ruby, it's…it's all gone."

The sound of her crying makes me weep harder, and

eventually, we hang up because what is there left to say? My phone slides onto the pavement and my fingertips squeeze my forehead around my eyes as I gasp and cry, my shoulders shuddering.

Hayley tugs me into her arms, and I rest my head against her shoulder, grateful for the way her perfume masks the horrid stench of smoke until, suddenly, a stronger pair of hands gently takes hold of my arms from behind.

Hayley lets go of me, and I'm pulled around and guided right into Dylan's warm chest, his palm cupping the back of my neck and his fingers sliding into my hair. "I'm sorry, baby," he whispers against my ear. "I'm so, *so* sorry."

Fresh tears glide down my cheeks, and I clutch onto him tightly, burying my face in his embrace.

"I came as soon as I heard," he says into my hair. "I'm so sorry I wasn't here."

"I'm so glad you weren't in the apartment," I barely get out.

"Me too. *Fuck,* I'm glad you weren't in the store." He squeezes me tighter. Hayley sits and breathes heavily beside us while I hold onto Dylan like a lifeline.

"Do you know what happened?" he asks softly, his lips brushing my shoulder when he speaks.

I shake my head. "Maybe someone set fire to the place because they're so sick of looking at it. They'd rather it was turned into something they actually want, like a cool café or a yoga studio."

He tuts. "Jade."

Another swell of tears wobbles in my eyes. "I know the store was struggling. I know that its popularity in this town has been on the wane for a while. But Quinn Brothers is part of my family, part of my childhood. Every time I go in there, I can still see my mom sitting behind the register, smiling at me." My tears burst free, and Dylan's palm scores lines up and down my back as he holds me.

"I know how hard it is to lose a mom," he says softly. "It's fucking horrible. I wouldn't wish it upon my worst enemy. But Jade..." He pulls back so that he can gaze right into my eyes. "Your mom isn't in there." He tips his head at what's left of the store, then flattens his palm over my chest. "She's in here. And even if the whole town goes up in flames, she's *never* leaving this spot."

My hand clutches his over my chest, and my shoulders convulse as I let out more tears: for the store, for Mom. A choked sob sounds from behind me, and I turn and reach an arm out to fold it around Hayley's shoulder so that I've got one arm around each of my two favorite Kings.

"I'm so sorry again about your mom and dad," I whisper to both of them. "This year has been..."

"A fucking horror show of historic proportions?" Dylan finishes, and I chuckle, releasing one arm to wipe my eyes. He then pins me in his blue-eyed stare. "But it hasn't been all bad, right?" he adds, tilting his head at me with a hopeful look. Clearly, he's talking about him and me. How could I have thought for even a second that this thing between us isn't real?

"You're right," I reply with a sniff. "The Italian fair was kind of fun."

A laugh bursts out of him, and he drags me into his chest again, resting his cheek against my hair. "I think the fire's finally out."

I lift my head to glance at the smoking, blackened shell that was once Quinn Brothers and then notice all the gawking locals standing around. Vera, the hairdresser, catches my eye from a few feet away. She brushes away a tear and steps over to where we're sitting.

"I'm sorry, Jade," Vera says. "It was a great store."

"I'm sorry too," adds Latisha, coming up behind her with her husband Phil, followed by Mrs. Felton.

"It was the best store in town," Mrs. Felton says, pointing her cane at me.

"Yes, it was," Mrs. Horne chimes in. "Jade always had fresh water for Minnie."

"I'm sorry," mumbles the shy bartender from The Rocking Horse, followed by Kayla, my yoga instructor, and then Mr. Chen.

"I'm sorry, Jade," says Carl, and Frank comes up beside him, echoing the sentiment. Mrs. Wilson offers the same apology before the family who run the gas station say the same.

One by one, the residents of Still Springs gather around me to pass on their condolences like some sort of bizarre funeral while I gaze up at each of them and say, "Thank you."

I try to smile at all their support, but on the inside, I'm thinking: *Where were you all when the store was here?*

CHAPTER THIRTY

DYLAN

Acrid smoke clings to the cool November air. The crowd that had gathered to witness the devastation has finally dissipated, leaving only a few rubberneckers who must've heard about the blaze too late and come by to see the damage for themselves.

I still can't believe the store is gone, so I can only imagine how shocked Jade must be feeling. I wish there was something more I could do besides offering the occasional word of support, but at least I'm here. It'd be awful to be across the country and have this happen to her. Even if I caught the first flight out of Austin like I did when I heard about Mom and Dad, it wouldn't be the same.

The more I think about leaving, the more I realize I don't want to go.

The folks still wandering around shoot me the occasional glare when I press a hand to Jade's back or rest her head on my shoulder, but I don't give a shit anymore. All that matters is Jade.

I steal a glance at her pale skin and tear-streaked face, still so beautiful it gives me a pain in my chest. On the other side of the yellow police tape, Robocop paces between more police officers and the weary firefighters taking a well-deserved rest on the curb.

Deputy Douchebag stops suddenly to duck beneath the tape right where we're standing. He shoots a glower at me, but his expression softens when he looks at Jade. "Can we talk in private?" he asks her.

The last thing I want is to leave Jade alone right now—especially with him. But I'll let her decide.

She steps a little closer to me. "I want Dylan here."

Nate blows out a heavy breath but nods. "I want you to know that there's going to be an investigation." The way he looks at me when he says the word "investigation" makes me want to introduce his face to my fist. "*If* the fire is ruled as an accident, there will be a hefty insurance payout."

Jade's brow knits. "What do you mean 'if' it was an accident?"

"It's common knowledge that the store wasn't doing well financially."

"Hold on," she says, holding up a hand. "Are you saying they think I did this *on purpose*?"

"We just need to make sure everything is above board," he counters.

And here I thought I couldn't hate this prick any more. To even suggest that Jade had something to do with the fire is so fucking infuriating. Can't he see the tears in her eyes? She's devastated. This isn't some act. She wasn't even here when the fire started. My hands ball into fists, and I know I can't hit him when he's on duty, but I really, *really* want to. "You've got a lot of fucking nerve," I say.

Jade squeezes my arm. "It's okay, Dylan."

"No, it's not." What if, by some twist of fate, they actually accuse Jade of setting the fire on purpose? My heart thumps wildly in my chest as all the disastrous possibilities flood my mind. What would happen to her then? Would there be a trial? Would she be wrongly convicted? Would she go to jail? Would the people in this town think she did it, even if she was cleared of any wrongdoing?

I force my fingers to stretch wide before stuffing them into my pockets. Since I can't hit the bastard, I may as well try to play nice. "Can we put our mutual hatred for one another aside for a minute and have an honest conversation?" I ask Nate.

His lips roll together as his gaze darts to Jade, but eventually, he bobs his head. "Fine."

I fill my lungs with smoky air and blow out a breath. "We both know Jade didn't do this." I look him square in the eye and add, "But sometimes the truth doesn't matter." Especially in Still Springs. "You said there's going to be an investigation. How long will that take, and how public will it be?"

"I can't comment on an ongoing investigation."

I should've known he wouldn't make this easy. "In general," I amend, "what are the procedures for cases like this?"

The walkie-talkie on his vest crackles loudly. He twists the knob on the top until the thing goes quiet. "We don't get a lot of arson around here, so I'm not sure how long it'll take," he says. "The Fire Marshall has been contacted and should arrive within the hour. He'll evaluate and document the scene. They'll collect and process evidence."

Jade's head swings toward the blackened shell of her family's store. "What sort of evidence?"

"Accelerants, tampered utilities, burn patterns, stuff like that," Nate explains. "Could take weeks or even months, depending on what they find."

Meaning that Jade needs to cover her ass in case this doesn't go her way. It kills me to do it, but I mutter a "Thank you" to Nate and grab Jade's hand, leading her up the street to where I parked my bike right on the fucking curb. Tickets be damned.

"Where are we going?" she asks me.

"To talk to a lawyer." I'll need to call Miriam to let her know we're going to be swinging by her office, but I'm sure she won't mind.

Jade tugs out of my grip, her face a mask of confusion. "Why? I didn't do anything wrong. I wasn't even here."

"I wasn't there when Miranda died, and I'm still dealing with the fallout twelve years later. It doesn't matter if you're innocent. All that matters is whether or not these people *think* you're guilty."

She glances over her shoulder to where two women with matching canes are watching us with a little too much interest. "That won't happen," she says. "Most of these people have known me my entire life. They know I wouldn't do something like that."

As if that matters when the Still Springs rumor mill gets hold of some juicy gossip. Back when I was twenty-one, I ran into my little league baseball coach in Austin, and I heard him call me a shitbag under his breath. "I really hope I'm wrong about this, Jade. But you need to be prepared, just in case. This could turn really fucking bad."

She shoves her hair back from her flushed face, a blush blooming up her throat. "I can barely afford groceries most of the time. How in the world do you expect me to pay for a lawyer?"

She couldn't pay for fucking groceries? I had no idea things were *that* bad. Why hadn't she told me? *Because she doesn't trust you.* My teeth clench so hard that my jaw creaks. "You don't have to worry about that. I'll handle it."

Jade's golden strands of hair fall right back when she starts shaking her head. "No. I don't need you to take care of me."

This woman. Of all the times for her to dig in her heels, why does it have to be today? I rake my hands through my hair, ready to rip it all out. "When will you get it through your beautiful head that I *want* to take care of you?"

Her eyes widen, and she blinks up at me, her expression carefully neutral. "Why?"

What kind of question is that? Why does anyone want to take care of someone else?

"So you can tell your sisters all about my failing store?" she asks.

I did what, now? "Jade—"

She holds up a hand. "It's fine, Dylan. I feel like a fool, but I'm not mad at you."

"I didn't tell them anything. Iris knew about the financial problems before I did. You know this town. People talk." All the more reason to make sure Jade doesn't end up getting raked over the coals after this fire. "Please, Jade. Let me help you."

More tears fill her eyes as she lifts her head toward the gray sky. "You heard Nate. This could take months. By the time they finish the investigation, you'll be long gone."

That had been the plan, but I'm not so sure it is anymore. "What if I'm not? What if I stay? What if we try to do this thing for real?"

At first, Jade looks stunned. But then she sighs and blinks away. "That's a lot of 'what if's', Dylan," she says sadly, running her finger under her eye to catch a falling tear. "And I have enough of those in my life already."

A tall firefighter steps around the corner. When he sees us, he waves a gloved hand at Jade. "Miss Quinn? Do you mind coming with me?"

She lets out a long sigh before walking over to him. I'm about to follow her when I start wondering if I should. She didn't ask me to come with her. Is that because she doesn't want me there?

Jade's constantly using the fact that I'm supposed to go back to Austin as an excuse to keep her distance from me. I've offered to stay several times, but she's never actually said that she wants me to.

Maybe that's because she doesn't.

My throat flexes hard.

Instead of returning to the mayhem on Main Street, I continue up the hill, away from it all. How easy would it be to hop on my bike and leave for good? That's probably what I should do, but I don't. I continue around the corner, not really having a destination in mind but knowing that I need some space to breathe and think.

I don't stop until I can no longer smell smoke other than what's left on my coat. When I glance around, my eyes catch on the town playground across the street. There aren't any kids playing today, so it shouldn't look creepy for me to sit on the bench by myself. Only I don't sit on the bench. I plop down on the uneven merry-go-round and give the rusted old thing a shove with my boot.

Leaves whirl through the air, landing on the wood chips beneath the slide and swings.

My head falls back against a metal bar, and I lift my eyes to the gray clouds looming above. Around and around I go, my thoughts spinning faster through my mind.

The more I think about leaving Jade, the harder it is to breathe.

My therapist's words come back to haunt me. *"If you aren't willing to give her what she needs, you need to let her find someone who will."*

She'd probably end up with some *nice* guy with a degree in finance and a golden retriever named Max.

Can I give Jade what she needs?

I *think* so. Assuming she wants me to.

One thing I know for sure is that the thought of leaving her behind—whether we're only friends or something more—makes everything inside me contract. And being that far away from my sisters and Ella sounds like the worst idea ever.

What if I decide to stay, not for Jade, but...for me?

Here I go again with the "what ifs."

I've been waiting for Jade to tell me what to do, to ask me to stay, to say that she wants me here, when I'm a grown-ass man who's perfectly capable of making the decision for myself. I could choose to stay, to make Still Springs my home once more, the same way Jade could choose to be with me or some smug-faced accountant and his dog.

Fuck that. I don't want anyone else to give her what she needs. I want it to be me.

Hopefully, she'll feel the same.

There's only one way to find out.

I press my heels to the ground that's still turning, carving a line in the wood chips until the merry-go-round comes to a stop. But when I try to stand, the world tilts, and I nearly fall flat on my ass. My stomach revolts against the chocolate-filled croissant I shoved into my mouth for breakfast.

All the spinning was a bad idea.

I bend forward and brace my hands on my knees, breathing deeply until the cold sweat across my forehead dries. *I will not puke. No, sir. I will swallow whatever bile climbs my throat so the joggers coming my way don't have to see me losing my breakfast all over the playground.*

With one final breath, I straighten, ready to tell Jade my decision, when I find a woman hovering beside the playground gate. My heart leaps into my throat.

Mrs. Williams.

Miranda's mom.

Our gazes meet, and there's no doubt that she's seen me. I really might lose my breakfast.

"Dylan?" she says as if she can't believe I'm really here. "Dylan King?"

My tongue feels so swollen that I can't speak. All I can do is nod. Sweat leaks down my spine, and my heart thrashes in my chest. Miranda would've looked just like her mom if she'd lived beyond seventeen. It's like glimpsing a future that wasn't meant to be.

Mrs. Williams grips the iron railing, and I seriously consider my options. I could turn tail and run all the way to my parents' house, get the keys to Dad's Mustang, and leave town. Hayley could pack up my shit in the waterlogged apartment and ship it back to Austin. It's the least she could do after the hell she's given me over Jade.

Jade.

My mom's and dad's endless devotion to each other taught me that you never give up on the people you love.

I gave up on Miranda.

I won't do the same to Jade.

So, instead of running, my boots remain glued to the wood chips.

"I heard you were in town," Mrs. Williams says. "You're staying above the old ice cream parlor, right? Next to where that awful fire happened today."

I nod once more. As painful as all this is for me, it must be excruciating for this woman to come face to face with the man she blames for her only daughter's downfall.

Her knuckles turn white where she's holding onto the gate. "I've...um...been trying to find the nerve to stop by to extend my condolences about your parents."

Oh, yeah. That. I haven't forgotten they were killed, but when I try really hard, I can convince myself that they're traveling somewhere in Europe or taking an extended vacation out west. Sarah wouldn't be impressed if she knew that, but it's helping me get through the hard days.

Hard days that didn't seem so hard with Jade by my side.

Mrs. Williams' head tilts the way her daughter's used to when she was being introspective. Such a silly thing to remember about a person.

"Maybe we could even reminisce," Mrs. Williams says. "There aren't many people left in town who remember my daughter the way we do. Back when she wasn't so...lost."

I manage to swallow past my heart that's still in my throat. If I'm going to stay in Still Springs, I can't have this hanging over my head any longer. With a deep inhale, I utter the words I've never been able to say until now. "I'm so sorry about what happened with Miranda."

Her brow furrows. "For what? None of what happened is your fault."

That isn't entirely true. My clammy hands tremble as I scrub them against my thighs. "She called me that night, but...I didn't answer."

Mrs. Williams's eyes flood with tears that streak down her cheeks in glistening lines. "She called me too," she says. "I answered, but it didn't make a difference. My baby was already gone by the time the ambulance arrived."

For a moment, I can't breathe. Knowing that Miranda had reached out to someone else—someone who had answered her call, who had been there for her so she wasn't all alone in her final moments—steals away the heaviness that has pressed against my chest for over a decade.

My legs finally unlock, and I rush forward to wrap my arms around Miranda's mother, both of us letting our tears fall like the leaves around us. My therapist was right. This is exactly what I needed. Why the hell did I put it off for so long?

Mrs. Williams draws away with a light laugh and dabs at her eyes. "Sorry for being such a blubbering mess. How long will you be in town?" she asks. "I'd love to meet you for coffee before you go back home."

Go back home.

Austin isn't home anymore—I'm not sure it ever was. This place, Still Springs, is where I want to be.

"I'm moving back, actually," I say, and the words feel like freedom on my tongue. "So we can grab coffee whenever you want."

Mrs. Williams and I make plans to meet up the following week and then part ways. When I tell Sarah about this, she's going to be over the moon.

Looks like Still Springs is getting a new resident.

Now, there's only one thing left to do: Go and get my girl.

CHAPTER THIRTY-ONE

JADE

I sit tightly wedged between Ruby and Dad in Nate's office cubicle, the space so tiny that my plastic chair scrapes against Dad's and my thigh presses into Ruby's.

Nate rests his elbows on his desk that's littered with crumpled papers, takeout coffee cups, and empty pretzel packets.

"Thanks for your time today," he says, and relief floods my chest because it looks like we're finally done here. Dad, Ruby, and I have given Nate all the answers we have about what happened before the fire and how it could've started—which was mostly a repeated cycle of "nothing out of the ordinary." Since Ruby arrived in town last night, the poor thing's been beating herself up over the fact that she was the last person in the store, but she can't remember doing anything differently.

"So, no leads at this point, then," Dad says gruffly.

Nate's cheeks stain pink. "Well. Just the furnace line of inquiry," he mumbles, studying the half-chewed pen between his fingers.

"Furnace?" Dad repeats, his confused frown mirroring mine.

Nate sighs and leans closer. "Look, nothing is official until we get the report from the Fire Marshall, but he did say this morning that there appears to be a path of fire originating from the furnace's electrical wiring." He points his pen at us. "But that's preliminary information, and you are obligated to keep it confidential until we figure out what happened and rule out arson."

I roll my eyes. He's still on about the freaking arson. And we've been trapped in this ice-cold office for an hour—why didn't he mention the furnace until now? Probably because he wanted to interrogate us without revealing all the facts in case one of us blabs about our evil plan. *Newsflash, Nate: This isn't gonna be a career-making arson bust for you. None of us did anything wrong.*

"The furnace in the store has been playing up for weeks," I say firmly.

"That's right," Dad adds. "Was it two times you had the service people out, Jade?"

I nod, feeling the boulder inside my chest finally beginning to loosen. During our meeting at the bank this morning, the loan manager agreed to freeze our commercial loan repayments until we have a resolution on the fire. Now, if the origins of the blaze can be traced back to a furnace that's on record as being faulty, I have every hope that everything's going to turn out okay. With an insurance payout, we'd be able to pay off what's left of the loan in one fell swoop *and* have a ton of money left over to cover repairs and, hopefully, Dad's medical bills.

Ruby and I get up and help Dad to his feet, and I pass him his walking stick that was leaning against Nate's desk.

"Uh, Jade, have you got a sec?" Nate asks.

Not for you. "Actually, we have to go."

"Go where, Jade?" Dad cuts in, clutching onto Ruby's arm. "We've got a few minutes. Stay and talk to the deputy, and we'll meet you outside."

He's probably right about playing nice, considering the situation we're in. Ruby gives me a wary glance before leading Dad away.

As soon as they're through the sliding glass doors, Nate says, "Why don't you have a seat?"

"I'm not staying long. What's this about?"

His hazel eyes cling to my face, his throat bulging as he swallows. "I don't get to see you much anymore."

What am I supposed to say to that?

"Would you like to have dinner with me this week?" he continues. "There's an Italian restaurant off the highway that I've heard isn't bad. You know I don't like Italian, but I'm happy to make an exception for you."

For fuck's sake. I lower my voice so none of the other officers can hear. "Nate, I need you to understand something. The thing we had between us is *not* going to be restarted. Please stop asking. Plus, you're investigating a fire at my business. Wouldn't that be a conflict of interest?"

He frowns. "You let me worry about the rules around here."

"I appreciate the offer," I say with a sigh, "but no."

He mutters a sound of annoyance. When I turn to leave, he says, "Is this because of that man-whore who killed my cousin?"

A flash of anger strikes my chest, and I spin back around to glare at Nate. "Don't you talk about him like that."

He smiles, but his eyes are as cold as this room. "You dumb blondes, all alike. Falling for the deadbeat with the ugly tattoos and the noise-polluting motorcycle who's got nothing to offer you except an STD."

My jaw grinds, and I fight off an urge to swipe that messy shit all over Nate's desk right into his lap. But that would be a stupid move, given the investigation, so I'll have to control my temper and try for reason instead.

"Nate, did you ever read the police reports into Miranda's death?" His mouth sets into a hard line. When he doesn't reply, I add, "How could you not have read the reports? You're a cop! Your cousin *died*."

His teeth clench. "I already know what happened. Excuse me if I don't want to relive it all over again."

"That's just it, you *don't* know what happened. And I'm sorry that it's still painful for you. I lost my mom much too young, and I can't imagine ever getting over it. But you need to read those police reports and learn the truth. Dylan isn't responsible for Miranda's death, nor is he some sort of criminal just because he has tattoos and rides a motorcycle. To tell you the truth, he's one of the kindest, smartest, most generous people I've ever met. Oh, and he's never told me to fuck off *or* called me a 'dumb blonde.' So there's that."

Nate heaves a sigh. "Shit."

I hold up a hand. "I'm not expecting you guys to be best friends or even shake hands. But if you don't lay off Dylan?" I clutch the edge of Nate's desk and stare right into his eyes. "You're gonna have to deal with me. And when I put my mind to something, I've got more energy and determination than you can even dream of. I *never* give up. My store had to literally burn to the fucking ground to be taken away from me. So, you think about that, Deputy."

With a glare of warning, I turn my back on Nate and stride out of his shitty cubicle.

Ruby rests her chin in her palms, watching me shovel another homemade brownie into my mouth. Mrs. Felton kindly dropped over a bunch of them to Dad's yesterday evening, and Flynn's sweet parents brought over three casseroles to freeze.

"What?" I say with a full mouth. It feels good to finally have some of my appetite back.

"What do you think we should do with the insurance money?" she asks.

I wait to reply until I've swallowed. "Geez, a bit of a big question for right now, isn't it?"

She tears off a corner of brownie and pushes it between her lips. "Given I'm heading home tomorrow, I have to ask some 'big' questions while I'm here."

I lift the lever on Dad's kitchen tap and run my hands under the warm water. "I don't know. I guess we'll all have to discuss it when the time comes."

Ruby hands me a paper towel. "Just to be clear, I don't need any of the insurance proceeds. Flynn and I are doing fine; plus, I'm no longer involved in the business. My only wish is for Dad to be able to retire after his operation next month and for you to use the rest of the money to set yourself up with something you love doing."

"I loved the store," I grumble mournfully.

She pouts. "I think you loved the *memories* in the store. And so did I. But those memories haven't gone anywhere, Jade. Lucky for us, they're fire-proof."

"I know."

"Is there something else you think you could enjoy doing as much?" she probes.

If we get the insurance money, we could rebuild and

reopen Quinn Brothers, but the store was struggling long before the fire. Who's to say we wouldn't end up back in another financial hole?

I rest my elbows on the counter and heave a sigh. What *do* I love doing?

"I like running a business," I say. "Although, I wouldn't mind running one that's profitable."

Ruby chuckles.

"And you know I love Still Springs. I don't want to leave this place."

Her lips curve up. "The old man lucked out there. He gets to keep the little one close by."

I glance at the hallway leading to Dad's bedroom, where he's having a nap. "Dad and I can look after each other. It's a win-win."

"What kind of business in Still Springs?" Ruby asks, folding her arms. "Another Quinn Brothers? Or a Quinn *Sisters*?" She arches a brow.

I smile because I know she's kidding. But when I give some real thought to the store and the parts of it that have been working well lately, it's really only two things: the online orders and the local artisan goods. Particularly Magnolia Sloane's macabre sculptures.

"You know how the Quinn Brother's website is still up and running?" I say, thinking out loud. "I wonder if I could keep selling the arts and homewares stuff online but get rid of all the groceries that take up mountains of space and need refrigeration. Plus, there are higher profit margins on the artisan stuff, and I only really scratched the surface for creatives in this area." Maybe there *is* a way to keep the business alive after all. Just in a different way that suits the times we're living in. In college, we called it "pivoting." It's considered good business to make a fundamental change to a company's direction when it's no longer meeting the needs of the market.

Ruby's eyes are sparkling. "That's actually a really good idea. The overheads would be super low."

"They would," I agree, a jolt of excitement striking my chest. "As long as I could find space at home to store the pieces, there'd be no shopfront to rent, no extra utility bills, or having to open on weekends."

"And don't forget about the insurance money. You'd be able to buy heaps of stock."

"No, I'd want to see how it all goes first. That's always the smart thing to do before investing in something new." I'd start with a few key collections and see how they sell. Plus, we need to pay off the commercial loan and what we can of Dad's hospital fees first.

"Sounds like a plan to me," Ruby says with a smile.

I reach for a third brownie, and she swats away my hand. I pout while she scoops up the tray from under my nose and carries it off to the pantry.

"So, there's another 'big' question I wanted to ask you before I go," Ruby says, padding back over to me. "What's going on with you and Dylan? And don't tell me that your stay in his cabin was a 'friend thing'." She makes air quotes.

My stomach jumps into my chest, stirring everything up. "Fine, yes, we've been seeing each other. But I think it's ending."

The disappointed expression on Ruby's face matches mine. "Because of Hayley?"

"No, Hayley's actually okay with it. It's Austin who's being a jerk."

"Who's Austin?"

"I mean the city. Dylan's going back home. Although,

after the fire, he did say something to me like, 'What if I stay here and we try something out?'"

Ruby's eyes widen. "He said that? So, what's the problem?"

"He sounded really uncertain. He was all, 'What if this', and 'What if that'."

Her brows bunch. "And you were expecting what—a marriage proposal?"

If I had a brownie in my hand, I'd be tempted to toss it at her. "Why does it sound like you're on his side? I thought you'd be happy to see the back of Dylan."

She leans her elbows against the counter, a trace of guilt in her gaze. "I won't lie; his reputation did scare me at first when you two started getting close. But then I thought about how people assumed the worst of me recently and how wrong they were. Plus, the few times I've been around Dylan, he's seemed so sweet and caring, especially towards you. I mean, gosh, the way he looked after you in the hospital. And then how he took you to his cabin so you could recover?" She sighs wistfully, and a tingling warmth spreads through my chest.

I miss that adorable jerk who's not actually a jerk.

I inhale a deep breath, trying to pin down what's really holding me back from this. "I'm scared of how I feel about him," I finally admit. "I've never felt this way about a guy. I have it so bad for him, and it's a really fucking scary place to be."

Ruby's smile spreads across her cheeks. "Welcome to my world. Isn't it wonderful?"

> ME
> R u at home?

SEXY NEIGHBOR
I'm over at Mom and Dad's. Come by?

> Be there soon. X

Gravel crunches beneath the wheels of my Honda Civic as I slowly drive down the Kings' driveway. After I pull over in one of the parking bays near the front stoop, my gaze snags on a huge pile of cardboard boxes resting on the concrete tiles. Beside them sits the Mustang that Dylan uses when he's not riding his motorcycle, the trunk wide open.

Dylan strolls out the front door wearing a vintage T-shirt and athletic shorts with a black cap sitting backward over his disheveled hair. I just about melt into my car seat while he walks toward me.

"Hey," he says when I fling the car door open. The second I get out, he reaches for me and pulls me up inside a heavenly hug, turning his nose into my neck.

When he lets go, my gaze drifts to the moving boxes, the sight piercing my chest. He wasn't supposed to leave for Austin until Christmas.

"How are you doing?" Dylan asks.

"I'm okay." As we take the few steps toward the house, I fill him in on this morning's meeting at the police station and the furnace revelation, leaving out all the shit that happened with Nate after.

When we reach the stoop, I wave a hand at the stack of boxes.

"So, this is it?" I ask, attempting to sound casual, but my voice is as tight as a fist.

Dylan's brow furrows. "This is what?"

"This is where it ends?"

He waits for more, then says, "Life as we know it? The universe? Ella's dance recitals which, apart from her sweet moves, are excruciating to watch? I need specifics."

I squint over a wry smile. "*Us*. You being in Still Springs."

He slides his hands into his pockets. "I'm not moving out, Jade; I'm moving in." He jerks his chin at the stunning home behind him. "The apartment's got smoke and water damage, and it's also kinda cramped. This place might be twelve sizes too big for me, but I'll figure out what to do with it, and my sisters will come and stay a lot. I'm also gonna be looking after Ella more now that I'm staying, and maybe the new baby too, so we'll need the space."

My mind is struggling to grasp all this. "You're *staying*?"

He throws a hand up. "Before you freak out, know that this decision isn't because of you—not entirely, anyway. I've thought about this a lot, and I genuinely want to be here. Okay?"

I nod, trying to catch the breath lodged in my chest. "Okay."

"Good." One side of his mouth quirks. "Now that that's settled, you should probably be my girlfriend."

My lips fall open, and my heart kicks into overdrive.

"I was planning to drive over to your place later to tell you that and a few other things." Dylan closes the distance between us and lets out a long breath. "Jade, I've always believed I was the worst man for you, but you make me want to be a better one. You have single-handedly replaced all the bad memories I had of this place with good ones.

And now, I want to do the same for you." He reaches for my hand, his thumb stroking over my wrist. "Let me be the one to help you rebuild the store if that's what you choose to do. Let me be the man holding your hand at the Italian fair. The one trudging through the mud by your side at the annual race. Let me be the one lying next to you when you fall asleep and when you wake up. Because if you don't, it'll get really awkward when we run into each other, and neither of us needs that."

Tears rise to my eyes, and my lips fight a smile. "That would be awful."

"Exactly. And since your best friend happens to be my sister, we'd be running into each other a lot."

I fake-grimace at that, and he smiles. When he reaches to cup my face in his warm hands like he can't help himself, I tilt into his palm. "I guess it's no secret that you came with a pretty big warning label," I say in a trembling voice. "Because of that, I kept waiting for you to let me down. But all you've done is lift me up. I know I'm not very good at accepting help, but you kept giving it to me anyway because you knew I needed it. Every day, I waited for you to walk away, but all you ever did was show up." I reach for his hand, and our threaded fingers drop to my side. "But Dylan, you're not the worst man for me. If anything, it's the opposite. You may be cooler and more confident than anyone I know, but sometimes I wonder if, deep down, you believe some of the bullshit that's been said about you. And while I can't buy you nice things—*yet,* or pretend to know anything about photography, maybe there's one thing I can help you with."

His eyes shine with affection as they move over my face. "What's that, baby?"

I gently lift both his hands and fold open his fingers,

stroking my thumbs over the words "Love" and "More" inked across his knuckles. I then guide his hands to his chest, holding them against himself.

Tears spring to his eyes, making them glisten a watery blue. He lets go of his chest to glide his hands around my lower back, pulling me close. "Yesterday, you said you had too many 'what ifs' in your life, too many unknowns," Dylan says. "But I couldn't live with myself if I didn't give you one more." He pauses for a moment, biting into his bottom lip. A gorgeous blush overcomes his face as he gazes right into my eyes. "What if I love you, Jade Quinn?"

My chest breaks open, liquid warmth rushing inside and filling up every part of me. "What if I love you too?"

EPILOGUE
JADE

My gaze roams over Dylan's bulging bicep as he grips the side of the cardboard box and peers into it. "Misplaced your dentures?" I tease as he sets the box down.

"Nah, just your pacifier," he deadpans, and I snort-laugh and lean forward to give him a playful shove. He catches my arm mid-strike and tugs me into his chest instead, wrapping his solid arms around me.

I tilt my face to stare up at him and soak in that rush of warmth I still get whenever he sets his blue eyes on me. "You know these age jokes are weird and creepy."

"But you love weird and creepy," he replies before lowering his lips to mine.

We sink into a deep, heavenly kiss, and right here on the concrete floor of his parents' old garage, we make out like teenagers until we're both left panting. When we eventually pull back, Dylan's hand curls tightly around my jaw, and my fingers stroke the soft tendrils of his hair.

Reluctantly, I untie myself from his arms. "Stop distracting me."

Sitting on my knees, I hunch over the box Dylan

opened and pull out a bubble-wrapped stack of hand-painted ceramic plates. "Oh yeah, this is the new set we have all those pre-orders for. Magnolia's new collection must be coming tomorrow."

The highest-selling artist in my online store is, hands down, Magnolia Sloane. Her gruesome sculptures have become so popular that an art gallery in New York tried to snap them up on an exclusive contract, but I managed to negotiate a deal to be her sole supplier nationally. Go me.

I sit back and assess the new stack of boxes that's going to grow even larger tomorrow. With the motorbikes in here that Dylan inherited, the existing stock sitting out in ordered piles, and the small desk I brought in to work from, we're officially out of room. Letting me take over the garage was such a sweet gesture, but QuinnStudio.com is roaring ahead, and the last thing I want to do is hold back the train.

"We need more space," I muse aloud.

"Are you saying you're ready?" Dylan asks with a smirk.

He's talking about the renovations of the old Quinn Brothers store that I've been planning for months. Since the fire, the store space has been rebuilt, but it's still an empty shell. With the hefty insurance payout and the website profits combined, there's more than enough money to start building. Dad keeps saying that he can't wait to watch the old space transform into a boutique art gallery and homewares store. I'll still keep the website, but it's time we have a physical presence for people to come in and view what's on offer.

With Hayley's help, I'm hoping to attract even more important artists from the area, and Dylan's going to sell his photos there too. Now that the Kings have opened a location next door where the old ice cream shop and Harringtons used to be, the area is buzzing with foot traffic.

"I'm ready," I say. Because I am. So freaking ready.

Dylan's smile widens. "I'll make that call to my contractor friend. It's time to get this gallery built and born."

Holy shit, speaking of born... I dig my phone out of my back pocket and check the time. Ruby's appointment must be over by now. Why haven't I heard from her? I dial her number, and she answers on the third ring.

"I was just about to call you." She sounds breathless and overjoyed. "The doc was running behind, so we only just came out. We're having a boy!"

"Oh my god!" I scream. Dylan's brows fly up, and I quickly cover the handset and explain, "Ruby and Flynn are having a boy."

He grins. "Congrats. I'll give Flynn a buzz later."

I rest my back against the garage wall, beaming while Ruby talks me through her latest ultrasound and how her morning sickness has finally subsided. Dylan and I still joke about how Flynn didn't waste any time, given their wedding was five months ago.

After Ruby and I hang up, I point my phone at Dylan. "You're not hogging this baby like you do Charli." Charlotte is Iris and Justin's adorable six-month-old, whom Dylan watches two days a week with Ella and is equally obsessed with.

"No promises. You know that all the little monsters worship me." He glances at his watch and climbs to his feet. "We better get going, baby."

"Yup." I slide my phone into my pocket and close up the cardboard boxes. Tonight, Dylan's taking me to the Italian restaurant where we went on this exact day last year for our first date. He wants it to be a yearly tradition, which is a super-romantic side of him that still amazes me (and him, I think). He even got us matching costumes for Halloween—a nurse's and a doctor's outfit covered in blood and gore. The best part is, he wants to be the nurse.

After helping me to my feet, Dylan laces his fingers with mine and brings them to his lips. "Still crazy 'bout you," he says, kissing each of my knuckles.

"Still crazy 'bout you," I reply with a dopey smile.

"Still love you," he says, weakening my knees.

"Still love you."

He gives me a once-over. "Still want to fu—"

"*Dylan*." I laugh, and he joins in.

"Too far. Got it."

With a wink, he lets go of my hand and heads over to get the bike and helmets ready. I grab my leather jacket from the chair behind the desk and reach up to pat the framed photo of Mom and Dad in Alaska that I had reprinted.

Dylan presses the remote to open the garage door before grabbing the photo album resting on his bike seat. The album is filled with pictures of his ex, Miranda, that he took back in high school. Her mom lives near the restaurant, so he's arranged to drop it off on the way as a surprise gift. Last month, Miranda's mom, Dylan, and I had dinner at The Rocking Horse, and she was really lovely and funny, even though her unimaginable loss can still be felt. That night, Dylan had joked about my "concerning" interest in horror, and it turned out that Mrs. Williams has actually visited the Island of the Dolls in Mexico! Dylan knows that place is at the top of my travel bucket list, and while we were leaving the bar, he'd murmured, "That death-doll island sure would make for an interesting honeymoon."

It wasn't a proposal—neither of us is really the jump-into-marriage type, as much as I know it's something I want.

But there had been a glint in his eye, a flush in his cheeks, and a tremble to his words.

And I'd known instantly, right in the center of my heart.

One day, this guy is going to ask me to marry him.

While I'm sure he'll do it when I least expect it, I have a secret wish that it happens in front of every judgmental gossip in town who wrote Dylan off and treated him like garbage over nothing more than a false rumor. Because then I'll get the chance to kiss the life out of him in front of all those naysayers and tell him that marrying him would be the greatest honor of my life.

I lean over the bike to stamp one more life-changing kiss on the lips of the best guy I know.

Screw the haters. All I have time for is love.

ACKNOWLEDGMENTS

Wow. Another book under our belts. Are you sick of us yet? Hopefully not, because we plan on writing at least a hundred more.

Publishing stories takes a village. And it's time to thank ours.

First, to Sam Palencia from Ink and Laurel: Our words may fill these books, but your artistic talent is what draws readers in. Thank you for creating the most stunning covers.

Our lovely beta reader, Megan Kitzmiller, thank you for wading through our early drafts and for your valuable feedback.

Andria Henry, thank you for helping us make this book even better—and for loving these characters as much as we do.

To Daniel and Sandra Burckhardt: Thank you for letting us pick your brains about the joys and pains of running a store. Your funny story about the clock collection turned into Mrs. Horne!

A special shout out to Jenny's street team, who helped hype this book and spread the word across the interwebs. And to all the bookish community for your constant love and support for us and our books.

A huge thanks also goes to the readers of *Hating the Best Man* who fell in love with Still Springs and wanted a book boyfriend to rival Flynn Hudson. (Did we do okay?)

Finally, as always, we thank our families for loving us

even when our heads are stuck in fictional worlds and for not holding it against us when we fall in love with every single MMC we write.

Hugs and HEAs,
 Jenny & Natalie x

ALSO BY JENNY FYFE & NATALIE MURRAY

Still Springs

(*Adult Contemporary Romance*)

Hating the Best Man

Loving the Worst Man

ALSO BY JENNY

The Myths of Airren

(*New Adult Fantasy Romance*)

A Cursed Kiss

A Cursed Heart

A Cursed Love

Prince of Seduction

Prince of Deception

The PAN Trilogy

(*Young Adult Sci-Fi Romance with a Peter Pan Twist*)

The PAN

The HOOK

The CROC

Omnibus Editions

The PAN Trilogy (Special Edition Omnibus)

YA Fantasy Romance

Married by Fate

ALSO BY NATALIE

Adult Contemporary Romance

Love, Just In

The Hearts and Crowns Trilogy

(*Young Adult Fantasy Romance*)

Emmie and the Tudor King

Emmie and the Tudor Queen

Emmie and the Tudor Throne

Omnibus Editions

(*New Adult Fantasy Romance*)

Emmie and the Tudor King New Adult Omnibus

ABOUT THE AUTHORS

Jenny and Natalie are romance authors living on opposite sides of the globe who found each other through fate and bonded over their mutual love for swoon-worthy fictional men and spicy books with loads of pining. They thought it could be fun to try and write one together, so they did and discovered that the only thing more addictive than writing about hot heroes falling hopelessly in love (with some hilarious high jinks on the side) was doing so with your writing soulmate. Jenny also writes fantasy romance as Jenny Hickman, and Natalie writes solo contemporary romance as Natalie Murray.